THE TRIUMVIRATE

Robert Banfelder

BB

~ ~

Broadwater Books

This book is a work of fiction. Names, characters, places, and incidents are the product of the author's imagination, or are used fictitiously.

Broadwater Books
141 Riverside Drive
Riverhead, New York 11901
E-mail: broadwaterbooksinfo@gmail.com

ISBN: 978-0-9915912-4-4

Cover Image: Igor Serazetdinov/123rf

Printed in the United States of America

10 9 8 7 6 5 4 3 2 1

Dedication

For Donna, who has always encouraged my passion for the written word.

Books by Robert Banfelder

Fiction

The Robert Redler/Liza Downs Series:

Dick, Richard, and I
The Signing

The Justin Barnes Series:

The Author
The Teacher
Knots
The Good Samaritans

Trace Evidence

Nonfiction

The Fishing Smart <u>Anywhere</u> Handbook for Salt Water & Fresh Water

PRAISE FOR THE NOVELS OF
ROBERT BANFELDER

THE TEACHER

"BRAVO! As a forensic psychologist specializing in psychopathy, I have been researching authors who write fiction in the field of forensic psychology. I am impressed with Banfelder's well-researched, credible, and unique plots regarding the criminal mind."
~ Dr. Jason Dunham, Forensic Psychologist

KNOTS

"THRILLERS THAT TAKE YOU AWAY TO A DIFFERENT PLACE, LIKE GOOD THRILLERS SHOULD. Just when you think you have figured out where the plot is going, Banfelder pulls out the rug from underneath you with heart-pounding effect."
~ Russell F. Moran, author, *The Time Magnet Series*

TRACE EVIDENCE

"A MASTER OF HIS CRAFT! . . . Banfelder captures the essence of the serial killer."
~ Linda L. Chase, Forensic Anthropologist Specialist

THE AUTHOR

"UNRELENTING IN HIS ABILITY TO MOVE YOU ALONG AND INTO HIS PAGES. You are running fast, and just when you think it might be safe, Banfelder hits you with another curve."
~ Patti Ann Bengen, author, *Sex, Danger in the Tulip Fields, The Devil's Dance, New Beginnings*

THE GOOD SAMARITANS

BANFELDER EXPERTLY WEAVES THE SUBPLOTS together at the end, and delivers a thrilling denouement. This book is one of the best crime thrillers I have read in a long while.

~ Russell F. Moran, author, *Justice in America: How It Works, How It Fails*, *The APT Principle*, *The Time Magnet Series*

DICKY, RICHARD, AND I

"I HIGHLY RECOMMEND this book to readers who enjoy the fast pace of a suspenseful and well-written psychological thriller with moments of humor and a surprising ending that is anything but expected." ~ Edward Fitch, Amazon Verified Purchase Reviewer, North Carolina

THE TRIUMVIRATE

Chapter 1

Angelica Ann Manns turned heads just as surely as the seedy sideshow barker lured pedestrian traffic toward the entrance of his brightly string-lit canvas tent, promising folks an unforgettable evening of *eyeful* viewing.

The man's nephew, situated in a booth directly across the narrow barren tract, stood before a group of grownups. Quite openly, the tall, thin figure hawked a series of colored, glossy 8 x 10 pornographic photographs of couples, along with decks of graphic vintage playing cards. Behind him stood a pegboard wall displaying rows of plastic, rubber, glass, and stainless steel adult toys and tools packaged in cellophane. An assistant rapidly converted customers' fantasies into instant cash—the merchandise immediately bagged then sealed in dark-brown paper pouches. Anyone who spent fifty dollars or greater received a 15%-off coupon toward the price of admission for the main event.

Back across the dusty tract, the carnival's main attraction was now being *feverishly* pitched by the vociferous uncle, vowing that the nearly sold-out show boasted three of the most provocative, unprecedented erotic carnal acts ever seen—live—on stage. One of the performances was to begin momentarily. No one would be admitted after the final call.

Consequently, if the evening's entertainment could be summed up in but a word, let alone a single syllable, it would undoubtedly personify the letter **X**.

Se**x**.

Summoning forth one and all.

In fact, virtually every male and female adult who gathered in that restricted, distant, dust-strewn cordoned-off corner of corruption milled about the area with prurient purpose of mind, all anxiously awaiting *showtime*. Sex for the price of admission is what the solicitor belied beyond the threshold of the prodigious tent. Sexual materials and items in all shapes and sizes, exhibited as though they were souvenirs, is what the prurient purveyors were offering in their booths and makeshift stalls.

Sex for sale or sheer unbridled abandon is what the salient, silent beauty boasted and immediately blossomed in the minds of the men and women who glimpsed or spied the tall, trim, well-tanned, short-skirted, curvaceous, tight-bodied, dark-haired, brown-eyed, twenty-two-year-old woman parading the fairgrounds on that sweltering star-filled night.

Angelica Manns would, in her own time and space, reveal the reality of illusion. Although not part and parcel of any festival performance, it was the exacting image Angelica had decided to portray that evening. The vision of a racy fairy princess on the prowl. A bejeweled-studded crown adorning a soft, sensational coiffure. A silver star-tipped wand held at the ready above a series of gold bangle bracelets worn along a slender wrist. A pair of glittery, strappy heels raising a light cloud of ankle-high powdery dusky dust.

Angelica had arrived at the annual event sometime after 11 p.m., parking in the far northeast section of the usually quiet, bucolic, blue-collar town outside of Lizella, Georgia. As she neared one attraction after the other, she most magically became it.

Before making her way toward the restricted ADULTS ONLY area, a crowd of men, women, and children turned and faced about. Angelica gave a comely smile to no one in particular, yet everyone in that instant felt the look had been cast especially for them. For in that moment, she had become all things to all people. To the young children she seemed something of a modern-day fairy princess. The older boys and girls simply saw her as someone especially cool. Several elderly women in the crowd thought her positively wicked in her ways, their disapproval underscored by a score or more of overt facial expressions. Men gaped, whistled, daydreamed, and remarked, all wishing she could be *theirs*, or—at the very least—their next-door neighbor. One gay fellow in the crowd expressed that very sentiment, but for quite a different purpose of mind.

"I'd simply love to rifle through her wardrobe," Jimmy Ober

put forth matter-of-factly. "Revealing, licentious, but oddly refined," he remarked quite appreciatively, admiring how everything about the female stranger somehow smacked of taste. "She part of the act, you think? Mattie's next headliner, maybe?"

"Nah, but look at 'em look 'er over. You just *know* he's thinkin' how to hook 'er, hawk 'er, and bed 'er for himself. He's fuckin' salivatin', man. Like Max, here," he said in comparison, grinning while staring down at his little panting dog, driveling from the heat and humidity.

The portly male attendant manning the tent had reluctantly stopped his pitch altogether, for no one was paying him any mind as folks turned their full attention toward the dark-eyed woman on the move, gracefully striding past concession stands, game booths and rides, picking up her pace as she headed back toward the parking area.

"Yes, siree, Jimmy. Sure would like to rope, rob, and ride that filly," the wiry middle-aged man, covered in an array of crude, faded tattoos, made clear. The indelible designs rooted above his narrow waist branched up his back and chest and along a pair of reedy limbs. "Indeed-ee-roo, I would." Carson Reynolds raised the container of cold beer to his lips, basking in the artificial light, saturating his ego on that torrid August evening.

"Tell you one thing for sure," Jimmy set forth in stone. "Those are very expensive footwear, shorts, and blouse. I shit you not."

"You say so. I know you know your stuff, Jim. How about the crown jewels?" he questioned with a hopeful grin.

"Get real, man. Those diamonds are paste. Base of the crown is copper."

"You can tell from here?"

"I was on her heels the second she pulled in. But drivin' a brand new black Jaguar. Pretty cat. 'Cock-and-balls,' my cousin calls 'em. Like some of them Corvettes." Jimmy smiled prettily and purred like a kitten. "Meow," he mimicked and giggled girlishly, bringing the tips of his fingers to his puckered lips.

"How about all them golden bracelets?" Carson asked anxiously.

"Well, in her case, all that glitters *is* gold, Carson," Jimmy replied. "Would bring a pretty penny."

A moment later, the tattooed man walked off in the young

woman's direction. "Come on, boy," the man called to his loyal companion. "Come on, you mangy mutt."

"Hey! Excuse me. Lady," Carson called out. "Hold up there a second."

Angelica turned around between two rows of cars.

"Man, you move like the wind. You goin' to a fire or a funeral, missy?" he questioned and grinned.

Angelica smiled warmly. "If I had the time, Carson, I'd go to yours for giggles. Your funeral, that is."

Carson stopped dead in his tracks and looked around, brushing the dog back with a sweep of his foot. "Say what?" he snapped menacingly.

Angelica stared coldly at the man. "You heard me, Carson."

"How do you know my name?"

The young woman looked dotingly down at the little terrier.

"Never mind the *doogh*, bitch. I asked you a fucking question," the tattooed man barked.

"*Doogh*, Carson?" Angelica mocked.

"Answer me, bitch."

"Your brother told me. He also told me how to find you," she answered, looking up from the dog and staring deeply into Carson's azure eyes.

"My brother?"

"Yes, Carson. Your brother," she repeated.

Carson looked back to the fairgrounds then all around the parking area. "Look. I'm going to make this easy for you. All right? I want those bracelets. And I want them now. You hand them over, and you won't get hurt. Fuck with me, and I'll put your head through a car window. Understand?"

Angelica placed her wand beneath the hollow of a shoulder before sliding several bangles off her wrist, dropping the items to the ground before Carson.

"Step back," he ordered.

Angelica raised her wand most magically and ran one of the pointed blades across Carson's cheek. Instantly, it bled.

The little dog barked as his master stepped back in horror with a hand to his bloody face. Carson stared in disbelief at the blood before he lunged at Angelica, but the woman easily brushed him off—as effortlessly as the man had swept his small dog aside.

"Oh, you're mine, cunt," Carson swore and stumbled. And as he reached for his fairy princess, Angelica drove the man's face into a driver's side car door window.

The dog barked away madly.

Angelica grinned. "Is that what you had in mind for me, Carson? Hum? You're even uglier now than when you started out after me." She laughed lightly before driving the wand-like arrow deep into the yapping dog's throat. "You won't believe what you're going to look like when I'm finished with the two of you."

Carson was about to scream for his life, but the woman closed off the man's windpipe in a flash.

"Shh," Angelica whispered, her thumb pressed solidly into Carson's larynx. "Butch-Lee told me all about you. About how you hunt all sorts of prey. About the big bowie knife you'd carry with you for skinning deer in days gone by. Your Arkansas toothpick, you'd call it. Overkill, Carson. You see the little star I carry at the end of this wand?" Angelica withdrew it from the voiceless, squirming animal. "Five tiny but super strong, sharp steel blades. Know what they're capable of doing in the right hands? You and your little friend here are about to find out. You and your d*oo***gh**," she said, enunciating the o in dog with a long vowel sound, holding the note before hitting the final consonant like a gong. "Why don't you kneel down here and give Max a kiss on the lips to say good-bye, Carson?"

Angelica removed three beige cable ties from her pocket.

Chapter 2

Robert Redler knew and loved boats. Robert and Liza Downs knew the Peconic River, blindfolded. Their home and dock were on it, just a stone's throw from the town of Riverhead, Long Island. They knew the backwaters and bays, too: Reeves, Flanders, the Great Peconic, and the Little Peconic. They knew the waters further east around Shelter Island and out to Gardiner's Bay. The couple was beginning a long-awaited and most needed vacation.

Robert turned and headed the twenty-five footer north through Plum Gut, taking a 352° heading across Long Island Sound toward Connecticut. Cruising at around 2700 rpms, they would reach the mouth of the Connecticut River at approximately 11:30 a.m., two and a half hours from home port. Liza felt that she was finally on vacation.

Summer was flying by quickly, and Liza had been complaining that they had done very little boating to date. And although she had had a respite from her sixth graders since the end of June, it really hadn't been much of a vacation for either of them. Much of their time had been spent doing never-ending but necessary projects.

"What time do you think we'll reach Hamburg Cove?" Liza asked excitedly.

"Should be there around one thirty," Robert answered above the sound of the single engine. "We've got to gas-up at Old Lyme Dock first. We're down to about a quarter of a tank."

It was the least expensive gas in the area and the reason why captains of big and small vessels alike made it a prudent point to fill up at the Dock on the east side of the Connecticut River, just between the bridges.

They arrived in Hamburg Cove at 1:30 p.m. sharp, and Liza was in the cool fresh water soon after they had picked up a mooring and secured the boat. Robert switched over from both batteries to number 2. He turned down the refrigerator from a high setting of 5 to number 3. It was a gorgeous day. Thursday, the 8th of August. Now, he, too, felt as though they were finally on holiday.

"V-A C-A T-I-O-N," Robert sang Connie Francis' recording as he bounded up the three steps from the cabin, past the helm area, down another and across the cockpit, then out and over Liza's head he flew, plunging headlong into the cool water that refreshingly shocked him, shooting to the floor of the nine-foot river's depth. Not impatiently, he headed for the surface.

Together, the couple sang a duo while treading water.

"That's not a swimsuit, Rob," she declared as he pulled himself up the ladder and onto the swim platform. "Where's your bathing suit?"

"Forgot it. No big deal as you can see," he joked and laughed.

Liza hadn't seen Robert smile but cursorily for some time now. But then there hadn't been very much to smile about of late.

Chapter 3

The police photographer knelt beside the body of Carson Reynolds, shot at point-blank range once through the back of the head after apparently having been tortured for quite some time. Carson's dog lay beside the man. The cameraman focused his close-up lens on a narrow beige plastic band that bound the tattooed man's wrists securely behind his back. A pair of bands fastened firmly around each ankle was tightly connected to the single band looped at the wrists.

"Cable ties," he stated.

"Yep," Sheriff Tom Hayes affirmed.

The deputy beside him stood transfixed.

"Let me know when you've got your pictures, Horace," the sheriff said, summoning his deputy back to one of the vehicles.

"You bet," Horace said enthusiastically, seeming to savor his assignment while oscillating between a degree of sadness and the pure sensationalism of it all. In all his twenty-three years in the business of bodies, he had never seen anything quite like this. As a part-time police photographer, as well as a full-time coroner for Bibb County, he thought he had seen everything.

"You get anything more out of Jimmy?" the sheriff asked his deputy.

"He's still hysterical," the man answered.

Sheriff Hayes grinned. "When is he not?"

Deputy Purty smiled and shook his head. "Told me just the same as he told you. He watched Carson and Max follow the woman from the fairgrounds toward the parking area then turned his attention to that water gun game with the balloons like he does every year. Loves that goddamn faggot game, ya know."

"Better not let Billy-Jo hear ya callin' that a faggot game," the sheriff warned with an even wider grin. "Billy just loves that game as much as Jimmy," he assured his deputy with a wink and a nod.

"I wonder if he heard about his kissin' cousin yet."

The two men looked back over at the mutilated naked tattooed body of Carson Reynolds, lying there in a God-awful position on the clumped earth next to his dismembered dog.

"You'd know it by now if he did 'cause Billy's gonna blow sky-high when he does hear. Listen, I want you to stay on Jimmy. What we got goin' for us is his description of the woman. He doesn't miss a trick, so to speak, right down to her shade of lipstick. When he calms down, he may remember something else."

"Right," the deputy agreed and nodded respectfully.

"What do you think we've got here, Tom?" Mayor Tom Harden asked, staring down at his speakerphone set on a highly-polished mahogany surface of the desk that had once belonged to a former governor of the state.

"Hard to say, Tom," the sheriff answered honestly.

Besides sharing same given names, the two men had shared most everything else over the course of many a year, dating back to a time the two boys languished to carry Millie Brown's school bag. The mayor won her hand in marriage. Through the decades, the two officials had conferred on all matters of importance, monitoring the mood of the town, the pulse of statewide politics, and the climate of the county. Tom-Tom, as the pair was known throughout the state, danced to a distant drummer: the governor of the great state of Georgia.

"Could be that Carson came on too strong with our mystery woman," the mayor put forth hypothetically. "She suddenly screams robbery and rape, then some nut case playing hero comes to her aid and gets carried away, taking Carson out for good. Or maybe the woman takes care of Carson by herself."

"But the dog, too, Tom? Just doesn't wash. This is gotta be the work of some raving lunatic. Remember that cult business that started up in New York, two years back? Circle of Friends."

"Sure I remember. Long Island. The mutilations. Richard Geist's nationwide assassination network. How could anyone forget? Mental patients and, in some cases, prisoners from across the country set free by Geist's people. Couple of our own local lunatics fled from Milledgeville. Authorities out there certainly had their hands full for weeks." The mayor sighed sadly at the memory before he brightened. "Got them all back but one, though. Right? Maybe, just maybe—"

"I know what you're thinking, Tom. I made an inquiry this morning. The guy was shot to death in a bar brawl over a year ago."

"Some of our neighboring states weren't so lucky. Could be any one of those nut cases."

"Sure could. Matter of fact, I'm on my way up to Milledgeville now."

Milledgeville was home to the Georgia State Mental Hospital.

"Got someone particular in mind, do you, Tom?" the mayor asked.

"More along the lines of someone's early employment there," Sheriff Tom Hayes answered, pausing for full effect.

"Care to comment at this point?"

"Carson Reynolds himself. I want to see his records."

"He worked over there?"

"Maintenance. Five years ago."

"I see. Well, let me know if you turn up anything interesting, Tom. All right?"

"Always do, ya know."

"Right."

"Regards to Millie, Tom."

"You betcha."

"Oh, almost forgot. Jimmy's cooperating with a sketch artist down from Atlanta re our mystery woman."

"Great." The mayor switched off the speakerphone then pressed the intercom. "Sally. Track down the governor for me, and tell him I'll be in the office till four."

"Yes, sir."

Chapter 4

Butch-Lee Reynolds was holed up in a modest single-family rental, situated along a quiet tree-lined block in a small New Jersey town. He awakened as soon as he heard a car pull into the driveway. Instinctively, he reached down for his semiautomatic, pressing the cool receiver to his forehead while he waited.

Angelica cut the engine and grabbed two newspapers off the front seat, noticing a curtain part at the neighbor's home next-door.

Butch-Lee heard the car door open then close, followed by footsteps coming up the walkway and onto the front stoop. A moment later, Angelica unlocked the door, entered, then closed, locked, and chained the door. She made her way through the living room then down the dark hallway toward the bedroom. Butch-Lee's pistol was leveled at the shadowy figure standing at the threshold in the glow of the night-light.

She was a blonde tonight, dressed in a beige gown and matching pumps. The newspapers hung at her side. The two peered at one another there in the penumbra.

Butch-Lee spoke first. "Done?"

"Wouldn't be back here if it wasn't."

"Done right?"

"Are you trying to insult me?" she snapped, stepping off into a corner.

He couldn't see her distinctly, but he could hear the rustle of papers and clothing.

"Did he suffer?"

"Oh, God, Lee. Did he ever."

He pointed the gun at the ceiling, giggling so satisfactorily. "And the dog?"

"Max?" she asked casually.

"Yes, Max," he practically shouted.

"Max is in more than half a dozen pieces."

"And you did Max first. Yes?" he questioned excitedly. "Yes?"

"Just as I promised."

"And what did he say?" Butch-Lee demanded.

"Max?" Angelica teased.

"Carson, you cunt!"

"That's exactly what he called me in the heat of the moment. Later, he said, and I quote, 'Oh, good God, girl. Why are you doing this to my poor *doogh?*' That's how he said dog. *Doogh.*" Angelica laughed lightly.

Butch-Lee grinned excitedly. "And?"

"And I said, 'Well, Carson. You see, I have my orders.' Then he said, in between a lot of crying and carrying on, 'Orders from who?' And I said, 'Not from *who*, but from *whom*,'" she elaborated while undressing in the dark.

Butch-Lee had his face buried in the pillow and was positively hysterical with fits of laughter. Angelica lifted a corner of the sheet and slid in beside him.

"Then, then?" he asked when he recovered.

There was a long silence between them, and she could hear his heart beating and his breath quickening. Suddenly, she felt the muzzle of the barrel pressing solidly against her skull.

"Well, bitch?"

"Well, then I told him that it was you who ordered it," she said, gripping his penis in both hands.

"His reaction?" he managed as she took his erection deep into her mouth.

Angelica sucked and stammered and gurgled and giggled and swallowed Butch-Lee again and again while he thought he'd die from the unbelievable suspense, the eroticism, the sheer hysterics of the moment.

"Now, tell me—tell me—tell me!" Butch-Lee insisted, the moment she brought him to climax.

"Tell me, tell me, tell me," she teased and tarried, warming herself up for round two.

"Did you cut him up good?"

"Ripped him a new asshole!" she answered, straddling Butch-Lee's lean frame while pointing the pistol smack between his eyes.

"Tell me everything," he pressed, squeezing her erect nipples between his middle and index fingers. "Orders from *whom*, and then what?"

"'Orders from your sweet brother, Butchy-Lee,' I had explained to him quite clearly." In the dim light, Butch-Lee could see Angelica's smile; and she, his. "Then he said, 'I don't believe you. Why would Butch-Lee want to hurt me?' So, I told him it was because Max crapped on your carpet when he was a pup. I think that's when he finally understood."

"So what did he say?" Butch-Lee demanded, twisting her nipples until she winced.

"'That was over fourteen years ago,' your brother cried, bawling like a baby. 'My brother's crazy. Surely you know that,' he wailed. So I said to him, then you'll forgive him for this deed. Yes? 'My brother's crazy,' he repeated, whimpering and whining till I thought I'd lose my mind."

"But you didn't kill him till he forgave me, yes? You promised me that."

"He forgave you, Lee. I didn't end his life until he forgave you," she outright lied.

"And the police?"

"They haven't got a clue as yet." She sighed and moaned so pleasurably, riding him ever so gently. "You can read all about it in the morning. I brought home a couple Georgia papers. We're miles ahead of them, Lee."

"Miles ahead of them, my angel. Miles ahead," he repeated, practically half asleep.

"God is dog spelled backwards," Butch-Lee barked delightfully, sitting at a small Formica table off the alcove kitchen, turning to page 29A of one of the two-day-old Georgia newspapers. His thinning, sand-colored hair fell to one side as he canted his head toward the hallway.

Angelica stood barefoot, poised in a powder blue cotton bathrobe. "Morning, Lee," she greeted.

"Morning, angel." He turned his attention back to *The Constitution*.

"That was quite a workout last night, fella."

"Hum," Butch-Lee managed, absorbed in the lengthy article

covering the hometown fair and the murder of his older brother.

"Coffee?" She ambled over to the kitchenette, taking in the belt at her waist.

"Dog is God. God is dog," Butch-Lee repeated, laughing delightedly, poring down the narrow newspaper column, taking in every word, biting his cuticle along the edge of a thumb, pumping a leg impatiently upon the linoleum floor.

Angelica ran water for the coffee maker then went over to a counter. "When do you want to get out of here?"

Butch-Lee giggled and shook his head violently.

"What's so funny?"

Butch-Lee smacked the paper with the back of his hand. "A terrier?" he said incredulously. "The fucking reporter is calling it a terrier!"

Angelica smirked. "After I got finished with Max, I'm surprised they even knew it was a *doogh*."

"God is dog, spelled backwards," Butch-Lee barked in repetition.

"Listen, baby. We have some time before we blow this place?"

Butch-Lee looked up. "Blow, blow, blow," he uttered and beamed brightly, closing his eyes and rolling his almond-shaped head clockwise in a lazy circle.

"Yes?"

"Sure, sugar. What do you wanna do? Make the bed and vacuum before we split?" He giggled.

Angelica was peering out from behind a kitchen blind. "No. I want to make a morning cocktail for Ms. Nosy-Body next-door."

Butch-Lee put his head back down in the newspaper.

"Ms. Nosy-Body drop by when I was busy butchering Max and coddling Carson, south of the Mason-Dixon Line, baby?"

Butch-Lee scrunched up his face.

"Well?"

"Woof!"

"I'll take that as a yes." She stared down at the empty bottles of Scotch and bourbon on the counter; the latter of which was Butch-Lee's poison. Certainly not the empty liter of Vat-69. "And because I know you don't dispense that piss-like liquid around here, Mr. Jack Daniel's. Girl got herself a vaginal vibe to trollop on over here and troll these waters while your baby's dogging it down in Moonshine County, I see."

Butch-Lee said nothing.

"Stay long? Fuck you silly? Tell you she needed a man around the house but that you'd do in a pinch, baby?"

Butch-Lee looked up from the paper with angry eyes.

Suddenly the newspaper flew from his hands and hit the ceiling fan. Butch-Lee was on his feet but for a fraction of a second. Down on the linoleum he laid, Angelica immediately behind him, holding him affectionately in a sleeper hold.

"Uncle, uncle," he whined, smacking his hand in surrender upon the flooring.

"Fuck your uncle and your brother, too," she cooed. "Tell me everything."

"Later."

"Every intimate detail?" she demanded, switching quickly to a stranglehold.

"Ahhh! Blow by blow," he swore.

"She here last night?"

Butch-Lee grimaced. "Yessss."

"Just don't fucking lie to me, Lee. It's the only thing I ever ask."

"All right!"

"Good thing I'm not a jealous woman, Lee baby."

"Good thing," he said then choked.

"Gonna have to waste her, you know." Angelica relaxed her grip.

Butch-Lee said nothing.

Angelica smiled. "Gonna let me referee a little?"

"I guess."

"You put it up her ass?"

"She won't do that."

"Wanna bet?"

"How you gonna make her do that, sugar?"

"Told you. A special cocktail for Ms. Busy-Body."

"Promise I get to put it up her ass?"

"Promise to be good and not to giggle?"

Butch-Lee giggled uncontrollably.

Angelica laughed. "What did I just say?"

Butch-Lee Reynolds catapulted from unrestrained giggles to an outright fit of laughter, the two of them rolling across the floor. He finally caught his breath and remarked: "You're the best goddamn sister a guy could ever have."

"Stepsister," Angelica reminded him.

Butch-Lee phoned next-door, spoke to the girl, then hung the receiver on the hook.

"Yes?" Angelica questioned.

"Little while," he replied. "Did you bring me back a present from the Peach State?"

"Yes."

"What?"

"You'll see in a little while," she promised.

Chapter 5

Angelica had packed her clothing into two suitcases and put them in a small closet. She busied herself with rinsing out cups and saucers, washing out the coffee maker, setting out three clean glasses, preparing for their guest.

"How old is she, Lee?"

"Says she's eighteen."

"More like sixteen, I'll bet. Vat-69, indeed!"

Butch-Lee shrugged indifferently. "Probably her folks'."

"Why'd she bring it?"

"Didn't like my Tennessee tonic."

"You feed her?"

"Hamburger and fries."

"When?"

"Friday."

"I'll bet the bitch was here the whole time I was gone. Wasn't she? You piece of shit."

"Just once before; I swear. The night you left."

"And what exactly did you tell her?"

"That you were my sister and that we were here—"

The front doorbell rang, and Angelica went to take a seat.

Butch-Lee went to the door and threw it open. "Boo!" he said in startling expression before giggling sillily.

"Boo, yourself," the young girl echoed, puckering her lips and brushing flirtatiously by Butch-Lee. "Hi there," she said, smiling broadly before the handsome woman seated on the love seat. "You must be Ramona."

"I guess I must be," Angelica agreed pleasantly.

"I'm Marade. Like parade but with an M. All my friends call me Mar."

Butch-Lee double-locked the door and slid the chain in place.

"That's an unusually pretty name," Angelica replied. "And you're a very, very pretty young lady. Come sit."

"Not so bad yourself," Marade complimented, brushing strands of long blonde hair away from her eyes. "Lee's told me all about you." She went over and took Angelica's hand, setting a slender frame upon the seat next to the woman.

"May I ask how old you are, Mar?"

Marade lowered her eyes. "Fifteen," she said quietly. "But I'll be sixteen in November. November fifth."

Angelica shot a look at her stepbrother. "Well, I think you look every bit of eighteen. And what a figure, girl. So there."

"All the fellas think I'm eighteen going on nineteen. At least that's what I tell them," she confessed.

Angelica took in the girl's long tanned legs and full breasts. White short-shorts with a matching cotton top. Tennis shoes from a dime store. Lacy-blue cuffed crew socks. "How about a cocktail, Mar?"

"Well, I'm a little hung over from last night," she said, smiling over at Butch-Lee. "We put away some pills and booze, your brother and I."

"Lethal combination," Angelica declared, getting up off the seat. "Got just the thing for you. Fix you right up. Just you wait and see." She scurried into the kitchen, holding her robe closed at the throat.

"God, she's gorgeous!" Marade swore. "You didn't tell me she was so goddamn gorgeous," she snapped, smacking Butch-Lee playfully across a shoulder. "You told me about all that karate stuff. I expected to meet some fucking dyke."

"No, that's her. One of Charlie's Angels."

"Who's Charlie?"

"TV show. Before your time, kid."

Angelica returned shortly with three tall glasses set on a silver serving tray. "Here we go. First for our lovely guest, Mar the magnificent."

"Thank you, Ramona."

"Lee."

Butch-Lee toasted the two. "Sis. Mar."

"What is this?" Marade asked.

"Fresh juices, herbs, and a little pick-me-up," Angelica explained.

"Scotch?"

"At ten in the morning, Mar? Get serious, girl."

"Oh, I could handle a cocktail or two, a.m. or p.m. But not after last night."

Butch-Lee grinned stupidly. "Mar put away a few."

"Not that nasty Jack Daniel's, Mar?" Angelica chided.

"God forbid. I don't know how he can get that shit down. Brought my own stuff. Actually, Dad's." Marade took a sip. "Hmm, good. What kind of juices?"

"Banana. Coconut. Cherry. All natural."

"What's with the flower?"

"That's the herb. Aster. It's edible. Drink up."

"Ramona's a health food nut," Butch-Lee explained.

"I'm a salad freak, myself," Marade confessed. "Gotta be careful, though, of all that fast-food crap. They spray all that chemical shit over everything. Don't know what we're doing to our bodies." Marade took a good-sized gulp.

"I like salad, too, Mar." Angelica said brightly, sitting down next to their visitor, enjoying the short-term small talk.

"You see the prices today of those ready-made salads in the supermarkets, Ramona? Outta sight. God only knows what they spray on them to keep them fresh looking."

"Not what you might think, Mar," Angelica started to explain, taking a sip from her own drink. "There have been scientific studies that show higher percentages of Vitamin C content in broccoli florets from those supermarket produce packs than what people cut up fresh at home. And those packaged mini carrots? Maintained one hundred percent of their cancer-fighting beta-carotene as compared to a bunch of Bugs Bunny-sized bruisers from the refrigerator."

"How do they do that?" Mar asked with genuine interest.

"Cold."

"Cold?"

"Very cold. Creating a state of hibernation. About five percent oxygen as compared to the air we breathe, which is around twenty-one percent," Angelica said knowledgeably.

Marade looked from Angelica to Butch-Lee then back to

Angelica. "What about all that chemical spray crap I hear tell about at those fast-food places?"

"That produce is usually washed in a chlorine solution, dried, and put into bags that allow the release of carbon dioxide. Nothing wrong with the fresh-cut market products, either. Just wash everything twice to be on the safe side."

"Ramona even washes her chicken before she cooks it," Butch-Lee chimed in.

"What Lee means is that I parboil it."

"So does my mom and dad!" Marade said excitedly. "Do you think you'll be around long enough to meet them, Ramona? You'd really like them."

"When are they coming home?"

"Late tonight. She and Daddy are visiting my aunt in Pennsylvania." Marade yawned.

"I'm afraid we won't be here to meet them. Lee and I are splitting soon."

Marade looked saddened and stared down at the floor. "When are you coming back, Lee?" she asked, looking up at her newfound friend rather languidly.

"Like I told you, sweetheart. By-and-by."

"Yeah, or more like bye-bye baby," she said with a forlorn frown, finishing her drink.

Angelica gestured, and Butch-Lee flew out of his seat to take Marade's glass. "It's not like that at all, Mar," he said. "Listen—"

"Let me get that," Angelica insisted, taking the glass and disappearing into the kitchen.

Butch-Lee was sitting on the love seat with Marade when Angelica returned. Her robe was open at the top, and she leaned forward, serving the girl another drink.

Marade pouted. "You know. Every time I meet someone I like, it seems they take a powder." She took a big gulp from her fresh drink. "Delicious," she said, setting her eyes on the front of Angelica's open robe.

"Doesn't have to be that way." Angelica smiled warmly, bending closer and kissing the girl on the cheek, her lips, her neck.

Butch-Lee put his hand between Marade's thighs and caressed her. Angelica brushed her breasts across the young girl's face.

"I feel dizzy," Marade whispered.

"Dizzy with desire very soon. You'll see," Angelica said softly, opening her robe at the waist, massaging herself gently.

"I'm not a lesbian," Marade said defensively, staring up at the beautiful form before her.

"Neither am I," Angelica said, unzipping the front of Butch-Lee's pants, kneading her stepbrother's prodigious penis, taking it out from the fly. Butch-Lee stood, and Angelica slowly guided Marade's head toward it. Angelica put her tongue in the teenager's ear. "Fuck him with your throat," Angelica whispered, taking the tumbler from Marade's hand.

Trancelike, Marade took Butch-Lee into her mouth as Angelica snaked the girl's top up her torso and along both arms, harnessing the garment around the slender neck, pulling her back gently while the fifteen-year-old moved mellifluously forward. In and out of her mouth Butch-Lee flowed.

"Deep. Deep. Take him deep down, darling," Angelica coaxed, massaging the firm young breasts.

"Humm," Marade breathed heavily, picking up the pace, allowing herself to be lifted slightly as Angelica removed the girl's shorts and panties.

"Here, take another sip—then I want you on your stomach on the floor."

Marade took another sip of the concoction and did as she was told, lying down on the plush carpeting.

Angelica kneeled and positioned a cushion from the love seat under Marade's hips, then softly stroked her inner thighs, summoning Butch-Lee down beside them. Opening the top of a small jar, Angelica swept up a finger-full of salve and began massaging Butch-Lee's large penis. Next, she smoothly traced the outline of Marade's anus with a middle finger before inserting it slowly and steadily inside her. "Kneel behind her," she told Butch-Lee.

Marade winced. "What's he doing," she whined, feeling the broad insertion as Butch-Lee put the head of his penis between the cheeks of her buttocks.

"Shh," Angelica sighed. "Lee wants so badly to fuck your ass. Yes?"

"Nooo," Marade shuddered. "Too big. Ahh. Hurts."

"Not if you relax and behave like the little slut you really are," Angelica said.

Butch-Lee held her hips and pushed himself in further.

"Ohhh," Marade moaned. "I can't—"

"Oh, yes you can, you little whore. Tell Lee to give you a little more." Angelica smiled, pressing her lips against the girl's ear. "Tell Lee to put half his cock in now."

"No, please—"

"Half your cock in, now, bitch," Angelica repeated, kissing Marade fully on the lips.

Butch-Lee withdrew then put himself partially back inside.

Marade let out a cry.

"Tell him," Angelica ordered. "Half your cock in, now, cunt," she insisted, tonguing the girl's ear and caressing her breasts.

"Half your cock in, now," Marade said breathlessly.

Butch-Lee thrust himself halfway back inside and almost came, catching his breath and sending his mind a million miles away.

Marade gasped and held her breath, contorting her face into a mix of pain and pleasure. Butch-Lee slowly moved himself back and forth, in and out of her anus. Marade groaned and Angelica shot her hungry tongue into the girl's mouth. Back out and into her ear.

"Want him all the way?" Angelica whispered.

Marade was breathing heavily. "Afraid," the girl whined and whinnied. Butch-Lee put himself in even further. Marade shivered and sighed.

"Want it faster in your aster?" Angelica recited sillily, brushing a nipple across Marade's mouth. "Humm?"

"Yes," Marade gasped.

"Can't hear you," Angelica teased, gesturing to Butch-Lee.

"Oh, yesss," Marade repeated.

"Want more you fucking little whore?" Angelica swore.

"More," Marade begged.

Butch-Lee thrust himself inside Marade, all the way up her rectum to his pelvic bone; the girl let out a gasp.

"All nine inches up your nasty little ass, Ms. Vat-69. You like?"

Marade's eyes glassed over before she closed them, sinking her polished red nails into the purple pile carpet. Butch-Lee was pumping her madly, prone against her shapely ass cheeks, sweat pouring off his bony chest. Suddenly, he exploded. Marade threw her blonde head of hair wildly from side to side, her body shuddering as she climaxed, too.

"Dizzy," Marade said, in what seemed a century later.

Dizzy and disoriented, the girl rolled off the pink cushion and gazed at the sand-painted ceiling. Drowsy, she closed her eyes and slept.

A quarter of an hour later, Butch-Lee tried to wake her. Angelica was going through the front door with her suitcases. "Come on, Lee. Let's get a move on."

Butch-Lee knelt close to Marade, putting an ear to her chest, then her mouth, finally pressing three fingers to the inside of her wrist, checking for a pulse. There wasn't any. He stood up suddenly and bolted to the door.

Angelica slammed down the trunk lid on the '96 Volvo and headed back inside.

Butch-Lee grabbed her by the wrist. "Marade isn't breathing," he said.

"Well, you certainly are," she replied, pressing her palm against his chest. "Feels like your heart is going to jump out of your chest."

"No, I'm serious."

"I'm sure you are," she said matter-of-factly, twisting her hand out from his grip.

"What the hell did you give her?"

"Double dose of GHB and juices. Now let's get out of here."

"What the fuck is that?" he snapped.

"Gamma-hydroxybutyrate,"

"Gamma who?"

"A date-rape drug, my peach. Also known as Georgia Home Boy. You asked me last night if I had brought you home a present. Anything else, dear?"

"Is she gonna be all right?"

Looking annoyed, Angelica walked over and stooped beside the body, pressing two fingers against the side of the girl's neck. A moment later, she closed Marade's eyes. Forever.

"What the fuck are we gonna do?" Butch-Lee bellyached.

"You? You're going to pack. Me? I'm going to get dressed and put on a little makeup. You don't want to travel with a witch, do you?" Angelica smiled winsomely and winked.

Butch-Lee stared back at Marade's body rather sadly.

Chapter 6

An unusually cool summer prevailed, finally giving way to seasonable temperatures immediately following Labor Day. Sand and sun worshippers relished the remaining days, with state park beaches extending their season for a fortnight. Otherwise, it was back to school for Liza Downs and her pupils. Back to the serious commencement of commerce for the nine-to-fivers. For the leisured classes, it was a time for contemplating to which distant corner of the world they would travel. For the criminal classes, it really didn't matter much what time of year it was. To law enforcement, it was business as usual.

Long Island's homicide detectives worked the unsolved murder of Riverhead High School's homecoming queen. A year earlier, Los Angeles authorities had paraded O.J. Simpson and the crime of the century. From coast to coast, it was the ordinary backdrop against the extraordinary.

For Police Chief Grear, the attractions and distractions of life and death were generally kept simple. You embarked upon a journey according to one's values and principles, then awaited judgment day. No deals cut in district attorneys' offices or sidebar conferences with some appointed judge. No fence-sitting politicians leaning one way one day, then in another direction the next. No haggling lawyers trying to snow a judge and jury. In Grear's ordered world, there was but one arbiter in the final hour of reckoning. Cut-and-dried. Only one practitioner: Our Lord and Savior.

Chief Grear's firmly embedded beliefs concerning man and God's role in the universe stood solely between his wife, Blanch, and him. Few knew that the chief was a profoundly religious soul. He rarely spoke of God or attended Sunday services. In all his fifty-seven years, he never met a person whom he believed *knew* God; that is, until the day he came to know Robert Redler. The police chief accepted that belief much like he accepted breathing. It hung within the untenable acceptance of his faith. That unshakable conviction remained a constant. Firm. Secure. Solid. And if the chief's tenets were ever in any way arguable or mistaken, he nevertheless felt content in the knowledge that he would remain a God-fearing, good man.

Good and evil. Light and dark. Black and white. Kept simple, life and death were relatively easy to deal with. It was the gradations of gray that on rare occasions created confusion and chaos for the man as a child of God, although he refused to question his faith. Chief Grear, Riverhead P.D., was soon to find himself in that gray area once again.

"So. Whatta we got?" Detective Sergeant Beau Hopkins asked with a degree of concern, draping his soaking wet raincoat across the back of a wooden bench just outside the chief's office. He placed two large Manila envelopes behind the coat. A volley of thunder sounded in the distance.

"What makes you think we've got anything?" the chief replied from behind his desk.

"That pensive look when you hung up the phone for openers," Beau answered, putting a foot across the threshold of the boss's office.

Chief Grear smiled. "Good thing I don't play poker."

"Gonna lay some cards on the table?" Beau pressed, placing a second shoe over the saddle and past the doorway.

"I'm not even sure I'm even anted in," the chief said rather absently.

"Stakes too high?"

"Might be nothing, Beau."

"That's why a federal prosecutor calls you two days running?"

"Nothing really unusual about that."

"From New Jersey?"

The chief swiveled ninety degrees in his chair, staring down the hall that separated him from the switchboard area. "Our Doris now the official *information* operator?" he inquired.

"I knew it had to be that Kelly guy again!" Sergeant Beau Hopkins declared and laughed satisfactorily. "So, now you've got one card face up, Chief."

"Snookered me, did you? And how did you know about yesterday's call? You bribing Doris with flowers, or candy, or what?"

"Hot chocolate. Goes right through her system—like that," Beau said, snapping his fingers. "I relieved her at the switchboard so she could go relieve herself. Legitimate coffee break," he swore. "Call came through at nine forty a.m. Pompous ass from Parsippany. It's that Pine Brook business, isn't it? Overdose. Right?" He studied the chief's face intently.

"You listening in on the line now?"

Sergeant Beau Hopkins looked wounded.

"Well, were you?"

"Not too good with all those plugs and lights, Chief," he admitted coyly. "Just got bits and pieces. I wouldn't exactly call it eavesdropping."

"You keep this under wraps, you hear?"

"Loud and clear," Beau promised.

"I mean it, Beau. Not really our concern." The chief's jaw locked.

Beau's grin grew from ear to ear.

"Damn it, Beau. Now listen—"

"Two cards face up—"

"But you're not going to see the whole hand. Not just yet."

"Well, then let me tell you what I think the dealer's holding. All right? You don't have to say anything. Okay?"

"I *won't* say anything. But you can have your say."

"Well, I'm not a fortuneteller like your friend, Robert Redler, but—"

"He's not a fortuneteller."

"Psychic. Clairvoyant." *Charlatan*, he wanted to add but didn't.

The chief sighed and shook his head patiently. "Redler's none of those things. He's been given an extraordinary *gift*, Beau."

"Whatever you say, boss. So, you gonna let me tell you what I've sort of stumbled across so that maybe you can give me a hint of what those Jersey boys got?"

"They've got a homicide. That's it."

"A homicide connected to Angelica Manns and her people? Circle of Friends."

Now he had the chief's full attention. Chief Grear grew still. "Go on."

"Well, I'm sure you know about that incident down in Georgia, few weeks back." The chief did not. So the sergeant filled him in quickly, bringing the man up to speed.

When Beau was finished, the chief scratched anxiously at an ear. "So what you're theorizing is that this tattooed guy, Carson what's his-name—"

"Carson Reynolds."

"—was murdered by the Manns woman down in Georgia, that she killed the guy's dog, headed up the coast to Jersey, killed the teenage girl found next-door, then split to parts unknown with some guy?"

"Not just any guy."

"No?"

Sergeant Hopkins shook his dark face. "No, but someone related to her. Her half brother."

"I thought a background search showed she has no living relatives, Beau."

"Well, the investigation failed to turn up the fact that she has a stepbrother who's still alive. A real cuckoo bird who some mystery woman recently helped get released from an institution in Europe. There's a history of insanity in the family dating back to The Crash of '29, when this guy's father flew out the window after losing millions. Still enough money around, though, to lend credibility to the chip off the old block's staged suicide. Along the line, someone committed a Leonard Ellis Harris, real name Lee Edward Reynolds, Butch-Lee to family and friends, to a sanitarium in Stockholm, while some poor soul had taken Lee's seat and a two-hundred-foot plunge into the Straits of Dover with the family car. Dozen witnesses saw the automobile explode. The only one left after the fifties to tell the tale, if she had a mind to, was the stepsister. And by no means an ugly one at that."

"Angelica Manns?"

"The one and only. Keeps turning up like a bad penny."

"What about our pretender?"

"Told everyone the factual account when he finally realized his confinement was final and that no one from the states was going to bail him out, so to speak. Of course, the administration there knew he was nuts to begin with and wasn't about to be making long-distance inquiries. So he sat and rotted in that asylum between attempted escapes."

"Escapes?"

"Eleven attempts over the past eleven years. Same person turned him in each time."

"Who?"

"His lover and confidante."

"Lover?"

"Twenty-nine-year-old female patient. Been there since she was seven."

"Why'd she turn him in?"

"Come on, Chief. Misery loves company. She didn't want to lose him. Nor did she believe his stories that he'd come back and get her out of there like he promised her he would. She told me he's hung like a racehorse." Beau laughed. "There's the real reason."

"Why would she tell you all this?"

The sergeant grinned from ear to ear. "Because I promised her I'd find him and bring him back."

"I see," Grear said, fingers combing back a graying mane with both his hands. "And when did you plan on telling me all this?"

"Just as soon as I knew her info was on the money," Beau said and nodded solemnly.

"And just how do you know, or shouldn't I ask?"

"Kelly's phone calls over the past two days. Edna, that's the patient in Stockholm, told me Butch-Lee Reynolds would be heading for New Jersey, and that he had some unfinished business in Georgia."

"Sweet Jesus." The chief exhaled, swiveling out of his chair like a whirlwind. He went over to the near wall and stood before a map of the United States. "Did she say where in Jersey or Georgia?"

"Nope. Just that he had a pile of money hidden in his basement somewhere in Jersey, and a brother in Georgia with a dog named Max that he wanted both dead."

"Jesus Christ."

Beau smiled. "All coming together for you, Chief?"

"That goddamn Kelly."

"Knows a lot more than he's letting on. Correct?"

"That Georgia business. You think it was this Butch-Lee?"

"Or the Manns woman, or both of them."

"But the Georgia murder went down first, you said."

"You putting all your cards face up on the table, Chief?" the detective sergeant asked bluntly.

Chief Grear fixed his eyes on Beau, then went back to his desk and opened up a drawer, removing a single sheet. "Faxed over early this morning," he said, handing it over to the detective.

The sergeant read the police report carefully. "So, she whacks this guy's brother for him while he's sitting in New Jersey on a pile of cash, waiting patiently for her return."

"With time on his hands to play around with the next-door neighbors' daughter."

"Marade Owens."

"Who incidentally got herself pile driven by this well-endowed creep it appears."

"Lee Edward Reynolds, a.k.a. Leonard Ellis Harris, Handson, and Hughs. Or affectionately known as Butch-Lee to his soul mates in the booby hatch."

"I'm afraid to ask how you came by *all* this information."

"I'm afraid to see Doris's face when she sees next month's phone bill."

"That's what I thought. Another thing. How did you get the administration in Stockholm to allow you to speak to this—?"

"Edna?" Sergeant Hopkins stalled.

"Yes, Edna."

"Well, I've got this long-distance romance going with the assistant to the director of the institution. She spoke very fondly of Butch-Lee." Beau grinned broadly. "Wanted to know how he was doing and all. Seems he did not discriminate between patients and personnel alike. I told her it was no myth about blacks from Brooklyn, too," he half-kidded.

"And how did she know to put you on to Edna?"

"She didn't."

"So, you just more or less conducted interviews at random with how many patients—never mind."

"Don't be too upset, Chief. I got a Mrs. Olsen in her eighties who swears she can close the books once and for all on Jack the Ripper."

"You got proof?" Grear asked with a straight face.

"Got us a full confession," he answered soberly.

"A patient there, I take it."

"Actually, no. Rather a parent down from Norway giving her fifty-year-old comatose daughter a piece of her own unsettled state of mind."

Grear laughed heartily. "Listen. I need not tell you that this is all together out of our jurisdiction. Am I right in that I need not tell you this?"

Sergeant Beau L. Hopkins handed back the fax then disappeared around the corner, returning a second later with the two large envelopes in hand. "Been thinking about doing a little investing, Chief."

"You mean investigating."

Beau brought his right hand up in a solemn pledge. "May Long Island lightning or LILCO's next rate hike strike me dead. Whichever comes first."

"Which means what?"

"Which means you won't find me sitting around here by the time you hear the next clap of thunder."

"What've you got there, Beau?" the chief asked skeptically, staring at the envelopes.

Several police officers came into the area, dripping wet, hanging their coats up on a long pine board lined with wooden pegs.

"These?" Beau smiled, raising the envelopes high above his head. "A secret hedge against inflation."

"Close the door behind you and take a seat," Chief Grear ordered, sounding rather official.

Beau turned to a woman officer drawing herself a cup of coffee from a large stainless steel pot sitting on a table just outside the doorway. "Privileges of financial wizardry," he whispered and winked at the pretty black cop.

"Yeah, sounds to me like you're about to get your ass chewed out," she whispered back. "And next time hang up your dripping wet coat like everybody else."

Beau smacked her playfully on the backside with one of the damp envelopes before closing the door and stepping into the police chief's parlor where many a web was spun. Beau sat down.

"Showing you all my cards. All right?"

Beau nodded.

"Parsippany police are treating this as a date-rape case gone as sour as it can get. However, Kelly's people are ruling it a homicide from the get-go. Lethal dose of Liquid-X."

"What the kids call Easy Lay."

"I must be out of touch, I guess."

"I'm just on the streets more, Chief—where all the action is. I think I know more about drugs than my pharmacist."

"M.E. said she'd been partying for days with pills and booze. That last drug supposedly put her right over the edge."

"GHB."

"Come again?"

"Gamma-hydroxybutyrate."

"Rolls right off your tongue, Beau. I'm impressed."

"They want Redler in on this. Right? That's why they're calling you."

The chief nodded. "Kelly told me there was a case like this in La Porte, Texas."

"Sounds like it belongs in France."

"Didn't have the high drama of this one, though."

"Nothing else in Georgia, or nearby?"

"Not that I know of."

"Kelly's real interest in this Jersey homicide is in how it connects to the Georgia murder of Carson Reynolds and that bizarre butchering of his dog," Beau proclaimed. "They want this Manns woman badly. Angelica Manns."

"Which brings us to the question of exactly how you found out that Angelica's stepbrother was alive and well—well not so well—in an institution in Stockholm, for Christ's sake?"

"Do you recall a Carl Gustafson, one of Dr. King's patients at the King Foundation? I'm going back some twenty-five years. A Swede who later turned up in Stockholm after making good his so-called *escape*?"

"Like it was yesterday," Grear said with a surprised look on his face. "Supposedly suffered from agoraphobia, yet he became the Foundation's groundskeeper and gardener. Part of Doctor King's cure," the police chief reminisced and laughed. "Gustafson claimed that his fear of open spaces lies just beyond the gates, so he remained behind them for many years, free to go whenever he chose."

"So one day he planned and executed his daring *escape*, winding up in Stockholm's hospital and hands. Carl mentions you in the letter. A lowly sergeant like me you were, once upon a time," Beau said behind a chuckle. "So, there's hope for me yet."

"What letter?"

"The letter Carl wrote to Dr. King from his rubber room in Stockholm. Apparently, he didn't know that Dr. King had died. Carl wrote on Butch-Lee Reynolds' behalf several years ago, explaining Reynolds' whole charade."

"How did you come across this letter, Beau? Or shouldn't I ask?"

"I'm a very resourceful detective, Chief. Can we just leave it at that?"

Chief Grear knew not to pursue it. Beau was telling him it was something that the chief really didn't want to know. Known to his peers as the Darling of Duplicity, Beau was a master at what he did. His transfer from a notorious Brooklyn precinct several years ago was Grear's godsend.

"So, you going to tell me about those envelopes you're holding?"

"Sure. N.J.A.H." He pointed to the logo in the upper right hand corner. "New Jersey Affordable Homes. Fifteen percent on your money, secured by a first mortgage lien. Better than a certificate of deposit sitting in a bank at six percent. They buy up existing homes, foreclosures, et cetera, at fifty to seventy cents on a dollar, fix them up then flip them."

Grear noted the Parsippany address. "And?"

"Well, if I'm going to be a potential investor, I'd have to see some of their homes and handiwork. Right? Got my eye on some property in Morris County. Gives me the excuse to snoop around the area. The state of New Jersey, if need be. Ask some questions. So on and so forth."

"Christ, and I thought you were going to ask me for plane fare to Stockholm, Beau."

Beau grinned. "Thought never crossed my mind."

"I want to see Carl's letter."

Sergeant Hopkins produced the letter and two cassettes with labels listing several patients' names including the assistant director of one of Stockholm's largest institutional warehouses. "Just skip over Janice's spiel on psychotropic drugs and get to the good stuff."

"Edna's interview?"

"That and Mrs. Olsen's confession to the murder of seven prostitutes in London's East End. The rest of the troops are just *plain* crazy. Your buddy, Carl, does the grand finale. Fucking lunatic rants and raves for a good thirty minutes."

"That's one of your faults, Beau."

"What's that?"

"No respect."

"That's what makes me a good cop, Chief."

"And immodest, too. That's another."

"You calling Redler in on this for them?"

"Probably."

"That's your one fault, Chief."

"How's that?"

"You're putting stock in this fortuneteller."

"You just can't stand the competition, Detective."

"He's a writer with a vengeance," Beau contended. "When you calling him?"

"You've got some lead time. They just got back from vacation."

"He and Liza on the high seas, were they? Or was he soloing around on his broom?"

"Don't mock these things, Beau," the chief warned rather sternly.

"Right. Listen. Thanks. If Angelica Manns and Butch-Lee Reynolds are still around, I'll find them."

"I know."

"Otherwise, Doris can book me on an international flight to where those square head blondies live and breathe, by God."

"Yeah, right." Grear smirked.

"I'll even fly second class, but I refuse to park my black butt in the back of the plane," he teased.

"I want to hear from you by Monday, Beau. But you call me earlier if you get anything. Hear?"

Beau stood up, saluted with an envelope, stepped outside the office and quietly closed the door behind him.

The area was ablaze with men in blue moving through the maze of offices: changing shifts, shuffling papers, drying off, downing coffee. Beau picked up his coat and headed down the hallway.

The woman sitting in a wheelchair at the switchboard was busy biting into a buttered bagel and stirring her hot chocolate. Beau removed an item from his jacket pocket, grabbed her shoulder, kissed her bouffant, then placed a ribbon-wrapped, gold foil treat upon her lap before heading toward the front door.

A call came through the board, but Doris ignored it for the moment, smiling up at her friend and colleague, crony and collaborator. With food still in her mouth, a phone plug jack held at the ready in one hand, a milk chocolate gun tied with a pretty pink bow in the other, she waved good-bye to Beau as he left the building.

Chapter 7

The two sat across from one another at a small metal table.

"You're a what?" The fat boy laughed loudly.

"A recruiter," the handsome woman answered and smiled.

"Like for Uncle Sam?"

"More like for our own form of government."

The lad leaned forward on his elbows, resting the folds of his chin in both palms. A guard seated in the far corner of the visitor's area looked over. The boy slid his big arms along the table's smooth surface, raised his buttocks and farted in the man's direction before planting his butt back down and smiling across at Angelica. The guard turned his attention back to a copy of *Ebony*.

"You sure are some kind of flaky broad," Darryl said, his flabby cheeks undulating like waves as he spoke.

"And you're a fat-assed fucking punk."

Darryl gripped both edges of the table in his meaty fists, scrunching up the corners of his mouth while taking on the appearance and even sounding like a grotesque bullfrog. "In the next three seconds, deary, I could crash this fucking table down around your ears," he whispered. "What do you think about that?"

"I think visiting hours would be over for you, Darryl. Still, you'd have to be quicker than that."

"Than what?"

"Three seconds."

"And why is that?" he questioned with a bored expression.

"Because in a fraction of a second, I could split your lip wide open."

"Could, could ya?"

Before Darryl knew what hit him, but then still wasn't sure a second later, Angelica had slashed the edge of her hand across that disrespectful mouth. Blood fell from the boy's face, and the guard was on his feet. Angelica halted the man where he stood, raising her hand, and with the other, handed over a handkerchief to Darryl. She made a gesture to the guard that she and everything else was going to be all right. The man bit his tongue, cracked a hint of a smile and sat back down.

"So, where were we?" Angelica asked, her eyes burning into Darryl's.

"You were telling me about your own fucking form of government," he said, sucking on and dabbing at his bloody lip.

"Ah, yes." Angelica broke out a small pad and pen from her purse. "Tell you what's in store for you when you get out. Glad you didn't make a scene, or that day would have been postponed for quite some time because of bad behavior, Darryl. From this moment on, you don't say anything you don't want heard. Just pretend you haven't got a tongue. Understand? You'll write everything down. Here's a shopping list of some things we'll need from you." She wrote out a long list, quantity needed, along with dollar amounts consisting of several zeros at the bottom of the page before turning the pad around. "Can you still pick these up in *produce*?" Angelica smiled. Produce was Darryl's euphemistic jargon for dealing in the production, confiscation, and redistribution of weaponry for death squad operations during apartheid assassinations in Johannesburg, as well as scores of arms involving the Mideast's holy wars. "The first figure is what we're prepared to pay you for *agricultural* expenses. The bottom line is just that, upon delivery."

Darryl scoured the list and smiled in bloody delight. He was in his element now. Angelica and her people wanted everything from sophisticated missiles to antiquated mines. Everything. Shoulder-fired grenade launchers: RPG's and Stingers; antitank and antipersonnel mines; tens of thousands of rifles; hundreds of thousands of pistols and silencers. Pipe bombs and plastic explosives. Trigger mechanisms for every conceivable type of explosive device known around the world. China. Russia. And good old Made in the U.S.A. Radar equipment, electronic communication systems. Angelica already had submarines, torpedoes, and sonar covertly covered. Finally, Darryl looked up.

"See any problem in getting any product, just point; don't

talk," Angelica stated.

Darryl pointed to the Stinger missiles where Angelica had requested one hundred. "CIA—"

"Shut your bloody mouth and write," she said softly, handing him a pen.

CIA-supplied, he scrawled.

"How many without the song and dance?"

Darryl held up ten fingers then wrote: *They're not like stun guns, deary. $38,000 apiece. Discounted, doll.* He pushed the pad toward her.

"I have an inside man who can help. I need a hundred. He'll call you when you get out. Any other problems on the list?"

Darryl shook his head.

"Good." Angelica took back the pad and pen and put the items in her purse. "Have a nice day, Darryl," she said, picking herself up from the table. "And if you ever refer to me as deary or doll again, I'll put a blade through your double chin."

Darryl smiled, still dabbing his lip. "By the way. Who the hell did you tell them you are?"

"Your probation officer, asshole. Who'd you think? Thought I'd pass myself off as your girlfriend?"

Darryl got up. "Thought you only toured booby hatches and halfway houses, Ms. Manns," he said, dropping his voice to a bare whisper.

"No, Darryl," she assured him, raising her dark glasses an inch above her brow, her back turned to the guard. "Now we're recruiting the cream of the crap. Bye." The twentyish-looking-year-old woman dropped her glasses to the bridge of her nose, faced around, then gestured to another guard standing by the door.

Chapter 8

The police chief pushed a button on the cassette recorder, fast forwarding the tape Beau had left him during their meeting. He stopped at a point near the end of the recording, hit PLAY, and once again listened to the familiar voice of a man he had met more than a quarter of a century ago. A remarkable patient. The most prejudiced man he had ever met in his life, capable of racial tirades lasting through an entire evening. Grear remembered the day he and his predecessor, Lieutenant Lark, had tried to question that loon suspected of murdering a young female patient. Wrong man. Another patient had framed Carl. Richard Geist. Long story. In short, Geist was one of the most brilliant psychopaths whom doctors and detectives had ever gone up against. Robert Redler had shot and killed the madman as well as one of his accomplices—and walked away unscathed, thank God. A jury had found him innocent.

Grear pushed REWIND, STOP, then PLAY, picking up Beau's voice near the beginning of the conversation with Carl Gustafson:

"—is a good morning there, Carl. My name is Professor Beau Hopkins, and I'm calling you from the United—"

"You a black man, boy?"

"Yes, sir. Brooklyn bred."

"What's your interest in Butch-Lee?"

"Well, I was his mathematics instructor when—"

"That tells me what you did, Sambo, not where your interests lay."

"Well, I'm trying to locate—"

"Tell me where you professed, Beau-wanna."

There was a brief pause in the conversation, and the police chief could picture Beau's black face burning brightly.

"Well, sewer rat got your tongue, boy?"

"No, no. N.Y.U., Carl. I retired in—"

"Butch-Lee's a southern WASP transplanted to Jersey. Why a liberal leaning toward such a faggot, Jew university?"

"Don't know, but—"

"Well, let me give you something that you have half a shot at, my spear-chucking Mr. Chips. Should be right up your tin-can alley if you get my meaning, boy. Here we go. Math question number one: If a nigger in Nikes from Newark left Broad and Market at nine in the morning, bounding ten miles an hour toward Flatbush—and a Bantu in bare feet from Brooklyn left Bushwick before noontime, flat out at thirty toward Trenton, who'd secure the sneaker endorsement and why?"

"Gee, Carl, you got me there."

"Answer: Neither, boog-a-boo, 'cause spooks, like cockroaches, don't scurry in a hurry 'fore dusk."

"Carl, listen to me. I'd like—"

"Math question number two. Ready?"

"Carl, please—"

"If a Reebok salesman from Hoboken had seven cartons of sneakers—Carl went on.

Chief Grear switched off the machine, sat back and shook his head. *Good ol' Carl*, he mused.

The Swede had wound up in America shortly after World War II, having fought in WW I as well. Confined to the King Foundation for more than a quarter of a century, the man had *escaped* and somehow found his way back to Sweden. The police chief firmly believed that if Carl Gustafson were back in the throes of society, he alone could and would initiate World War III. Yet, the good doctor had found Carl harmless, giving him the title and responsibility of caretaker. And what a beautiful job Carl had done with annuals and perennials through the years, Grear recalled . . . as if camouflaging the crazy world within the confines of the Foundation with bursts of splendid colors and arrangements. Such symmetry and balance in the unbalanced world the chief had visited that day so long ago.

Books and beauty were Carl's love. Loony as hot summer days are long but as brilliant as his blooms.

Mental illness. Who knew? Grear pondered. The chief's own sister sat in a home in upstate New York after having worked for the Pentagon for twenty years. Thirteen people she had once supervised.

One day, for no apparent reason, she suffered a nervous breakdown. Full disability. A kiss-off followed by eighteen hundred dollars a month for life from the federal government. Some life! The doctors had assured him that in time she'd be able to lead a *normal* life. What life? It wasn't a month after her collapse that she fell into what was later learned to be a feigned catatonic state, never ever breathing a single word about what had happened to her. Not a clue. Rape? Grear didn't think so. He had a feeling that Kathleen had seen or learned something she was not supposed to see or know. He had suspicions. He believed that the government doctors at Walter Reed had done something to her. No proof. Probably his own paranoia. Yet, he couldn't shake the awful feeling. He'd probably never know.

Where was Beau? he wondered and worried. No call. It was a week and not a word.

Chapter 9

Robert and Liza were enjoying the day taking care of her nephew.

"Aunt Liza?"

"Yes, sweetheart."

"Who's Uncle Rob talking to?"

"Police Chief Grear, a friend of his." Liza smiled, removing a piping hot casserole from the oven and placing it on top of the stove.

"Does he have a big boat, too?" the five-year-old boy asked.

"No, he goes out on your uncle's boat every once in a while."

"But then why isn't he a captain? I heard he was a captain once. I thought all captains have their own boats."

Liza waved a pair of oven mitts through the air before cupping them around her nephew's ears. "You ask complicated questions," she said with a warm smile.

"What?" David questioned and giggled, squirming away.

"You see, at one time he was a police sergeant, then a police lieutenant, and then he became a police captain before becoming chief of police here in Riverhead."

"Then how come he doesn't have a policeman's uniform?"

"Well, he does, but he doesn't always wear it."

"Don't all policemen have to wear them?"

"Not everybody."

"Why not?"

Liza smiled, removing her apron and tousling the boy's hair. "Well, for a couple of reasons. Like when they're off duty for instance. And then there are plainclothes police detectives like Dick Tracy who are still policemen, too. Right?"

"How come some policemen wear suits and not uniforms all the time?"

"Because they don't want bad people to know that they're really policemen."

With two hands, David pulled a stool out from under the island, climbing up and onto the seat. "Then how come *all* policemen don't wear suits if they don't want the bad guys to know them?"

Liza homed in on the tip of David's nose with a missile-like finger. "Now that is a very good question, which I think we'll save for Police Chief Grear. What do you think?"

David nodded. "What are we having for dinner, Aunt Liza?"

"Something with snails and puppy dog tails."

David giggled. "No, we're not. Tell me what we're having."

"Hungarian galoshes," she teased.

"No, we're not!" he blurted and laughed, swinging his legs to and fro.

"Salisbury snakes."

"No, we're *not!*" he insisted, shaking his head back and forth for emphasis.

Liza put a finger to her cheek in thought. "I know!" she exclaimed. "How about shepherd's pie?'

"Yes!" David cried out in delight, climbing down from the stool and heading for the stove, peering at the simmering contents cooking in the Pyrex dish. "My favorite," he reminded his aunt, pointing a finger inches from the glass.

"Careful, that's very, very hot."

"When I get bigger, Mom says I can help her in the restaurant."

"Well, right now you can help me by bringing this salad to the table. All right?"

"You bet. Want me to mix it up?"

"You can do that just before we eat."

"Roger Dodger. Aunt Liza?"

"Hum?"

"How come you and Mom don't like each other?"

"Oh, it's not that we don't like one another. It's just that we have differences of opinion, I suppose. That's all."

"What differences of depinion?"

"Opinion. That's when I think one way—and someone else thinks another way—and we can't agree."

"Dad says it's because you make her take her shoes off before she comes in the house, which she doesn't like to do."

Liza laughed lightly. "Everyone takes their shoes off before stepping foot into my home. That's the rule."

"If my mom took her shoes off, could she come in and you'd be friends?"

Liza held out a handful of silverware and dinner napkins. "Help me set the table," she suggested, smiling down at her sister's boy.

"Roger that. I know where everything goes, too. Forks on the left, knives and spoons on the right. Mom likes to put the napkins in front of the plates . . . like this. She doesn't follow rules. Is that a good opinion?"

Liza followed her nephew into the dining room then suddenly swung him up and into her arms, setting him upon the table. "And where do we put you, young man? Hum?"

"In front of the mashed potatoes," he answered without hesitation.

"So. Is it just the mashed potatoes you're after? Or all that good stuff underneath?"

"Both. Because it's the only way I eat my vegetables. All mushed up. And I have a request."

"A request?"

"Yep."

"Pretty fancy word. So, what's your request?"

"May I have a little wine with my dinner?"

"Wine?"

"Yes. Mom always lets me have a little wine with dinner."

"Always?"

"Well, sometimes just a little."

"Show me what a little is."

David showed the space of an inch between his thumb and forefinger.

"What do you think the chief of police of Riverhead would say to that?"

As if on cue, Police Chief Grear kicked off his boat shoes in the vestibule then stepped into the kitchen. "Say about what?" the chief asked, peeking around the corner and into the dining room.

"Tell him it's grape juice," David whispered in his aunt's ear.

"That's what Mom tells everyone in the restaurant who sees me."

"Oh, really?" Liza helped David down from the table and turned to her guest. "Chief, this is my nephew, David. David, this is Police Chief Grear."

The man took the boy's hand. "I'm very pleased to meet you, David. Your aunt's told me many fine things about you."

"Why don't all policemen wear suits so that the bad guys won't know that's them?" David asked, carefully taking his hand back from the chief's grip.

"I see we have an inquisitive one here," Grear remarked and laughed.

"Wait till he gets to know you. I feel like I've just finished playing twenty questions. Problem is they can't all be answered with a simple yes or no."

Grear turned his attention back to the young boy. "Well, the fact is, policemen have different jobs. Some do wear suits."

"Detectives."

"Right."

"So the bad guys won't know them."

"Right again."

"But how come *all* policemen don't?"

"Well, not everyone is bad, right?"

"Right."

"So, sometimes it's good for good people to see a policeman in uniform. If they need help, they can walk right up to a man in blue and get the help they need."

"If I'm good, will I know if a man in a suit is a detective?"

"If he wants you to."

"Why wouldn't he want me to?"

"Sometimes it helps him to do his job better if people don't know he's a detective. Even good people. Understand?"

"Would a detective put a kid in jail?"

The chief glanced at Liza then looked for something further in David's eyes. "Depends what for."

"Say, for drinking wine."

"Well, we do have laws against drinking for those who are under the legal age."

"What's the legal age?"

"Here in New York, it's eighteen, but some places won't even serve a person an alcoholic drink, like wine, unless that person's twenty-one."

David's eyes widened. "Wow!"

"Where's Robert?" Liza asked.

"Straightening up some hunting equipment in the garage. He'll be in in a moment."

David went back to finish setting the table, turning as quiet as a clam.

"Rob tells me you're a regular Annie Oakley with a rifle, Liza. And not too bad with a bow, either," the chief said with a smile.

"Oh, we do a little shooting at the range in Calverton from time to time. Bow and arrow in the backyard." Liza laughed. "Our neighbors thought Rob was nuts the first time they saw him shooting arrows from the roof of the garage."

"The garage?"

"Practicing for deer season. Simulating shooting from a tree stand."

"I see."

"Hear from Beau, yet?" she asked rather inquisitively.

"Not a peep."

"Aunt Liza?" David called out.

"Yes, sweetheart."

"Can I sleep over when Mom and Dad go to Bal'te'more?"

"That's not for a while yet."

"Will it be before I'm eighteen or twenty-one?"

"Way before then," she said and sighed, cupping and rocking her head with both hands as though she had a splitting headache.

"Good."

"He doesn't stop with the questions. He must have asked me a million since this morning."

"Maybe a wee bit of wine will quiet him down," Grear suggested with a wink.

Liza giggled. "You know, I'm half tempted."

With the tips of his fingers, the police chief covered his ears, his eyes then his mouth. "Hear no evil, see no evil, speak no evil."

Liza laughed lightly. "Yes, I just may."

Chapter 10

Beau Hopkins strained with all his might against the cable ties that bound his hands and feet, focusing on the single bottle of Jack Daniel's sitting on top of the basement refrigerator.

"So, Detective. What are we to do with you?" Angelica Manns asked politely. "Hum?"

"I say we do him like Marade," Butch-Lee suggested excitedly. "I never did no nigger in the can. Get it? In the can?"

"That's 'cause all us niggers did you, dickhead," Beau barked, instinctively drawing his body into the fetal position as Butch-Lee's foot made ready to kick him in the groin. The blow glanced off the stocky man's knee. Butch-Lee about toppled, catching onto a lolly column for support.

"Easy, Lee," Angelica said, moving around the naked black body lying on the concrete basement floor. "Easy." The woman's foot shot out of nowhere but with half the force of Butch-Lee's, landing squarely in Beau's lower back. The man let out a shriek like nothing Butch-Lee had ever heard before. "Nice and easy. See?"

Butch-Lee moved toward the man's face and delivered three brutal kicks, one of which broke most of Beau's front teeth. "See, you have finesse and patience, sister. But I have steel-tipped boots. Trouble is you can't reckon the damage because the motherfucker's a wall of black and blue to begin with. So you got to make him bleed and spit his pearly whites."

"I'm going to ask you again," Angelica swore. "Just one more time. How did you find us, Detective Hopkins?"

Beau knew that he was close to death. There was no denying that. He also knew that he would take Butch-Lee Reynolds with him.

Angelica pulled a Beretta .380-caliber pistol from a holster clipped at the small of her back, threading on a 9mm silencer, fixing its muzzle firmly against Beau's temple, promising him a painless finish if he told her what she needed to know. A *no* from Beau would mean an unnecessary painful death at the hands of an artless thug.

Beau closed his eyes and mumbled through broken bloody teeth that Butch-Lee had bragged and broadcasted to a Stockholm patient about the whereabouts of the loot for which he and Angelica had come to New Jersey to retrieve.

"Ask him about Edna Robinson as well as an administrator at the institution in Stockholm, neither of whom had taken him very seriously. We didn't, either," Beau added incoherently. "But we have to check every lead. Your stepbrother told them who you were and that you'd be coming to take him home soon. Pine Brook, New Jersey."

"That's a lie!" Butch-Lee screamed.

"Shut up," Angelica snapped.

"How else could I have known about the car accident and that you were his stepsister?"

"I never told no one," Butch-Lee shouted, driving his boot into Beau's body. "No one!"

Beau watched the pistol fade from his face.

"No one!" Butch-Lee repeated.

"Leave him be," Angelica said calmly.

"I told no one," Butch-Lee insisted.

"You had to have told someone, Lee," Angelica reasoned.

"Only that I didn't belong there," Butch-Lee confessed. "And that I had—"

"That you had a brother in Georgia and a dog you wanted dead," Beau managed, a river of blood spilling freely from his mouth.

Suddenly, something sounded in the far corner of the basement. Angelica snapped the weapon in its direction as the dehumidifier kicked on.

Butch-Lee went on above the humming sound, digging himself in deeper. "Listen, I only told Edna. But not where the money is. I swear."

"Only thing you didn't give Edna was the exact address, Butchy-boy," Beau swore.

"I didn't even remember the address. Just how to get there. That's the truth. I was in there for eleven long fucking years, sugar. You were my guiding angel. The only hope of freedom I had."

"The rest was easy, asshole," Beau went on. "I just passed

around your release photo locally till someone remembered you walking out of a Pine Brook liquor store, heading down the street with an open bottle of Jack Daniel's. Our forensic boys analyzed stains from the bedroom carpeting. Jack and some Vat-69 that Marade's parents said went missing from their cabinet. They told us their daughter said you'd be laying low somewhere nearby and that you'd be in touch. Keasbey, New Jersey. Woodbridge Township. Middlesex County. Western end of Perth Amboy," Beau outright lied. "So I just started hitting the local liquor stores again. It wasn't long before—"

Detective Beau Hopkins heard the muffled report from the handgun. A second later, Butch-Lee Reynolds was lying beside him. There was no need for further discussion. Beau closed his eyes again, said his prayers silently and waited. He didn't have to wait very long.

Chapter 11

Ms. M smiled down from the stage of the auditorium. Fifty new recruits smiled back at her warmly. She wore a wide-brimmed khaki hat, baggy khaki pants, and a matching long-sleeved shirt buttoned up to her throat. Turning slowly from her troops, she placed a hand on her hip, displaying the outfit like a fashion model. Shifting her weight to one leg, she brought the heel of a black leather field boot smartly across the other.

The young women gave mild approval while the men made merriment with wild applause and whistling, laughing up a storm. Angelica Manns took a modest bow then briskly crossed the stage before bounding down the steps toward them, tossing her hat aside.

"So. This will be part of your survival issue for the next several weeks in desert-like conditions. The *desert*," she emphasized, pointing to a female in the first row. "Sharon. Tell me what came to mind when I said desert."

Sharon started to stand.

"From your seat, dear," Angelica said. "This is not a military academy, although many of you will think so before the week is out. But right now I want you to relax and think. Sharon?"

"I think of a hot place."

"Peter?"

"Cactus and sand."

"Philip?"

Philip wore a grin. "I think of banana splits when I think of *dessert*, teach," he said, searching the room for approval and applause. But no one so much as cracked a smile. The auditorium was as quiet as a corpse.

"A punster in our midst," Angelica finally acknowledged. "This is a course in survival, and I'm wondering if you're going to survive the first day, Philip."

Philip's grin was gone.

"Karen," Angelica continued.

"Hot, like Sharon said—with lots of lizards and scorpions running around," Karen added, displaying a squeamish look.

Several recruits smiled and stirred uncomfortably.

"A desert is a hostile environment," their instructor began. "It can kill you in a few days if you don't know how to survive." Angelica let that thought sink in before she continued. "The days are scorchers. Envision one hundred and fifteen degrees for openers. Nights can be downright cold. In order to survive in the desert, Danny, what is the one item you would want to have in great supply?"

Danny looked around the room for some support. There wasn't any.

"Danny? What is the one element we humans need to stay alive?" Angelica coaxed. "Forget about the desert for a moment."

"F-f-food," Danny answered.

"What else, Danny? Think. We can live for days without food. But we have to have . . . ."

"Wa-water," Danny swallowed. "We haveta have water s-so we can live."

"That's exactly right, Danny," she nodded emphatically. "Water! And we will have an abundant supply of water when we head out on maneuvers this week."

Danny bravely raised his hand.

"What is it, Danny?"

"H_2O," Danny said without stuttering.

Everyone but Philip laughed and applauded Danny for his courage to raise his hand and speak out voluntarily, something he had not done since the day he became a member of the organization.

Angelica's methods were a far cry from her predecessor's, but she was in charge now, and she would lead the way, giving her new recruits the encouragement most of them so sorely needed.

"That's very good, Danny," she offered.

Danny was pleased with himself. "Th-thank you," he practically whispered.

"So, here's your situation," Angelica went on. "Our water supply truck is blown sky-high. Reserves are bone-dry. There isn't a drop of water to be had. We're scattered. You're on your own out there. You need water to stay alive. How do you get it?"

Danny's hand flew up. She had created a monster, she told herself. Not the kind she needed at the moment. Not yet anyway.

"Yes, Danny."

"Ca-cactus."

"What about cactus?"

"You c-cut in-into it and g-get water."

"There is no cactus to be had," Angelica said decidedly. "Then what?"

Philip raised his hand.

"Philip?"

"Y-ya d-dig d-down in-into a d-dry st-streambed, Ms. M," Philip mocked and imitated Danny, waiting for a response.

Several students bowed their heads out of embarrassment for Danny. Others bit their lips to keep from giggling. Danny's face was as red as new brick. Angelica's expression was as expressionless as a blank sheet of paper.

"There are no streambeds to be found anywhere in the area," Angelica stated flatly. She waited patiently for the answer to her question. "Well?"

"C-can you g-give us a hint?" Philip continued his antics.

Several recruits snickered. Others tried to contain their laughter but could not.

"You're digging your own grave, Philip," Angelica said matter-of-factly. "But I'll give everyone a hint as Philip suggested. Plastic."

"What?" several students said simultaneously.

"Plastic," she repeated.

"Plastic?" Sharon questioned.

"Sheets of plastic to pull water from the sky," Angelica elaborated.

"How?"

"That's what we're going to learn in just a moment. Philip. Grab some of those shovels in the corner. Danny. Grab the rest. Karen, take that bag by the door. Everyone outside." Angelica strapped on a holster and gun.

Fifty students stood along the sandy beach, waiting with curiosity as Angelica explained what they were about to do.

"You can't count on plants or nonexistent riverbeds to cut into like Danny and Philip suggested. But what you can count on is a solar still to save your life. Danny, I want you to dig a hole in the sand right here. About two feet across and two feet deep. Doesn't have to be a work of art."

"Yes, ma'am."

"Philip, I want you to start digging a hole over there, and don't stop until I tell you. Sharon, I want you to dig one like Danny's over there. Guadalupe, same thing. Spread yourselves out. Peter, over there. Let's see, now. Several more over there. Wanda. Carol. Junior. Harold. Next to Peter's. Sharon, bring the bag over here and open it up. The rest of you can gather up some good-size stones from along the beach."

The ninety-degree temperature on that mid-day afternoon bore down on the group mercilessly, and everyone thought they had a good idea of what another twenty-five degrees would do to them, especially without the benefit of water.

"All right. Everyone but Philip gather around Danny's hole. Philip, continue digging, please." Angelica removed a sheet of folded plastic and a wide-mouthed can from a canvas bag. She placed the can down in the center of the hole, then unfolded and spread the 3 x 3 foot sheet of clear plastic over the opening. "Now, I want some stones placed all around the edge of the plastic to hold it in place. We don't want a sudden wind lifting up the cover."

A moment later, a series of stones framed the plastic sheet, holding the cover in place as Angelica sealed its edges with shovelfuls of sand. Finally, she placed a single stone upon the center of the sheet, suspended directly above the can.

Philip had stopped digging, staring over at the demonstration with interest. "How deep do you want this hole?" he called out, standing in it up to his knees.

"Just keep digging, Philip," Angelica answered, turning her attention back to the still and her students. "Note," she said. "The heat from the sun creates water vapor beneath the surface of the plastic sheet." Almost immediately, the underside of the cover was clouding over with vapor. "See the condensation? As this process continues, the water will run to the center of the sheet where it's weighted with the stone, then down into the can. Any questions?"

"How much water will it make, Ms. M?" Guadalupe asked.

"This still will produce between one quart and three quarts every twenty-four hours. If you can find any kind of vegetation whatsoever, put it into the hole. It will accelerate the process."

"That's a lot of water," someone said.

"Don't you believe that for a minute," Angelica said with utmost seriousness, "or you'd be dead. Each and every person here is going to build four stills." Angelica looked back at Philip digging deep into the hole. The sweat was pouring off the nineteen-year-old. The others looked on, too.

"Is Philip's going to be one gigantic solar still, Ms. M?" Karen asked.

Angelica didn't answer. "What's important to keep in mind is that you build these stills in the early part of the morning or late in the afternoon. At night would even be a better time. But never ever during the heat of the day. Why?"

"Because it's too hot?" someone answered.

"Because you'll sweat to death, like Philip over there," Sharon swore.

"Yes, but why?" Angelica pressed.

Peter had his hand up.

"Peter?"

"Because your body will give up more water than the solar still can produce."

Angelica looked deliberately into every face. "'Because your body will give up more water than the solar still can produce,'" she echoed Peter's words.

"I knew that," Sharon whispered kiddingly to another girl.

An hour later, Angelica told everyone to take a break.

"Now, let's go over and see how Philip is doing to help illustrate Peter's earlier point." Everyone followed Angelica to the site.

"How much bigger you want this hole to be, sweetheart?" Philip questioned, standing in the pit up to his waist. "Am I digging a solar still for some elephant, or a fucking latrine for fifty assholes?" Philip finished, throwing down his shovel and climbing out.

"I told you when we were all inside, Philip."

"Told me what?"

"That you're digging your own grave. Now, get back in your

hole, asshole."

"Say what?"

"Did I stutter, Philip? Danny, please tell Philip the last order I gave him."

"Ms. M said to get back in-into your hole, asshole," Danny said, nearly without a flaw.

Philip laughed. "You can't be serious."

Angelica's eyes showed that she was quite serious.

"Bitch," Philip snapped, grabbing for the shovel, raising it level with his shoulders.

Angelica's foot flew into Philip's face as the boy was about to swing the implement like a bat. Philip fell backwards but bounded to his feet. The shovel was firmly in his grip.

"Danny told you what I said. Now, get back in," she repeated calmly.

The beach clung to Philip's body like sandpaper. Perspiration poured from his pores. The boy drove the pointed blade of the shovel toward Angelica's face, intent on sending it and her sailing across to Fisher's Island Sound. The sound that followed was that of Philip's arm cracking at the elbow. Philip screamed in pain, cursing up a storm. "You f-fucking cunt," he cried out. "I'll kill you, you g-goddamn bitch," he stammered. But the look on Philip's face and Angelica's told everyone that the heat of the battle was over. "No, please," Philip suddenly begged.

The lead from two bullets blew away the fear in Philip's eyes. His body fell but a foot away from the grave of his own making.

"Bury him deep," Angelica ordered, staring directly at Danny.

Danny nodded anxiously.

"The rest of you finish the other stills. I want to see a pint in each before we break for dinner."

Everyone but Sharon did as they were told. The girl just stood there trembling, meekly raising her hand.

"Yes, Sharon."

"I'm scared," she cried, suddenly dropping to her knees. "I think I'm going to be sick."

Angelica holstered her weapon then went over and knelt beside Sharon, taking the girl gently into her arms. "Look at me and listen carefully," her instructor said. "Remember why you ran away from home and what you told me?" she reminded. Sharon nodded. "Well, you just pretend that Philip over there is your brother lying in that hole. Then you'll be able to stomach it. All right?"

"Yes, Ms. M," Sharon said through a shiver.

"You're already a survivor, Sharon," Angelica assured her. "And now we have to teach others how to cope and overcome adversities. So, back to work."

"Yes, ma'am." Sharon wiped the tears from her eyes and got up. She walked past Danny who stood over Philip's grave, anxiously throwing shovelfuls of sand upon the boy's bloodied body.

Chapter 12

"This country is practically lost, Mr. Redler," the mousey-looking, ferret-faced, sixtyish-year-old man declared. "Kaput. Going down the crapper hard and fast. Mideast terrorists at every turn, hatching plots against us around the globe as we speak. South and Central American drug traffickers moving their never-ending shipments of shit across our borders. It's just a matter of time before we see our nation collapse. But not on my watch if I can help it. Problem being is that our little group needs a lot of help," he soured. "No law enforcement budget in the millions is going to curtail this deadly business because business is in the billions. And the business of violence is becoming as big as the businesses I'm speaking of; they walk hand in hand.

"We're in the middle of a war, Mr. Redler. I call it the In-and-Out War; oil and drugs. We're warring over those two commodities and being destroyed from the outside as well as from within. Bottom line? As always, megabucks. Every thug around the globe is fighting for a piece of the pie. Many of our so-called legitimate businesses are fast becoming as corrupt as our federal, state, and local governments. The American people are handed the Bill of Rights in one hand and a bill of goods in the other. All the average person knows about the oil crisis is that their home heating costs went up from fifty-nine point nine cents a gallon last September, to well over a buck this fall. At least that's what my wife says she paid here on Long Island, as she pays all the bills while I'm away trying to save the Free World," he stated matter-of-factly. "Cup of coffee?"

"No, sir."

"No damn good for you anyhow." The Man leaned in toward his desk. "Oil and drugs, Mr. Redler. You don't have to be clairvoyant to see that, do you?"

Robert Redler said nothing.

"The whole world is a war zone. The Mideast wants and has us over a barrel, holy wars fought for the crude oil kind. Religious wars and drug wars. They're all interconnected. Arms and ammunition coming in from the east. Coke and heroin up from the south. And that prevailing northeast wind? Even the weather has turned against us," the wispy man mocked. "We're surrounded," he added solemnly. "These times are the harbinger of a world-wide revolution. Mark my words. Right around the corner. On the horizon. It's imminent," he concluded, punctuating the air with the point of an expensive ballpoint pen.

"Why am I here?" Robert asked.

"You're supposed to know why you're here. You're supposedly clairvoyant. No?"

Robert smiled uncomfortably. "No, not really."

"Ah, yes. A *gift*, I believe you call it. A gift from God, no less. Listen, I know you worked pretty closely with Police Chief Grear on that other business," the frail man remarked. "I also know you're a decent chap. Even something of a hero. I'm pleased you blew those two bastards away. Would have done the same myself had I been in your shoes. Would have given up a month's vacation for the privilege. You're smiling. What?"

"It's just that another person might have said a month's salary."

"I see." The Man paused, smiling, too. "I guess what you have to understand is that, here, we pay ourselves a salary far greater than any of us or our families would ever need in several lifetimes. Keeps us honest," he explained quite candidly.

"How?"

"You mean, how is the program funded?

Redler nodded.

"You, for openers, the taxpayer."

"And then?"

"And then from great reserves set aside for a rainy day—like today."

The writer didn't press.

"You know what they call us, yes?"

"The Three Musketeers."

"That's right. What else do you know about us?" the little man asked, seemingly amused. "You see, you have me at a disadvantage. I've never dealt with a person such as yourself; a person with an extraordinary *gift*. Usually, we know everything there is to know about a person we deal with. What intrigues and at the same time concerns us, though, is the fact that we don't know exactly how much *you* know about *us*."

"I know that you ran the show back then. Even had the feds against the ropes. And that Chief Grear trusts and respects the three of you. That's about it."

"Well, I'm not so sure that's all of it. But it doesn't much matter now because I'm going to confide in you in order to gain *your* trust."

"To what end?"

"To the end of Angelica Manns and her Circle of Friends. To the end of Barbara Giordano and her drug empire."

"What about the oil and terrorist situation in the Mideast and its impact on our economy here?" Redler tested. "Sounds a bit more important. No?"

"My two associates are handling that quagmire."

Redler believed the man was serious. "Just how powerful are you three?"

"Most powerful, Mr. Redler."

"But you cannot turn the tide."

"Time is our enemy."

"Time?"

"Time to recruit incorruptible people like yourself."

"To do what exactly?"

"I just told you. Death to Manns' death squad. Death to Giordano's drug cartel," the thin-framed man said as casually as one might suggest doing lunch.

"Can we win the war on drugs?"

"No."

"Why?"

"Just like that prevailing northwest wind, Mr. Redler. Prevailing liberal wink-and-nod policies," he said and winked and nodded. "Sure, a skirmish here and a skirmish there. Hang a bloody victory sign out for a battle won every now and then. But to win *the* war?" The Man shook his head omnisciently—as if *he* were clairvoyant.

"What about Manns and her followers? Can you win?"

"We."

Robert Redler shifted in his seat. "We?"

"We can win, meaning, with your help, perhaps."

"What are you going to ask me to do?"

"Don't you mean, what do you *want* me to do? Hum?"

"Last time I cooperated, your victory was followed by my trial."

"You murdered two people in cold blood and—"

"I was kidnapped."

"And you walked away unscathed."

"Because a jury acquitted—"

"Because we let you walk! Think about it. Did you ever see such a wishy-washy prosecutor in such a high-profile case before?"

"Public opinion was on my side."

"Public opinion? I set public opinion. I write the words that make the whole world sing, Mr. Redler. Not Barry Manilow. Editors slant for me what I ask them to. I don't ask often. I never tell. Just ask. Only once. Like I'm asking you now." The Man waited for a response.

Redler knew The Man was serious, but was he sane? A moment had passed between them. Somehow the writer felt that The Man sitting across from him was, indeed, both very serious and reasonably sane.

"What do you want me to do?" he finally asked.

"Find the two of them for us, Rob. May I call you Rob? Just find them."

"You're not asking me to kill them?"

"We didn't ask you the last time out. Did we? That act was of your own volition. A public enemy and a public servant. Albany wanted to award you a medal, posthumously of course, for slaying the dragon. But only after having you shot for assassinating an aide to the governor."

"Michael was corrupt."

"So is Bill Clinton. So was Nixon. So what?"

"Michael had people killed."

"Your attorney didn't prove that. *You* were on trial, not Michael."

"The district attorney had the sworn testimony of the chief of police as well as—"

"Two corpses that couldn't argue otherwise."

"And what if I find Angelica and Barbara and find my back against the wall again?"

"You'll kill them like you killed the other two, I suppose. I'm sure you won't discriminate just because they're women. Now would you?"

"You know that I'm still experiencing fallout from the last trial."

"There won't be a trial for you this time around. That's a promise I make to you now."

"Then why was there one last time out?"

"Because we weren't fully prepared for you."

"And now you are?"

"You know something? You ask far too many questions for someone who's supposed to be, shall we say, *knowing*."

"Well, before I fully commit to anything, I'm going to be asking you many more."

The Man firmly shook his head. "No. And no fodder for the current book you're writing. You'll pass all your writings on to me. That's how you somehow *see* certain things from what I understand. You write things down, and they come to pass. Is that not so?"

"Sometimes," Robert admitted. "How come you didn't stop the presses on my last book?"

"Read like fiction. This time, people know you. They'll be reading between the lines. Watching your every move."

"How will I be able to operate?"

"You'll have something going for you that you didn't have before."

"The Three Musketeers?"

The slight figure shook his head. "Just me. For the time being, anyway. Oh, there's something else I have to mention."

"What?" the prospective recruit asked suspiciously.

"Liza. I don't want her to know about this talk or place or anything connected."

"I could tell you yes, but how would you really know otherwise?"

"Your word."

Robert Redler thought hard and fast before he gave his hand. "The word is mum."

The Man smiled genuinely. "Good, Rob. Very good."

"One question?"

"Go ahead."

"Do you believe in preternatural powers?"

"Not one bit," The Man said without hesitation.

"But then why me?" Robert asked, a bit befuddled.

"I believe in Chief Grear, and it is *he* who believes in *you*."

"Isn't that kind of—"

"The same thing? No, not really. To tell you the truth, it's my wife's best friend who believes in the supernatural. So, I thought I'd give it a shot."

"May I ask what you firmly believe in, sir?"

"That's four questions. But I'll answer you. I believe in two things. I believe in this country, for one."

Redler waited a moment. "And the other?"

"Results. Now, that's about it. Glad you're on the team. Good day, Rob." The Man lowered his head to a pile of papers and immediately went to work with his Monte Blanc pen.

Robert didn't have to be omniscient to know two things. One, that the meeting was over. Two, that he would be contacted shortly.

Chapter 13

At an undisclosed location on another continent, two women met at a secluded backwoods cabin. Neither of them resembled their passport pictures. Barbara Giordano was the first to speak.

"You are drawing considerable attention to yourself," the middle-aged mother of two declared, hanging her hat and coat on a hook behind the door.

"If you're referring to Carson Reynolds or his younger brother, Lee, you have to understand that they had become liabilities," Angelica explained evenly, sitting in a comfortable chair, her arms folded and legs crossed.

"Let's begin at the beginning with that dog you butchered. What was the point of all that?"

"I made a promise to Lee. We wanted his cooperation. Correct? I was dealing with a nut. So, I had to do some nutty things. Okay?"

"What about the girl in Jersey? What about the cop?"

"The cop made the connection and found us. Lee fucked up. The girl simply had to go."

The woman digested Angelica's explanation before she spoke. "So, where are you finding new recruits these days?"

"Here and there. Prisons. Schools. The streets."

"I like that approach much better than the way you went about collecting them before. Remember. You're not Richard Geist. You can't *heal* the lot like he did. Geist had a talent. Now, the question is, do you think you can keep his followers in check, or do we have to resort to genocide?" the older woman put forth plainly and perhaps half-jokingly.

"Look who's talking about drawing attention to ourselves. There are no problems there. They're soon to become seasoned soldiers. The elders keep the younger ones in line."

"Then maybe we should hold the line right there."

"No," Angelica said emphatically. "I'll soon have scores of leaders training hundreds. Hundreds will soon be training thousands more, my way. Geist had tens of thousands under his control in less than a decade."

"We lost the best explosives man in the business when we lost Lee."

"Get real. Lee was rotting in an asylum for more than a decade. He wasn't up on the latest technology. The nut house didn't offer remedial or advanced study courses," Angelica retorted with a smirk. "Lee would have been useful. But that's all. He wasn't indispensable."

"No one is. Just remember that."

Angelica held her tongue, perfectly aware that she was simply a pawn. At least for the moment.

"All right. What's done is done, Angelica. Damage reports state that risk is at a minimum."

"Meaning what? That your attorney, Mr. Laddington, can bail me out of this one if the authorities ever pick me up?"

"The authorities have nothing solid. I guess you took care of all loose ends." Barbara dropped herself into the chair across from Angelica. "So what did you turn up here in Frankfort?"

"Well, I haven't found us an explosives man to replace Lee, as yet. But I've got us an NBC man who's just dynamite," she quipped.

"NBC?"

"Nuclear, Biological, and Chemical warfare, Barbara. If they ever put you before an investigating committee, dear, they're just going to have to believe that you're simply the little ol' homemaker from Long Island that you say you are. I think you're your best defense."

Barbara smiled banally, accepting the rather left-handed compliment. "Sweet of you to think so. So tell me. What do you have?"

"Gold. Thirteen plus pounds of sarin stored in each of the one thousand sixty rockets taken from an army bunker in Iraq. That's seven tons of trouble."

"What is sarin?"

"Nerve gas."

"I'm nervous already. How did you come by this stuff?"

"Our NBC man. U.S. Army Corps of Engineers was supposed

to blow the bunker back in ninety-one. Instead, he blew those boys away and stockpiled the weapons for a future date."

"Who is this guy?"

"One of the enterprising engineers," Angelica said discreetly. "A week later, he tried to get his hands on another load at an ammunition dump nearby, but he was too late. Army Corps had blown it to smithereens, accidently sending tons of sarin over fifteen thousand American troops."

"You're kidding."

"That's Desert Storm for you, Barb."

"War *is* hell."

"So it is."

"What were you doing in Rhode Island last month?" Barbara inquired.

"Initially, looking in on Redler and his lady. Loved Watch Hill. Tail end of their vacation. So I went back and forth. Training fifty more."

"Good potential?"

"They're learning to feel their way."

"I don't want to hear about any more bodies suddenly turning up, my angel. Right now I need for you and your Circle of Friends to keep a low profile. Hear?"

Angelica nodded her understanding, turned and stared coldly out the cabin window.

Chapter 14

The strap slid toward her, running diagonally across Liza's shoulder and chest as she pulled the passenger car door closed. She locked the secondary belt across her lap. Robert pulled the Camry away from the curb at the railroad station in Speonk. Liza smiled, leaning left and receiving a kiss hello.

"So?" she said.

"What?"

"You know what."

"No, I don't. What?"

"Are you going to do it?"

"Do what?" he asked with some annoyance.

"What they asked you to do. Get involved again." She was staring straight ahead.

"I promised I wouldn't talk about it."

"Good. I'll do the talking and you'll do the listening. All right?"

"If you remember, you're the one who asked me to cooperate the last time out."

"You know that was quite different. You were the one who was in trouble. You really didn't have much of a choice. Now it's over. Richard Geist is dead. We put that all behind us. So let's get on with our life."

"I don't know that it's really over. Angelica and Barbara are still out there."

"That's not your business anymore. Start meddling around in theirs, and you might just wind up dead this time. You were lucky before."

Robert sat quietly, heading north to their Riverhead home.

"Did you forget what you put us through?" she persisted. "Did you?"

"What your daughter put us through, you mean."

"No, my daughter is dead. I'm talking about your obsession with this, this—"

"Gift?"

"Call it what you want. It will destroy us if you continue to use it the way you did. That's *my* prognostication."

"God gave me this gift for a reason, Liza."

"And you used it for better or worse. Now let it go. Let the authorities handle this."

"Handle what?"

"Angelica Manns and Barbara Giordano, for Christ's sake! What do you think, I'm stupid? That I don't know what's going on? You've been in an agitated state for weeks. I know the signs. I've lived with you for twenty-five years. Don't you think I know you? If you're not thinking about yourself, then think of me. These people can snatch either of us off the street at any given moment. We don't have the protection we had before."

What if we did? he wanted to ask then tell her everything. About his first meeting with the man. The existence of the omnipotent musketeers. The power of their being. He wanted to tell her all about his second meeting last week. He wanted to tell her that he had their full support; all their resources at his disposal. But he couldn't tell her anything.

"Listen. It's Friday. We both had a heck of a week. I've got a two-inch-thick Black Angus porterhouse from Riverhead Beef and a fine bottle of Cabernet. You'll take a shower; I'll fix us a salad then fire up the grill. How does that sound?"

"Sounds like we may make it through Friday night, Rob. But what about our tomorrows?"

Robert said nothing for the remainder of the drive home.

Chapter 15

Robert Redler wrote and rewrote then passed his work on to The Man through an intermediary, a single chapter at a time. Nothing happened. Nothing came to light. Perhaps he had lost the gift. He even prayed to God he had. And then it happened. The grandest scheme and largest known theft of combat equipment and vehicles ever to be removed from a United States military base. Seventeen armored personnel carriers, complete with TOW anti-tank missile launchers; one hundred and eleven other combat vehicles; even a Vietnam War-era Sheridan tank.

Robert had set the scene in Fort McCoy, Wisconsin. It had all been fiction. One week later, Ted Wasky of the FBI's Madison office was talking to reporters, handing them the facts, not fiction, for a federal grand jury had already returned indictments against seven men. ARMY THEFT RING BUSTED. The story was given a quarter-page in *Newsday*, picked up by the Associated Press. Robert had presented his prose the week before—before the event made headlines—before the event ever came to pass.

It was the first weekend in October. A cold snap had already plummeted the mercury into the thirties for the past few nights. Robert and Liza were busy Sunday morning with yard work. She was fussing in the garden, tending to the last of her vegetables. He was toying with the idea of putting their boat to bed early this year, thinking ahead to bowhunting season. There was a message on the answering machine when they went back into the house for lunch. It was from Beau Hopkins' wife, asking—no—more like begging for Robert to call her as soon as possible. He called her while Liza prepared a light lunch.

"Mrs. Hopkins?"

"Yes."

"This is Robert Redler returning your call, ma'am."

Immediately the woman began to weep. "Oh, thank God you called, sir. My husband was the one, the one they found . . . ."

"I know who your husband was, Mrs. Hopkins," Robert said in a consoling tone, "and I'm deeply sorry. Police Chief Grear spoke very highly of him. The chief said he was a brilliant detective and had grown very fond of him," he added awkwardly, realizing that he was overusing the past tense and turning his condolences into a eulogy. "A good man."

"You're a good man, too," she said through her tears. "Po·lice Chief Grear promised me he was gonna find the person responsible. But I says to 'im, 'Sir, how can you promise me a thing like that?'" the woman went on between her weeping. "I says, 'Maybe you can promise to do everythin' in your power to *try* and find the person, but you can't promise me you're *gonna* find 'im.' You knows what he did, Mr. Redler? We was at the funeral parlor and he took me firmly by the shoulders and says, 'No, Flora, I'm gonna find the person responsible 'cause I gots a special man to help me. A friend. A man who can help me get this thing done.' I knowed right then 'n there he be talkin' 'bout you 'cause I read 'bout you in the paper. Then I says to the chief: 'And what you gonna do when you find this person?' And he says, 'I can't tell you what I'm gonna do when I find this person or persons, Flora. I can only tell you what I'm gonna haveta do soon after I do.' So, I says, 'What?' And he says, 'Retire from the force.'

"Now, I's not a stupid woman, Mr. Redler. I know I's not educated like ya-all and that you knows you talkin' to a low-class black woman when I get mad. Beau get mad at me when I don't watch my speech—says I's talkin' like a nigger. I's been an embarrassment to 'im on mo' than one occasion at those po·lice functions. But he never hit me, and he never forgot from where he comes. Off those mean streets, Mr. Redler. He come off them mighty hard. That's why he was a good detective. That's how he found that bitch."

"Mrs. Hopkins—"

"No, let me finish. I knows that Beau was after 'er. That Manns woman. I knows it in my heart. I knows that the po·lice chief knows it, too. He kept playin' 'round with the word, '*person* or *persons*.' The '*person* responsible.' But we both knows it was that bitch. I could see it in the po·lice chief's angry eyes."

"Mrs. Hopkins, please—"

"Now, Chief Grear gonna get his self in a heap o' trouble if he's not careful. So, that's why I's callin' you. You find and kill that evil bitch, Mr. Redler, like you did her boyfriend, Richard Geist, and that accomplice of his. Killin' her ain't gonna bring my Beau back. I knows that. But it gonna stop a whole lot more killin'. And that's a fact. Now, I'm not hangin' up on you; I'm just hangin' up 'cause I don't want you to say nothin' that can and will be used against you if certain parties be listening in," she continued just as calmly as she could through a stream of tears. "God bless you, sir," Flora Hopkins said, terminating their conversation, resolutely setting down the receiver.

In silence, Robert put down the phone.

"What was that all about?" Liza asked.

"Oh, just some good Samaritan asking another for a favor."

"Asking what?"

"Asking me to commit murder for her is all."

"Mrs. Hopkins asked you that?" Liza asked incredulously, carrying two bowls of soup carefully to the table. "You know, I think I'm going to lose my mind soon," she added. "I really and truly do."

"Well, first we have to eat then finish pruning. Next, we have to thatch the lawn. I'll run the machine; you rake. After that, you can help me hatch a plot," he half-teased, making light of the matter he knew was truly getting out of hand.

Chapter 16

Barbara Giordano paced the modest studio apartment. Angelica sat with her legs drawn up on the sofa, studying the angry woman quietly.

"First it's the armaments you hauled off that army base in Wisconsin, and now it's the money-laundering scheme gone to pot. The feds just happened to have walked right around our so-called fail-safes, and without warning, fell in on five of my key people. Not decoys or fall guys, mind you. No! Five of my front office fixtures. That's just not dumb luck on the agency's part. They had to know exactly how to go in without alerting others. And that is next to impossible. The operation is set up like a labyrinth, with land mines all along the way."

"How did the money-laundering scheme work?" Angelica asked, now that the charade was over and that the boss woman would have to find new ways to funnel her funds.

"I guess it doesn't matter much at this point, does it?" Barbara scowled.

"Maybe I can spot a flaw."

"Oh, really?"

"I might surprise you. Besides, you're really going to have to trust me more and more as we move further along the line."

"Trust is golden, Angelica. First you have to show me that you shine."

"Tell me how you laid it all out, and I'll show you where the problem lies."

Barbara shook her head at the young woman's audaciousness. "It's complicated," she said.

"I like complicated."

"A member of my cell—"

"What cell?"

"Twelve associates, including myself, and don't interrupt," Barbara snapped then began again. "An associate of mine with contacts in Columbia would approach legitimate businessmen who import goods from the United States, offering them American dollars for Columbian pesos at a favorable rate of exchange. The pesos are then handed over to the Cali drug cartel people with whom my other associates deal. *Comprende*? The drug money that I collect here, in U.S. dollars, of course, is used to purchase the exported goods through a network of dummy corporations."

"So, the Cali boys get their money, the Columbian businessmen get a good deal because they actually pay less for their imports, and your drug dollars never really leave your bank account, technically speaking," Angelica clarified.

"As smart as you are beautiful. Already you pose a threat to me," Barbara said, forcing a smile.

"So what do you think went wrong? A bogus banker in your midst?"

"Couldn't happen. We only deal with banks and people we control. I told you before. We're impenetrable."

"You *were* impenetrable."

"It was impossible for the feds to infiltrate. Every associate is a member of a cell."

"Yet five of them are sitting in one."

"As we speak. And six more are being sought."

"Which makes eleven and leaves one member of the cell . . . ."

"Left in the lurch. Me."

"Can it come back to you?"

"I say no. I can't see how. But then again, I don't know how they fell on the others."

"I think I do," Angelica said. "I think you truly do, too."

"Robert Redler?"

"Robert Redler," Angelica repeated, swinging a pair of shapely legs off the sofa.

"My protégé."

"Your protégé. Your brainchild."

"Believe me. He knows nothing."

"Maybe. But he *sees* things. True? Look. Granted you managed to get yourself off the hook concerning a certain faction of the Mob.

But I don't think you're going to be in their good graces if any of these five associates of yours, or the six being sought, sing. Do you?"

"They can't put a name to me. Just my instructions. That's the way I set it up."

"You hope."

Barbara Giordano said nothing.

"I want to teach Redler a lesson," Angelica remarked.

"We don't know that he brought the heat."

"There is a way of finding out, Barbara."

"You might make matters worse."

"Do nothing and things *will* get worse. If it's him, I know how to make him stop."

"How?"

"By having a little talk with his domestic partner, Liza."

"First you and I have to have a long talk," Barbara said.

"Think about it, Barbara. Impenetrable, you said. Yet you still got fucked."

Barbara Giordano thought long and hard before she opened her mouth. "Let me hear what you have in mind," she finally said, sitting down beside Angelica.

Chapter 17

Mondays through Thursdays, Robert drove Liza to and from the train station in Riverhead for her commute into upper Manhattan. On Friday evenings, he'd pick her up on the South Fork, waiting for the eastbound diesel. The only problem being that the recalcitrant caboose would invariably block the roadway until the engineer decided it was time to pull his weight. Usually, it was a full five minutes before the train moved again. By then, two long lines of vehicular traffic would string the north and south routes while peeved drivers waited impatiently for the gates to rise . . . waited for the train to pass . . . waited to step on the gas and be gone.

Robert had recently remedied that situation. He simply parked and waited for Liza in the turnoff just before the railroad crossing. As she'd approach the rear of the train and start to cross the tracks, he'd back the car onto the northbound lane, pop the trunk for her to toss her bag inside, and in seconds the couple would be homeward bound.

But things happened quite differently on the third Friday of that mid-October evening. Robert had been in a meeting most of the afternoon and had driven the truck to the station in lieu of the sedan. As usual, the train arrived promptly at 6:25 p.m. He sat and watched for Liza as the passengers stepped lively onto the platform, heading easterly for the ramp. Although he couldn't see her distinctly through the train's filmy windows, he watched her step from the last railcar and walk westward along the platform, heading for the closest set of stairs. As she started down the first flight, he saw her drop something; her tote bag, stooping to pick it up. Robert waited a good minute before sensing that something was wrong.

Robert threw the vehicle into reverse and hit the accelerator. The truck flew rearward, snaking around the railway gate. Along the border of the track he sped. As he veered toward the rear of the train, he braked. Not a soul was there—neither Liza nor her bag.

Suddenly, the signal sounded. Red lights alternately flashed along the rising white arms of the wooden railroad gate. The train was pulling away. Slowly at first. And then he saw her again, seated behind the filmy window, back in the last railway car. Her face contorted. Her hands waving hysterically above her head as if signaling for help. Robert was out of the truck and running towards her. Running fast and hard. The train was picking up speed. More speed than he could possibly muster. He glanced from the vehicle back to her window seat. She was gone. Robert went bounding for the phone at the station and called 911. Moments later, he was scrambling and stumbling toward the truck.

The next station east was Westhampton, but Liza wasn't there or anywhere along the route. She had vanished into thin air. The police brought Robert in for further questioning and paperwork.

The two men sat across from one another at a small table in a corner of the room.

"Why would you let her cross the tracks alone?" the police sergeant asked Robert. "Don't you realize how dangerous that can be?"

"She was in my sight practically the whole time," Robert railed defensively. "I could see her head and shoulders then the hem of her open coat at the knees." He looked at the man's unsympathetic face, realizing how ridiculous that sounded. "Look. It's not like there's a third rail. It's a diesel, for cryin' out loud." That's exactly what he felt like doing. Crying out loud. "This is the country, for Christ's sake. The South Fork."

"And things like this aren't supposed to happen here. Is that what you're telling me?"

"What I'm telling you is that she can take care of herself. She works in Harlem, for God's sake. Twenty some years. She's street-smart. This isn't—"

"She works where?"

"Harlem."

"And she commutes from Speonk?"

"From Riverhead. I drive her there and pick her up. On Fridays, I pick her up in Riverhead—I mean Speonk."

"Listen, Mr. Downs."

83

"My name is Redler. The woman you're supposed to be out there looking for is Liza Downs."

"You told me she was your wife back there."

"If I told you she was my domestic partner, you would have—"

"Whoa! Let me get this straight. Is Liza your wife or not?"

"We live together, but it's like we're husband and wife. Twenty-five years we've been together," Robert offered lamely.

"I see," the uniformed man in his forties said, a frown creasing the fleshy corners of his mouth.

"You see nothing," Robert added with heightened agitation.

"No, I see plenty. For instance, I see a man before me who *thinks* he saw someone snatch his girlfriend's purse."

"Bag, not snatched, dropped." *Are you even listening to me?* he wanted to shout.

"Next thing you tell me, she's back on the train sitting behind a dirty window with her hands waving all around her head. And then she suddenly disappears into thin air again. Then you tell me your wife was kidnapped, only it turns out she's not your wife. Now she's your domestic partner. When you go home, Mr. Redler, you're going to find that your friend missed her train and—"

"Now you listen to me," Robert insisted, taking the sergeant's wrist in a firm grip. "I know what Liza looks like. I saw her drop her tote bag; a boat bag in which she carries books and papers. I watched her heading toward the stairs at the rear of the train. She was on the staircase going down, I'm telling you. But she never made it because someone put her back on that train. Had to have."

"And I'm telling you to remove your hand from mine unless you want to spend the night in a cell."

Robert relaxed his grip and took his hand away, touching his brow in frustration.

"You told me when you reached the tracks, she was gone."

Robert nodded.

"Disappeared."

Robert nodded again.

"How could that happen, Mr. Redler? You said that you had backed up all the way to the tracks, looking over your right shoulder all the while."

"I was focused on that last car where I saw her waving. Not at me but with her hands above her head."

A plainclothesman approached the table where the two were seated. "Mr. Redler?"

Robert turned around abruptly. "Yes?"

"I'd like you to come with me, please."

The sergeant interrupted. "We have a bit more paperwork to finish, Matt."

"You're finished for now, Ted," the detective said plainly. "Mr. Redler, if you'll follow me."

Robert had a sickening sensation in the center of his gut. He followed the man into a private office down the hall. The detective pushed a button on the phone and handed over the receiver, directing Robert to take a seat before leaving the room and closing the door behind him.

"Hello?"

"Rob?"

"Yes."

"You alone?"

"Yes."

"Do you know who this is?"

"I think so."

"I write the words that make the whole world sing."

Robert started to tear. "Yes."

"What happened?"

Robert Redler blurted out the whole story in one fell swoop. Uninterrupted. When he finished, the man on the other end of the line asked him a single question.

"Why Speonk at that hour, Rob?"

Robert told him why. "To get home a little earlier. To have a little more time together," he said quietly. "We decided to do that on Fridays. I told you that." Then he began to weep. "You were supposed to be watching her—every step of the way."

"We were. My people watched her change at Ronkonkoma, bound for Riverhead, Rob."

"But she didn't take that train to Riverhead. She was on the diesel headed for Speonk. She had to have changed at Jamaica. Had to."

"No, Rob. I'm afraid not. She took a later train. Changed at

85

Ronkonkoma. The electric. She got off in Riverhead at 7:38 and got into your Camry."

"That's impossible! The Camry is sitting in the garage. I've got the truck with me."

"Well, you got that right. The Camry *is* sitting back in your garage."

"What the hell is going on? Liza never said anything about a later train. Did you check the house?"

"I have a man inside right now. Nothing. So don't bother calling there," he ordered, anticipating Robert's reaction. "I want that line clear."

"If that wasn't Liza I saw in Speonk, who in God's name was it?" There was a momentary silence before things began to sink in. "Jesus Christ."

"They want to traumatize you by a show of force, Rob. Plant a picture firmly in your mind. They won't hurt her. If they did, you would have found Liza's body on the tracks. They want you to live with that fear."

"How can you be so goddamn sure they won't hurt her or that she's even . . . ." He couldn't bring himself to say it.

"She's alive. We'll just have to wait for a call. In the meantime, I want you to go tell Sergeant Wilcox that you and Liza got your signals crossed on where you were to pick her up and when, that Liza phoned me—your uncle—and that she's all right. Tell him you're a writer with an active imagination that's on overload, that when she didn't get off the train, you came apart at the seams, assuming the worst. He'll buy that. I don't want anyone else but my people going over that train. Got it?"

"Won't be hard. He already thinks I'm a fucking nut."

"Good. Go find that detective first and put him back on the line. Not another word to him or anyone, other than what I told you. If there's a problem, call the number I gave you earlier, which is what you should have done in the first place. You don't involve the police. Are we clear on everything?"

"Clear." Robert hung up the phone, swearing to himself that if Liza were still alive, this business would be over. He was very clear on that.

Chapter 18

Liza had been released by her abductors just as suddenly as she had been kidnapped. She was about to be questioned in the living room of their Riverhead residence. A unit of armed men in SWAT uniforms and tactical gear had declared the premises and perimeter secure. Robert came in from the kitchen with a pot of coffee and fixings. Several uniformed men and women wearing white coveralls and carrying what appeared to be pest control equipment had finished a thorough sweep of the couple's home and property, searching for hidden electronic surveillance equipment: mini-microphone bugs, transmitters, cameras and such. From room to room they seemed to roam, though methodically examining every nook and cranny— inside the entire structure as well as out: top to bottom, upstairs, attic, roof, downstairs, each and every closet including clothing, basement, garage, vehicles, shed, dock, boat, bushes. The area was deemed uncompromised, and the team finally left.

For Liza's and Robert's protection, four men, none of whom Robert had ever met, introduced themselves as federal agents, assigned to guard the couple 24/7. They were, in fact, The Triumvirate's people. Liza's abduction was to be treated *unofficially* as a kidnapping— classified, of course, because of its sensitive nature. Liza said she fully understood. A full investigation was under way. The interview was about to be conducted by a man and his associate.

"Ms. Downs, I know that this has been a long and trying day for you. Think you're up to answering a few questions?" The stocky well-dressed man introduced himself as Bill Collins.

"I'm fine. I'm alive, and Robert's alive—and I thank God for that," Liza said, wiping away her tears.

"Why did you change your initial plans from being picked up in Speonk tonight to the Riverhead train station?" he asked matter-of-factly.

"I didn't. Before I left work, there was a message, supposedly from Rob, saying we'd meet in Riverhead at seven forty instead of six twenty-five in Speonk."

"We understand from Mr. Redler's police chief friend that your captors dropped you off by boat."

Liza nodded. "At the Moose Lodge dock. It's right around the corner from here." She pointed in an easterly direction from her seat on the couch.

"That's the lodge that Mr. Redler belongs to?" the other man asked.

"That's correct."

"And you went over to the pay phone and called . . . ." Collins was looking at his notes.

"Chief Grear at police headquarters here in Riverhead. He came and got me."

"You didn't call home, here."

"They told me not to."

"Who told you?"

"I don't know. I was blindfolded. Voices of two men."

"Jesus Christ," Robert interrupted. "That's exactly what they did to me back when—"

"Please, Mr. Redler," Bill Collins' associate spoke up sternly. "Let's do this one at a time. Shall we?"

"Go on, Ms. Downs," Collins instructed calmly. "Please continue."

"They left me on the dock and put change in my hand. Told me to count backwards from one hundred then to take the blindfold off and call the police and tell them how well I was treated," Liza scoffed.

"What else?"

"Not to stop counting or move until I got to one or they'd shoot me from a distance." Liza sniffled, putting a handkerchief to her nose. "Excuse me, I don't mean to carry on like this."

"You're doing just fine, Ms. Downs," Collins said encouragingly. "Let's go back to the beginning, from the moment you got off the train in Riverhead and walked up to the car. Did you see or sense anything suspicious?"

Liza shook her head. "I just got off the train like I usually do and headed for the car."

"The Camry."

"Yes."

"And what happened?"

"The trunk popped up, and I put my bag inside. I closed it, came around, and got in." Liza started sobbing.

"Go on."

"Can't you see that she's upset?" Robert snapped, going over to Liza's side.

"Take a seat, Mr. Redler," the other man ordered. "Over there." He pointed to a single chair.

"Take a sensitivity course, asshole," Robert Redler blasted.

"All right!" Collins said sharply. "This is your home, and I respect that, Mr. Redler. But this is our investigation. Do you want to do this elsewhere? Either way, this is going to be done civilly."

Liza spoke up. "I'm sorry, gentlemen," she said, addressing the pair. "You have no idea how we somehow managed to get through two years of hell. I know you must have a good idea of *what* we went through, but you have no idea *how* we handled it all. Not very well," she emphasized. She turned to Robert. "Rob, let them ask their questions. Let them do their job. I'm all right," she assured him. "Really."

"It might be a good idea if you wait in another room," Collins' partner suggested quietly.

"I'm not going anywhere," Redler made clear.

"Can we do this calmly, Rob?" Collins asked patiently.

"Be good, Rob," Liza said, forcing a little smile. Then she faced her interviewer directly, avoiding Robert's angry eyes. "After I got in the car, I leaned over for a kiss. It was dark. I didn't see his face, at first, but I knew it wasn't Robert. A strap, a belt, or something came across my throat from behind. I tried to fight, but a voice from the rear told me that I was going to die if I put up a struggle. The car had already pulled away, I think."

"Did you lose consciousness?"

"I thought I might, but I didn't. As she relaxed the strap, I relaxed my body. I mean I was shaking all over, but I didn't struggle."

"You said, she."

"Yes, a woman."

"Did you see her face or the driver's?"

Liza shook her head, biting her bottom lip.

"Ms. Downs. A moment ago you said of the driver: 'I didn't see his face, at first, but I knew it wasn't Robert.' What did you see?"

"Masks."

"They wore masks?"

Liza nodded.

"Did you recognize these masks?"

Again, Liza nodded.

"Well?" Robert asked, interrupting the man's flow.

Liza turned to Robert. "They were of you and me."

"My God!" Robert exclaimed.

"Ms. Downs?"

Liza returned her attention to Collins. "Yes?"

"Did they say or do anything else?"

"The black man behind the wheel said nothing. The woman behind the front seat did all the talking."

"Black man?"

"His hands. On the steering wheel."

"I see. Go on, please."

"Like I said. The woman did all the talking. Should I say exactly what she said? I mean, the foul language and all."

"As best you can. It could be helpful. Either way, I'm good at filling in the blanks." Bill Collins smiled and waited patiently.

Liza put her head down as she spoke. "She said Luther wanted to blank me in the backside and would if I didn't do as I was told. There was someone sitting next to her in the back seat. I couldn't see."

Robert stood up. "Did they rape you, or hurt you? This I want to know," he demanded. "Then I'll go wait in the kitchen."

Liza never lied to him and wasn't lying now. "No," she said succinctly.

Robert went into the kitchen and held onto the edge of the sink. The other man was at his side.

"This is why these things are better handled like I suggested out there. No hard feelings?" he asked, extending his hand.

"No hard feelings," Robert answered, taking the man's hand. "It's been a fucking nightmare. I thought I lost her."

"They want to fill you with the fear of the devil. Got a beer, Rob?"

"Beer? I thought you guys weren't allowed to drink on duty," Robert said sourly, opening the door of the refrigerator.

"I've officially signed myself out," the man decreed with a grin. "My partner can ride with coffee for a while. Then I think he'll need a double."

Rob handed him a bottle of Budweiser, taking one for himself. "Can I speak off the record?"

"Not with the FBI you can't."

"Can the crap; all right? I know who you are, and I'm telling you I want them fucking dead."

"Never heard you say that."

"I'll tell you something else."

"Sure you want to do that?"

"You tell the three blind mice who you really work for that they better never ever fuck up like that again. Hear me?"

"You bet," the man toasted, taking a long pull on the ice-cold beer.

Ten minutes had passed when the two men standing in the kitchen heard a hearty laugh from Liza. As they stepped into the living room, even Collins seemed nonplused. Liza was pointing to the floor, barely able to control herself.

"What could be so goddamn funny?" Robert Redler insisted, genuinely upset.

"I forgot, I forgot—" Liza could barely catch her breath. "I forgot to have all of them take their shoes off," she said in sheer hysterics, doubled over in her seat.

"Healthy sign," the man said to Robert, handing him the empty bottle. "Like they say in the movies, we'll be in touch."

Liza was still laughing when Collins and his colleague left. That night, Liza did nothing but cry until she finally fell asleep in Robert's arms.

The following morning, Liza and Robert sat in the dining room with their coffee.

"We have to talk," Liza said.

"There's nothing to talk about. We did all our talking last night. I put you at risk two years ago, and you could have wound up dead last night. They made their point. Angelica Manns and her people. That's it. I'm out. The agency will find them, and that will be that. In the meantime, I'm going to see to it that you continue to have door-to-door and around-the-clock protection."

"Really?"

"Really."

"In exchange for what?"

"In exchange for nothing. All right?"

"Robert. Look at me."

Robert looked.

"Let's bring these bastards down. I mean all the way down and straight to hell," she said with such hatred in her eyes.

"That's anger talking."

"Oh, you are so goddamn right. Anger and fear that if we do nothing, the same thing could happen to us next week or next month, or maybe not at all. But what about other innocent people? I've looked death squarely in the eyes, and I don't want another soul out there to go through what I went through last night. I was lucky because they fear and want your gift. You can *see* where others cannot. You can point the way so that the authorities can take them down."

"I didn't *see* this coming last night."

"You didn't see every single step along the way when you brought Richard Geist and Michael no-name down, either. Did you? But you saw enough. Now, listen carefully to me. I don't know what you did to set those freaks in motion. But I know you had to have done something for them to pull a stunt like that. I know how principled you are. I know you can't tell me things because you promised somebody you wouldn't. And I want you to keep that promise. The less I know, the better, probably. You use this gift, this power you possess. God gave you this ability. Where the authorities fall short of protecting us, God will. I honestly believe that. I would not have believed that before last night."

"That's a lovely little speech, Liza. But what if you're wrong?"

"What if I'm not?"

"Oh, Liza. I don't know. I'm really scared this time around."

Liza got up and came around the table to give him a hug and assurances. "Whatever you decide, Rob. I just want you to know my feelings. Okay? Whatever you decide," she repeated.

He felt very strange that morning. Liza was somehow gaining

strength and courage, whereas he was surely losing his nerve.

Chapter 19

Halloween was still a week away, but parents in the area wanted their children to remain home, safe and sound.

Watch Hill, Rhode Island police authorities exhumed the body of a nineteen year-old male Caucasian, identified as Philip Glover, missing since August. High school dropout. Troubled kid since grade school. The boy had been a handsome youth. *Had been* was the operative phrase. Two bullet holes had blown out the back of the boy's skull after tunneling their way through a pair of once sea-blue eyes. Although forensics at the scene had no physical evidence to lead them to any definitive conclusion as yet, even-money was wagered that the caliber that caused the damage could have been a .380 fired at point-blank range, reminiscent of the close-up cruelty that Carson Reynolds, Lee Edward (Butch) Reynolds, and Beau Hopkins had suffered.

Barbara Giordano was not a happy boss. "I had said no unnecessary killing. Didn't I? Why did you waste that boy, Angelica? Why? Tell me."

"Reasons? He was not the type to benefit from after-class instruction," Angelica calmly offered in explanation. "He was becoming a discipline problem. Set a bad example for the others. I could give you several more reasons. But what would be the point?"

"He was just a kid for Christ's sake."

"So now Christ can deal with him. I cannot have anyone jeopardize my operation."

"I think *you* are doing just that."

"No. Let me tell you what *I* think. I think Liza Downs should have gone down for the final count. But we did it your way. If we did it my way, Robert Redler would be weeping over her headstone or babbling away in a home someplace. No way could the cops have found that kid without some help from someone."

"Probably from one or more of your pupils who believed you'd have shot theirs out for simply whispering from their seats," she quipped. "I'm sure they fear you, Angelica."

"No. They've become positively fearless. We have mutual respect for one another. Redler is the meddler. I say we take him out."

"I think you're out of control."

"Come to one of my sessions. Spend a day. See if you walk away with that impression."

Barbara Giordano looked deeply into Angelica's sea-green eyes and saw a deadly serious stare. Not one of anger or defiance, but of definitiveness, determination, and drive. What she saw were the signs of a gifted leader. Barbara smirked and slowly shook her head. "I wonder if I'd walk away at all."

"That's not what I meant."

"I'm glad. It would be a shame to have to let you go. And I do mean that."

Both women sat across from one another on a seesaw. Barbara was looking down at Angelica. Angelica suddenly pumped her legs and rose as Barbara descended, the soles of her black knee-high boots touching the well-worn barren strip of earth.

"Heard you lost a rather large shipment of Acapulco Gold last week," Angelica stated.

Barbara nodded.

"Do you attribute that to bad luck, poor timing, or do you think the feds got themselves a good tip?"

"I don't know what to think anymore. It's uncanny."

"A word you could attribute to the likes of Mr. Robert Redler, don't you think?"

Barbara pushed off, but Angelica leaned far forward, counterbalancing the weight until the two were perfectly level, staring directly across at one another.

"You'll never get near either of them," Barbara swore. "If he's still doing what you think he's doing, he's well-protected by now."

"Then let me send a message that will get through to at least one of them this time," Angelica affirmed.

"No more shootings. I mean it."

"Believe me. They'll barely hear a sound, Barbara," Angelica said solemnly.

Chapter 20

The metal through-the-wall mail chute at the Redler/Downs residence measured 5½ x 4½ inches. It was the perfect passageway in which to deliver Angelica's message. As the couple's mail was being intercepted by the Triumvirate's team on a daily basis as a precautionary measure, searching for letter bombs, virulent spores and such, a special surreptitious delivery, therefore, arrived in the wee hours of the morning. It was handled with utmost care and cunning, lifted boldly from the beige canvas mailbag and placed into the sufficient opening.

A doleful moan of wind ran rampant between the homes off the body of water fifty yards behind the house. Inside, Robert and Liza were sound asleep upstairs. One floor below, a bed of embers smoldered behind the safety of the glass fireplace doors.

Through the chute and down the interior wall a shiny, large-scaled serpent came, slithering quietly across the sea-foam carpet, exploring the width and length of hallway. Along the stark-white baseboard the python swept. A body black and gray and brown. Into the living room it wound, uninvited, drawn instinctively to the warmth of the gray slate hearth. For half a minute, maybe more, it lay as still as rope; all fourteen feet.

Suddenly it moved, passing an electrical outlet, winding its way to the leg of an open convertible sofa. Up it rose and onto the blanket it slithered, resting beside the warmth of a body less than a quarter the length of its own.

Liza's five-year-old nephew, David, stirred slightly and seemed to sense a presence. He gradually sat up from a deep and satisfying sleep. Without warning, the cold-blooded creature coiled its constricting mass about the child's chest, steadily crushing his rib cage amidst the terrible scream of terror.

Out of a sound sleep, Robert hit the floor with both feet, and

Liza hit the light. Down the stairs together they flew. Robert switched on a hallway light and stepped into the semi-darkened room. Liza switched on the living room light. The boy greeted them with silence, bleeding profusely from his mouth and nostrils, locked in the deadly embrace of the hungry snake. The scene seemed so surreal, Robert wondered for an instant whose bad dream it was as Liza was already tearing away at the powerful hold of the vertebrate.

A figure in a brown bomber jacket had already bolted through the back door. Out front, another member of the team lay dead. Robert, Liza, and the security guard pried and pulled the python off the bloody boy, moving the one hundred plus pound reptile toward the hearth.

"In there!" the man hollered and pointed. Liza ripped open the fireplace doors and screens.

The two men hurled the snake inside and slammed the glass doors closed. Liza immediately ran back to her nephew.

Within ten minutes, Emergency Medical Service personnel arrived, and a paramedic was performing cardiopulmonary resuscitation on the unconscious boy.

An eerie white cloud of ash rose from behind the fireplace doors as a steady sickening rhythm and stench ensued through the burning embers. Robert stacked a series of heavy logs against the glass.

EMS workers suddenly rushed the boy outside to a waiting ambulance. Riverhead police and a swarm of other professionals filled the front yard. The phone kept ringing incessantly inside the home. Liza sat at the dining room table in a sort of trance, rocking herself to and fro in a steady, sturdy chair after being told by an officer that she could not ride to the hospital with her only nephew.

David was pronounced dead on arrival at Central Suffolk Hospital; 2:45 a.m. Cause of death: thoracic suffocation. Robert stood beside the boy, crying, holding his little hand.

Back on Riverside Drive, Emergency Service Unit officers removed the remains of the Burmese python from the fireplace and secured the house.

At David's funeral, no words were exchanged between the immediate families. Only the tears of their tragic loss were shared among the grieving parties. As for other family members and friends, they all stood at Liza's sister's side. Robert Redler had no family to speak of; Liza alone held his trembling hand. The chief of police was in attendance. So were fifty federal agents, Suffolk County homicide detectives, state troopers, deputy sheriffs, and uniformed police— spread out everywhere. Bill Collins and his team were standing on the sidelines. The collective lot was now officially Robert's and Liza's unofficial family.

Robert swore that if the nameless little man he met two months ago showed his ferret face, he'd smash it for him. He told Bill Collins exactly how he felt.

Liza stood at graveside, her mind and heart filled with more venom than a hundred thousand lethal snakes. Robert stood beside her, worried sick over her well-being. She wasn't eating, sleeping or showering, nor saying very much without his prompting. He had never ever seen her in such a state. There, standing before David's grave, Robert Redler swore absolute revenge.

Liza took a few personal days off from work, followed by several sick days before putting in a request and being granted extended sick leave.

Sheer hatred consumed Robert to the very core as he wrote a minimum of twelve hours a day—every day—with a vituperative, venomous pen. Within a week, a middle-level player of Barbara Giordano's was arrested for delivering a large shipment of drugs at a recycling plant in Brooklyn.

Chapter 21

Angelica Manns slipped on a pair of Royal Robbins khaki BlueWater shorts. Pockets everywhere: bellowed cargo pockets in front that contained better than a pound of bulky items; deep-seated pockets in back with a web strap sewn just above the right rear, one through which she secured the handle of a heavy hammer. A D-ring secured a set of boat keys that hung from a rawhide lace. She placed her bare feet into an expensive pair of dark brown Sperry boat shoes, pulled on a skintight loden-green cotton top, tied her red wig into a ponytail, framed her face behind large tortoise shell sunglasses then left the stateroom.

Topside, she addressed her troops.

"Today you will see, firsthand, how looking hot can sink a yacht. Or in this case," she said and smiled broadly, nodding toward the cove across the bay, "a smaller vessel."

Robert and Liza's white and blue cabin cruiser sat at anchor, sixty yards off the distant shore. The two were out in their inflatable, heading toward a village to clear their minds and stretch their sea legs. They planned on doing a little shopping, picking up some odds and ends; perhaps enjoy a light lunch in the early afternoon. Robert felt he needed to get Liza away from the house for a while. He was becoming more and more concerned about her mental state.

The *Write On* rocked gently among several other boats anchored some fifty yards apart. Her bow held steady to the south in seven feet of water. Angelica handed a pair of binoculars to Guadalupe.

"The one with the radar arch," the pretty pirate pointed.

Guadalupe acknowledged with a nod behind the rubber coated glasses.

"You know what to do," Angelica said to the others.

Everyone knew the drill. Guadalupe went below and inserted a tape into the cassette player, switching on the external speakers, cranking up the volume. Their vessel headed toward the cove at several knots.

As the fifty-footer slowly approached the other boats, two dozen young women aboard her removed their shirts or blouses, dropped their shorts and mooned those tied to moorings. Men were going topsy-turvy from port to starboard and fore to aft, gawking at the naked bodies jiggling their breasts in concert to the blaring of Beethoven's Fifth.

Angelica dove quietly beneath the chilly surface off to starboard, swimming underwater toward the writer's anchored craft. She came up directly in front of the partially submerged swim ladder, grabbed a rung then pulled herself up and onto the swim platform. Off to port, she could hear the men cheering; certainly not the dead composer, she mused. She quickly headed toward the hatchway, hammer in hand.

Angelica swung the head of the hammer high and hard against the center of the thick, locked Lucite folding door then took it off its hinges with two swift kicks delivered from the ball and heel of her foot. Down a step, then another, and into the cabin she stooped. Standing midship, she stood and lifted two Velcro tabs that secured a bulging pocket on her shorts. Withdrawing a handful of tapered steel spikes, the saboteur quickly went to work, piercing the floor of the fiberglass hull in strategic locations. Up along the port wall she continued, driving a dozen more spikes below the water line. Slowly, the boat was starting to fill. Opening her other pocket, she turned to starboard, taking up another handful of nails before banging away with wild abandon.

Surveying the damage around her, Angelica seemed satisfied. She exited the craft the same way she had come, swimming beneath the water, back to her gang of girls. Guadalupe put down a foldable boarding ladder. Angelica climbed aboard, and the crew got under way.

A male captain and crew from another nearby vessel lined the railing, loudly expressing their disappointment over the young women's sudden departure. One fellow from a sailboat insisted on knowing the ladies' port of call. An elderly couple on a trawler smiled and waved good-bye to the group. Another pair bid the girls good riddance, turning their attention back to the Sunday *Times*. Several wives and girlfriends standing in the cockpit of a large pilothouse shook their heads plaintively at their respective mates, exchanging knowing looks that told that they had somehow hooked up with a ship of fools.

No one saw the twenty-five footer listing hard to starboard, already a good foot and a half below her water line, sinking steadily. No one saw the vessel until it was too late. Finally, one woman turned and called to her husband, pointing to the radar arch disappearing beneath the surface.

I'm glad we were able to squeeze in a little boating," Robert said and smiled peacefully, taking in the ambiance of the cozy corner cafe. "God knows we both need this. Not too many days left like these before we put 'er away in mothballs. Last hurrah," he added, trying to start a conversation.

Liza sat with her salad, picking away quietly.

"Sure you don't want a glass of wine with that?"

Liza forced a polite smile. "I'm fine."

"No, you're not fine. And I'm not fine, either. But we have to find a way to heal, Liza. I thought this little trip might be good for us. We had to get away," he said, fussing with his fish and chips.

"I miss him so, Robby."

She rarely called him Robby. It almost sounded strange.

"I know," he mumbled, pushing his plate aside. "They say, time."

"What?"

"Time. It's going to take time."

"If only I didn't put him downstairs. But he insisted, wanting to sleep by the fireplace. If only—"

"Now, stop it. We've been over that a hundred times."

"I have such hatred in my heart."

"Not healthy."

"Fuck healthy!" she snapped with a vengeance. Several people looked over and were staring in their direction. "South Shore snobs," she carped, making eye contact until they looked away.

"Jesus Christ," he whispered. "Get a grip."

"Around their fucking evil throats," she swore loudly. "Manns and her Circle of Friends."

He had never heard or seen her behave like this. Never had she used the f word. She hardly ever had an unkind word for others, let alone vent her anger before perfect strangers.

"Do you want to go?" he asked.

"No." And with that she stood and walked up to the folks she had made uneasy.

Robert got to his feet, perplexed.

"I apologize for that scene a second ago," Liza said, standing between two tables. "People don't have a right to make others feel uncomfortable, especially here in a public place."

One of the women smiled and nodded nervously, her companion rising halfway from his seat. Robert was immediately at Liza's side, taking a firm hold of her arm.

"I just want to explain—let go of me!" she snapped.

"Come on back to the table," Robert coaxed, leading her away.

"NO!" she shouted. "I want these people to understand."

Robert held her firmly. "Come on, now."

"I want them to understand that some horrible people killed my five-year-old nephew with a fucking fourteen-foot constrictor snake. It crushed the life right out of him," she screamed. "And here we are sitting and eating in a charming little place in Sag Harbor as if nothing's happened." Suddenly, she started throwing her arms wildly about. "I said to let go of me!"

The maître d' was fuming, and the bartender switched his role to one of bodyguard/bouncer. Customers were buzzing all around.

"We're going to have to ask you to leave," the employee said in a thick brogue, standing in front of the headwaiter that dramatically dashed off a check and handed it to Robert from over the bartender's shoulder.

"We're out of here," Redler said, ignoring the check, placing a twenty and a ten on the table, finally pulling Liza from the establishment.

Neither of them spoke a word during the dinghy ride back across the bay, heading toward their boat. As the two approached the small cove, a large inflatable boat came out to meet them. Robert immediately recognized the orange craft. A sickening feeling filled his gut as his eyes scanned the shoreline: the other boats, the men in orange vests. Liza's back was to them. One of the men waved him over. Robert pulled alongside. The two inflatables brushed together. Liza looked over. Robert was handed a line.

"Tie this to your bow ring, sir," the Coast Guard official ordered. "You're both coming aboard."

"What happened?" Robert demanded.

"Your boat's sitting on the bottom in nine feet of water is what happened," the man remarked.

Liza began laughing hysterically. She couldn't stop. Suddenly, she started crying, cursing like a sailor, carrying on as a crazy person might. Robert believed, indeed, she was . . . or at the very least, temporarily insane.

Chapter 22

Chief Grear, Robert Redler, and all Three Musketeers held a meeting at Riverhead Town Hall. The five men sat around an oval oak table. Matching chairs with padded armrests were drawn toward the table's border like a magnet. A pitcher of water and inverted tumblers sat on a cork and plastic tray.

"So," the mousy, ferret-faced man began. "You want to know why you're here. Well, it's really very simple. Like a bird dog working the brush, we're going to help you flush Barbara Giordano and Angelica Manns out of hiding. We're going to help you, help us."

The other two musketeers sat in stone-faced silence. Chief Grear picked up the conversation.

"What these gentlemen are getting at, Rob, is that they have been carefully weighing your gift. Somewhat skeptically, of course. But no one here can argue the accuracy of the information you've provided thus far. The only problem is its scope."

"To get right to it, Rob," the mousy man picked up, "the chief feels that if you had access to, say, sensitive information we've been collecting concerning certain drug operations both here and abroad, other stolen armaments and whatnot, it might put you more in touch with your sixth sense, so to speak. Heighten your awareness. Help you develop your insights more keenly. Move things along for you and us. Give you something more tangible rather than something tangential to work with. Am I putting things into their proper perspective, Rob?"

"You're very clear," Robert said benignly.

"So, is the chief's assessment of this situation on target? Will this help you home in?" the man asked.

"Do I get the files? I mean everything?"

"You'll get what we feel is necessary. Now, in answer to my last two questions. Is the chief's assessment—"

"Yes, to your first, and maybe, to your second."

"Explain the maybe."

"The more I'm privy to, the more I glean. The more I glean, the bigger picture I see. It's as simple as that."

"Oh, I think this vision of yours is anything but simple," the musketeer said. "Nonetheless, we're prepared to hand you a particular file right now. It concerns Mexico's Gulf cartel. It appears that Ms. Manns is operating just south of the border from Brownsville. Matamoras. Branching out on her own."

"With the blessings of Barbara Giordano? Or is she going behind her back?"

"Maybe *you* can tell *us*," the man said, picking up and pushing an accordion file across the table toward Robert. "Go home now, and look this over. See what you can see. The chief will escort you."

"How's Liza doing?" the chief asked as he pulled around the driveway to the back of the two-story home.

"About the same."

"We're going to nail those two bitches, Rob."

"Goddamn right we are. And thanks for trying to wake those guys up back there," Robert said, stepping out of the car and picking up the heavy accordion file, secured in a locked steel case.

"To tell you the truth, I had very little input. It was the guy sitting across and to your right whose wife is best friends with the wife of the man in charge. I think you've got two women on your side."

"I think maybe that women should rule this land," Redler said straightaway.

"They do," Grear said half-seriously. "I read somewhere that most of the country's assets are in their names."

Robert smiled. "Where's the key?" he asked, holding up the hefty box.

"Two keys. I've got one; here you go. And your doorman's holding the other." The police chief gestured toward the man.

Jack, a member of Triumvirate's team, stood at the back door of the house.

Robert sighed. "All this cloak and dagger."

"Let's get this business behind us so that we can go out fishing sometime, Rob. How does that sound?"

"Yeah, in what?" Robert questioned, gesturing toward the

empty dock where the *Write On* had sat peacefully.

"When we find them, we'll confiscate that reported fifty-footer, and fish on her till kingdom come," Grear promised with a smile.

"That would be nice."

"That would be poetic justice."

Robert Redler went inside the house to read the file. He could hardly wait.

Grear headed back to headquarters, reflecting to a point in time that he had made detective second grade . . . a million years ago or so it seemed. He had been on the case involving Richard Geist. As a young sergeant, Grear had used the word *glean* (as Redler had used it moments ago in the office with the musketeers) to make a point and perhaps impress his predecessor, Lieutenant Lark. He recalled with amusement the proverbial mill his boss had put him through for having used such a show-off verb, gleaning more about police work in a single month with the veteran detective than he had during his years at John Jay College of Criminal Justice in Manhattan and the police academy combined. He recalled with great sadness Lark's modest game plan after retirement, the retirement he never got to enjoy. It was a simple plan, more along the line of a wish concerning a boat and a fish. A lifetime spent catching career criminals, and all the man had wanted to do was catch a cagey game fish. A trophy. A billfish he would have proudly displayed on his den wall one day.

Taking his right hand from the steering wheel, Grear reached into his coat pocket and fondled the scrimshaw-handled folding knife that the cancer-ridden cop had bequeathed to him from bedside. The heirloom had been handed down for generations in the man's family. The man who had treated him like a son. It was the knife with which Lieutenant Lark had cut Richard Geist's tongue out of his head at the North Shore State Hospital in Havenwood, a hospital for the criminally insane.

Chapter 23

Barbara Giordano and Angelica Manns sat together on a hilltop in a clandestine corner of South America. The older woman spoke softly, as if her words might possibly travel down the hillside and awake the sleepy village.

"You have to understand some things. I control the largest empire in the Empire State, Angelica. I buy down here as well as all through Central America," Barbara added. "I operate with virtual impunity. If I were ever taken into custody, which is highly unlikely, I'd be granted immunity. Immediately. I *own* officials whose careers were built on the largess and support of my people in Albany, D.C., L.A., Houston, and yes, even here. I ship via Montevideo, Managua, and Mexico, and I am untouchable because I can have the long arm of the law broken off at the elbow, just like that," she said, snapping her fingers judiciously. "I deal in multibillions of dollars and pay out paltry millions for protection. Got it? Protection for profit. Anyone from a field hand to the producers of pure white powder is on my payroll. Anyone who turns greedy or self-righteous turns up dead. I am responsible for the deaths of forty some-odd officials over the course of a decade. So I'm no stranger to violence. But that stunt you pulled on the water was sophomoric. You hit a man in his heart, his head, his home, you let it lie. You made your point. You don't keep hammering away, literally, like your latest stunt. He's got the message and its meaning. Now, let it go. If he continues, that's another story."

"You may be protected from the long arm of the law, which probably means you won't sit a day in jail or even stand before a judge," Angelica acknowledged. "But what about a second bullet in your brain? You're not immune to that."

"No, you're quite correct on that account. That is why I used Redler the way I did back then. He was my insurance policy. When you play with the big boys, you've got to have an edge. I took a gamble, bet on Redler, and gained the upper hand. I had other plans for him as well."

"But he wouldn't join you."

Barbara shook her head. "Robert Redler is an idealist. He sees things as he believes they should be; not how they actually are and always will be." Barbara laughed softly. "And in that lies the great irony for one who is supposedly *gifted* and sees so clearly."

"He sees too damn much."

"But he didn't see how I was using him. Now did he? Not until I showed my hand. So he doesn't have a crystal ball, Angelica. He sees but half a sphere."

"He saw well enough to put a bullet into Richard's and Michael's brains. And at the end of his second book, which you so diligently promoted, I might remind you, he promised to put a bullet into ours. Therefore, my dear, I say we waste him. I think we'd both sleep better at night."

Barbara shook her head again. "No. You had your chance to charm one of them into oblivion with that snake, but it wound up and around the boy instead. I have a way to deal with Mr. Redler, writer extraordinaire, if he persists. We have too much at stake to stick our necks out now. That business in Georgia, Jersey, Rhode Island, and Long Island is done with. Redler is on hold. No more unnecessary violence. No more bodies buried or boats sunken off a beach. You are valuable. Not indispensable. Just remember that, and you'll keep your head. If you want to screw around with teenage girls, then kill them off for kicks, let me know. If you want a guy like Butch-Lee Reynolds hanging around because he's hung like a racehorse, let me know that, too. I'll provide you with your most perverse propensities. But jeopardize my operation with stupid stunts, and I'll *sink* you. Go behind my back and try and make a score for a paltry two-point-two mil like the last official, and I'll have you shot. There will come a time when I need you and your people. But I can't have screw-ups or screwballs. I have to have professionals. All right?"

"I understand."

"All right?" Barbara repeated.

"All right," Angelica answered.

"Good. Now, we're both going to a party down there tonight. I'm here to finish up a little business first, and then it's time for W.R."

"What's that?"

"Wild Recreation. Kind of like R & R, but without any inhibitions or rest involved. You'll see soon enough. And then I'll get to see what kind of stuff you're really made of. It's all been rumor up till now."

"Sounds hot."

"You have no idea, my dear girl. You haven't lived until you've been to one of Don Violeta's happenings."

Don Carlos Violeta's home was his castle, literally, lost among an imposing entanglement of tropical vegetation. Travel in and out of the area was by plane, or not at all. Uniformed soldiers guarded the majestic fortress from within as well as just outside the circular granite walls. What force lay hidden beyond the border of the jungle could accurately be classified a legion. What walked and talked and dealt behind the walls of the one-hundred-fifty-room mansion was a living legend.

That evening, one hundred of Central and South America's most beautiful women paraded themselves before the elite associates of Don Violeta. A pair of studs [comprised of eight legs] stood off to a corner, lashed to a marble column. Several young men stood masturbating over a shapely naked girl of no more than fifteen years of age. She held her legs wide open, giving them inviting stares.

Another girl, gorgeous and somewhat older, recoiled in the corner as one of the august animals was untied and drawn forth. Two bare-breasted maidens stroked the horse's prodigious penis while another woman massaged the girl's vagina before pouring on an ounce of fragrant oil. Four muscular Spaniards, each in different colored serapes, wearing nothing more, stepped forward, lifting and gently setting the teenager upon an open-sided wagon, wheeling her toward scaffolding in the center of the room. Her long, shiny black hair swept the floor as she lay flat on her back on the wooden cart.

Looking down into a pair of the loveliest, frightened dark eyes she had ever seen, Angelica backed her buttocks into the crotch of the man who stood behind her.

Two Spaniards left the wagon and led the stud to the middle of the scaffold, lifting its front legs high up and onto a sturdy wooden frame. The three women quickly followed. The first two continued stroking the magnificent Thoroughbred male. The third masterfully massaged the girl. Drums sounded in the background as the cart was put before the horse, its lengthy member planted firmly between the girl's long and lovely legs, inches away from her quim. She squirmed as the cart was suddenly ushered forward, the head of the creature's sex inserted within her shaven lubricated outer sheath, the animal's turgid erection held steady by pairs of helping hands, guiding the awesome organ in deeper.

The girl's eyes shone fearfully before she closed them tight. Her horse was halfway home and riding high. The scaffold creaked ominously from the massive weight upon it while the naked body writhed beneath. More of the horse drove forward, and its rod rode firmly in and out. The girl took it with an agonizing cry and had to be held down. The cart was steadily inched ahead. The horse reared heavenward on its haunches, its hooves hugging the hardwood floor. White powder was whisked into the girl's nostrils, and those of the distended steed flared.

The drums pounded away furiously until the horse and the girl were one. The lights in the room slowly dimmed, and the scaffolding took on an eerie glow. The smell of incense, oils, and perfume clogged the air. Clouds of opiates hung heavily around the tops of a hundred marble columns. Articles of clothing lay strewn across the area.

Angelica held one hand behind her, gripping the man's firmness in her fist. With a free hand, she undid her skirt and let it fall freely to the floor. The man unfastened the heavy belt buckle to his pants then pushed them down before kicking off his shoes.

The girl on the cart was frenzied, writhing and sighing heavily somewhere between the respective depths and heights of pain and pleasure as the stallion was driving her wild. The three women both fought with and fondled the girl. One of the male Spaniards climbed upon the wagon, straddled the girl's shoulders then thrust his tool past her hungry darting tongue. The other man stepped in closer to the cart, putting his sex in her hand. Her other hand groped the woman closest to her side.

Angelica marveled at the spectacle before her, her skin crawling with desire. The man abruptly turned her around toward him and put her back flat against a marble column, pulling off her panties. Angelica tore open her blouse, lifted her bra and pushed her breasts towards the Columbian's mouth. The man nipped one of her rock-hard nipples between his hot wet teeth and heavy breath. Angelica threw her head from side to side. The man reached down and pulled the belt free from the loops of his trousers. He picked up another pair near his feet and removed that belt, too, threading one end through the buckle of the other, lashing the straps around the column and across Angelica's throat, tying them off squarely. She closed her eyes and moaned. The man quieted his guest with his mouth upon her own. Down the front of her body his tongue traveled until it came to a fork in the path. Angelica leaned forward against the strap, lifting her feet off the floor and around the sides of the pillar, hanging there like a crucifix; arms extended outward; her hands, palms up. The Columbian knelt before her, speechless. His face was partially hidden between her legs. Yet, with eyes wide open, he stared up at the angelic face. In that moment, Don Carlos Violeta worshipped her.

The horse reared again, snorted, and shook the scaffold mercilessly. Sweat poured off the young girl from every pore. There came a round of wild applause. The two male Spaniards at the wagon were changing positions. Semen covered the teenager's face. She set her heels against the wooden surface and arched her back as the cart was pulled away. The steed's steaming organ hung to the floor. Finally, the animal was led away. Another stud was suddenly brought forward and put upon the wooden structure in the other's stead.

A moment later, a second wagon was wheeled into the area. On it, knelt a breathtaking black beauty in her twenties, seductively rising to all fours, knees and hand planted solidly upon the wooden platform. Her breasts were large and hung as gourd-like fruit. Her buttocks bore the firm and fleshy cheeks of a goddess groomed and promised for the darkest, deepest pleasures of a single kind. Her lips were full yet as proportioned as her figure. Her mouth a monument to man. Teeth as white as the powder the two ladies-in-waiting whipped into her nostrils before backing the wagon up to the snowy stallion. Her eyes burned as brightly as any jungle cat's.

Liberal amounts of oil were applied simultaneously to the woman's backside and all along the horse's sex: an organ seemingly larger and longer than that witnessed during the first performance. The animal reared at the sound of the starling drumroll. All the lights went out except for the spot on center stage. Two natives of Montevideo came forward in loincloths and climbed upon the table before the nubile creature. Immediately, she took the male pair into her greedy mouth, swaying her buttocks seductively to the beat of the pounding drums. The crowd went wild.

Angelica could plainly see over the Columbian's shoulder while he plowed her hard against the terra-cotta column, her arms and legs locked around the man's body in a powerful embrace.

"Fuck me, Don Violeta. Fuck me faster while the beast shoves it further up her ass," she whispered, taking in the scene. Angelica could see the woman's eyes. Bulging. The quarter horse was more than a quarter of the way in. "Oh, God! Yes, faster. Fuck me hard," Angelica groaned, straining against the strap across her throat.

Two men at the scaffolding pulled the cart toward them. The woman cried out to her god. One of the men on the table ejaculated; down her face his semen ran. The other man drove his member back into her mouth and down her throat. She gagged. The cart was pulled forward even further. The racehorse rammed the human female's fleshy cheeks while the native steadily pounded her mouth.

Men and women were engaged in foreplay and fornication all around the entertainers. The guests were fast becoming an integral part of the act. It was audience participation night of the most carnal and capricious kind.

Angelica begged for the likes of what the gift horse was giving the girl. She whinnied as though she were a mare herself in heat. Releasing her legs from around the stocky Columbian, she turned and faced the column, pressing a flushed cheek firmly against the cool marble, biting the rein that held her to it. Undulating her sensual backside in a rhythm that would summon forth Satan himself, Angelica's request was quickly granted, her erotic appetite nowhere near satiated; but no matter, for the night was young and her passion for desire unbridled.

With the help of handmaidens, the horse had gotten its fill, the beast's amazing length of cock buried deep inside the stately amazon, the Nubian slave shrieking away in a union somewhere between sheer agony and ecstasy, suddenly collapsing hard upon the cart. The native kneeling before her pulled her head up roughly by the hair, commanding in Spanish that she finish what she had started, whipping his thick crop of manliness repeatedly across her striking face. Catlike, the swarthy six-foot-two creature rose to oblige him, taking his testicles deep into her mouth while masturbating him furiously until he climaxed in an upward shower of semen that brought the act to its conclusion. Wild applause and approval went on forever.

Suddenly, the spotlight swept the room and fell upon Don Violeta and his lovely guest. Angelica was fingering her hungry mouth while her host continued hammering away from behind until he came. Slowly, she slithered down the column to the highly-polished doweled floor. The leather noose around her neck held her at the base of the support. She whispered something to her lover. Don Violeta had stepped back and made a gesture.

One of the women from the wagon came forward with a blindfold and covered the Anglo's beautiful eyes. Another woman stepped up and unfastened the strap at the American's nape. Angelica's sleek form suddenly rose as a cobra's from a basket, slender fingers clicking away like castanets, chiseled arms tracing the outline of her body as though she were charming a fascinated snake, assigning its rhythm, immediately signing for the accompaniment of drums. Instantly, a beat began and followed her measured movements as she slithered blindly along the floor. Most magically, it seemed as if she were shedding a scaly skin, peeling away the remnant of her sequined top. Simultaneously, she was transformed into that of a jungle cat, its nocturnal instincts traversing an entanglement of a savage yet seemingly familiar terrain. Past the piles of clothing and coveters she cavorted. Around the shadowy pillars she swept. Dramatically, the dance changed composition. A series of deadly kicks Angelica boldly delivered, barely missing the vertical supports, which nonetheless, yet metaphorically, brought down the entire house.

Exuberant applause and words of wonder accompanied her kata as she flew about the floor. One man had the audacity to smack her backside as she came full circle, seductively slipping back into the skin of the serpent, passing her taut body snake-like up and down a polished pillar, teasing it deliciously with the tip of a serpent-like tongue. Again the man reached out to her. In a flash, the insolent Yankee was on his face.

Angelica never touched him. One of Don Violeta's men had the senator in a hammerlock and was escorting him off the floor. It was as if nothing had happened; Angelica went on with her performance, never missing a beat, never touching her blindfold, demonstrating her uncanny ability for a full fifteen minutes before she finally stopped. Only after she had finished her number did the orgy truly get under way, continuing through the wee hours of morning.

Chapter 24

Tom-Tom, as the two men were called, drove up to Atlanta and were immediately ushered into the governor's office for a meeting. They made themselves comfortable, seated across from the portly man.

"So, gentlemen. What do you think the feds have got?" the governor asked, tamping his pipe tobacco into the Grecian briar bowl.

"Got themselves a situation to be sure," the sheriff said out of the corner of his mouth.

"Tom?" the governor queried, addressing the mayor.

"Don't rightly know for sure yet. The New York office has put the lid on tight," Mayor Tom Harman hedged.

"But why the renewed interest in Billy-Jo's cousin, Carson Reynolds?" Governor Atkins pressed.

The two Toms looked askance.

"Come on, gentlemen. This is not an inquisition." But that is exactly what it was. "Shed a little light on the subject. I can't sit here in the dark on this."

"Well, it's the kinds of questions they keep asking Billy-Jo," the mayor said. "Repeatedly. Interviewed him several times since August."

"Go on."

The mayor looked at the sheriff. "Tom."

Tom Hayes stared across the desk at the governor. "Bombs."

"Bombs?" The governor lit his pipe.

"They keep wanting to know about Carson's younger brother, Butch-Lee. What his interests were. Childhood friends. Family. Questions concerning his hospitalization for the past eleven years. If anybody might have visited him abroad. Stuff like that."

"What's your take on all this? Where do you think they're headed?"

"First, I think it's important that you understand that Billy-Jo knows very little about Carson's brother, Butch-Lee, apart from the fact that he was insane," the mayor piped up.

The governor looked at the sheriff for confirmation.

"That's so, Governor. Billy-Jo knows nothing beyond that. Said his cousin rarely spoke of Butch-Lee. When Carson did, it was about his brother's craziness."

"What's with the feds' questions about bombs?"

"Butch-Lee made them as a kid," the sheriff unfolded. "Became an obsession it seems. Graduated from a Gilbert chemistry set to mail-order materials from suppliers. What he couldn't afford, he'd steal. Blew up the school's laboratory because they wouldn't let him join the chemistry club."

"I'll bite. Why couldn't he join the club?"

"He was only a sixth-grader at the time."

"Probably would have made a great governor, given the proper grooming and direction," the governor kidded, puffing on his pipe. "Only thing I blew in school was my stack. Three days' suspension. My father, may he rest in peace, blew a gasket." The governor's expression suddenly changed from lightheartedness to seriousness. "If I ever see any of this in print, I'll have the two of you thrown out of office. Hear?"

Both the mayor and the sheriff laughed.

The governor laughed, too.

"Then what happened, Al?" the mayor pressed.

"Blew a big test. Didn't know how to study at the time. Probably didn't care, I guess. Anyhow, how does this Butch-Lee's demented childhood translate into today's situation? Anything we have to concern ourselves with?"

"Not a thing to worry about, Governor. Polls say you're a shoe-in for reelection for the next two terms if you don't first die of lung cancer," the sheriff joked.

"That's pretty funny, Tom. You better pray I finish this term out before this landfill scandal buries us all."

The mayor took a dim view of the sheriff's sense of humor, or at least his sense of timing. "Tom, let's get back on track, all right?"

Sheriff Tom Hayes nodded. "Like I called it from day one," the man said boastfully. "This Reynolds thing has got to do with that business up in New York, couple years back."

"You mean Geist and the Manns woman?" the governor questioned and puffed on his pipe.

"Right. Only now it appears that Angelica Manns is back on the playing field."

"Playing with whom?"

"Well, my contacts in Dallas tell me she may be hooked up solidly with that Giordano dame."

"A reputed anarchist and a drug magnate, Tom?" the governor asked rather skeptically.

"A revolutionary leader is what we read about Angelica Manns in the newspapers, Al," the mayor chimed in. "But her real cause is whatever benefits Angelica Manns. Follow the money trail, and you'll find Ms. M, as her familiars call her, sniffing somewhere along the greener path."

"And you're sure it was the Manns woman that Jimmy Ober saw at the fairgrounds, night of the murder?"

"Sure as shootin', Gov.," the sheriff said. "Same height, approximate weight, build, bone structure, and those unmistakable eyes. Only she wore brown contacts then, Jimmy said. Said he'd recognize her at a cross burning," he added for emphasis. "Hood or no hood."

"Come on, now. Seriously. How come so sure?" the governor inquired, appreciating the analogy.

"Her perfume. Very rare. Quite expensive. And . . . ." The sheriff's upper body heaved as he hooted with laughter.

"And what?"

"Jimmy said she'd be the only one on the lawn in a designer sheet; 'four hundred twenty threads to the inch,'" the sheriff quoted, smacking the arm of the chair in sheer delight.

The governor pointed the stem of his pipe at Tom Hayes for the full effect. "So why do you suppose she came down here and took out Carson Reynolds and cut up his goddamn dog?"

The two Toms exchanged uncomfortable glances.

"Well? Is this a secret you're keeping from your benefactor, boys?"

The mayor squirmed uncomfortably in his chair. "Of course not, Al. It's just a shot in the dark. Tom thinks . . . well—"

"Put it out on the table, boys."

"Well, Tom believes that a Lee Edward Harris, who was found shot to death alongside the body of a New York detective two months ago in New Jersey, is actually Lee Edward Reynolds, Carson's brother, as well as Angelica Manns' stepbrother."

"What?"

The mayor nodded.

"She had a stepbrother?"

"Yep," the sheriff answered succinctly.

"But I thought your report said—"

"That she had no living relatives. The few who knew she had a stepbrother believed that he was dead for more than a decade. Turns out he was institutionalized in Sweden for the past eleven years."

"Tom believes it was Angelica Manns who got him out," the mayor interjected, getting to the point.

"Because?"

"Because he was one of the best bomb men in the business," the sheriff continued.

"And maybe because of something else Jimmy Ober said," the mayor added, nodding to Tom. "Tell him."

Sweet white clouds of cherry-scented tobacco billowed then wafted across the governor's desk while he waited patiently for the news.

"Jimmy believes Ms. Manns is actually a man," the sheriff said flatly.

The governor drew on his pipe then shook his head perplexedly. "I don't get the significance of it, gentlemen. Number one, this Jimmy Ober, by your own admission, is a fag. So we got one fag calling another fag a fag. So what?"

"A transsexual, if you will, Al."

"If I will what, Tom? They're all the same to me. I lump them all together in one big pot of perversion. Degenerates. Destroying this country. But not this great state, by God. Not while I'm still around. And don't you start lecturing me on who's a fag in public office. I know each and every one of them, by God!"

"Is that in the familiar sense?" The sheriff chuckled, striking the heel of his hand upon his knee.

The mayor raised his eyebrows and shook his head.

"That's all right, Tom. Let him have his fun," the governor said good-humoredly. "If he wasn't my niece's husband, I'd have him policing county parks and dog pounds. Better still, I'd use him as a scapegoat for the landfill/carting dilemma I'm in—in over my head, I'll add."

"Goats! Now, that's an idea, Gov. We can use them at the site. Eat up every inch of trash. Everything from household garbage to tin cans to hazardous waste." The sheriff tittered.

"Not funny, Tom."

"Al, if what Tom is piecing together for us turns out to be accurate, its significance could be monumental. Politically speaking."

The governor gradually grinned. "Is there any other language worth a lick?"

"You might be in the catbird seat to negotiate some kind of deal concerning your dilemma as you put it."

The governor looked both men directly in the eyes. "Tom, Tom, do you guys realize that in the past five minutes the two of you have brought up the KKK, fags, and transsexualism? And now I'm getting a hint, just the tiniest, mind you, that you want me to put certain parties in a compromising situation via delicate information that you may or may not be privy to."

"Let's just say that based on what we have, it would be to your advantage to hint to the feds sooner, than for you to plea bargain later," the mayor suggested.

The governor weighed the suggestion before he spoke. "How good is your information right now?"

"Not good enough to move on anything as yet, Al."

"When do you think?"

"Just as soon as a Dallas friend of mine returns from a clinic in Sweden," the sheriff said.

"A clinic where they perform those kinds of *fag* operations," the mayor added.

"Just be sure to see that your friend has all of his or her parts upon returning," the governor said with outright disgust.

Tom Hayes winked. "I'll be sure to pass along your concerns."

"Feds onto what this Jimmy Ober seems to believe?"

The sheriff shrugged. "At least not from Jimmy, they don't or won't."

"I'm sure I'll have a million more questions for the two of you after I've had some time to think on this," the governor considered.

"And those questions, for now, are better left unasked, Al," the mayor said flatly.

"All right, gentlemen. I get the picture."

An 'all right' from the governor was a green light, but with a precautionary blinking-yellow down the road. There would be several more meetings before he'd allow them to put any plan into action.

"Thank you, Al."

"Thank you, Governor."

"Just one quick question before you go, boys."

"Yes, sir?" the sheriff acknowledged.

"That Redler fellow somehow involved in all this?"

"Right up to his crystal eyeballs," Tom Hayes answered matter-of-factly.

"I see."

He really didn't. He didn't see how Jimmy Ober's juicy tidbit gave them a distinct advantage concerning the feds. He didn't see how that mysterious morsel might provide the upper hand. He didn't completely understand the Swedish connection and its overall significance. What he did understand, however, was that the two men had offered him a glimmer of hope in bailing him out of the boondoggle he alone had initiated, and that bailing out early would be a whole lot better than having to post bail at some later date.

Tom-Tom had never failed him, and they would not fail him now, the governor firmly believed. *Yes*, there was a merciful God . . . he truly prayed.

Chapter 25

It was a crisp fall evening. A Friday. Robert and Liza drove to Huntington for the second time that week. The couple was two of eight judges for the first Miss Armenian Beauty Pageant to be held in the United States. Wednesday evening had been a preliminary meeting at the Huntington Townhouse, where the judges had asked questions of and viewed the thirty-one contestants in three categories: photogenic quality, personality, and overall appearance. The young ladies ranged in ages eighteen to twenty-nine. Tonight, Robert and Liza would enjoy dinner, entertainment, then go to work judging the contestants in business attire, formalwear and, once again, overall appearance.

Liza seemed to be coming out of her shell, slowly, and even spoke of returning to school to resume teaching; however, there were periods through the day when she remained as quiet as a clam. Robert rather rationalized the situation to a degree, attributing her reticence to the long hours they had both been keeping lately: he with his prolific and prophetic writings for the musketeers; and she—getting very little sleep—indefatigably examining his work like a student studying for the bar.

Wednesday night, especially, had knocked them out. Tonight's event was expected to continue until 2:30 a.m.; the irony being that no one since Wednesday, (particularly the contestants), had gotten their beauty sleep. Everyone was exhausted but too excited to rest properly.

The Kezerians, who had orchestrated the contest, were drained, too. But no one complained. Second winds were gotten with the help of caffeine, camaraderie, and genuine concerns. Everyone was nervous. Thirteen hundred guests were filing into the building. The entertainers and the girls were waiting in the wings.

Sylvia and George Kezerian, together with their children, were a special family. Wonderful people. They, too, had lost a loved one of late. Their middle son. The innocent young man had been unfairly trapped between the crushing powers of a criminal justice system hellbent on exacting its pound of flesh, while another more sinister force set out to claim the tortured soul. Terminal cancer had reduced the gentle giant's six-foot-four, two hundred-forty-pound frame to skeletal remains.

Robert Redler had written a score of scathing editorials in defense of the young man's innocence; family, lawyers, and friends fought against the system's injustices; a renowned TV commentator put it before the public's eye, with the end result amounting to a Pyrrhic victory, followed by the death of the twenty-seven-year-old a year later. Robert and Liza were treated as members of that family. It was an honor to be asked to judge the pageant.

Liza had made the comment on Wednesday evening that it was nice to see Sylvia in something other than black, for the woman had mourned the death of her son for more than a year in appropriate and respectful attire. Liza, too, had worn black since the day her nephew, David, died. Still, tonight she wore a black but scintillating beaded dress. Robert thought that the outfit was at least a positive step.

The pageant was an absolute success. Robert and Liza arrived home at 4:30 a.m. Liza went to bed immediately, but Robert felt compelled to write. He wrote until his fingers cramped, yet went on to near collapse. When Liza awoke at noon, she found Robert asleep at his writing desk. She gently pulled the yellow legal pad from under his arms then went downstairs to transpose his handwritten copy on the computer, for Robert Redler did not type:

****

"That's why there were no records on Angelica Manns when authorities picked her up on Long Island in ninety-four."

"She, or should we say, he, was born Angelo A. Reynolds, Stockholm, nineteen seventy-four."

"Raised by loving parents."

"Father, European. Mother, German-Jew."

"Both naturalized here in the United States."

"The parents took the boy from Stockholm to Oslo for the operation when he was fifteen."

"Shortly afterwards, they were murdered."

"Angelo had given himself a new name and a whole new identity. Female. Angelica Ann Manns."

"So it's easy to understand why records showed and authorities believed that there had been a foul-up when they turned up prints belonging to a male Eurasian, years older, but supposedly deceased."

"Easier to report no record than admit to a screw-up and open an investigation.

"Especially across a continent."

"Not the first time Interpol blew it."

"Bureaucracy is bureaucracy everywhere, I guess."

"Couldn't have had better cover than if he'd been in the witness protection program."

"Only better. This he/she, now Angelica, managed to kill off her parents who had kept that dirty little secret quiet. She made it look like daddy committed suicide and that mommy had met with a most unfortunate boating accident."

"Which then left only one person alive who knew the truth."

"Lee Edward Reynolds."

"His stepbrother."

"Who became his stepsister."

"Who someone had committed to a mental institution eleven years earlier."

"Christ. This is complicated." [third voice]

"Angelica loves complicated."

"It's no wonder Butch-Lee went crazy." [third voice]

"No, he was crazy long before that."

"Their incestuous childhood probably exacerbated Butch-Lee's condition, though."

"Although Angelo's return as Angelica probably didn't help matters much, either."

"According to Billy-Jo's cousin Carson, Lee was bats from birth, bawling incessantly from the day his parents brought him home from the hospital. An incubator baby. Almost didn't make it."

"Noise was certainly his thing though. The louder the better."

"Hence, his fascination with bombs, I suppose. The bigger the better."

"Then one day, Carson's dog laid a bunch of little bombs on Lee's carpet during a family get-together. Lee went berserk and killed the pup. Blew the dog to smithereens with a plastic explosive fastened to its collar."

"So Carson went out and bought another. But Lee insisted it was the same dog reincarnated and blew that one away, too—which led to a heated discussion as to whether or not animals such as dogs actually have souls. Lee had this insane notion that any and all dogs were the embodiment of God. Dog spelled backwards. Carson told Billy-Jo that Lee had killed three of his pups over a period of years."

"Each time, Lee begged for his brother's forgiveness, promising never to do it again. The last time out, Carson refused to grant forgiveness, obtaining an order of protection to keep Lee away. Lee swore revenge. Carson didn't get himself another dog until Lee dropped out of the picture. You know the rest of the story."

"But why are the two of you dwelling on this Lee character? He's dead." [third voice]

"Because he's part of a jigsaw puzzle I'm trying to piece together. Ever hear of the name, Baceni?"

"Baceni?" [third voice] The man seated behind the desk shook his head. "Never heard the name. Why?"

****

Liza saved the file, backed it up, ran the printer then put both the typed and penciled pages upstairs on Robert's desk. The writer stirred.

"Who's delivering the dialogue?" Liza asked with interest.

"Don't know," he said, yawning and stretching his arms toward the ceiling.

"Police?"

Robert shrugged. "Really don't know."

"Think it will make sense to whomever it is you give this to?"

Robert hunched his shoulders with indifference.

"What's the matter?" she asked, putting her arms about his shoulders in a genuine hug.

"All morning and only two-and-a-half goddamn pages that make no sense," he said with disgust.

"All night with no sleep. What do you expect?"

"Something more than this."

"You feel it's good, though." It wasn't a question.

"I don't know. Makes no sense," he repeated.

"Why don't you give your mind a rest and go back to this tomorrow, fresh?"

Robert picked up a pencil and started scribbling away on his pad. Erasing. Absorbing a thought. A phrase. Struggling with an idea.

"How about some tea?"

Robert didn't answer. He heard the offer from some distant corner, but it didn't register. *Who are they? Two people telling the third a story. Who?*

"Come on, now. Let this go for now. I think you're doing just fine."

"Others know."

"Know what?"

"That she's a man—or was."

"You mean . . . that's not fiction what you wrote?"

Robert Redler shook his head. "I'm not sure."

"Jesus. I thought . . . . Rob, when I was in the car with my captors . . . ."

He looked up at her. "Go on."

Liza shook her head in confusion. "Well, I had the strangest feeling."

"Like what?"

"Right along the lines of what you're saying."

"What?" he pressed.

"No, it's stupid."

"Tell me."

"Like she wasn't real. I mean, she was wearing a mask of me, but it wasn't me, of course. Or Angelica, either, for that matter. Yet it was. I had the queerest feeling that if I could tear away that mask of me . . . I'd see—"

"See what?"

Liza had a faraway look in her eyes that sent a shiver through him. "A hermaphrodite," she unfolded.

"Yes . . . androgynous . . . functioning as both male and female."

"Then it's true." It wasn't a question.

"Yes." He stared at her for a good moment before turning his attention back to the ambiguous dialogue. "Their names are Tom," Robert finally said, focused, thumbing quickly through the pages.

"What?"

"There," he said pointing. "The dialogue. The two men speaking to a third. Their names are Tom. Both of them."

Liza stared down at the pages then back at Robert.

"Tom-Tom," he said anxiously. "I don't know who the third party is." The two names pounded between his ears like an internal and insistent drummer. "Yes!"

"Tea?" she repeated.

He stared up at her then back down at the pages, nodding satisfactorily. "Sure."

Chapter 26

Sheriff Tom Hayes straddled a chair in a private room at the Georgia State Mental Hospital in Milledgeville. He rested his beefy arms atop the back of the solid wooden frame, staring across at the eighty-three-year-old patient seated cross-legged.

"I told you I wouldn't speak to you again," the wizened prune-faced man said plaintively.

"Oh, you'll speak to me all right, you crazy ol' coot."

"If I'm so crazy, why are you back here, Tom?"

"Sheriff Hayes to you, nigger. And don't—"

"You're a white nigger, and your mother was a whore. Only thing you ever accomplished in your miserable little life was to marry into respectability. Had everything handed to you on a silver platter from then on." He watched the veins in the sheriff's neck swell.

Tom Hayes shook his head and stood, took hold of his chair in both hands, raised it high then brought the back across the man's right shoulder, sending the skeletal figure to the floor.

Laughing, yet in obvious pain, the old fellow managed to pick himself up, right his own chair, then seat himself properly, staring defiantly at the law officer. "Does your woman know what a monster she's married to, Tom? Does Millie Brown know what a snake she married when she married the mayor and his manor? And do the people of this state know that they have a criminal for a governor?"

"It's that kind of talk that put you here, Zack. You know that, don't you?"

"I know what I know. And I know that I'll take what you need to know to the grave with me, Tom turkey."

Tom Hayes picked up his chair and sat back down, deciding to take a different tact. "Listen to me, Zack."

Zachariah Ballard shook his shaven dark head. "Listen to the sound of your heart, Tom. Seventy-seven beats a minute. Almost as fast as a woman's. As we speak, you have twenty-three million, nine hundred sixty-three thousand, nine hundred and forty beats left. That translates into two hundred and seventy-three days, Tom. Two hundred and seventy-three days left to make your peace. Why waste them trying to ferret information from me? It's not going to change a damn thing, ol' foe."

"Now, you listen to me."

Zachariah shook his head again. "No, sir."

"I can get you out of here."

"You told me that back in seventy-eight. Remember? I told you things you wanted to know then. But I'm still here. See?"

"I can get you out in thirty days, Zack."

"No, sir."

"Look." The sheriff took out several stapled sheets of paper folded widthwise in thirds. "Look here. Your release paper. Signed by the governor of this state," he said, unfolding the pages. "All you have to do is sign it and tell me what I need to know, Zack. What do you say?"

"I say you sound rather desperate."

"You want to die in this place, Zack? Is that what you want?"

"Ol' foe, I've been dead inside here for years," the old man declared, tapping his bony breast through a tattered cotton shirt. "Since the day the government put me in here."

"You put yourself in here with wild talk, Zack."

"I was injected with plutonium 239 during the winter of forty-five in a Rochester hospital in New York, as part of secret human experiments carried out by physicians and scientists. I suffer from urinary tract infections and quite painful osteoporosis. My bones feel like peanut brittle, Tom."

"You've been singing that same song for fifty years now, Zack."

"And apparently it reached God's ears, ol' foe," Zachariah said and smiled, taking a folded copy of an article from his shirt pocket and handing it to Tom.

"What's this?"

"Read it in your leisure. The tests were finally publicized, turkey."

Sheriff Tom Hayes read the headline. GOVERNMENT

COVER-UP. RADIATION VICTIMS REVEALED. *The Democrat &
Chronicle*, one of Rochester's newspapers, carried the story. "This is
nonsense, Zack."

"Is it?"

"This is some right-wing rag."

"This is the paper and the reporter I've been secretly writing to
for years. She got first crack. By tomorrow, every newspaper in the
country will have it. Bill Clinton will soon be forced to issue a formal
apology. The United States government will eventually make a
landmark settlement. I'm telling you this because if anything happens
to me, reporters are going to know right where to look."

"And where is that, Zack?"

"At Georgia politics, starting with Bibb and Crawford Counties
and its sheriff; the city of Macon and its murdering mayor; and on up
to Atlanta and its corrupt governor. You know I know things, Tom
turkey."

Sheriff Hayes studied Zachariah Ballard with keen interest. The
patient had the law officer's anger building rapidly.

"I want to know whatever information you have in connection
with Carson and Butch-Lee's stepbrother, Angelo Reynolds, before he
became their stepsister, Angelica Ann Manns. And I want to know it
now," the sheriff ordered.

The emaciated black man smiled with a good degree of
amusement. "In due time, ol' foe. In due time it will all come out."

"I won't ask you again," the sheriff said threateningly, glancing
over at the door before standing and picking up his chair by its seat
again.

"Don't suppose you will. So I'll leave you with a couple of
skeletons you'll have trouble putting back in your closet. My son never
paid your mother a penny, Tom. She did him for free. When Al came
home and found them in the pantry, his white maid and black butler, he
went berserk."

"Shut up."

"Senator Al Atkins was paying your mother handsomely for
services rendered, while my boy was doing her regular-like for
nothin'."

"I said shut up!"

"But the senator couldn't afford a scandal, so he had young

Tom mastermind their murder, and you, the cover-up. You know Tyrone didn't shoot your mother, Tom. He loved her, fool that he was."

"That's all a goddamn lie."

"Now, why would I lie to the law, Tom, when you know you're lying to yourself? Hum? I have respect for the law, but none for you or your kind, ol' foe. You're just a co-conspirator standing behind a tarnished shield, about to take the law into your own hands once again."

"I said I want to know about the Reynolds connection. I also want to know about Baceni. I know you know."

"Thought you'd like to know about your own family misfortune. You framed my son for a murder he never committed then claimed self-defense, saying that he attacked you. You know he was dead before you ever got there. I know you know that. Otherwise, maybe it's you who belongs here."

The sheriff slowly lowered the chair.

"You're a bad man, Tom turkey. You, and Tom, and Al. I know the three of you were in the Klan. I also know that the governor of this state is responsible for the deaths of two civil rights workers."

Tom Hayes went to the door and unlocked it. "I need to know, Zack. I'll give you a day to think about it. No more. So you better listen up."

"No, you listen. Listen to those heartbeats, pounding like a drum, Two hundred and seventy-three days, Tom turkey. Go make your peace."

Sheriff Tom Hayes waved the papers in anger and disgust and exited, locking the door behind him.

Chapter 27

Angelica Manns drove a yellow school bus past the second set of iron gates and around the circular drive.

"Wow!" a dozen voices sounded while three dozen more recruits held to silence, mesmerized by the sprawling estate.

"These are your training grounds for the next nine weeks," Angelica stated. "Any questions?" she teased.

Forty-eight hands shot up.

"Only kidding. Only kidding. Of course you all have questions. And very soon they'll all be answered. But for now, I want you to file in and greet your benefactor. She's anxiously waiting to meet you. And remember, no smiles. I'm the only one who gets to smile because I'm very, very proud of each and every one of you. You've come a long way, troops. In three months, you've accomplished what takes years for many a soldier to achieve. In nine more, no enemy in the world would want to mess with you. So. Through that entrance over there," she directed. Angelica hit a button on the panel, and the bus door opened. "Let's go troops. Look sharp."

The young men and women grabbed their gear and moved in no-nonsense fashion toward a secluded Connecticut structure and grounds of mammoth size and proportion. Colossal would be deemed an understatement. More of a fortress than a residence; one of several homes throughout North America belonging to Don Violeta.

Danny noted men positioned like pillars at the corners of the property.

Descending a spiral stone staircase then passing through a columned court, Barbara Giordano entered a vast room. Like an inspecting general, she viewed Angelica's troops, looking each recruit in the eye, randomly scrutinizing every detail of dress and demeanor.

"Name."

"Ma'am. Number Four of forty-eight, ma'am."

"Specialty."

"Karate and jiu jitsu, ma'am."

"Ka-ra-te and jiu-jit-su," their benefactor mocked. She turned and summoned her most seasoned bodyguard. Facing forward, Barbara Giordano confronted Number Four. "Demonstrate," she ordered, then stepped aside.

The bodyguard came forward and took his stance. Number Four stepped from the ranks and bowed politely as the bodyguard's fist shot forward like a missile but was intercepted by a block, swiftly followed with a powerful kick and a devastating blow that caught the man in the groin and solar plexus, buckling the form in half as she drove the ball of a foot into her opponent's face, sending him head over heels before the rank of statuesque recruits staring straight ahead. Springing forward and into a roll-out, Number Four withdrew a spring-loaded commando boot knife sheathed at the top of the man's pant leg. In an instant, Guadalupe brought the razor-sharp edge of the black stainless steel blade a fraction of an inch from the bodyguard's throat.

Barbara raised her hand, and Angelica immediately brought further action to closure with a silent command.

"Very impressive," Barbara stated. "Now, what am I to do with *you*?" she asked, looking down at her incapacitated henchman lying on the floor in pain and humiliation with a broken bloody nose. She made a single gesture. Two men immediately came forward and helped the man to his feet, leading him out of the area. Barbara turned back around. "Name."

"Ma'am. Number Se-seven of forty-eight. Ma-ma'am."

"Excuse me?"

Number Seven of- f-forty-eight. Ma'am."

"You're a stutterer, son?"

"Yes, ma'am."

"Specialty."

"Ca-communications."

Barbara Giordano grinned from ear to ear. "Communications you say."

"Yes, ma-ma'am."

"Isn't that rather ironic?"

"No, ma'am. N-not when I'm on the radio."

"I see," she said and smiled pleasantly, snapping her fingers for security. Several men appeared on the spot. "Give him your radio," she commanded to one of her soldiers, dismissing the others. The man turned over his hand-held.

Angelica gave Danny a wink and a nod.

"Demonstrate," Barbara ordered.

Without hesitation, Number Seven pressed the button on the transmitter. "Alpha, Bravo, Charlie, Delta. Copy?"

Four voices came back sharply. "Read you loud and clear."

"Perimeter one, report."

"Clear," a voice reported.

"Perimeter two."

"Clear."

"Perimeter three."

"All clear."

Perimeter four."

"Clear."

"Position of a yellow bus."

"South-southwest corner."

"Condition."

"All clear, I said," security at the main gate responded.

"The bus."

"Code blue."

"BULLSHIT," Danny shouted.

"I checked it," the voice crackled.

"Check it again, asshole."

"What?"

"Red Alert!" Danny exclaimed to the man standing off to a corner. "I repeat. Red Alert. South-southwest corner. The bus. Back seat. Driver's side. Bring the intruder in. Go! Go! Go! Go!" Number Seven ordered, pointing to and directing the others scrambling after him. "Move it!"

The men ran off in a single direction. Barbara looked at Angelica. Angelica feigned ignorance.

A few minutes later, eight angry men with red faces escorted a young woman wearing only a three-quarter jacket belonging to the senior security officer.

"What in hell? Where are her clothes?" Barbara demanded.

"She doesn't have any," the officer fumbled. "She's one of them. Found her in back of the bus without a stitch," he added reluctantly.

"You mean to tell me you secured the area, but you idiots couldn't see a naked woman in the back of the bus?"

"She was lying down," the man offered lamely.

"Oh, I see. That makes it oh so clear," Barbara said with disgust, waving them off anxiously. "When we are done here, I want Number Seven put in charge of security until I can make other arrangements. Think you can handle that, young man?"

"Ma'am, y-yes ma-ma'am."

"Matter of fact, you can start right now. My own Mel Tillis of talk radio. Priceless." Barbara turned back to the troops once again, making her way down the line. "Name."

"Ma'am. Number Eleven of forty-nine. "Ma'am."

"Forty-nine, now, is it?" Barbara acknowledged, noting that the half-clad woman had joined the rank.

"Yes, ma'am."

"Specialty."

"Plastic explosives, ma'am."

Barbara Giordano looked the recruit in the eye. "I'll bet you're even prepared to demonstrate your skills if need be. Is that correct?"

"Yes, ma'am."

"Think you could bring this compound down if you had to in a hurry."

"Yes, ma'am."

"How fast?"

"In a heartbeat, ma'am," Peter assured her.

"I bet you could," Barbara said quite seriously. "I'll just bet you could." She turned to Angelica before continuing down the line. "I love them already, Ms. M. I'm very much impressed. So far."

Angelica accepted the compliment with a nod.

"Number Forty-nine. Front and center," Barbara called out.

Sharon stepped forward smartly, made a left-face, walked right up to her benefactor then came to attention.

"Ma'am. Forty-nine reporting as ordered. Ma'am."

"Specialty."

Angelica immediately drew her pistol and fired a shot that jerked Sharon's body backward before she fell to the floor. A stream of blood ran from the corner of the young girl's mouth. Security had their guns drawn, but Danny ordered them put away.

Barbara looked from Angelica to the body, then back to Angelica. "I—"

"Actress," Angelica answered for Sharon, stepping forward to the body and turning it over with the toe of her boot. "Get up."

Sharon sprung to her feet between the two women and stood there at the position of attention, red dye dripping down the front of the borrowed security officer's coat.

Barbara shook her head in amazement. "Well, I declare," she avowed then laughed. "All we need now is the theme from *Mission Impossible*." And then she really laughed, uncontrollably so.

All forty-nine troops resolutely disobeyed a direct order in front of their commander in chief. They were smiling. Each and every one. A few of Barbara Giordano's security men were smiling, too, shaking their heads in disbelief. Still laughing, Barbara put her arms around Angelica and Sharon.

"That was truly a consummate performance. For a moment, I thought you really lost your mind, my angel." Barbara turned from Angelica to address the young woman. "My dear, dear young lady. Number Forty-nine. You were terrific. The four of you were terrific. You go back to the others now," she said to Sharon. "Ms. M, I don't know how much more drama my poor heart can take," she joked. "Are you all so theatrical?"

"We do what we have to do to get the job done. I take it you approve," Angelica said, stepping forward of her troops.

"If I could sell tickets, I'd pack the house," Barbara whispered.

"I'd like to dismiss them and get them settled in."

"By all means. You and I will have dinner tonight at nine so that we can talk."

"I'm in bed by nine. Up at five. Can we make it earlier?"

"My, my. Such discipline. But I fully understand. How's seven then?"

"Seven's fine."

Angelica Manns went back to the group, and Barbara Giordano took her leave.

"At ease," Angelica commanded, and forty-nine bodies assumed the position. "I want all of you outside by the northwest corner of the compound at fourteen hundred hours, sharp. Bring with you all gear packed in boxes marked with the letter A. Mrs. G's staff will meet you through that door to my left and all the way down the corridor to your right. Dress appropriately as it gets cooler once the sun goes down. That's it for now. Troops, ten-hut! Dismissed."

Chapter 28

"There is a black man sitting in a mental institution in a town called Milledgeville, not too far from Atlanta," Robert stated emphatically. "I'm thinking of going—"

"Zachariah Ballard," Liza said and nodded knowingly.

"Who?"

"God is renowned," she answered.

"What are you talking about?'

"What God wants us to do."

"Us?"

"Yes. You and me."

"God's talking to you now, is He?"

"Through us."

Robert shook his head. "Listen, this business the other morning about—"

"Tom-Tom?"

"Yes."

"The names mean something to you now, I suppose."

Robert didn't say anything.

"But you can't tell me. Fine. Then I'll just go see Zachariah myself."

"Who is this Zachariah, Liza?"

"The black man who sits waiting in the mental hospital."

"Where did you come up with the name Zachariah? Snatch it out of thin air?"

"Snatch." Liza giggled, grabbing at the air.

"With all due respect, Liza, I think you are, *indeed*, heading for an institution."

"Oh, I am indeed. The one in Milledgeville. With or without

you, dear."

"You're going to Georgia?"

"Yep."

"No. *I'm* going to Georgia. That's what I started to tell you before you hit me with this Zachariah nonsense."

"Well, that's his name, dear. You'll see."

"What's this *dear*? You haven't called me dear in twenty years."

"That's his name, grumpy," she said smilingly.

"And what's this 'God is renowned' business when I asked you where you got the name?"

"That's what Zachariah means, Rob. From the Hebrew."

Robert studied her for a moment before he spoke. "So, how did you happen upon the name Zachariah, or did you first come up with the phrase and then connect it to the name?"

"Am I on the witness stand? You sound like a prosecutor."

"I'm just trying to—"

"I was looking at the Bible. All right?"

"You've been doing that a lot lately."

"Well, pardon me for breathing."

"What the hell does that mean?"

"It means you're acting like an ass."

"Ever since David died you've been at that Book."

"Oh, I guess I'm supposed to hold fast to just one author around here. Is that it?"

"Try the Book of the Month Club."

"Try expanding your horizon."

"How? By—"

"By getting on a plane with me."

"I don't fly."

"With two martinis you do. Figuratively as well as literally."

"Where did you come up with the name, Ballard? God give you that one as a handicap?"

"You're bordering on blasphemy, bozo."

"Got an answer?"

"I called."

"Called who?"

"I called the Georgia State Mental Hospital in Milledgeville and asked about a black patient named Zachariah. 'Oh, you must mean Zachariah Ballard,' a sweet southern voice answered immediately. The one and only, I replied. You don't happen to have another, do you? I asked. 'No, but we got us a Jeremiah' she went on. 'Believes he's a prophet. More fun than the other one who thinks the government injected him with radioactive stuff some fifty years ago.' Then there was a bit of commotion in the background and some nasty old snip got on, telling me that they do not give out patient information to strangers over the phone," Liza mimicked in a positively exaggerated southern accent.

"How did you latch on to Milledgeville?" he pressed, wondering if she may have gotten it from his notes or the manuscript but then realized that Milledgeville had been committed to memory. He hadn't recorded it anywhere.

"Same as you."

"What does that mean? Tell me."

"That maybe we could be a team."

"How did you know about the black man, Liza?"

"How did you?"

Robert was getting impatient and angry. "Look. This thing cannot be explained rationally. All right?"

She smiled. "Maybe not to our friends or what family we may have left. But perhaps we can help explain it to each other."

Robert shook his head. "*I* don't even understand it."

"Therefore, how can I? Right?"

"That's not what I meant. Now, look. I—"

"No, you look and listen. What happened to you back then was an ordeal in the strictest sense of the word. God saw your pain and reached out to you. I lost a daughter, but He didn't reach out to me. Want to know the reason why? She was evil, and God does not like ugly. Now He's reaching out to me, too, because He sees justification in it."

"You want to believe that?"

"I do believe that. God wants us to deliver those two down to the very gates of hell. Angela Manns and Barbara Giordano. Just like you did Richard Geist and Michael. Ever wonder why the government did not attach a name to Michael's body, Rob? An aide to the governor of New York?"

"It's officially called a disavowal. No true record, they claim."

"Just like Angelica, up until the trial. But Manns is not her real name, either. I know you know this. Just like you wrote down the other night. We're locked out from the truth, Rob. But you and I both know who holds the key." She nodded solemnly.

"I was going to drive down there tomorrow."

"We can get a flight out of Islip this afternoon. Then a connecting flight from Durham to Atlanta. Rent a car there, and we're on our way to Milledgeville."

"And how do you propose we get to see Mr. Zachariah Ballard if you were cut off at the pass by phone?"

"Easy. We get a letter of introduction from the powers that be. Any of The Three Musketeers I'm sure will help you," she added. "Or have one of them have someone call ahead. All their resources at your fingertips, you said. Remember?"

"How in God's name do you know about that?"

"You just answered your own question." Liza giggled.

Robert Redler thought hard and fast. "Book a flight," he said finally.

"We're on an eleven-thirty flight. And yes, they serve martinis aboard. So, pack. I've already finished."

Chapter 29

Angelica addressed her forty-nine relatively new recruits who sat quietly in their seats, absorbing the information like a sponge.

"You all have your new bows now. They are not toys. In the months ahead, you will become totally familiar with this elegant weapon of soundless destruction. You will learn that silence is golden. A far cry from what you've been used to for the past several months." She caught Peter's eye and smiled appreciatively. "Over the next nine weeks, you will become quite proficient with this sweet stringed instrument. Some of you will be capable of delivering lethal flights out to forty yards; however, most of your kill shots will be between fifteen to twenty yards.

"Now, you will note that your bow is a good deal shorter than some of the others you may have seen. Approximately thirty-six inches, axle to axle, is what you have before you. It weighs a mere three and a quarter pounds. To begin, I want you to observe the difference between the two so-called wheels at either end. Harold?"

"Well, the upper one is round, just like a wheel. But the lower one is somewhat egg-shaped, Ms. M."

"Oblong. Good. These wheels, collectively, are called eccentrics. Everyone say it."

"Eccentrics," forty-nine voices repeated simultaneously.

"The establishment would say that we are eccentric; that is, odd in our behavior, or off center. In a very short period of time, we are going to show them how on-target we really are," she assured everyone. "These wheels are also referred to as radicals. How fitting.

"Let's look carefully now at that oblong wheel or, as Harold noted, egg-shaped in design. It's actually called a cam, as opposed to a wheel. So, we have a wheel at the top, and a cam on the bottom. A single-cam bow has several advantages over a compound bow, which has two identical wheels. Everyone with me?"

Heads nodded and yesses chorused across the classroom.

"The weapon that you have before you is called a single-cam bow. They are positively the easiest to tune because the eccentrics are working in concert, not against one another as with wheels, which require precise synchronization for optimum performance."

Peter and Guadalupe were nodding, fully appreciating the dynamics being presented clearly and concisely. Most of the others got the general idea.

"Of course, we'll go over everything very clearly in the field. For now, I just want you to have a basic understanding. If I've lost some of you, don't fret. It will all come together in time. Like golf, fly-fishing, and martial arts, it's all a matter of timing and technique.

"Okay. Let's see if some of you peeked at the literature I handed out last night."

A hand went up in the last row.

"Priscilla?"

"Is this a test, Ms. M?" the freckled teenager asked rather nervously.

"Do you want it to be a test?" Angelica questioned pleasantly.

"No, ma'am."

"Then this is not a test. Okay?"

The girl nodded anxiously.

"This is a long quiz," Angelica teased.

Priscilla took a deep breath.

"Only kidding, gals and guys. Relax. Before I give a test, you'll all be well-prepared. You should know that. Right?"

Everyone, including Priscilla, sighed happily. Even Peter, who relished tests and quizzes, settled back.

"All right, Priscilla. How many fletchings on an arrow?"

"Three," she answered.

"Name the two common types. Danny."

"V-vanes, which are plastic, and feathers which are, ah, f-feathers," he explained with a smile.

"You're sure?"

Danny nodded knowingly.

"All right." Angelica walked to the second row and put her hand on Sharon's shoulder.

"Name the three common materials from which arrows are

made."

"Wood, carbon, and aluminum."

"What will we be shooting?"

"Aluminum."

"Why aluminum when carbon is a lighter material and will fly faster?"

"Good question. We will be using them shortly, but for now it will be aluminum because we have them in great supply. Your draw length, Sharon?"

"Twenty-nine inches."

"Explain how it is then that you will be shooting a twenty-seven and a quarter inch arrow."

"My bow will be equipped with an overdraw."

"Which accomplishes what?"

"Which allows me to shoot a shorter, therefore, lighter arrow."

"That does what?"

"Travels to my target with a flatter trajectory."

"Which translates into what?"

"Greater velocity."

"One more question, Sharon. Answer this accurately, Number Forty-nine, and you're all free agents for the rest of the afternoon. How late did you stay up studying your material?"

"Ms. M," Sharon groaned in an exasperated tone.

"Oh, you're such an actress, my dear."

The entire class broke out in laughter and applause.

"Well," Angelica pressed. "I'm waiting, Sharon."

"Zero-three hundred hours," Sharon said quietly.

"Three a.m.," Angelica said, shaking her head. "Your sleep and what you eat are of paramount importance." She was addressing everyone. "I can monitor the latter. I have little control over the former. Am I getting through?"

"Yes, Ms. M," forty-nine students answered simultaneously.

"Good. On your feet." Everyone stood. "Troops, ten-hut. Dismissed."

Chapter 30

The old man was escorted just outside a room at the Georgia State Mental Hospital and directed to a table where Robert Redler and Liza Downs were seated. It seemed a circumscribed space, antiseptic and depressing, yet its pale walls appeared to brighten the moment the man took his seat. The orderly who had brought the patient to the threshold left immediately with not so much as a blink.

"That's Mr. Shapely," the elderly man offered, grinning from ear to ear. "Stoic as well as being a repressive bore." He laughed lightly, extending both hands across the table to his two visitors who were already getting halfway up for introductions. "Sit, sit," the old man said happily. "No need for formalities here."

"I'm Robert—"

"I know who the two of you are. Even know which one's which," he kidded and laughed. "Liza, I'm happy to see you."

Robert and Liza sat back down after releasing the old man's bony hands.

"Do you know why we came here, Mr. Ballard?" Robert asked politely.

"'Course I do, Rob. And you're just as pretty as I knew you'd be, Liza," he added warmly.

"Thank you." Liza smiled with a bit of embarrassment.

"Did they tell you we were coming, sir?" Robert asked, glancing over his shoulder toward the entrance.

"Nope. Didn't have to neither."

"No?"

"Nope. The good Lord sent you to me in my time of need. 'Course you needed a little help from Liza, here," he declared with a wink. "You call me Zack. Everybody does. Friend and foe alike."

Robert looked at Liza, and Liza spoke.

"Zack? We're here to ask you about—"

"Angelo."

"Yes. Now Ms. Angelica Manns," Robert said excitedly, "who was once Angelo Reynolds, I believe."

The old man waved the name away with a flagrant flap of his wrist. "Deceivers, the lot of them. Forget that name, or they'll have you running ragged across three continents. Means nothing. Nothing at all. Made up name is all."

"Do you know the name, Baceni?" Liza asked.

"Nope. Don't know no Baceni. Don't matter, either. I know what you need to know. That's why you're here."

"And what is that?" Robert asked patiently.

"Think, Rob and Liza. Open up your minds. You're so close to the truth that you're blinded by its light."

The couple glanced at one another, then back at the patient. Robert shook his head. Liza looked deep into the man's soul, searching for something behind those lucid steel-gray eyes.

"What was the boy's given name?" the black man coaxed.

"Angelo," Rob answered.

"And the girl's chosen name?" the old man asked.

"Angelica," Liza said.

"Which are?"

"Variations of the word angel," Robert answered. "So?"

"So?" the ancient figure thundered. "So it's so damned simple, man. Open your eyes, by God."

"Fallen angels," Liza offered quietly.

"He may be a former college English professor, Liza, but it's you who is passing the test here with flying colors, my dear. Go on."

Liza racked her brain for further understanding, finally yielding to Robert, reluctantly giving up the game. "Rob's the one with the truly extraordinary gift, Mr. Ballard," she said, shaking her head rather slowly and unassuredly.

"Not of late, Ms. Downs," he countered, his teeth two gleaming rows of whiteness.

"Sorry, Zack," she apologized. "I'm not getting—"

Robert interrupted. "Are you saying . . . you don't mean . . . ." Robert faltered.

"Ever wonder why God delivered Richard Geist and Michael into your hands, Rob? You don't really believe that God asked you to take a human life, do you? 'Vengeance is mine,' sayeth the Lord. Not yours, Rob. Not yours, Liza. Not even over your loss of little David. No, He did not, leaving me to wonder how the two of you can be so blind." He waited for their eyes to open and see the light.

"You're not suggesting—"

The old man smiled broadly. "I'm not suggesting anything. Now, that would be very presumptuous of me. After all, I've been in a mental institution for most my life." He nodded affirmatively. "I know what I know, and I know that I have to go now and make my peace with God because I don't have much time left. I haven't exactly been an angel here myself for fifty years, just God's messenger today. No, it's with you folks now, and I know you'll do the right thing. There's one thing I know for sure that I can comfortably share with the two of you. And that is that God loves you both so very much. So much so that He gave me a message to give to Liza before I go." The old man stood and smiled benignly, bringing the tip of a bony forefinger an inch away from his thumb. "God and David shared a little wine together most recently." The old man smiled sincerely before he turned and walked away.

"No, wait. Please don't go," Robert called after him.

Liza sat there numb, tears suddenly streaming down her sunken cheeks and right on past the corners of what Robert perceived to be a smile; an ambiguous, ambivalent smile filled with pain and pity and hope and happiness. In the next instant, Liza hands hid all emotion, and her shoulders heaved as she wept uncontrollably, leaning forward of the table.

Robert sat there in a daze, his arm around her, his eyes searching the empty doorway for the orderly who led the old man away.

A moment later, a figure appeared in the entrance. A stranger. Yet, somehow, Robert sensed he knew him. The stout man with wavy chestnut hair made his way to the table in a confident stride, hesitating at the look he got from Liza as she lifted her head, setting her palms flat upon the table.

"Crazy old goat got her all upset, didn't he?" the man said, setting his eyes on Robert.

"Who are you?" Robert asked in a somewhat hesitant tone.

"Sheriff Hayes, Bibb County." He smiled, extending his hand

to Robert. The sheriff's eyes, however, went immediately back to Liza. "Look, ah, I just want you to know that if I can be of any assistance to you folks while you're down here, you just holler, hear? If I can't help you myself, I'll have someone point the way."

"And in which direction would that be, Sheriff?" Robert asked with an edge to his voice he couldn't hide.

"Oh, I guess in any direction you like," the man came back abruptly.

"These walls have ears, Sheriff?"

Sheriff Hayes seemed at a loss for words, taking in the two narrowly before he spoke. "Mister, you're a long way from home," he finally said. "You don't seem to appreciate the hospitable nature with which I've greeted you."

"You tried to block this interview, didn't you?"

"With Zachariah?" The sheriff laughed. "Now, why would I do that? Got a call from New York to assist you and your friend here in any way I can." He smiled sardonically.

"Why did Zachariah run off like that? I think he knew you were coming."

"I wouldn't know about that, Mr. Redler. Like I just said, I knew you and this lady were coming, though. Just drove here from Macon to see if I can be of any help."

"Help? And you're telling us that's why you're here?"

Sheriff Hayes appeared agitated by being put on the defensive. "Well, I'll tell you how it is, Mr. Redler."

"Please do."

"Seems New York and New Jersey got themselves a few unsolved homicides that apparently you've attached yourself to. Now you're down here asking questions."

"Of Mr. Ballard."

"A mental patient here in Milledgeville. A very sick patient at that."

"You qualified to make that judgment?"

"You bet."

"He's dangerous?"

Sheriff Hayes did not answer.

"I guess not, having sat with us with no attendant or anyone else present."

"A person can be dangerous without exhibiting violent behavior, Mr. Redler. Zachariah Ballard is a danger to himself."

"How's that?"

"I'm not going to stand here and debate with you what qualified doctors have determined concerning Mr. Ballard, Mr. Redler."

"I'm not looking to enter into a debate, Sheriff Hayes. Just a simple answer to a simple question."

"Mr. Ballard has been delusional for the past fifty years, claiming that the government injected him with radioactive material as part of a plot."

"They did," Robert declared in a calm voice.

The sheriff laughed uneasily. "What are you talking about?"

"Well, on our drive down here from Atlanta, they announced it over the radio, releasing the names of about a dozen patients around the country who had been human guinea pigs in experiments conducted in nineteen forty-five. Guess you were busy listening to country-western, Sheriff. Oh, and those were medical not mental hospitals. Zachariah Ballard was one of nine patients who were injected at Strong Memorial Hospital in Rochester, New York. Poisoned with plutonium 239. Fifty years ago."

Sheriff Tom Hayes acted surprised. He stared at the pair then down at the black and white tiled floor before turning away and walking slowly toward the door he had entered.

"That's him," Liza said. "That's one of the Toms."

Robert put a finger to his lips. "Not here," he whispered. "Come. Let's get out of here."

"What about Zachariah. He's not safe."

"He'll be all right for now. We'll talk about this in the car."

"There is something very wrong, Rob," Liza stated, staring out the back window of the rented sedan.

"Wrong?" Robert asked, about to pull the car out of the visitor's parking area.

"Don't go yet."

"What?"

"We've got to go back."

"Why?" Robert put the car in park.

"Zachariah."

"I told you he'll be all right. They won't touch him after that newscast earlier. Reporters will soon be swarming all over the place. Probably headed here right now. He's no threat to anyone. Crazy old man. We flew all the way down here to listen to a story about fallen angels, for crying out loud."

"That wasn't Zachariah."

"What?"

"That man wasn't Zachariah."

"What are you talking about?"

"The sheriff *is* one of the two Toms, but the black man was not Zachariah, Rob."

"Then who the hell was he?"

"I don't know. All I know is that Sheriff Tom Hayes and others do not want us to meet the real Zachariah Ballard. And that imposter was trying to throw us off track."

"Look. That old man may very well be crazy, but he did have certain insights. Yes? He knew about the Angelo/Angelica Manns business. He knew of your recent ability; 'of late' is how he put it. Christ, he even knew about David and the wine."

"He knew because someone told him what to say."

"Liza. Come on now. Granted someone else could know about the Manns connection. Even about David and the wine. But this man knew about *your* gift and the fact that you talked me into coming down here. How could he have gotten that?"

"From the real Zachariah Ballard," Liza said firmly.

"How do you know that?"

"I don't. But like you, I'm beginning to sense certain things."

Robert hunched his arms over the steering wheel indecisively.

"Please," she pleaded.

"Why didn't you tell me this back there?"

"I tried."

Robert saw a woman in the rearview mirror hurrying toward them, waving frantically. "Someone's coming."

Liza turned. "That's the woman who was at the reception desk. Put down your window."

Robert hit the power button, and the window lowered noisily.

"Mr. Redler?"

"Yes?"

"I was by the desk when you came in asking for Mr. Ballard," the young woman said in a melodic drawl that belied her anxiousness.

"Yes, what can we do for you?"

The woman looked over her shoulder toward the building, then down at the two of them. "My name is Bridget." She smiled nervously.

"Hi, I'm Liza," Liza said, reaching across Robert to take the woman's hand.

"I know. We spoke on the phone early this morning."

Liza nodded. "You were trying to help me before that—"

"That fat old cow got on the line." Bridget glanced nervously back at the building anew.

"Bridget, what's going on back there, sweetheart?" Liza coaxed.

"I could lose my job if they see me out here talking to you guys. But maybe it ain't worth saving if somebody might get hurt."

"What are you talking about, Bridget?" Robert pressed.

"Remember my tellin' you 'bout Jeremiah, ma'am?"

"Yes, of course. The one who believes he's a prophet."

"Yeah, some prophet. Missed his calling, though. That wasn't Zachariah Ballard you just met with." The woman shook her head solemnly. "That was Jeremiah Jones. Loves to playact. Pretty good at it, too. Sheriff Hayes said he gave a four-star performance during rehearsal this morning."

"Sheriff Hayes was here this morning?" Robert asked.

"Showed up shortly after Liza's call."

"Where is Zack, Bridget?" Liza questioned with grave concern.

"Don't rightly know. Mr. Shapely, that's one of the attendants, took him down from his room the minute Sheriff Hayes showed up. I haven't seen him since. He wasn't in the dining room. And it's rare that Mr. Ballard doesn't show up for lunch. Hardly eats anything; loves to chat. Everyone missed him at breakfast and then again at lunch. That's when patients and staff were wondering what happened to him, asking if he was sick or something. I checked the infirmary myself. No Mr. Ballard. Then I saw the register and noted that you guys had an appointment scheduled for this afternoon. The patient who they brought to you was not Mr. Ballard. It was Mr. Jones," she repeated.

"You're positive about that?" Robert queried.

"About as sure as a pregnancy test marked proof positive. I was coming out of the lavatory and saw Jeremiah coming out of that room. Saw the two of you, too. And that's another thing."

"What is?" Robert asked.

"Well, in the six years that I've worked here, I never saw no visitors and patients together except in the visitor's lounge."

"And what room were we in, Bridget?" Liza asked.

"The old library section, moved within the last year or so to another wing. Mr. Ballard would spend half his day reading the Bible and other religious books, the other half gabbing about God and what the government did to him fifty years ago."

"How would you characterize Mr. Ballard's condition, Ms.—"

"Oh, O'Reilly. Took back my maiden name," she explained, looking back over her shoulder. "I'm not really qualified to say. I'm just a file clerk and gofer here. But I'll say this much. Outside of all that being poisoned with radiation nonsense, I'd say he's the dearest man in this whole wide world of ours. And I've really got to be getting back now."

"Apart from carrying on about this radiation business, would you say Mr. Zachariah Ballard could be considered sane?" Liza questioned.

"Aside from that and his sermons from the mount, about as sane as you and me, I guess. A man with most of his marbles. But who am I?"

"At this moment, Bridget, about the most important person in the whole wide world to us," Liza assured her with a big smile. "How can we get in touch with you if we need to? I mean, beside calling or coming back here. We certainly don't want to put your job in jeopardy."

"May we contact you at home if the need arises?" Robert said directly.

"Oh. Sure. I'm in the book. Only O'Reilly on Maiden Lane, next to the post office. I'm really worried about that old man."

"We're going to do something about that, Bridget," Liza assured her. "Aren't we, Mr. Redler?" Liza said, putting emphasis on her question.

"Damn right we are. What time do you work till?"

"Six."

"You're going back to the reception area?"

Bridget nodded.

"Wrong. You're going back to the ladies room. You've got a bad stomachache. Anyone comes in, you flush the toilet and stay put. Flush it a hundred times if you have to. Just stay put until Liza comes to you. I don't want you in the reception area so that they can put two and two together. Did the sheriff leave after us?"

"Left his boot print on the paneling. Mad as hell about something."

"I'll bet."

"He left by a side exit shortly after you guys."

"You go back inside now, Bridget," Liza said. "And try not to worry. Believe me you did the right thing coming out here." She nodded, assuring Bridget that Robert and she would somehow set things right.

Liza and Robert appeared back at the front desk. He asked to see the supervisor.

"Excuse me. Did you forget something Mr. Redler?" the stern figure standing off to the corner asked coldly.

"No, ma'am. But it's nice to know that you remember me."

"Well, I could hardly forget you, sir. You only left a few minutes ago."

"Then apparently you'd have no trouble remembering a patient who spent fifty years here, now would you? A Mr. Zachariah Ballard, for instance. The person who we came to visit."

The tall woman stepped over to the reception desk, peered down at a green register and, with practiced scrutiny, ran her finger vertically then horizontally along the page. "Says here you saw Mr. Ballard at four forty and that he was returned to his room at four fifty-two, Mr. Redler," she said, looking Robert squarely in the eye.

"Was he, now?"

"That's what it says here," she repeated.

"That precise? Hum. Only problem is that wasn't Zachariah Ballard. That was another patient, Ms. . . .?"

"I'm sorry, sir. But that's what the register shows."

"I'm sorry, but I didn't get your name."

"Didn't give it," the woman said defiantly.

"Have a problem with that?" Redler asked, taking out a small notepad and pen from his raincoat pocket, scribbling down meaningless words with presumed purpose.

The woman didn't flinch. "Mr. Redler."

"How about a title, or are you averse to telling the public what it is you do?"

"Mr. Redler. What do you want?"

"What my associate and I flew down here for. A visit with Mr. Zachariah Ballard."

"I'm sorry, but visiting hours are over for today. It's past five, so you'll have to come back tomorrow morning after ten."

"We're not going anywhere, Ms. Whatever your name is," Robert stated firmly. "And what I can assure you is that you will be named as a hostile witness in an investigation involving the impersonation and sudden disappearance of Mr. Zachariah Eddington Ballard," Robert Redler said, raising his voice.

"Sir, how do you know that the person who you and your associate met with wasn't Mr. Ballard? Can you tell me that?"

"Because there's a news reporter from *The Constitution* sitting in his car parked next to mine at this very moment who showed me a picture of Mr. Ballard. And guess what? It's not the patient we just met with. Now, Mr. Jack Carancoat is extending me professional courtesy simply because we arrived here first. He doesn't know that I know that that wasn't Zachariah Ballard. I'm sure you know why he's here, ma'am. Soon this place will be swarming with reporters, and unless my associate and I see the genuine article within the next five minutes, you're going to be reading a hell of a one come the morning edition. We clear?"

The woman looked from Robert to Liza. Liza nodded politely but firmly, indicating to the woman that Mr. Redler meant business.

"Apparently there has been some sort of misunderstanding," the woman said, forcing a rather disingenuous smile. "Mrs. Cook, I'm sure, can straighten out the confusion," she added, gesturing down the hallway.

Bridget O'Riley was being escorted back to the reception area by a heavyset woman in her late fifties. The older woman was practically on Bridget's heels.

153

"What's all the commotion," the stocky woman demanded. "I can hear you all the way down the hallway from the bathroom."

"Mrs. Cook, there seems to have been some sort of mix-up. Mr. Redler, here, and his associate claim that the person they were visiting with earlier was not Mr. Ballard, which is whom they wish to visit."

"That so?"

"That's correct, Mrs. Cook," Robert said, taking his eyes off the matron and fixing them on Bridget. "And you, young lady, were standing here when we came in. We made it quite clear that we were here to see Mr. Zachariah Ballard, not some deceiver who—"

"All right, now. Hold your horses," Mrs. Cook said steadfastly.

"Are you the supervisor?" Robert asked with indignation.

"I am, buster."

"Well, I want to know this young lady's name," he demanded, pointing an accusatory finger at Bridget, giving her half a wink. "And this tall drink of water over here refuses to give us *her* name."

"You just pipe down a minute. Miss O'Riley has nothing to do with the patients or this area. Mrs. Thompson, can you tell me what's going on here, please?"

"Mr. Shapely escorted Mr. Ballard to the visiting area, but Mr. Redler says that it wasn't Mr. Ballard. Says a reporter sitting out there in his car showed him a picture of Mr. Ballard, and that unless I let him see him—"

"Whoa! There's a reporter where?"

"Sitting out there in his car."

"That so?" the woman asked surprisingly, walking over to a corner window and peering out into the visitor's parking area.

"Said that I'll be named in an investigation."

"Threats, Mr. Redler?"

"None of them idle if anything has happened to Mr. Ballard."

Mrs. Cook caved. "Call Mr. Shapely and have him bring Mr. Ballard down here, Mrs. Thompson. Bridget, you go on home, now. I hope you feel better, dear."

"Thank you, Mrs. Cook." Bridget took her leave immediately.

"There now. Why don't the two of you have a seat in the visitor's lounge, and let's see if we can straighten this business out. All right?"

Robert and Liza turned to the right and started walking back

154

down the hallway.

"The visitor's lounge is this way," Mrs. Cook stated, directing the two in the opposite direction. "End of the hall, first doorway on your right."

Robert and Liza looked at one another then proceeded down the corridor.

Liza whispered. "This is not the way—"

"No shit, Sherlock," Robert snapped.

"Calm down, now. We're doing great. Save your anger for Mr. Shapely and crew. Don't take it out on me."

"Right."

A few minutes later, Mrs. Cook and a middle-aged muscle-bound creature appeared in the lounge.

"Mr. Shapely. This is Mr. Redler and Ms. Downs," Mrs. Cook said.

"What the hell is going on here?" Redler barked.

"Introductions, buster. You're one rude dude. Anybody ever tell you that?"

"That's not the person who escorted the patient to the door," Liza jumped in matter-of-factly.

"And this isn't the lounge that we were first directed to either," Robert added irately. "I want to see Zachariah Ballard, Mrs. Cook. And I want to see him now."

Mrs. Cook glanced at Mr. Shapely.

"I'm afraid that's not possible, Mr. Redler," Mr. Shapely said in a very soft and sad spoken manner.

"Oh, my God," Liza said, dropping her voice to a murmur.

"Mr. Ballard passed away in his sleep a little while ago," the man stated. "I'm so sorry," he added sincerely.

Mrs. Cook brought her hands to the side of her face, slowly shaking her head from side to side.

Liza went over to a couch and sat down quietly.

"When, a little while ago?" Robert asked caustically.

"I'm afraid I'm going to have to direct you to our legal department for further comment, Mr. Redler," Mrs. Cook declared. "I'm not at liberty—"

"Liberty? Neither was Mr. Ballard at liberty, Mrs. Cook. Do you understand what's going on here? Do you? Some impostor pretending to be Zachariah Ballard was escorted to a fictitious visiting area by a man the dissembler named as Mr. Shapely."

"I brought Mr. Ballard down from his room for visitation privileges. But there was no one here. I was told they left and to take Mr. Ballard back to his room not ten minutes later."

"By who?" Mrs. Cook asked.

"Jenny," Mr. Shapely answered straightaway.

"Is Jenny a bleached blond with tobacco-stained teeth and poor posture?" Robert snapped.

Mr. Shapely nodded.

"That's the woman who directed us to the area at the other end of the building," Robert said to the supervisor before turning his attention back to the attendant. "I'm going to ask you again, Mr. Shapely. When did you find Mr. Ballard permanently asleep?"

Mrs. Cook was shaking her head halfway through Robert's question. "Don't answer that, Stanley."

"Tell us where Jeremiah Jones is now, Stanley," Robert insisted. "Is he in his room?"

"Not when I—"

"Shut up, Stanley," Mrs. Cook ordered.

"Why?" Robert bellowed. "Don't you get the picture?"

"What picture is that?" the woman stalled, unsure of what tact to take.

"That someone went through a great deal of trouble to have us believe we were visiting Zachariah Ballard, when in fact we were sitting down with Jeremiah Jones. Your register shows our visit from four forty to four fifty-two. Twelve minutes in which he told us things he was instructed to tell us, did so then couldn't wait to get away. Two seconds later, Sheriff Hayes shows up. Didn't seem to know about the fact that Zachariah's contention of being poisoned in a Rochester hospital with plutonium 239 fifty years ago is well-founded, documented, and has recently been reported to an outraged public. I'm sure you may be able to keep a cub reporter or two at bay. But wait until the news teams descend on this place with camera crews and around-the-clock coverage. They're going to get their story, and I'm going to have to give them a version of mine."

"Which is?"

"That you and your people are involved in a murderous cover-up, designed to silence the last survivor of a government plot."

"That's preposterous."

"The media is the message, darlin'. That's what I'm going to feed them, Mrs. Supervisor of the Georgia State Mental Hospital here in Milledgeville. 'Uncooperative, deceptive, and deceitful is how I see it, gentlemen of the press,' is what I'll tell them."

"Who the hell do you think you are?" the woman hammered out syllabically.

"An intermediary assigned and empowered by the State of New York to investigate a matter of national security," Redler responded in his best Walter Mitty recitative interpretation of character, which was true enough in part. "Here's the phone number of the agency from which Sheriff Hayes was called and instructed to cooperate. I implore you to call it. Now!" He handed her a card.

"What time did you bring Zack down, Stan?" Mrs. Cook inquired.

Stan said nothing.

Liza got off the couch and went directly up to Stan Shapely, who stood with his arms folded across his chest. "Accessory to murder, Stan. What does that carry in this state, Rob?"

"Don't know. But I'll bet Stan does."

Stan started to cry. "I didn't kill anyone; I swear."

"What *did* you do, Stan?" Liza asked, putting her hand around Stan's bicep as if she were locking it with a wrench.

"Just what Sheriff Hayes told me to do."

"Which was?"

"Bring the patient down—"

"Which patient?"

"Zack."

"Go on."

"To bring Zack down at four forty for visitation."

"This lounge here?" Liza continued gently, her hand still on the attendant's arm.

"Yes."

"And?"

"And about ten minutes later, he told me to take Zack back up."

"The sheriff told you?"

157

Stan nodded.

"What else did the sheriff say?"

"Nothin'."

"What did Zack say, Stan?"

"Nothin'."

"And what did you do?"

"Took him back up to his room. But he was fine when I left him. I swear it."

"I believe you, Stan," Liza nodded, taking her hand away.

"And when did you find Zack dead, Stanley?" Robert picked up.

Stan looked at this boss.

"It's all right, Stan. Tell him," the supervisor said. "We have nothing to hide," she said decidedly.

"Just now, when you asked me to get him."

"Stan," Robert said.

"Yes, sir?"

"Stan, we both know there's a middle part to this story. Yes?"

Again, Stan looked at Mrs. Cook.

"It's all right, Stan. Tell him everything you know."

Stan hesitated, biting his bottom lip. "Well, sir, I brought Zack down at the same time Troy and the sheriff brought Jerr down."

"You mean Jeremiah Jones?"

"Yes, sir."

"Troy Travis is one of our other attendants," Mrs. Cook explained.

Robert nodded.

"Jeremiah told Sheriff Hayes not to worry, that he had his part down pat."

"What did the sheriff say?"

"Told him to shut up. Troy took Jerr down the other end of the hall to the old library, and I took Zack here. Like I said, ten minutes later, the sheriff told me to take him back to his room." Stan Shapely was physically shaking.

"Get it all out now, Stan," Robert pressed.

"When I took Zack back to his room, Jerr was sitting on the bed."

"Zack's bed?"

Stan nodded.

The supervisor was slowly shaking her head in disbelief.

"Anything wrong with that?" Liza pushed.

"Jerr can fly off the handle at any time," Stan explained. "He's supposed to be locked in his room at all times or under watch if he ever had a visitor. Zack, on the other hand, is nonviolent. But Troy told me to lock him up with Zack. Said Zack attacked the sheriff with a chair. Zack was arguing that it was the other way around."

"So what did you do?"

"Locked them up together as Troy ordered. Senior attendant. You don't ask questions."

"Jesus, Mary, and Joseph," Edith Cook said, shaking her head back and forth incredulously. "Why didn't you come to me?"

"Troy said you knew all about it."

"When you went back up to Zack's room just now," Robert asked, "was Jeremiah there?"

"No, sir."

"Was the door locked?"

"No, sir."

"Tell me what you saw when you entered the room."

"Zack lying on the bed with a hypodermic needle resting on his chest."

"Mother of God!" Mrs. Cook exclaimed.

"Where is this syringe now, Mr. Shapely?"

"I put it in Zack's bureau next to his bed."

"What was in your head, Stan?" Mrs. Cook asked.

Stan shook his head searchingly. "The sheriff and Troy had already left. So I figured I'd ask Troy what to do in the morning. Zack hadn't been feeling all that well. Didn't go to breakfast or lunch. I figured no one would bother till morning. Thought maybe everyone would think he just died there in his sleep. I thought he committed suicide. Wasn't really sure."

"What do you think now, Stan?" Robert asked.

"I think Jerr killed him." The man sobbed.

"Why do you think that now and not before?"

"Because of something I remember Jerr saying to the sheriff just before all of us got into the elevator."

"What was that?"

"Jerr said, 'Just remember what you promised, Sheriff.' Then Jerr turned to me and said, 'Sheriff Hayes promised me I could play doctor later on.'"

Robert, Liza, and Mrs. Edith Cook stood silently before the frightened attendant.

"Am I in big trouble?" the man asked, taking a long moment to look into all three faces.

Robert stepped forward and put his hand on the man's shoulder. "Nothing that a good defense attorney and a hundred thousand dollars couldn't remedy," the writer bruited about quite knowingly.

Chapter 31

Thanksgiving was three weeks away, and already Barbara Giordano had a lot to be thankful for. So, too, did Angelica Manns. The pair courted health, wealth, and power. Although Barbara had taken a bullet in the head several years ago, her personal physician assured his patient that she had made a remarkable recovery. That was not the case the year before; however, doctors at that time were cautiously optimistic, yet remained guarded, unable to forecast even a short-term outlook. Somewhere along the line, their prognosis became sound. Her bright future had been restored via a series of medical explanations couched in a framework of cranial gobbledygook.

Angelica Manns was another story.

"I wouldn't let a doctor near me if my life depended on it," she told Barbara in the sitting room. "Two types of doctors will never touch this body till I'm dead. Medical and dental. Not too long ago, however, I allowed a podiatrist to take a look at my foot, which blew up like a balloon after tangling with several feds who arrested me on Long Island, who had the gall to stage my death in order to draw Richard Geist out."

"I remember that all quite well, of course. All I'm saying is that you should have an annual physical. But you do as you like. So. I understand you have some good news to report."

"Oh, better than good, Barbara. Fantastic would be the word."

"Robert Redler has had a fatal heart attack?" Barbara threw out good-humoredly.

"Robert Redler would certainly have one if he could see what I've arranged."

"Please don't keep me in suspense."

"We've expanded our weapons program to include thirty some odd shipments of anthrax to a warehouse not far from here."

"More nerve gas, darling?"

Angelica smiled. "That was sarin; chemical. These are pathogens; biological. We need to develop them into doable battlefield munitions."

"Pathogens?"

"Disease-causing spores."

"And what do these spores do?"

"Devastating things."

"Such as?"

"Initially they cause high fever, chest pain, and breathing difficulty, eventually leading to blood poisoning and death, dear."

"And how do you deploy these little devils, my angel?"

"By delivering them in the warhead of a Scud rocket."

"Which we have."

"Which we have," Angelica assured her.

"And how did we come by these shipments of anthrax?"

"By way of Iraq in a rather round-about way. If you'd care for me to elaborate . . . ."

Barbara gestured affirmatively, pouring herself a drink.

"Well, a firm down in Maryland produced it along with some other lethal goodies. Sent them off to Iraq between nineteen eighty-five and eighty-nine. Government approved by the U.S. Commerce Department during the Reagan years."

"Is that right?"

Angelica nodded. "Seventy shipments in all. We just got thirty plus back. What I need from you is the use of a facility and the funds for further development."

"Anthrax into warheads?"

Angelica grinned. "Actually, a bit more of a kick than that."

"How do you mean?"

"A combined biological and chemical battlefield cocktail."

"Sarin gas and the anthrax spores?"

"A double whammy for double jeopardy."

"What a hangover," Barbara said and saluted, downing her shot of port. "Have to come up with a clever name for that poison. Now. Sit back. I've got some very exciting news, too."

Barbara poured herself another port then set the crystal decanter in front of Angelica.

"I don't think I'd better. Got to be up early with the troops."

"You're pushing them hard, dear. I haven't seen you give them a break in weeks."

Angelica said nothing.

"Listen to me. I want you to give your people a day of grace. And I'm not taking no for an answer. Thanksgiving is in a few weeks, and I've taken the liberty of ordering eight twelve-pound turkeys. My staff will be preparing everything from soup to nuts for your magnificent fifty."

"Forty-nine."

"Sharon's pregnant. Only teasing. Forty-nine, and you make fifty. You all deserve a day of rest. You're pushing them too hard, Angelica," she repeated.

"Do I tell you how to run your cartel?"

"No. But until now, you haven't had a say."

"What does that mean?"

"It means, my dear, that I secured the Burma connection. Think you can handle a little more responsibility?"

"Burma?" Angelica repeated.

"Yes, Burma. You know. Northwest of Bangkok. I believe you special-ordered a snake from there not too long ago."

"Oh, believe me, I know Bangkok. Number one producer of heroin and opium."

"A long, long history, my dear."

"A long way from home."

"So, now I expand the operation to the Asian front. Do you have any idea at all of the kind of revenue this will generate?" Barbara said excitedly.

"Millions, I would imagine."

"Your imagination is arrested. Billions within the next few years. My Columbian contacts? Two hundred billion combined worth as we speak. Gilberto and Miguel? Fifty billion easy. They'd pale as paupers by comparison. The point is I need someone that I can trust. I need someone smart."

"A good man is hard to find is what you're telling me?" Angelica asked and smiled handsomely.

"Interested?"

"What about my operation here? My troops."

"When will they be ready?"

"Seven, eight months. Maybe earlier. But not if you keep giving them holidays off."

"Thanksgiving, Christmas, and the Fourth of July. How's that? Think they'll be ready by then?"

"For fireworks for sure," Angelica put forth most assuredly.

"The facility and the funding you just asked me about?"

Angelica bristled at the thought of the woman's procrastination. "Yes?"

"Done deal."

"Just like that?"

"Just like that. You with me on this Asian deal?"

Angelica beamed. "Done deal."

"So. How about that drink?"

Angelica reached for and poured two fingers of the expensive port into a thin-stemmed glass. Barbara raised her own.

"I guess we both have a lot to be thankful for, Angelica."

The two smiled and toasted to their good fortune and future.

Chapter 32

"All right. Here is my speech and proposal," Ms. M said, speaking formally before her troops. "On the surface, we are a demonic cult. Not a coed scout troop. Mrs. G operates a notorious drug cartel. Not a corner convenience store. Her business is to limit competition, period. There will be reprisals of course. In a joint effort, we shall help protect and ensure our benefactor's aggressive goals. In essence, we will augment her team. But I promise you that we will not lose sight of our own objective. For in fact we are a highly-paid band of assassins, fifty strong, serving in but one of many factions throughout the country. A faction that will soon motivate and train others to do what no network of professionals has ever accomplished. And that is, the overthrow of an imperialistic government of the United States that is in no way 'by and for the people' of this great land. The reality is that the monies needed have to come from someplace in order to accomplish this feat. Our cause is fueled, funded, and funneled by drug money.

"A cartel and a cult will rule this land in time. We are neither demonic nor angelic. The light which we shed neither comes from beneath nor above. The light comes from within each and every one of us. A collective light called truth: the truth of who we are and what we stand for. And what is that single truth?"

"Strength for freedom," forty-nine voices answered in unison.

"The law of the land is presently one gigantic lie. In our studies, we have witnessed the truly good convicted in our courts. We have seen the truly wicked walk. Justice here in America is a two-hundred-year-old joke. Our actions are not for others to judge. We are the gatekeepers of right and wrong. Any outsider who threatens the will of this coalition will be dealt a fatal blow. You will not be ordered blindly to execute your strengths in such a situation. You will be asked.

However, you will not thwart the will of our group once a majority vote has been taken. In that respect, we will act democratically. If an individual declines to take action, for whatever reason whatsoever, he or she will simply step aside until the next assignment arises. Once committed to a cause, you will rise to the occasion.

"Within our core, we have an army of highly-trained soldiers who *shall* execute our will blindly. They cannot and will not question my authority. Robotic beings are an essential element of war. Orders must be carried out without question. You, however, as you now know, are part of an elite corps. Collectively, you will carry out policy. I want it crystal clear in your minds that you are privileged in that you have a choice to participate or not to participate in any operation. Once a deciding vote is cast, silence shall be your prudent partner. Your objections will bear no weight.

"For your services, you shall be granted the gift of unparalleled securities, free from the poverty that binds an entire underclass, pacifies the center, satisfies the upper echelon, yet never satiates sovereignty. You shall be replete and regal. Your salvation, your reward, will be received here on earth, today, not set aside on layaway like a pension fund. From this day forth, you shall amass wealth beyond imagination. Your kingdom is here on this planet, now.

"I want you to go over these materials carefully this afternoon as a group. Write down any questions you may have. In this single packet, you are offered the opportunity for power, wealth, and well-being. Read it then decide. That's it for now. Get plenty of rest tonight. We have a busy day ahead of us tomorrow."

Millions of leaves from hundreds of majestic oaks and maples blanketed the outer boundary of the swamp. A burnt umber carpet crunched beneath their boots as Angelica's troops trekked forward. It was a bright, crisp autumn day.

"All right," Angelica said, raising her hand and commanding her troops to halt. "We can all take a break. Put your gear down and relax. Don't get too comfortable, though, because we want to reach the other side of that swamp before we lose the light."

Twelve of the forty-nine bodies collapsed.

"Okay, we're tacked in a good ten miles. When we head back

tonight, you'll see how brightly they pick up in artificial light. I also like to use these limb-ties." Angelica held up a small package. "Very much like what is used in the kitchen to tie off plastic bags," she said, tearing off a narrow strip.

"Twists," Sharon said.

"Exactly. Only these little guys give you three hundred sixty degrees visibility. You simply wrap them around small branches. Just like your tacks, they shine up brightly when the beam from your flashlight hits them. But let's just suppose you don't have tacks or twists or flashlights. Suppose you have to get from point A to point B without any such aids; for instance, from south to north. It's easy enough to get turned around and lose your direction during daylight hours. Evening can be a nightmare," she assured everyone. "But let's assume it is daytime. No stars out to show direction. No compass to point the way. How could you find a northerly direction?"

Number Thirty-seven's hand shot up. "Moss grows on the north side of a tree?" the young man offered questioningly.

"Billy, in about ten minutes we're going to be in that swamp, setting up our tree stands. You're going to find moss on any given side of a tree. Anyone else?" No one appeared to have a clue. "All right. I'm going to teach you all a little trick. Elizabeth, get me four sticks about three feet long. Willie, gather up five small stones. Let's focus on this spot." Angelica swept away a large area of leaves with her boot, exposing a dark, bare space. "We're going to create a makeshift compass and clock. Now, stick one stick into the ground, Elizabeth. Straight up. Willie, take one of your stones and place it at the very tip of the stick's shadow. Good. Now, we're going to wait a few minutes. And while we're waiting for our hour hand to move ahead, I want you all to shade your eyes and squint up at your old friend Sol, the sun. Never stare directly at it." Pairs of eyes followed Angelica's to the bright, sunny sky. Several soldiers remained staring down at the shadow-stick. "A watched hour hand never seems to move," Angelica said and smiled. "So, all peepers up to Mr. Sol." Everyone raised their eyes heavenward. "Someone tell me how the sun moves across the sky." Peter had his hand up high, smiling and shaking his head knowingly. "Peter is about to tell us that the sun really doesn't do that. That it's fixed. Right, Peter?"

"Right, Ms. M."

"Go on, Peter."

"Well, we, that is the earth, rotates on its axis once every twenty-four hours and orbits the sun once a year."

"I'm the sun, Peter. You're earth. Show everyone how you rotate."

Peter nodded then turned around very slowly. "Like this."

"Note that Peter has made a full turn counterclockwise. The equivalent of . . . anyone?"

"One twenty-four hour day," a dozen or so voices answered up in sum and substance.

"But for all intents and purposes, in what direction do we see the sun move *across* the sky?"

"From east to west," three quarters of the group replied.

"Correct. Maybe tomorrow we can ask Peter to rotate *and* orbit for us," Angelica joked good-naturedly.

Several of the girls giggled. Guadalupe raised her hand. "Ms. M?"

"Yes, Guadalupe."

"Maybe Peter could do that for us in a camo leotard," Guadalupe suggested with a twinkle in her eye.

"Yeah, maybe he can pirouette around a campfire like Peter Pan," Alice announced then guffawed. Her laughter turned infectious. Half the girls were rolling upon the forest floor.

"Yeah, maybe you can rotate and orbit this," Peter said, raising his middle finger before Alice.

After several minutes of playful banter, Angelica called for order among the troops. "All right, troops, time to get back on the stick," she punned and redirected their attention, pointing down at the ground. "Let's note where that shadow is now. Willie, mark it with another stone. Great. Elizabeth, place one of the sticks across the two stones. Alice, tell me the direction of movement between the pair of stones." Angelica waited but a moment for the girl's response. "Earth to Alice."

"Clockwise, Ms. M. Sorry."

"The first stone is on a line to the west; the second is to the east. Guadalupe."

"Yes, Ms. M?"

"From the base of our shadow-stick, take and lay another stick directly between the two stones." Guadalupe took a stick from Elizabeth and set it carefully down as instructed. "Perfect. Peter. In what direction is the stick that's intersecting the west/east course pointing?"

"North."

"Sharon, start heading off in that direction." Sharon walked about ten paces. "Stop. Turn around and come on back. What direction are you now heading?"

"South, Ms. M."

"Any questions, troops?"

"Are there any wolves in these woods, Ms. M?" Priscilla asked anxiously.

"All in sheep's clothing, my dear," Angelica swore and grinned, baring her teeth. "Now, I told you that this shadow is also an hour hand. Not a Swiss timepiece by any stretch, but a pretty good clock. Questions. Yes, Doug?"

"What if it's cloudy, Ms. M?"

"You're fucked. Now pay attention. Danny, over here."

"Yes, ma'am."

"Lay the last stick parallel to the east/west direction along the base of the shadow-stick."

Danny stared down at the ground vacantly.

"Well, Danny?"

"I'm n-not sure wh-what you mean by p-p-parallel, Ms. M." Danny did not raise his eyes.

"Danny, look at me. Get your bow." Danny did so. "String an arrow and take aim." Danny removed an arrow from his bow quiver, nocked it, and drew rearward. "Fine. That invisible line between your eye and your sight pin is parallel to the arrow just below it. Got it?"

Danny nodded, released the tension, put the arrow back in its quiver, took the remaining branch from Elizabeth, then stooped down and placed it at the base of the vertical stick on a parallel plane to Guadalupe's east/west indicator.

"Excellent, Danny," Angelica affirmed. "While you're there, I want you to draw me a semicircle—half a circle—between the two parallel lines, *centering* it on our shadow-stick. Perfect. Once again, troops, the shadow also serves as your hour hand. Six a.m. is at the west tip of the semicircle. Twelve o'clock noon is your north line. And six p.m. is at the east tip of the semicircle. Mark them for us, Willie, with the three remaining stones. Wonderful. Danny?" Danny's head popped up. "Approximately what time is it?"

Danny's head dropped as suddenly as it had risen. No one said a word. He studied the problem for a good half a minute before he finally answered. "F-f-f-four p.m.?" he questioned, his eyes betraying a growing shadow of doubt.

"Well, it could be closer to five before you ever finish answering, Danny," Angelica teased. "But I've got four-ten by my watch," which she held up for everyone to see.

Danny's face lit with astonishment.

"Way to go, man," Doug encouraged Danny with a thumbs-up followed by a high-five, finally concluding his animated praise by embracing the younger boy in a playful headlock.

Danny felt like he had just made a winning touchdown for his team.

Chapter 33

Robert and Liza's motel room was small, tidy, and comfortable. It sat on the outskirts of Milledgeville.

"Well, we know one thing for certain," Robert said.

"And that's what?" Liza asked, gazing into the mirror, having finished combing her hair then plopping herself upon the bed.

"Somebody doesn't want us to learn about the Reynolds or Baceni family tree."

"That's for damn sure."

"Doesn't want us to harm a single hair on Angelica Manns' or Barbara Giordano's head, either."

"How long are we going to stay in this motel?"

"Just long enough for us to get a good night's sleep before we pay Jeremiah Jones a visit tomorrow morning."

"Don't you think we're going to run into a problem with the authorities, seeing as how they're at the starting gate of a murder investigation?"

"Not a problem."

"How do you know?"

"When you were in the shower, I was on the phone."

"Who with?"

Robert didn't answer.

"I see."

"Don't worry about it. All right? We're set to see Jeremiah Jones tomorrow morning at seven."

"How come so early?"

"Before everything else falls apart."

"You mean before they classify it as a homicide?"

"It's going to be reported as a suicide."

"Are you kidding me or what?"

Robert shook his head.

"You know, earlier this afternoon I was scared for Zachariah. Right now, I'm scared for us."

"You shouldn't be afraid. People are watching out for us."

"Yeah, right. Like they were supposed to be watching out for me at the train station."

"That won't happen again."

"Really? We got on a plane then drove down here alone. Who's looking after us?"

"On the plane, another couple sitting two seats behind us on the opposite aisle. Driving down here, a helicopter and a car in constant radio contact, above and behind us."

"What about when we took the inflatable over to Sag Harbor, across open water?"

"Two agents were tagging right along."

"And what about our goddamn boat? That could have been booby-trapped instead of sunk. Where the hell were they then?"

"Coast Guard was watching it," Robert offered lamely.

"Watching it what, go down? In case you didn't know, Rob, the Coast Guard is currently under the auspices of the Department of Transportation. Even my sixth graders know that."

Robert couldn't help but smile. "The Department of Transportation, you say?"

Liza nodded in disgust.

"I didn't know that. Good thing I took the power squadron course," he teased, trying to lighten the moment and allay her concerns.

"Now, *there's* a protection agency for you. Bunch of beer-bellied captains who'd rather be carousing with their dockside chums than sitting home with their homely wives." Liza swung her legs off the edge of the bed and sat up straight, staring ruefully into the mirror.

It was that kind of nonsensical talk and behavior that Robert was seeing more and more of lately. He stroked her long brown hair, studying their images in the mirror.

"Don't," she snapped. "I just combed it." Liza turned away.

The phone rang, and Robert picked it up on the first peal.

Jeremiah Jones was brought into a secured area situated somewhere on the south side of the building. A high, arched ceiling along with its rust-colored stone walls and iron bars gave it the paradoxical appearance of a medieval church. In a small room with a metal table and four chairs in its center sat a man (The Man), waiting patiently. Robert and Liza sat across from him.

"Inside," a security guard ordered gruffly, guiding the patient by the arm.

Jeremiah stepped into the room. In lieu of a straitjacket, the man was secured in leg irons along with handcuffs that held his wrists locked in back of him; he bowed forward from the waist.

"Cha-cha-cha," the patient/prisoner chanted and grinned, shaking his head from side to side, rattling his chains while doing a little in-place dance. "Jig is up," he announced and curtsied, pointing his chin in an affected manner toward a corner of the room. "Cha-cha-cha."

The guard spoke. "Jeremiah—"

"—was a bullfrog," Jeremiah sang out loudly. "Was a good friend of mine. Never un-der-stood a single word he said, but I helped him drink his wine. He always had some mighty fine wine. Cha-cha-cha." Jeremiah laughed aloud, shaking his head back and forth rhythmically before suddenly snapping his chin sharply back toward the corner.

"You ready to settle down now and answer some questions?" the frail-framed, ferret-faced figure seated at the table asked.

Jeremiah went up and down on his tiptoes.

"Well?"

Jeremiah turned and cocked his head arrogantly toward the mousy-looking man. "They call me J.J.," the patient responded in no uncertain terms. "What's yours?"

"I don't happen to have one."

Jeremiah burst out laughing. "You don't happen to have a name? Oooo, dat bad," he sounded off and smiled broadly, tucking his chin down tightly against his collarbone. "Dat's positively bad. Then I'm gonna hav'ta give you one. How's dat? You now officially, The Man. What you got, my man?"

"It's what *we* don't got, Jerr," The Man said, glancing over at Robert and Liza. "Time, patience, and answers."

"Then I wouldn't be hangin' 'round here wastin' my time, my man," Jeremiah made clear.

"Please wait outside," the musketeer said to the security guard. "And lock the door behind you."

Without hesitation, the guard disappeared. The door to the room was pulled closed on its rusty hinges, the metallic sound of the key turning in the lock ominously foreshadowing a note of finality.

"Watcha gonna do, man? Beat me in front of this woman and her beau, bro? I don't think so," Jeremiah jawed and winked, staring fixedly at the mousy figure who tipped the scales at perhaps a hundred and twenty pounds.

The Man suddenly stepped forward and plunged a knife into Jeremiah's chest. The patient immediately went to his knees in pain and disbelief. Liza turned her head; Robert looked straight ahead in fascination. With one hand pushing down firmly on the handle of the knife, The Man placed his other hand squarely around Jones' throat. Blood soaked the front of the patient's pajama top.

"Next stab won't allow you to tell me anything, even if you wanted to," The Man in charge assured him. "So. Do you want to cha-cha-cha or chat? Infirmary might be able to save your black ass if you hurry." The musketeer suddenly withdrew the blade. Blood ran into Jeremiah's pajama bottoms just before he collapsed to the floor.

"Oh, God . . . ." Jones shifted his head and focused keenly on his bloodstained top and bottoms.

The Man kneeled and flashed the five-inch bloody blade before Jeremiah's eyes before putting it to his throat. "Talk."

"Tom Hayes," Jeremiah squealed, "told me to do it."

"I don't give a flying fuck about Hayes. Tell me about Angelo Reynolds. Tell me about Baceni."

"I don't know. I swear to God."

"Talk or I'll kill you in the next two seconds."

"I don't know no Reynolds or Baceni. I don't know the sheriff's game," Jeremiah squealed. "Sheriff gave me a script and I delivered," the black man bawled.

The Man pushed the point of his blade against the patient's throat.

"No, no, I swear. Lord, spare me. Please. I'm bleeding," Jeremiah pleaded.

"You kill Zack?"

"Yes."

"How?"

"Hypodermic."

"Filled with what?"

"Air."

The Man pressed down harder until a spot of blood appeared at Jeremiah's throat.

"I swear! Air into the bloodstream the way the sheriff told me. Pleeeeeease," Jeremiah pleaded and sobbed.

"Last chance, Jerr. Who are Reynolds and Baceni?"

"I swear to God I don't know," he screamed.

Liza was up from the table and over to Jeremiah and The Man, moving the musketeer's hand back but an inch, placing her other hand on the patient's shoulder. "He's telling you the truth," she said quietly.

The Man stood up and knocked twice on the door, announcing orders. Moments later, the heavy door opened and a gurney was wheeled into the room by two bewildered attendants who rushed the patient away. The security guard holstered his weapon. The musketeer ran the blade of his knife through a clean white handkerchief, pushed the spring-loaded stainless steel blade back into its handle then put it away inside his coat pocket. "He'll be fine. Just a superficial wound. A good inch away from his heart," he said casually. "Bled like a pig though, didn't he?"

Liza looked at him severely. "You're a fucking nut-case who probably belongs right here with all the rest."

"Ms. Downs," The Man said gently. "My wife couldn't agree with you more. To tell you the truth, and you can lay your hand on me for confirmation, there are times that I'd concur."

"Is this one of them?" Liza asked in anger.

"Good day, Ms. Downs," the little man replied. "I want to see you downstairs, Rob."

Robert nodded abruptly.

Back in the motel room, Liza threw the few remaining articles of clothing and other items into her suitcase. A TV commercial droned monotonously in the background.

"Listen, I tried," Robert argued.

"Like hell you tried."

"I did. He wouldn't hear of it."

"Sure. You asked. He said no. That was the end of it."

"You call the guy a fucking nut-case and you expect him to embrace you?"

"I could have accomplished the same thing he did without jeopardizing a man's life."

"The man's a professional, for God's sake, Liza. Jeremiah's life was never in jeopardy. The man's a pro."

"What is he, one of your heroes now? He's a puny little punk; a pipsqueak who everyone probably pushed around as a kid. Gets off on power. Pro, my ass. What are you? Some kind of fucking fan?"

"You don't pamper people like Jeremiah and expect to walk away with the truth, for crying out loud."

"No, you stick them with a knife instead."

"It had a one-inch blade, Liza."

"I got the truth from Stanley without playing Brutus, Rob."

"It's not the same thing and you know it."

"No?"

"No. We're talking about a lunatic here. Jeremiah's crazy. You don't reason with a person like that."

"That was just another performance of his, Rob. Jeremiah convinced a psychiatrist and a jury that he's a fruitcake so he didn't have to go to prison. The Man, or whatever the hell his name is, saw through his act is all. But you don't stab a person with a knife whether it's a one- or five-inch blade. This is not Nazi Germany," Liza concluded, shaking her head in disgust. "We are nowhere," she resounded. "We're right back where we started."

"No, we're not. We know that the sheriff's interests surround this Reynolds/Baceni business. Serious enough to put a man up to murdering Zack."

"But the sheriff didn't get what he wanted from Zack," Liza said.

"Why do you say that?"

"Why? Because if he had, he'd have had Jeremiah silenced, too."

"All the sheriff wanted with Jeremiah was to throw us off the trail. Let us believe there was no family tree to leaf through."

Liza shook her head. "Whatever knowledge the sheriff collected, he learned through Jeremiah. Bits and pieces probably. Over a period of time. If Jeremiah had full knowledge, he'd be long dead. If this information is important enough to kill for once, it's important enough to be kept secret at all costs."

"So you think Jeremiah might be able to shed some light?"

"If he can, I'm sure he's sealed himself up tighter than a drum, especially after your buddy got finished with him."

"You want a shot at him, don't you?"

"Who?"

"Who. Jeremiah. That's who."

"Of course I do. But that's not going to happen because you didn't push that pip-squeak hard enough, if at all. And I'll tell you something else, Mr. Clairvoyance. In case you haven't noticed, I'm seeing things you're just beginning to entertain."

"Believe me; I've noticed."

"Well?"

"Well what?"

"Talk to him."

Robert put his hands up in frustration. "All right. I'll talk to him tomorrow—"

"Not tomorrow. Today."

"All right. Today. Right after—"

"Shh. Listen."

"What?"

Liza turned up the volume of the TV.

". . . a patient, Zachariah Eddington Ballard, whose suicide death came after fifty years of confinement in a Georgia State Mental Hospital in Milledgeville, was the last survivor of a government experiment conducted in the mid-forties at a hospital in Rochester, New York, whereby medical records show that Mr. Ballard had been injected with plutonium 239. Two officials, Tom-Tom, as Sheriff Hayes of Bibb County and Mayor Harden of the city of Macon, respectively, are affectionately known, were unavailable for comment concerning related questions raised by a watchdog committee monitoring a series of bizarre events. We'll have more on this story as it unfolds. And now back to . . . ."

"Tom-Tom," Robert said.

"Sheriff Hayes of Bibb County and Mayor Harden of the city of Macon," Liza recited.

"Now it registers!" Robert exclaimed. "Grass-roots politicking at its best and worst. A sheriff and a mayor. Rumor is those two run the state along with a figurehead governor whom they helped elect to office. They're the power behind the scenes. Have been forever from what I understand."

"Rob. I just got one of my feelings. Strongest ever."

Robert sat on the edge of the bed. "Just relax. Let it come, Liza."

"Oh, it came and went. Like that," she said, staring at him oddly.

"Tell me."

"I don't think The Man is telling you everything."

"Maybe he can't."

"Or won't. Why don't we find out?"

"First things first," Robert said firmly. "Tell me exactly what you felt."

"Real fear," Liza said and shuddered. "Sheer dread," she concluded with certainty.

Chapter 34

It was a quiet morning at police headquarters in Riverhead. The desk sergeant signaled Robert ahead, and an officer led him around a corridor. Doris was sitting in a wheelchair at the switchboard reading *Newsday* and drinking hot chocolate from a Styrofoam cup. She looked up and smiled sadly then continued reading.

"The chief will be with you in a moment," the officer said.

Robert Redler disregarded the comment and let himself into the police chief's office.

"Hey!" The officer followed after Redler, but the chief, sitting bleakly behind his desk, waved the officer off. Robert pulled up a chair.

"So much for formality or procedure—yes?" Grear snapped.

Robert launched into his spiel. "Who did you happen to mention the story of David and the wine to, trusted friend and public servant of the people of Riverhead? Well, Mr. Chief of Police? Who are you really serving? The people? Yourself? The Musketeers? Who?"

"And a good morning to you, too, Rob." Grear frowned.

"Morning, my ass. You ask for my help. But you hold things back."

"What things?"

"Don't play that game with me. I had some lunatic in an institution down in Georgia passing himself off as another patient who winds up dead as a coffin nail. Practically snapped Liza's mind with a story that only you, Liza, and I knew about. You were at our home the day David asked for wine before dinner. Liza told you that story. No one else. Now, I was onto something down there. I had a lead that went up in smoke. Zachariah Ballard. Conveniently cremated. A homicide listed as a suicide. I've got people purposely pointing us in the wrong direction. You're not giving me everything. Not only that, but you're—"

"Would you like a cup of coffee?" the police chief interrupted.

Robert stood up to leave.

"Sit back down," Grear ordered. "Goddamn it. I said sit down."

Robert Redler glared at the captain. "I'll sit down. But you'll tell me everything you've got. Starting with the day you assigned Beau Hopkins to this case."

"Sit. I didn't assign Beau to anything. He assigned himself, unofficially. He made the connection between the murder down in Georgia and that Jersey homicide. Beau actually had a line on Butch-Lee Reynolds through a lover of his in a mental institution in Stockholm. Another patient. Edna Johnsen, s-e-n. Norwegian."

"She still there?"

"Isn't going any place."

"You get me there."

"Don't have to."

"Why is that?"

Captain Grear took an audio tape and a letter out of his desk drawer and handed it over to Robert. "Beau taped her as well as others. Everything she knew is right here."

Robert took the tape and letter. "Who did you relate the story to about David and the wine?"

"The Man."

"Why?"

"This is a murder investigation, Rob."

"Meaning what?"

"Full cooperation."

Robert laughed. "What do you know about Reynolds and Baceni?"

Grear shrugged.

"That's what I thought. So much for cooperation."

"I don't know the name Baceni," the captain said truthfully.

"Want a flash? The Man does," Redler said, getting back up.

"Where are you going?"

Robert straightened the chair. "Got work to do," he answered, holding up the items. "I'm sure you've got copies?"

Grear nodded.

"How long you had these?"

"Since September."

"I want *all* the files. Everything."

"Can't."

"You mean, won't." Robert shook his head and left.

Three hours later, Robert sat before The Man in an unimpressive office in Queens.

"You get us on a plane to Stockholm," Robert insisted.

"Us?"

"Liza and me."

"Why?"

"She's got the gift."

The Man smiled. "I meant, why Stockholm?"

"Carl Gustafson."

"What about him?"

"I want to interview him."

"He's dead," the musketeer said evenly.

"What?"

"Hearing problem?"

"How did he die, and when?"

"Aneurysm. Yesterday."

"Yesterday? Don't you find that a bit coincidental?"

"I'm really busy, Rob. Unless you have something specific—"

"I want to speak to Jeremiah Jones. And I want Liza there with me. Arrange it."

"No."

"I insist."

"The answer is no." The Man picked up his pen and put his head down in paperwork. "Good day, Mr. Redler."

"Who are Reynolds and Baceni, and how are they connected, sir?"

The Man said nothing.

"Who did you pass the information to concerning David and the wine?"

The Man simply shook his head.

"Unless we pool our information and work from the center, we're sunk."

The Man picked up his head and put down the pen. "*We*, Mr. Redler? You are a civilian. Need I remind you? You feed me your insights; I do the police work. I share what I can. That was our understanding. Good day."

"But I can shoot those two women down for you in cold blood. I'm good enough to do your dirty work. Correct? You do remember that conversation, don't you?"

"You have my blessings, should you ever get the opportunity. Good day, Mr. Redler. I won't say it again."

"Liza was right. You are a little twerp," he managed.

"A puny little punk; a pipsqueak is what she said. Get it right. Very important to intelligence work. Now, for the final time, you're out of here."

Distraught, Robert turned on his heels and left.

Robert grabbed Liza by the arm and led her into the shower with all their clothes on.

"Have you lost your mind?" she hollered, standing there soaking wet, the shower running full blast.

"They're bugging us."

"Who?"

"The Man. That's who."

"He's been bugging me since day one."

"He knows you called him a pipsqueak and a punk in the motel room."

"God, I hope he didn't have a hidden camera, too," she said, pushing the showerhead away.

"This is nuts."

"Good boy. That's the first sign of sanity I've seen because this *is* nuts," she agreed, pointing to the blasting water. "What are we doing?"

"Talking so they can't hear us."

"Why in here?"

"I saw it in a movie."

"Well, I saw one where they simply turned up the radio."

The two of them looked at one another before suddenly laughing hysterically. It was a full minute before they quieted down.

"We have to be serious now," Robert said.

"Make the water a little warmer, and I'll get serious," she swore, putting a fingernail brush in front of her lips like a white mustache. "Think he'd recognize me?" She giggled like a little girl.

"Only without a trench coat." He chortled, sounding like a loon.

"Now look at who's not being serious." She turned off then stepped from the shower, getting out of her wet clothes.

Suddenly he was serious, realizing how long it had been since the two of them made love. Not since the night that David died—the night that stole a piece of their heart and soul.

The two lay naked in bed with a flannel sheet pulled up to their necks. They plotted and schemed in a low voice, muffled by the sound of the radio announcer guaranteeing any homeowner listening, instant mortgage money:

"If your bank says no, Champion says yesss," the man promised in a loud tone.

Robert quietly renamed the musketeer Mickey. "Mickey the mouseketeer," he brayed beneath the blanket.

"Ferret-faced polecat," Liza decided, snickering into the sheet.

"Rotten little rodent!" Robert howled louder than a hound dog.

Chapter 35

Late that evening, Bridget O'Reilly opened the door to her modest but immaculate home. "Come in. Come in. How was your flight?" Bridget asked anxiously, her eyes red from crying.

"I hate flying, so an uneventful flight is still a harrowing experience," Robert answered, stepping into the living room behind Liza.

"The flight was fine," Liza said, taking Bridget's hand in hers and giving the young woman a kiss upon the cheek. "We had a little problem renting a car, but everything is all right. How about you? Are you okay? Did anybody bother you?"

"Nope," she said then began to weep again. "They're saying it was a suicide, but I know Zack would never take his own life. It was all true what he said about the government. It was on the news. I feel so ashamed."

"Hey. You're not to blame," Liza stated firmly. "Robert and I know that there are many—Bridget, please listen to me. There are a good many people out there sitting in prisons and institutions who are as innocent and as sane as the three of us. Our government, to a large extent, is corrupt. Period. Zachariah was a very smart and good man who somehow learned what they were up to. So they shut him down by locking him up in a mental hospital for fifty years here in Milledgeville. That's not your fault. Do you hear? Come on now. Let's sit down and talk. We're going to expose them. All of them. But we need your help."

Bridget composed herself and led them to the kitchen table. "Please sit down. I'll put up coffee. Decaf okay?"

"Decaf is fine," Liza said.

Robert nodded. "Bridget, we need for you to think of a way that we could somehow see Jeremiah Jones again," he began, coming immediately to the point.

"Slow down, Rob," Liza ordered, raising her hand like a caution sign. "Rob believes that Jeremiah may know things that Zack told him in confidence, Bridget."

Bridget laughed and shook her head. "Zack hated Jerr. He wouldn't give him the time of day," she swore.

"But Jeremiah Jones may have learned certain things that only Zack could possibly know," Robert insisted.

Bridget shook her head again. "It may be that Jerr *tried* to get certain information from Zack. But Zack would never tell him anything. Believe me, but he told that woman reporter plenty though."

"You mean the one in Rochester, New York?"

Bridget nodded.

"Carol Ling," he added for confirmation.

"Yep. That's the one."

"I spoke to her," Robert elaborated. "She said she wouldn't and couldn't discuss the matter. Said she was doing a feature story for her paper."

"*I* could probably write that story," Bridget set forth sadly, sitting the two of them down at the kitchen table. "We'll have coffee in a few minutes. Can I make you a sandwich? I just bought some nice fresh cold cuts this afternoon that will probably see Christmas if we don't eat them." She sniffled, wiping her eyes and nose.

Liza and Robert were staring at one another.

"What?" Bridget asked. "Did I say something dumb?"

"What do you mean *you* could write that story, sweetheart?" Liza asked while experiencing a queer sensation.

"Well, from the day I started working there, we talked."

"You and Zack?" Robert questioned.

Bridget nodded. "He was the dearest person to me in the whole world. And now he's gone." She bit her upper lip, not wanting to carry on in front of her two late-night visitors.

"I thought Mrs. Cook said you had nothing to do with the patients."

"Officially, I don't. Unofficially, I'd visit with Zack before and sometimes after work. He always hung around the first floor. Loved to chitchat," she explained. "I used to think all his stories were all made up. Now, I'm not so sure."

"What kind of stories, Bridget?" Liza asked.

"Stories about Governor Atkins, Mayor Harden, and Sheriff Hayes."

"Did Zack ever mention the name Baceni?" Robert pressed.

Bridget laughed. "Practically every day."

Robert and Liza locked their eyes on one another before setting them back on Bridget.

"Can you share those stories with us, Bridget?" Liza asked in earnest. "It would really help tremendously. Then we wouldn't have to question Jeremiah, who probably wouldn't see us anyhow."

"You can bet good money he wouldn't. Besides, I don't know how I'd get upstairs anyways. They have him under heavy guard."

"Do you know who's guarding him?" Liza asked.

Bridget O'Reilly shook her head. "Strangers. Several well-dressed men in suits, different shifts, three times a day, I hear. Never saw any of them though."

"Will you tell us about Baceni?" Robert asked almost pleadingly.

"Zack told me never to tell anyone," Bridget said, staring blankly at the stove, not wanting to disappoint. "He said it was his insurance policy."

"Zack's dead!" Robert reminded her in no uncertain terms. "They murdered him, and I have good reason to believe other innocent people may be killed who are somehow connected to this cover-up. How many people know that Zack confided in you?"

"No one that I know of. Like I told you. It was either early or late when we talked. Maybe Mr. Shapely saw us talking once or twice. But then Zack acted like you did the other day. He started hollering at me, pretending he was mad about something. I don't think anyone knew Zack told me secrets."

"I don't either, Bridget," Robert said. "And do you know why?"

"Because maybe I'd have turned up dead?" Bridget was beginning to get the picture.

"There are people out there who are not playacting," Robert assured her.

Bridget stepped over and took the pot of boiling water off the stove. "You didn't give me an answer about a sandwich. I have ham and turkey and—"

"Tom turkey," Liza interrupted.

Bridget turned on her heels. "What?"

"Tom turkey," Liza repeated. "That's what Zack wants me to say to you, sweetheart."

Robert looked nonplused.

Bridget stood trembling.

Liza was smiling and nodding her head assuredly. "Zack doesn't want you to be afraid, Bridget. He knows that you would understand."

"Oh, my God!"

Liza was on her feet, taking and holding Bridget closely in her arms. "It's all right."

"That's what he'd call Sheriff Hayes. Tom turkey." She laughed anxiously. "That was our private little joke. Zack told me how mad the sheriff would get when he called him that. He just spoke through you. Didn't he?"

Liza nodded. "What can you tell us, Bridget?"

"He trusts you," she said and wept through her laughing, tearing eyes.

"I think he knows we're here to help," Robert offered.

Bridget bit her bottom lip.

"You sit," Liza insisted. "I'll get the coffee. You tell us what you can."

Robert stood and pulled out a chair for Bridget. The woman sat while Liza tended to the pot of coffee and fixings.

"You ever hear the expression, 'passin'?" Bridget asked.

"You mean like to die?" Robert asked.

Bridget shook her head in nervous laughter. "No, not that kind of passing," she drawled. "Passin'," she repeated. "A black person who is light skinned and doesn't have any of the, you know, usual features of that race, and chooses to mingle among white folks without telling anyone of his or her ancestry is said to be passin'. Zack told me that," Bridget explained.

Liza nodded. "I've heard that term used in the ghetto where I teach," she recalled.

Robert nodded in understanding.

"Well, Sheriff Hayes has been passin' through these parts for years," Bridget disclosed.

"You're telling us that Sheriff Tom Hayes is part black?" Robert asked incredulously.

"Not like this cup of coffee, of course," Bridget said, accepting the mug and waving off Liza's offer of half-and-half and sugar. "But he's got black blood coursing through his veins for sure. Only a few folks down in Macon know that. Those who do, don't dare breathe a word of it to anyone. What they don't know, and I never believed a word of it till now, is who Sheriff Hayes' grandfather really is—or rather was," Bridget added, shaking her head slowly back and forth in such sweet sorrow, the tears streaming down her face like tired plumbing having suddenly given way to the force of gravity.

"Who?" Liza asked, already cognizant of the answer.

"Zachariah Ballard," Bridget answered flatly.

Silence swept the room for a good fifteen seconds.

"Does Sheriff Hayes know this?" Liza asked quietly, taking both of Bridget's hands firmly into her own.

Bridget shook her head. "Zack said that Tom Hayes must never know," she said and sobbed. "He told me, 'I'm so ashamed of him, but he's still my grandson.' Said that Tom forsook his people but that he never murdered anyone by his own hand, but might just as well have. Said, too, that the sheriff never had any children of his own for fear they'd turn out dark."

Robert stirred in a teaspoon of sugar without a sound, setting the utensil down upon a napkin. "Getting back to Baceni, Bridget," he urged.

"Baceni was a shortened name from one I can't quite remember. But it really doesn't matter because it was a made-up name anyhow, belonging to three brothers whose identity remains a great secret."

"Did Zack share this secret with you?"

"Zack said that was one secret that must follow him to the grave; that many innocent people would die if the truth be known."

Robert sat truly disappointed.

"You said Zack told you stories about the governor," Liza prodded.

Bridget nodded. "Very bad stories."

"Please tell us, sweetheart." Liza could clearly see the pain written across Bridget's face.

"He's a murderer," she whispered.

Liza moved her chair closer to Bridget's. "Exactly what did Zack tell you?"

"That the governor, Senator Atkins at the time, killed both Zack's son and the sheriff's mother when he found them doing you know what in the pantry of his home. She was the senator's white maid; Zack's son was his black butler. Zack said the senator had put the sheriff, Deputy Hayes at the time, up to claiming that Zack's son shot the sheriff's mother and that the sheriff had to shoot the man in self-defense," which the senator actually did. Shot Zack's son, Tyrone, in cold blood."

"In other words, Tom Hayes' own father," Liza clarified.

Bridget nodded. "Only Tom Hayes didn't know it was his daddy, of course. Still doesn't," she reiterated.

Robert shook his head, clearing away the cobwebs. "You're telling us that Zack's son, Tyrone, who was the senator's butler, was fooling around with a white maid who was Tom Hayes' mother?"

"Yes, both employed by Al Atkins and living under his roof. Zack said the woman and Tyrone made lots of trouble for everyone, but that there was a great deal of money around to make the problems go away and that all the dirty little secrets were locked away across three continents."

"Did he say which three?" Liza asked.

"Europe, Asia, and North America. He'd always say, 'Ms. B,' that's what he liked to call me, 'you're privy to more than one of the state government's top secrets.'"

"Did Zack ever mention the name, Angelica Manns?" Liza asked.

"Yes, he did. Zack said she was related to the three brothers; that she was their niece. He also said that like his own kin and kind, the Baceni family tree had lost most of its branches. Those were his exact words, which he must have repeated to me a million times."

"Anything else that you might remember?" Robert pushed and prayed.

Bridget shook her head.

"Can you tell us anything about the mayor?" Liza asked.

"Oh, yes. Zack said that he was the truly dangerous one of the lot. Worse than a murderer. Said the governor and the sheriff were stupid, but that the mayor was a snake. Strike when you'd least expect. He said the mayor seems harmless, like your garden variety, but that it was his second set of fangs hidden back further in his mouth that you'd have to be concerned about. He must have told me that a hundred times."

"Did Zack ever mention the name Angelo Manns?" Robert quizzed.

Bridget shook her head.

Robert took out a notepad. "Stop me if any of these names rings a bell. All right?"

"All right."

"Lee Ellis Reynolds. Lee Edward Harris."

Bridget shook her head.

"Carson Reynolds."

"Nope."

"Butch-Lee Reynolds."

"Nope. Wait!"

"What?"

"What was that last one again?"

"Butch-Lee or Butch-Lee Reynolds?"

"Yes. When you said those other names . . . Lee something . . . say them again."

"Lee Ellis Reynolds. Lee Edward Harris?"

Bridget curled a lip and shook her head slowly. "But Butch-Lee Reynolds. Zack spoke of him, I'm sure. Yes. Something about the boy growing up around these parts. About his family . . . I can't remember. Wait! Something about a neighbor's family that wouldn't let their kids hang out with him because they said he was crazy. Butch-Lee had a sister, though. Actually, a half sister. Beautiful girl. It was only when she came around to visit that Butch-Lee was allowed to socialize with her and the other kids. I guess she was able to control him or something. Is that important?"

"I don't know," Robert said truthfully. "The only thing I know for certain is that their lives are somehow intricately intertwined and that a great secret is being kept at all cost. Zachariah had the key to unlock it. It seems he shared a good part of it with you."

"I wish I could be of more help."

"Believe me you have, Bridget," Liza assured her.

"You know, I just thought of something," Bridget said. "I know someone who might be able to help you."

"Who?" Liza asked excitedly.

"Zack spoke of her on and off. Mildred Brown, known as Millie B. 'Sweetest and prettiest girl in these parts,' Zack said. Knew everyone. All the families."

"Does she still live around here?" Robert asked.

Bridget brightened. "She certainly does. Married now," she went on, holding back something she knew would be sure to surprise. "Big ol' house on a hill down in the city of Macon. Largest estate in that area. Never been there, but I've seen pictures in newspapers and magazines." Bridget held her tongue in the hollow of her cheek, knowing this news was good.

"What?" Liza asked, studying the indomitable pose.

"Did she know the two Toms?" Robert cut in.

"Well enough to take a decade in deciding which one she was going to marry," Bridget said in a declaration of ambiguity.

"She's married to one of the Toms?" he asked and answered his own question with obvious surprise.

"Yep," she said, pursing her lips together in a satisfied expression.

"And you're going to make me ask you which one," Liza said, also drawing out the moment. "Aren't you?"

Bridget beamed. "Yep."

Liza laughed. "Okay, which Tom did this Millie B. marry, Bridget?"

"Millie married *the* man."

"Which man?" Liza asked impatiently, quickly growing weary of the game.

"She means the sheriff," Robert concluded.

Bridget laughed. "Not *that* man. *The* man. Millie married the mayor of the manor as Zack used to say. The mayor of Macon. Mayor Tom Harden." Bridget paused. "You're looking at me like I have two heads."

"No," Robert said. "I'm looking at you like maybe Mayor Tom Harden wears more than one hat."

"Bridget, did Zack ever mention the mayor apart from being the city's chief official?"

"Not that I recall. No."

Liza came back to the table with more coffee. "Listen. I know it's late, but do you mind if we ask you a few more questions?"

"Where are you guys staying tonight?" Bridget asked instead of answering.

"Probably the motel we stayed at last time."

"No, you're not. You're staying here tonight. I'm supposed to be the hostess, and you're busy pouring coffee while I'm sitting on my butt like I'm helpless," she said, removing herself from the table. "I'm going to make us sandwiches as I suggested earlier, while you ask me all the questions you want. All right on both counts?"

Robert looked at Liza then nodded.

"Great. Now you go sit back down, Liza. Ham and turkey and Swiss cheese?"

"Fine," her guests said simultaneously.

"Rye or whole wheat?"

"Whole wheat," the two rejoined.

"Mayo or mustard?

"Mayo," Liza and Robert chorused.

"Me, too," Bridget said, taking out several items from the refrigerator. "What's your next question?"

"You got a beer with that sandwich?" Robert asked, receiving a poke from Liza.

"One beer coming right up."

"Bridget, he had martinis on the plane."

"One martini coming right up," Bridget replied.

Liza laughed. "That's not what I meant."

"Two martinis coming right up," Bridget went on, reaching from the counter to a cabinet.

"Bridget!"

"Oh, all right. You talked me into it. I guess I'll join you," she acquiesced with a mischievous wink. "And I want you to know that I make the best martini north of the Macon County line. I ain't an O'Reilly for nothin' you know."

"A woman after my own heart," Robert affirmed and nodded contentedly, eyeing the top-shelf liquor. "Before I forget, did Zack ever mention The Three Musketeers? I don't mean the novel or the movie. I mean . . . ."

Bridget's face seemed suddenly to turn to stone. She set the bottles of vermouth and vodka down on the countertop. "You mean the men who were responsible for injecting him with radioactive material, for warehousing him here in Milledgeville."

Robert said nothing. He didn't have to.

"Then *every* single word Zack said was true! Wasn't it?"

"That's what we're going to find out," Robert answered straightaway.

"Bridget."

In a trance, Bridget turned to Liza.

"Make mine a double," she said soberly.

"Ditto," Robert agreed.

Bridget took down three good-sized tumblers. "I got us covered."

A few minutes later, the three raised their glasses to the memory of Zachariah Eddington Ballard.

Chapter 36

Addressing her troops, Angelica held center stage. "In memory of Richard Geist, founder of this network of which you have the privilege and honor to belong, I'd like to pass on his philosophy concerning a noble creature for which he had the greatest respect. So much so, that he referred to it as the ultimate challenge when pursued with a bow. 'Harvest deer with a bow on a regular basis, and you'll outwit the cleverest of men,' he'd sign. Like most of you sitting here today, I didn't take much stock in that belief. Later in the game," Angelica emphasized, "I ate those silent words. Ate venison for the very first time, too," she said quite fondly.

"We had spent a rather uncomfortable winter with the deer, hiding from federal, state, and local authorities. The woods were our home through blinding blizzards and torrential downpours. Temperatures at times fell well into the teens, and with the wind chill factor, forget about it. I'm talking cold. But we survived.

"Then along came a persistent police chief and a writer with a gift. A gift reaching beyond the five senses. The two men became Richard's nemeses. Police Chief Grear of the Riverhead Police Department and Robert Redler, writer extraordinaire. Ironically, Mrs. G was once Redler's benefactor. She used his gift to her own advantage. In the end, however, Robert Redler defeated Richard Geist with a bullet to the brain. In his second book, he avowed the same for Mrs. G and me."

Peter's hand shot up.

"Peter."

"Why not simply waste him?"

"First off, I don't think it would be that simple," Angelica made clear. "Secondly, we're not sanctioned."

"Is this Robert Redler a definite threat to our organization, Ms. M?" Karen asked.

"I'm afraid he is," Angelica affirmed.

"Then the powers that be have to be made to understand that," Harold stated, "followed by a plot to take Redler out."

"And if the powers that be, along with Mrs. G, fail to understand that?" Angelica put forth hypothetically.

"Then, for the good of the whole, the power of authority must be put into the hands of those who wish to survive," Harold said forthwith.

"Peter. If someone proposed something that you disagreed with adamantly, would your disapproval run along the lines of treason?"

"If what someone in authority proposed jeopardized the *well-being* of our organization, probably not. If that proposal seriously threatened *annihilation* of our organization, I'd be plotting a mutiny against that force within the minute."

Karen and Harold deferred to Peter's wisdom with nods of understanding.

"Why so long a period of time, Peter?" Angelica teased and tested with a winning smile.

Peter smiled down at this desk.

"Of course, we're just speaking hypothetically here," Angelica said, a sinister smile forming upon her handsome face.

"Of course," the three agreed in unison.

Chapter 37

The Triumvirate sat in judgment on the top floor of a dumpy downtown six-story hotel in Atlanta. A heavy set of drapes was drawn across a large window. One of the musketeers stood, pouring himself a brandy from an antique crystal decanter. Another stooped and scratched his knee repeatedly through a rip in his shabby trousers. The third sat with a green highlighter fixed between his teeth, paging through Sunday's editions of *The Atlanta Journal-Constitution* and Rochester's *The Democrat & Chronicle.*

"Getting too old for this crap, gentlemen," the unshaven, thin-faced, frail man declared, setting himself down into a high-backed leather chair with his drink.

"Not your fault Redler's resourceful as hell. He pulled the same shit couple of years back at the Giordano home when the feds had it staked out. Probably went up and out her goddamn chimney disguised as smoke," the mercenary mocked, straightening out his pant leg.

"Actually, he walked out her front door in drag. No, it's my fault. I let him know that he was being bugged, and it bugged him. Stupid of me."

"Gotta have faith," the monsignor said, the marker still in his mouth as he spoke. "They'll turn up."

"Yeah. Like a bad penny," the gray-haired mercenary swore.

"So, what do we do with them when they do show?"

"Fuck her; dispose of him, I guess."

"And he does mean, fuck her," the ill-dressed man declared and laughed.

The youngest circled a four-line death notice before taking in an obituary.

"The added concern is that she's able to *see* certain things now, too. Redler wanted her on the team. I shot him down."

"I say they're both expendable."

"I don't know."

"They could be useful. Maybe hold on to one of them."

"Both of them walking around together are like two fucking time bombs."

"What the hell are the odds of those two having the gift; working in concert under the same goddamn roof?"

"What do you think they know?"

"At this point, not a hell of a lot. Let the energy secretary put the onus on the Army's Manhattan Project, and maybe it will come to rest there. It's amazing to me that no one has figured this out yet."

"Let's consider ourselves lucky."

"Fifty people terminated fifty years ago, and no one makes the connection."

"At least our forefathers were smart enough to mix things up a bit."

"Yeah. Six deadly substances. Yet no one had the foresight to arrange even a fucking traffic fatality or two if only to cast suspicion under a different light."

"Gotta remember the times, gentlemen. Most of the patients thought they were positively going bonkers. Several suspected what was going on. Even fewer of them ever spoke about it for fear that their family and friends would have them committed."

"And then along came Zachariah Ballard."

"Came and finally went, thank God."

"May be thanking the wrong party. But special thanks does go out to Sheriff Hayes for his decisive action, after a little push from Al."

"We going to hang the sheriff out to dry?"

"No. Law enforcement is getting a bad enough rap," Karl kidded. "We'll let Zack's death stand as a suicide. Fifty years of an uphill battle; the so-called truth uncovered. The old man just finally fell to pieces and put it all to rest. It flies. Besides, Hayes has other problems on the horizon, which will inevitably take their toll. So. Agreed?"

"Agreed," the clergyman shrugged.

The merc nodded in the affirmative.

"But what about Manns and Giordano, and how it affects our agencies?"

"Simple. I say we sit back and see what transpires. You can't argue that it won't be entertaining. We'll step in at just the right moment. If you think that we enjoy autonomy now, just wait. Talk about a shot in the arm for a failing economy."

"What about Mr. Jeremiah Jones?"

"What about him?"

"Ties to Mr. Ballard. Self-proclaimed prophet. Could he possibly know anything at all about this Baceni business?"

"Nothing, I can assure you. Allow me to add that Mr. Jones profited greatly from the experience of having met me. And think about it; Redler and Downs even witnessed me trying to extract the truth from Mr. Jones about Baceni. How much more convincing can I be that I must be totally in the dark, too?"

"Yeah, and what if Jones did know we are the Bacenis and said something in front of them? Then what?"

"A crazy old coot locked away in a mental institution? Who's going to believe such an incredible story? No one. Not even Robert Redler or Liza Downs."

"I don't know, Karl," the merc said. "I like the old adage that says, 'Dead men tell no tales.' And that would include Liza Downs."

"Look. In the highly unlikely event Jones should know more than what I give him credit for, he'll keep his mouth shut. Trust me on that. He's scared shitless and he knows nothing that can hurt us. We do not want to raise another red flag. Sheriff Hayes can do just so much for us. Besides, there's still another layer someone would have to penetrate beyond the Baceni shield. A shield that protects who we really are as well as our successors."

"Well, I guess that about wraps it up for now," the monsignor said. "But we do have to talk this Redler/Downs business through, though. Thoroughly."

"I'll call you as soon I get word on them."

"Any word from her school as to when she might be coming back?"

Karl shook his head. "Got accumulated sick leave up the kazoo. Even after Redler's trials and tribulations, she's got a bank of days built up. Yet, she elects to take a leave of absence. Tells us what? Believe me; she's not worried about the money or her job."

"Fucking teachers," the merc bellyached. "They work a

hundred and eighty days a year and can still afford to go out on extended leaves of absence without a worry in the world. Fucking unions. Somebody ought to put a bullet in that UFT president's head."

"You work on that," the little man jokingly suggested with a bright smile.

"Yeah, right. See you two *mañana.*" The merc started to leave the room.

The monsignor put down the newspaper and shook his head in disgust, staring in their cohort's direction.

"What?"

"Those pants of yours."

"What? The Bowery. A dollar ninety-nine."

"I'm surprised they even let you in the building like that."

"Did you open your eyes coming in here?"

"I took the elevator."

"There is no elevator."

"The freight elevator. Out back."

"I didn't know the building even had one."

"Anyhow, the stairs could be dangerous."

"Why's that?"

"Why, I could wind up splitting the seat of my pants," the merc bantered, popping a Certs into his mouth.

Chapter 38

The library was about to close.

"Here it is," Robert whispered, pushing two alphabetized lists, A and B, of Holocaust names, under Liza's nose: Victims ~ Survivors. Treblinka. Extermination camp in Poland. "Read."

Liza scanned the list. "I don't see the name Baceni anywhere."

"You won't. But you do see the name Bacenowitz; survivor. And on this list, the name Hannah Abramowicz, victim. Bacenowitz was Hannah's brother's wife's maiden name. Hannah Abramowicz is in some way connected to The Triumvirate."

"How in the world can you possibly know that by looking at those two lists?"

"I can't. But when Chief Grear gave me that file to work from, he wrote down two names that his so-called crazy sister swore would shed light on a secret of national security, begging him to use it wisely."

"The sister institutionalized in upstate New York."

"Exactly. And these are those two names."

"Well, I'm sorry to bust your bubble, good buddy. But do you have any idea how common those two surnames are?"

"With given names of Hillel for the brother and Betya for the sister?"

"Hum. Maybe the librarian could somehow help us."

"What's the matter with you? I don't want anyone in this town to know what we're after."

"So what do we do? We've already been through two dozen phone books and half a dozen libraries in five different towns."

"Keep your voice down."

"Anyhow, I think we can pretty much rely on Angelica Manns

being born Angelo M. Reynolds. So at least we've got something to work on. I say I march right on up to the mayor's mansion like Bridget suggested and sit for high tea with Millie B. Harden. Would I refer to her as Mrs. Mayor, Mildred, or Mrs. Harden? Or better yet, I could just ask her for her Christmas card list and see," she kidded.

Robert had Liza by the hand and was leading her along the stacks and past the information desk.

"Where are we going?" she asked once they were outside.

"Post office."

"I knew that," she teased, not knowing what Robert now had in mind.

When they were a block away from the post office, Robert spoke in earnest. "Do you remember a couple of days before the Miss Armenia contest when I had a meeting with the Kezerian family?"

"Of course I remember."

"Well, what I probably didn't tell you is that I forgot their street address in Bayside. It had been some time since I was there last. I drove around like an idiot for thirty minutes before I decided to get help at the post office."

"And?"

"And nothing. They told me about a recent federal law that prohibits them from giving out addresses."

"So how did you finally get there?"

"Had to backtrack a bit. Started from the college, the route I used to travel to their home after teaching. Things suddenly came back to me. Finally, I found it. The point is the people in the post office here probably aren't going to be of much help, either."

"So why are we going there?"

"Because *you're* going to put on your charm and accost a mail carrier or someone *outside* the post office, where you stand a better chance. I'll wait here. See that flag? That's the Macon City Post Office on Mulberry Street. Behind me is the Bibb County Court House, where I'll meet you on the corner of Second Street."

The pair formulated their plan. Liza hiked her skirt above the knees then tugged the top of her sweater, exposing a slender shoulder as Robert stepped from the rental. "How's this?" she asked with a grin.

"I said to put on your charm, not to take off half your clothes."

Liza gave him a Bronx cheer and rummaged through her

pocketbook for a mirror, comb, and makeup.

Liza slid behind the wheel and drove the sedan along the busy street, looking for a place to park. There wasn't any, so she turned on Third Street, heading toward the rear of the post office building. She pulled into a private parking space in back, adjacent to a loading platform.

"Hey lady, can't you read?" a burly figure hollered.

Liza stumbled out of the car. "Hey, buddy. You read this?" she burped, giving the man on the loading dock the finger and a great big sexy grin.

"Hey, you a wacko or something?" he said, bounding off one end of the loading platform.

"Wack, wack, wack, or something," she stammered and giggled, staggering up to him with four white envelopes clutched to her chest, revealing an inch or so of cleavage. "Mayor Harden wants me, oops," she slipped, stepping out of a high heel and grabbing hold of the man's arm. "Sorry, wasn't supposed to mention his name."

"The mayor?" the man questioned.

"Shh." Liza hiccupped, looking all around them. "Mayor wants me to send these off to the Baceni family for Thanksgiving; only I lost last year's Christmas list with all the addresses. Those families," she said, putting the envelopes in the man's hands before holding up four fingers, "are going to be pissed, not to mention the mayor," she concluded, rocking backward on one foot while the other found its shoe.

The man stared down at the envelopes. "Baceni? I don't know no Baceni."

"The Baceni brothers. I think they're in moving and storage or something." she swore.

"Hey, Joe!" the man called out to an old-timer coming out of the back of the building. "Come on down here a minute and see if you can help this lady out."

"Hey, Joe!" Liza waved, putting on her biggest and brightest smile.

The old man squinted and found his way along a railing, heading toward them.

"If anybody'd know, it'd be Joe."

"Hey, Joe. Whattaya know?" Liza leaned to the left and

laughed.

"Hi. What can I do you out of?" The old man grinned.

"Well, if I were only a little older, Joe, maybe more than you bargained for, you ol' rascal you," Liza said, flirting unabashedly.

The younger man put the envelopes in Joe's hand. "Lady's from the mayor's office."

"I don't have my glasses here, George," Joe said, holding the envelopes at arm's length.

"Baceni," George said. "B-a-c-e-n-i."

"By George, I think he's got it!" Liza remarked and giggled, poking George playfully in the ribs with an upright thumb.

"You're going back in time, Missy," Joe said rather quietly, running a thumb and forefinger along the side of his chin.

"Back, back, back," she repeated, resisting the urge to temper her charade.

"Way back, actually."

"Told ya. If anybody'd know," George assured her.

"Would you excuse us a second, George," the old man said, handing the envelopes back to Liza.

"Sure thing, Joe," George said, somewhat surprised, stepping around the woman before taking his leave. "I think he wants you all to himself," he whispered, giving her a pat on the backside.

When George was back on the platform, Joe turned to Liza. "Who are you, Missy?" he asked plainly, any expression of friendliness dissolving before her eyes.

"I'm here to find out—"

"Come clean, now. You're not from the mayor's office, are you?"

Liza shook her head.

"Law enforcement?"

"No, no. Nothing like that," Liza said, dropping the act and setting her teeth firmly against her upper and lower lips.

"Reporter?"

Liza shook her head. "Joe. I'm at the end of a trail. The forest is all around me. Only I don't know in which direction to face to clearly see the trees." Tears filled Liza's eyes; they were real tears.

"Only thing I know about you is that you're a lousy actress, lady. But I don't think you're acting now. Am I right?"

Liza nodded abruptly.

"And I guess you really can't tell me what this is all about, can you?"

Liza shook her head.

"Well, in that case, I'm going to ask you one more question. All right?"

Liza nodded, looking toward the heavens in sheer frustration.

"Are you a good witch or a bad witch?" the old man inquired.

Liza looked back down and laughed.

"Well?" the man said. "I'm waiting for your answer."

"Oh, Joe. I'm a very good witch," she assured him.

"And I believe you. So I'll tell you some of what I know."

Liza brightened. "Oh, thank you, Joe," Liza said, putting her hands together as if in prayer.

"Which Baceni would you like to know about?"

Liza pulled her hands apart, flagging them indecisively.

"Why don't we start with the one who went off to the seminary," Joe suggested.

"The seminary?"

Joe nodded. "Monsignor. Keeps a low profile. But a very powerful man. Assigned to the Vatican. An emissary, of sorts; but a very powerful man."

"Please go on, Joe."

"One of the other two brothers was a mercenary soldier. Good for whichever way the wind blew."

"Soldier, you say."

"Yep. The other brother, oldest of the three, rules the roost."

"Rules the roost," Liza whispered. "How do you mean exactly?"

"Like you, Missy, I really can't say," he said sadly.

"But then . . . at least tell me how you know these things," Liza pleaded.

The old man bent close to Liza's ear. "I used to read their mail," he whispered. "Long time ago."

Liza drew back with a face void of expression.

"Several of us did," Joe shrugged. "Not a nice thing, I know. But we kept our secrets to ourselves. More than I can say for the monsignor."

"What do you mean, Joe?" she practically begged, taking him by the arm, tacitly declaring herself his confidante.

"The confessions he heard daily were not as privileged as one might think. Certain declarations were shared with those in power to great advantage."

"My God!"

"Probably the same noble sentiment that pulled some good God-fearing folk down, Missy."

"Who is this eldest brother?" Liza pressed. "Please tell me more."

"The keeper of dark secrets. A powerful ruler as I said. A most evil man. The power behind the throne."

"What do these three brothers want, Joe?"

"Can you give me their names?"

Joe shook his head so sadly. "All that I can tell you is that they are of a single Godhead."

"Godhead?"

"Yes. An evil sort of Trinity, if you will."

"Does this Trinity have a name or title, Joe?"

"Yes."

"Please, Joe. Please tell me."

"The Triumvirate. The most powerful ruling body of three."

Liza nodded knowingly that what Joe was saying *was* indeed true. "Can you put a face to these three men?"

"Well, Missy, you're not going to find them on the wall in the post office; and they're certainly not on any postage stamps."

"But if you could describe them—"

The old man shook his head. "Never really saw them. Really never want to."

"Joe?"

"Missy?"

"Did you know a Zachariah Ballard?"

"Yes."

"My God! Did Zack know these three men?"

"He knew them. Up close and personal."

"Do you know why Zack was poisoned with radiation?"

"To make it look like he and fifty others were part of a scientific experiment to see how radioactive substances react in human beings."

"You're telling me they weren't?"

"They were. But they were not solely poisoned for that reason."

"Then why?"

"Because we had the gift."

Liza stood stunned. "Oh, my God, Joe. When were you going to tell me?"

"I'm not sure that I was."

"Then why now?"

"Too old to care anymore, I guess."

"Oh, Joe," she said, taking the old man to her bosom.

Suddenly, the two were aware of a presence.

"Joe. Joe. Joe. Joe. Joe," several postal employees chanted from the top of the loading dock. "Go, Joe."

Joe turned away from the woman and faced the harmless group. "Get back to work, the lot of you, or I'll— What will I do to them?" he asked, turning back to the woman.

"Have them for breakfast," Liza whispered.

"—or I'll have you for breakfast," Joe hollered, bobbing his head in total satisfaction.

Joe left Liza with a final piece of information referencing The Triumvirate and its reign.

Chapter 39

Liza drove to the corner of Second Street and Mulberry. Robert was waiting and could clearly see that she was brimming with excitement. The door lock posts popped up, and Robert came around to the driver's side to change places, sliding in behind the wheel.

"Pay dirt," Liza declared.

"What did you learn?" Robert asked excitedly.

"That the one we're concerned with sits in the seat of power."

"Mayor Harden?"

"Hardly."

"Then who?"

"Your Man. The man with the blade who knifed Jeremiah Jones. Karl, your *mouseketeer.*"

"Jesus Christ!"

"More like the anti-Christ."

"You're sure?"

"Sure as I'm sitting here."

"Tell me everything."

"Better grab hold of your seat."

"Got it."

"Not only do I now know about this monster and his two cohorts, I also know why fifty people died in that related Manhattan Project scandal."

"Because some mad scientists wanted to know about the effects of radiation—"

Liza shook her head, cutting him short. "Real reason? Because all fifty had the gift."

Robert looked at Liza in amazement, slowly going off in thought.

"Listen to me," she said. "There's more. Every twenty-five years, The Triumvirate—"

"Who?"

"The Triumvirate. That's what they're called. Your Three Musketeers. So don't play stupid. Now shut up and listen. Every twenty-five years the guard changes. Those three now rule the roost. They have ultimate power. But soon that power changes hands. You and I and Zack and Joe—"

"Joe?"

"The postal worker."

Robert glowered. "Have you been licking the glue on those postage stamps?"

"I'm dead serious, Rob."

"I'm going to share something with you, Liza."

"Gee. That's nice."

"I know how powerful those men are."

"No you don't."

"I do."

"Don't."

"They control this country."

"Wrong. They rule this world. The monsignor is headquartered in the Vatican. Joe says it's presently the seat of evil."

"Did Joe escape from Milledgeville?"

"Joe knew Zack."

"There you go."

"Stop it!"

Robert let out a wind of exasperation. "I know you know how all this sounds."

"Crazy."

"That's an understatement."

"Kind of gives you an inkling as to how those fifty-one guinea pigs, including Zack, must have felt. Kind of explains the state of the world right now; doesn't it?"

Robert said nothing.

"Popes and presidents, monarchs and madmen have been placed in the highest offices throughout the world."

"By the Big Three?"

"The Triumvirate."

"Not the American car companies?"

Liza was climbing out of the car.

Robert braked and reached for her.

"Get your goddamn hands off of me, you son of a bitch," she screamed, slamming the car door. "You knew about The Triumvirate!"

"Hey. Hey. Hey," Robert shouted. "In name, yes; not in deed. All right?"

A patrol car cruised on by, reducing its speed a hundred or so yards ahead. The officer behind the wheel studied the situation in his rearview mirror before driving away.

Liza was pacing the pavement. "I hate you."

"I hate you, too. Now get back in here and settle down. We've got work to do."

Liza got back in the car and sat there quietly . . . a statement of Joe's gnawing away at her. She pondered it, rolling the words over and over in her mind. Why couldn't Joe tell her *everything*? What piece to the puzzle was being held back?

Like you, Missy, I can't say, Joe had said. It was the only question he had veered away from.

"Why?" Liza asked aloud.

"Why what?"

"Just shut up," Liza snapped.

"Why would such a powerful man put himself on display like that back at the hospital, Liza?"

"I said I'm not talking to you."

"Can't answer that, can you?"

"Sheer arrogance. All right?"

"Did you ask Joe how Angelica was connected to this business?"

"He said he didn't know and didn't want to know. Said he told me far too much already and just wanted to forget the past. Said the gift was his curse."

Chapter 40

The merc grinned from ear to ear when he heard the news.

"We found them."

"Where?"

"Macon. Second Street and Mulberry, near the District Court."

"They still there?"

"No. They're heading east in a rental on the Interstate."

"What were they doing back in Macon?"

"Fighting. One of the patrol officers spotted them."

"That's healthy. How are you set?"

"Chopper."

"Good. They're probably heading up to Durham for a connecting flight back to Islip. That's why you missed them in Atlanta. They drove straight down."

"You want them picked up?"

"Just keep them in sight. Had you checked *all* the hotels and motels like I asked, you could have taken care of business then."

"We checked everything. Train stations. Private airports. Bus depots. We don't know where they were holed up. They could have been sleeping in the car."

"I think it was your guys who were doing the sleeping."

The merc held his tongue.

"Don't lose them this time. Call ahead to Durham. See what you come up with."

"Right." The merc hung up.

Late that afternoon, the merc made a second call.

"What the hell do you mean you lost them again, Ed?"

"Their rental showed up a little while ago with an elderly

couple behind the wheel. Apparently, Redler gave the old gent a hundred dollars and instructions to take the wife out dancing and to a nice dinner before returning the car."

"I thought you had an eye on them."

"We did."

"And you couldn't see that you were surveilling two senior citizens, for cryin' out loud?"

"We thought they were incognito."

"You better be incognito in the event I show up in your office on Monday."

The merc hung up. "Piss, shit, and corruption. Sandra!" the merc shouted.

"Yes, sir?"

"Put my retirement papers through."

"You know you don't have any such papers, sir," Sandra reminded him with a smile.

"Well, then draw up a virgin set right now," he chided.

"Would you like a cup of coffee instead?" she asked, still wearing her pleasant expression.

"Get me Bill on the line."

"He's finishing up vacation in Argentina, sir. Fly-fishing. Fly-in. No phones. No cell. Should be in contact shortly, though. I called the lodge. How about I make arrangements for you to join him next time? He's always suggesting, you know."

"No, just get me two aspirins."

"Tylenol, sir."

The merc put down his pen and looked up at his Washington secretary. "How long have we been together, Sandra?"

"Twenty-three years this January, sir."

The man reflected. "Do you know that if I had people out there," he said, pointing toward a windowless wall, "half as competent and on top of things as you, why, this world would be in the greatest shape it's ever been."

"If you say so, sir."

"I say so."

Sandra stepped just outside the office to get a glass of water and two Tylenol.

"Oh, and dig out an FBI ID badge and credentials, cipher-lock combination and key," he called out. "Put Bill's code to it and messenger the parcel to his drop in Seattle. He may have to exchange his collar for a necktie and suit, soon."

"Package coming from where, sir?"

"That KGB guy's office, in case it's intercepted. Stanislav or something, on New Hampshire Avenue."

"Lunev."

"Right."

"I'm afraid he's dormant but about to be resurrected. Not a good idea right now. How about that former handler, Yuri Shvets?"

"The author? Good. I hate authors. Especially turncoat hacks. What was his book?"

"*Washington Station.*"

"That's it. Would serve them both right."

"Here are your Tylenol and water."

"Capsules? I hate capsules. They remind me of the one I had to carry behind the Curtain."

"I'll get you caplets next time. Swallow. Drink your water." Sandra waited. "All of it. Good boy."

"Now, let me get some work done."

Not five minutes later, Sandra buzzed him from the outer office.

"Yes, Sandra?"

"Bill just called; he's been briefed."

"Fantastic. Forget what I said about the package. I'll hand it to him myself when he returns."

"Hold on a second. Clarence called, too. He wanted me to tell you where the targets are headed. They're on their way over here right now."

"Redler and Downs are on their way *here*?"

"Yes, sir."

"Instead of that package, Sandra, send a pipe bomb to Redler's home address," he half-kidded.

"What do you want me to do when they get here? And I think they're here already."

The merc expelled an exasperating column of air.

"Wait. Something's very wrong here," Sandra said. "They're a very young couple. Teenagers. And they're with two men," she added.

212

"Recognize them?"

"*Washington Post* and *The New York Times*."

"Shit. Tell them I'm not in and have Clarence run interference. Let Karl know immediately what's going on."

"Right."

"Then set up a three-way conference call as soon as possible."

"I'm on it."

The merc was informing Karl and Bill of Redler and Downs' *coup de grâce*.

". . . and in stroll two teenagers and two reporters that the dastardly duo sent," the merc continued, setting down his coffee. "Sandra was nonplussed. Can you picture Clarence's face when the two reporters told him they had good information that the office was fronting for a child pornography ring?" he roared.

"Talk about rings; those two are certainly running circles around us," the monsignor made clear.

"Two actors and two innocent kids. Sandra said the guys were spitting images of Tyson from the *Post* and Gilbreth from the *Times*. The kids say they got fifty bucks apiece; the actors did it for the publicity," the merc went on.

"I'd have had the whole bunch locked up if not for the real press we'd have gotten," Karl blasted.

"I still maintain that it's a damn shame to waste them both, but I see Ed's point, too. They came as a pair, so I guess they'll have to be returned as a set."

"You want it Ed?" Karl asked.

"Might as well. You're too involved personally, Karl. Warned you about that. Bill, you'd probably go soft and want to join them in holy matrimony before you pulled the trigger. And forget the agencies. They fucked this one up royally."

"So all we have to do is decide how we want it done," Karl put forth.

"How about a traffic fatality?" Bill suggested.

"Both of them?"

"Why not?"

"Why don't the two of you get a good night's sleep and read about it in the morning paper," the merc yawned.

"What morning?" Karl asked.

"What paper?" Bill added.

"How about Monday's *Wall Street Journal*? 'Couple Clobbered as Market Crashes,'" Ed recited, assigning the headline in deadpan.

Bill laughed. "Hey, I like that. Who do we hang it on?"

"Harold Greenspan," the merc came back without hesitation.

The three of them giggled like children.

"Who do you want to give this to, Ed?" Karl asked straightaway.

"One of our locals."

"I don't want to read about 'suspected foul play.' And forget about any more suicides."

"A nice fire while they sleep," Ed decided. "Got just the man."

"I'd prefer a boating accident. But this can't wait till May or June."

"Relax."

"Relax, he says. First we've got to find them, Ed. And don't underestimate those two."

"If they're under a rock, I'll find them."

"Yeah, just make sure they don't hit you over the head with it," Bill warned good-humoredly.

"You change those pants from last time, Ed?" the monsignor teased.

"Different pants, same shop."

Bill smiled and shook his head before the speakerphone.

"Hey, baggy is in, boys."

"So, why don't you wear them down around your ass like a wigger? Walk that walk and talk that Ebonics shit. You could have Clarence as your sidekick," Karl put forward good-naturedly.

"What the hell is he talking about? Wiggers and Ebonics."

"White niggers speaking black English, strolling down busy boulevards with boom boxes on their shoulders and their ass cheeks hanging out. Where you be, my man?"

"Better part of town, I guess. Ebonics? You shittin' me or what?"

"Oakland school board is trying to declare it a second language. District's got fifty-three percent black."

"Second language? When are they going to learn the first?"

"You got that right," Bill bantered.

"Put them all back on the boat," Karl murmured.

"But I'd keep Clarence around," Bill said. "Good man."

"Good man, indeed," Ed agreed.

"But would you want him as your next-door neighbor?" Karl taunted playfully.

"He *is* my next-door neighbor," Ed reminded him.

"I thought they burned him out once or twice."

"They did. Came back with a sign that is still on his front lawn. 'I'M BLACK, BAD and BACK.' They haven't bothered him since."

"Who did the fire? One of your guys, Ed?" Bill kidded.

"If Ernie did the fire, believe me, Clarence would be history."

"Ernie, the arsonist. Isn't that the guy who burned his own house down while smoking in bed? Tried to collect on two policies?"

"Nah, that was Arnie," Ed said.

Karl and Bill were hysterical.

"What?"

"Er-nie, Ar-nie," Karl sang out concordantly.

"Ar-nie, Er-nie," Bill chorused.

"Let's call the whole thing off," the two harmonized hysterically.

"Yeah, you guys laugh now. But wait and see what Ernie comes up with concerning those two birds you want barbecued," Ed admonished.

"Yeah, just don't call Arnie by mistake," Bill positively pealed with laughter.

Chapter 41

Thanksgiving had come and gone, Angelica's troops having thoroughly enjoyed a special day the likes of which many in her band of followers had never experienced—*excess* being the single word that perfectly described their celebration. Barbara Giordano had spared no expense in presenting the finest in fare for her fifty guests.

The following weeks flew by with many classes, drills, and highly-specialized training sessions. Morale was high among Angelica Manns' young men and women. Winter was two days away. Peter addressed the group informally. Everyone gathered around the room in long-sleeved camo shirts. Lightly starched utility trousers stood neatly bloused at the tops of spit-shined boots.

Peter smiled handsomely. "Make yourselves comfortable."

Everyone dropped to the carpeted floor and faced forward. Sharon leaned a shoulder against Harold's. He draped an arm casually around her hip.

"Everybody comfy?"

"Hungry," several answered.

"Later," Peter reproved. "And when we do eat this afternoon, it's going to be light. You don't want a bellyful of food on tomorrow's predawn run. This is not an exercise. This is for real. It's our chance to show what we have learned and what we're capable of handling. Anyone here who wants to bow out on this first assault, for any reason, let me know now."

Betty raised her hand. "I have a cold," she kidded.

"Sneeze and you're fucking dead." Peter wasn't kidding. "Anyone?" he asked again, taking in the entire room. "All right. Zero two hundred hours we gather in the compound and push out. I want every piece of equipment and gear checked, checked again, then triple-checked beforehand. Are we clear?"

"Clear as a bell," Harold said.

Everyone acknowledged.

"Especially those batteries," Peter added.

"He's got batteries on the brain," Malcolm whispered.

"Speak up, Malcolm," Peter snapped.

"I said you're the brain," Malcolm said grinning.

"Batteries run our vehicles, our radios, our laser sights, and our GPS. Yes, I've got batteries on the brain."

"Fuckin' guy's got ears, too," Malcolm whispered in an even lower tone.

"Speak up so we can all hear you, Malcolm," Peter insisted.

"I said I hear you, man. NAVSTAR stuff and all."

"All right. Everybody got their part down pat?"

Everyone acknowledged in the affirmative.

"Okay. Now let's talk real world." Peter paused until he knew he had everyone's rapt attention. "There might be some casualties in such a siege. How well we do our job will impact greatly on the success of this mission; however, the fact remains that it is possible we could suffer losses," he reemphasized. "Again, I'm going to ask if there is anyone here for any reason who wants to sleep in. No questions asked."

Again, Betty had her hand up. "I really think I've got the flu," she said through a giggle.

"Ms. M going to be there with us?" Janice asked, sounding nervous.

"Wouldn't miss it. Right up there in front. Leading the way." Peter waited. "All right then. It's a go."

Forty-eight fists punched the air high above their heads. Peter felt the power and put his fist up, too.

Priscilla waved her hand in earnest.

"Yes, Priscilla."

"What did Ms. M say about us, Peter?" was her question.

Once again, Peter waited until he had everyone's full attention.

"Shh," half the room insisted of the others.

"Ms. M said, and I quote, 'They're nowhere near ready for the big time, but this operation will whet their appetites. However, the troops are no longer recruits; they are soldiers. Soon they will be seasoned soldiers.'"

Ninety-six hands applauded, and even Priscilla seemed

satisfied.

It was a bitter cold morning. The twentieth of December. Not a star was visible. The troops woke up to flurries; the wind was out of the west at twenty-five miles per hour. Nineteen degrees with the wind chill factor. The sky was jet black above a frozen ground covered with a thin blanket of snow.

Peter threw up the hood of his parka and flattened the Velcro strip at his throat. In those next few minutes, fifty warm bodies boarded the bus. An hour later they arrived, parking the vehicle fifty yards off the North Road. The troops went in on foot, balaclavas covering their faces. Through the pitch-black woods they trekked; due north to the bluffs. Toward the Villa they swept. Twelve of the fifty assault cadre scaled the fourteen-foot walls with rope ladders after killing the electric fencing. A dozen soldiers were over and within the perimeter. Twelve more rose from four directions. Another twenty-four surrounded the retreat run by a group of nuns.

Janice and Priscilla remained behind in the bus: Ol' Yeller.

Four armed guards within the walls fell silently as single arrows pierced their nape or throat. Two others toppled over like wooden end pins off a bowling alley, cups of coffee staining the snowy floor. Another guard caught a movement and had his automatic weapon well into his shoulder as Sharon sliced the man's throat with a blade the breadth of which could easily spread butter in a single application along the length and width of a good size loaf of French bread.

Danny signaled, and two dozen troops moved from the courtyard into the convent without a solitary sound. Karen was the last one in and closed the door behind her.

"What the fuck?" were the man's last words as Betty put an arrow through the agent's heart. Through was the operative word. For it entered and exited his body like a whisper, assuring that he was surely dead. The man fell off to one side. The noise brought another. Harold put a silencer to the man's temple and told him mum's the word. But the man did not listen, so Harold shot him dead in the eye.

It was not a quiet death. Not so noisy as to wake the nosy neighbors had there been any. But it was enough to raise the curiosity of a nun.

Peter put a finger to his lips as she stepped into and through an archway. Miraculously, the woman hesitated, taking in the scene without making one. Peter moved her ahead and into a large area.

Two dozen troops went in pairs from room to room on the ground floor, disarming three men and a female FBI agent, indicated by three large capital letters on the back of her jacket.

Carol and Tanya set aside four handguns then searched the quartet for other weapons.

Half a dozen nuns were rounded up along the hallway, which made seven.

"Now, how many are you all together? Outside and in: guards, feds, nuns, and the civilian witnesses," Peter asked the female agent, pointing a pistol at her pretty face. "I'll ask you only once."

"Twenty-eight in total," one of the male agents answered-up immediately.

"I think he likes her," Peter said and smiled beneath the warm woolen hood, covering all but his eyes.

With hand signals, Guadalupe had given Peter a headcount as well as a current death toll suffered by the opposition.

"So, there are seven dead outside; two dead within; seven nuns now standing over there; and the four of you makes twenty. Where are the other eight warm bodies?" Peter demanded.

"There is no one else here," one of the nuns shouted, taking a step toward Peter.

Peter raised his pistol and shot the nun between the eyes. "Probably the sister of the sister who hit me on the knuckles as a boy," he announced playfully. "What a bitch on wheels she was.

"Now, we know that there are civilians here who are a part of or planning on entering into the witness protection program. Sister, pay attention, please. Get her away from that body, Number Twenty-seven."

Carol helped the sister to her feet. "Stand over there," she insisted.

"Distractions. So where was I? Ah, yes. Same question. Where are they?" Peter asked patiently.

"Sleeping," another nun answered quietly.

"Sleeping," Peter echoed. "Sleeping where?" Peter turned and addressed the pretty-boy of the group. "Get this one right and you get to live. I'll ask you only once."

The man shook his head.

Peter shot him on the spot. "And then there were three."

The female agent had completely lost it, screaming hysterically, having to be held at bay by her two colleagues. It was clear that she stood on the threshold of death's door.

"If not for your own safety, then for the safety of your two remaining pals, tell me where to find these people. Otherwise, it's sayonara, baby."

"Downstairs," she screamed, kicking and biting her two associates who held her life by a thread.

"How many?"

"Eight," one of the men answered. "Wine cellar; west end of the building."

Peter gestured.

A full five minutes had passed before Betty and several others returned with six men and two women, all wearing civilian clothing.

"All right. Put the nuns in that corner," Peter ordered. "You three, over there," he directed. "Number Twenty-nine; handcuff one to the other and take these witnesses outside. Where is his coat?" Peter suddenly questioned, aiming his pistol at the tall figure at the end.

"He said he doesn't have one," Allan said.

"Bring him over here."

Allan brought the six-foot-three man up to Peter.

"Take his wallet."

Allan patted down the man's pockets. "He doesn't have one."

"Where's your wallet?" Peter asked.

"Lost it," the man replied, staring down at the two bodies.

"Put your hands on top of your head," Peter demanded. "Do it."

Allan searched the man thoroughly, in and around his crotch. "He's clean," Allan said. "I searched everyone."

"Yes, but I don't think this guy's a witness," Peter surmised, sizing him up carefully. "Roll up your sleeves."

The man rolled up one sleeve and then the other, extending both hands, palms up.

Peter grabbed the man's wrist, twisting his forearm. A faded tattoo of a bulldog with U.S.M.C. initialed just below it verified what

Peter suspected. "I do believe you're in the wrong group, fella. Yes?"

The man said nothing.

Peter put the gun to his head. "I'll ask you one more time."

A hand reached out of nowhere and snatched the gun away from Peter.

"You. Over there in the corner with your cronies," Angelica ordered, pushing the tall man toward his ilk. She handed the gun back to Peter. "Put it away," she said calmly, assuming command. "Except for these seven, tie everyone else up and put them in the cellar under lock and key," she directed. "Like Number Eleven just said, Number Twenty-nine, do handcuff one to the other and take these witnesses outside on the double."

Danny radioed the perimeter. All twelve stations came back in code. Danny nodded. Once outside, the file of five men and two women were brought through the woods, heading toward Ol' Yeller. Janice and Priscilla had given Danny a green light at a precise interval, and the eight prisoners were led aboard and directed to the rear of the bus. They were instructed to lie face down on the floor, heads in the aisle, legs beneath the seats. The eight were told that if anyone so much as twitched, they would all be executed.

Peter, for the life of him, could not understand why Angelica had only taken the witnesses, leaving the others behind to live. He would have done things quite differently. He would have executed the nuns and feds, or at the very least, taken them along as hostages. Peter was about to learn an important lesson in restraint. He was about to learn from the very best.

Chapter 42

Barbara Giordano beamed, stepping forward to the edge of the stage, looking directly at her audience. "So, I understand that you had a most busy morning. And a rather successful one at that. First, I want to congratulate each and every one of you. You did yourselves proud. What you contributed to the organization is invaluable. You cannot put a price tag on what you have accomplished. But I'm standing before you this evening to try and do just that. Each of you has been assigned a numbered account in one of the strongest banks in the world with assets in the multibillions of dollars. And you won't have to wire Switzerland to check your balance, either," she assured them with a sincere smile. "Besides which, they pay out such paltry interest," she added gleefully. "Your monies, and I do mean yours, are secured in the Cayman Islands, where all of you will be vacationing before long. Bottom line? One million dollars each. No strings attached. And no taxes to worry about. We don't pay them, so why should you. Not bad for several months training and preparation. Not bad for one night's work. Wouldn't you agree?"

Everyone present applauded their good fortune, many of them shaking their heads in total disbelief.

"Now, some of you may be wondering why we took those seven civilians who are either in or were about to enter into the witness protection program. Why didn't we kill or take the feds as hostages? Why not the nuns? Answer. Unnecessary blood; we got what we came for. Also, because the United States government does not negotiate with terrorists in a hostage situation. Why did we steal those seven witnesses? Simple. Secrets. Secrets are invaluable. Two of the seven hold a secret that I've been trying to unravel for many years." Barbara glanced at Angelica who was busying herself with paperwork behind a podium. "In a minute, I'm going to turn you over to your commander who wants to say a few words. But before I do that, I once again want to say what a splendid job you did. The fact that there was not a single casualty on our side speaks volumes as to your professionalism. If this morning could be looked at as a test, as far as I'm concerned, you'd all received an A plus. Thank you."

Wild applause filled the auditorium for a solid minute.

Angelica stepped to center stage and glowed. "What can I say that Mrs. G has not already said?" If Angelica was glowing, her troops were positively radiant; all forty-nine of them. "In a few minutes, we are going to begin our interrogation of the witnesses. The process will not be for the squeamish. Anyone who wants to stay behind may do so. That's it."

"Troops, ten-hut," Peter commanded.

Everyone came smartly to their feet. Betty sneezed.

Peter shook his head ever so slightly. "Dismissed."

"O-one m-mil-million dollars!" Danny roared.

"Nothing to sneeze at," Peter joked, hitting Betty playfully on the shoulder.

"Good thing I didn't do that back there in the courtyard," she swore.

"I thought you were kidding about a cold."

"I was. But I felt something coming on though."

"You wanna bow out of this and get some rest?"

"Are you kidding? I wouldn't miss this for the world."

"You're a sick puppy."

"Not half as sick as you, Peter," she assured him with a grin.

"Let's go."

Angelica and her troops filed into another room annexed to a small building adjacent to the compound. It was cold and dark inside. Barbara's people directed a container wheeled along a narrow passage leading to a row of bleachers, pointing the way with tiny beams of light. Fifty soldiers took a seat, forming a horseshoe around a rectangular wooden box that sat on a concrete floor no more than ten feet away. There was no doubt that something alive was contained beneath its cover. A dull, knocking sound came from within at random intervals.

A gradual illumination appeared some twenty feet above the crate, the beam of light increasing in intensity as it descended slowly from the ceiling, flooding the box and floor. Suddenly it stopped, its diameter narrowing until it sharply shrouded the ebony cover. Two men with crowbars appeared out of nowhere and pried off the lid. The figure inside lay still, partly covered with a rich pitch-black loam. Something odd was happening. The earth around the body was moving in such a way that ripples would disturb a stagnant pond. The eyes of the creature told something of the hours of terror. The bed of night crawlers told it all. The woman suddenly heaved her legs over the side of the high-walled coffin-like container. The wrap of rope that bound her wrists and ankles remained somewhat indistinguishable from the coil across her shoulder. Finally, the long black snake slithered to a corner of the box, then out and down its side, hanging but a foot off the floor.

One of the two men holding crowbars assisted the thirty-year-old woman from the bin. The other man roughly ripped the wide strip of duct tape from her mouth. The woman sobbed and shook violently, expelling filth and sucking air in steady spurts until a single breath filled her lungs with renewed life and meaning.

"Ready to talk now?" Barbara asked, walking nonchalantly to center stage.

The woman's head pounded up and down like a pneumatic drill.

Barbara nodded appreciatively. "Good girl."

The woman lost her balance and toppled to one side, crying and shivering on stage from fear as well as from the cold.

"The tall man with no coat and no credentials?" Barbara questioned. "Who is he?"

The woman couldn't bring herself to speak, her wails and whining resounding off the chamber walls.

"Put her back in the box," Barbara ordered sharply.

The woman shot her bound hands outward, tossing about a filthy head of hair as if it were a tattered flag flapping mercilessly in a sixty-mile-an-hour wind. Dirt flew in all directions. "Agent," she managed in a shaky incoherent shrill, struggling to stay on her feet.

"Excuse me?"

"Federal agent."

"Honest injun?"

The naked woman nodded hysterically, staring off in the

direction of the clearly visible five-foot limbless length.

Barbara acknowledged the woman's concern. "Nonpoisonous is my understanding. Would stay alive for weeks on worms is what I'm told. You, too, they tell me. Until *all* the worms were gone. Then it would burrow where it pleases for nourishment."

The woman fell then immediately struggled to her knees. "Ple-e-e-e-ase," she bleated. A clump of dirt fell from her body.

"The identification we found in your purse. Is that you, Jo Ann? Or is that your new name?"

"New," she swore.

"Then what is your real name?"

"Joan."

"Joan. Joan what?"

Joan looked at the box behind her. She trembled. "Joan Blaton."

"Would you like to tell us where you're from, Joan?"

"New Orleans."

"And where were they going to relocate you?"

"England."

"Where in England?"

"I don't know."

"You don't know?"

"Mr. Addington said—"

"Who's Mr. Addington?"

She shivered. "The agent who was with us at the convent."

"You were saying?"

"He said I'd know soon enough."

"You mean you had no say in the matter?"

The woman shook her head.

"Why were you entering the witness protection program, Joan?"

Joan started crying quite loudly. "Are y-you going to k-kill me?" she stammered, shaking from head to toe.

"I'm going to let the snake take care of that, little by little, if you tell me even the tiniest lie. All right?"

"I won't lie, I swear it."

"That's good, Joan. Now tell me why."

"I know you're going to kill me when I do."

"No, I'm not."

Joan nodded. "I don't care. I beg you to shoot me. I'll tell you everything. Just don't put me back in that box."

"No one is going to shoot you. And no one is going to put you back in that box if you tell me the absolute truth." Barbara waited.

"I was witness to a shooting."

"Fatal?"

Joan nodded.

"Who shot who?"

"Mr. Giancano shot a police captain last month in Florida."

The Miami murder had been highly publicized in all the papers. Mr. Giancano was a Mob boss who the authorities could not land behind bars—although the feds had tried for years.

"Mr. Giancano, you say."

The woman bobbed her head.

"Gene Giancano?"

"Yes."

"And who are you to Mr. Giancano?"

"His mistress," she said succinctly.

"His mistress?"

Joan shivered in the affirmative.

"Why would you hand the government Mr. Giancano's head?"

"Because the state of Florida said they would send me to the chair if I didn't cooperate."

"What was your role, Joan?" Barbara asked with special interest.

"I lured a police captain to my apartment and fixed him a drink to make him sleep."

"You mean a Mickey," Barbara said rhetorically.

Joan nodded.

"And for this they told you that you were headed for the electric chair?"

"I thought he had passed out, but he was on his cell when I was inside changing."

"And?"

"And Mr. Giancano let himself in with a passkey and shot him in cold blood."

"What was the game plan, Joan?"

"Just for Mr. Giancano to talk to him when the captain came to. To reason with him."

"And you believed him."

"I was a damn fool."

"Is there a trial date set?"

"Sometime in February, they said."

"And you're their whole case?"

"Yes."

"What had the captain told his people on the phone before Mr. Giancano shot him?"

"Where he was. That's how they found me, they said. Mr. Giancano had the body moved from my apartment, but it made no difference."

"What about the others?" Barbara asked carefully. "The five who were to be relocated?"

"I don't know." Joan shook violently. "We were told not to discuss our situation."

"By whom?"

"By Mr. Addington. He stayed with us night and day."

"And you can't tell me anything about the others?"

Joan shook her head. "Just that the older couple is together; husband and wife. That's all I know, honestly."

"The other three are alone in this like yourself?"

Joan nodded.

"All right. Untie her and stand her up," Barbara said, turning her back to the woman. "Hose her down and put her in a cell."

Joan managed to stand firmly on her feet as two men came forward with hoses and hit her with a steady stream of water from both sides. A moment later they led her away.

Several lights came on in the room, and Barbara was facing the troops.

"We once had a man lose his mind in half an hour in that box. That woman is very strong-willed. Her information will undoubtedly prove invaluable. In a few minutes, we'll see a demonstration of a different sort. Not as dramatic, perhaps. But certainly effective. Why don't we take a break?" Barbara turned to one of her people. "Get that snake the hell out of here. Christ, I'll have nightmares," she said, turning back to the group, smiling warmly at Angelica.

Fifteen minutes later, Carlos Saveranti was carried out on a massive wooden cross then placed on the concrete floor by four of Barbara Giordano's men. The overhead lights turned blinding, shining down on the outstretched figure bound at his wrists, ankles, neck, and the trunk of his body with five-eighths-inch nylon rope. Carlos was raised as if crucified rather than resurrected, the base of the cross planted in a space provided within a huge concrete block. Eerily, the man resembled the figure of Christ, suspended in what appeared to be a large cloth diaper covering his privates.

"Jesus!" Sharon said and received a poke in the ribs from Harold.

Barbara walked up to the cross. "Carlos. I'm hearing reports that you are being most uncooperative," she said, looking up at the man.

Carlos slowly cocked his head toward Barbara then spit down upon her.

Barbara wiped the shoulder of her paisley blouse with the opposite sleeve, calmly gesturing to the men before her. The four figures left then returned a moment later with two 4 x 8 sheets of three-quarter ply. Each board was spiked with one-inch galvanized nails spaced no less than three inches apart. The sheets were placed end to end lengthwise upon the floor, nail side up. One of the men left then returned in less than a minute with a chainsaw. He pulled the starter cord, and the saw fired up immediately.

Barbara gave the signal, and the man noisily cut a narrow wedge in the base of the fourteen-foot crucifix. There was no question as to which direction the cross and Carlos would start to fall if given the lightest crosscut touch.

"Well, Mr. Saveranti, or whatever your real name is," Barbara said above the steady low-speed idle. "Are you ready to rise to the occasion, or do you choose to experience the true meaning of what it's like to be nailed to the cross? Metaphorically speaking, of course."

Again, the man spit at Barbara but missed. Barbara turned her back to the figure. The man with the chainsaw hit the throttle. Carlos, his cries, and the cross came down thunderously upon the nail bed. Seconds later, the stage went dim and became as quiet as a church.

Barbara faced the troops. "When he regains consciousness, I can almost assure you he'll tell us what we want to know."

The lights came on in the room, and the troops were staring at Barbara Giordano as though she had completely lost her mind. Their eyes traveled from the bloody figure lying motionless on the plywood board, back to their benefactor.

"Oh, we've done this thing from time to time," Barbara assured everyone. "Especially effective with Latinos and Spaniards. We've never lost a single soul on the fourteen footer; have we?"

The two men standing on either side of Carlos shook their heads simultaneously.

Barbara smiled knowingly. "It's the eighteen footer that's the killer. No one's come back from the dead on that descent. Not even Jesus Christ would want to go through such an ordeal. Believe me. They do talk."

Sharon was crying quietly. Guadalupe placed a hand on her shoulder from behind. Karen gave the tearful girl a knock against the knee.

Barbara picked up on the scene. "That's all right. No one's asking any of you to digest this all in a day. Takes some getting used to. Took me years."

Sharon wiped her eyes on the back of her sleeve.

Barbara made a gesture, and in a matter of minutes, the area before them was attended to.

"Now. We saw how Joan had a change of heart after being left alone for ten hours in a box to think things over. And you witnessed how we had to fight with Carlos tooth and nail before we brought him back down to earth. Well, we're going to bring out a couple in a moment that didn't put themselves or us through any unnecessary grief. I think you'll find their story remarkable. It begins sometime before the end of World War II, a little more than a half a century ago.

"I'm going to let them tell you their own story. I'm just going to set the scene. Buchenwald. A concentration camp in East Germany. You are to be their interrogators. I want you to concentrate," she began to explain. "I want you to draw the story out of them. I'd like everyone to participate. Emma and Emil Jewett have agreed to answer all your questions. They will volunteer very little at first. All right. I guess we can begin."

Barbara summoned forth the elderly couple who was directed to two chairs set in the center of the room. Emma and Emil took a seat.

All the lights around the room dimmed. The stage was bathed in a soft light from behind.

Peter got right to it. "Why were the two of you brought into the witness protection program? Mr. Jewitt."

"Our government is trying to learn the identity and location of a person they believe to be a threat to the nation," Mr. Emil Jewitt said forthrightly in a thick Yiddish accent.

"Who is this person?" Harold asked.

"I don't know," the old man answered truthfully.

"Then how can you be of service to the government?" Guadalupe challenged.

"By providing them with background information they feel is pertinent to their search."

"Mrs. Jewett," Betty said.

"Emma."

"Emma, we're told that your story begins near the end of the war; that is, World War II."

Emma nodded her wavy, gray head of hair.

"Precisely at what point was that?"

"Shortly before the liberation; nineteen forty-five."

"And what exactly were the two of you doing at that time that's relevant to this matter?" Betty continued.

Emma deferred to her husband.

"Before I was arrested, I was part of the underground, trying to save Jewish children from being sent to death camps."

"And where did they send you?" Steve inquired.

"Buchenwald."

"I thought Buchenwald *was* a death camp," Karen said.

Emil shook his head. "Buchenwald was not an extermination camp. It was a work camp. Although many of us died there."

"How?" Gerald asked.

"From the work. From the beatings. From disease. From a broken heart," Emil Jewitt answered.

"Wh-what k-kind of wo-work did you do, Mr. Jewitt?" Danny asked with interest.

"I worked in the quarry."

Danny looked toward Karen for amplification.

"Stone mine," Karen whispered.

"How could that kill you?' Priscilla pressed.

Emil smiled. "We had to carry very heavy stones up one hundred and forty-eight steps. You couldn't rest. If the stone was too big, you wouldn't last. If it was too small, you might be beaten, or even shot for laziness."

Priscilla put her head down.

"How many children were in the camp?" Greg put forth.

"Seven hundred by the end of the war."

"Wow!" Charlotte exclaimed.

"How many children had you saved, sir?" Billy asked with reverent respect.

"Many," was the man's succinct answer.

"Getting back to the information you provided concerning the identity of this person that the government is interested in, what does it have to do with those war years?" Peter queried.

"One of the men whose sister died in an extermination camp in Treblinka survived the war and eventually married a young woman who had survived the horrors of Auschwitz."

"Where's Treblinka?' Carol asked.

"Town in Poland," Emma answered. "Death camp."

"And what is so significant about the brother and his wife, aside from their ability to survive?" Peter pressed.

"The significance actually lies with the murdered sister," Emma said. "Murdered by the Nazis."

"Go on."

"Unbeknownst to the young brother and most of the outside world, a child was born to the sister. A child whose identity is shrouded in secrecy," Emma explained.

"What was the mother's name?" Peter asked impatiently.

"Hannah Abramowicz," Emil answered.

Angelica's eyes fell upon the old man like an anvil.

"And her husband?"

Emil shrugged. "She didn't have one."

"And her brother and his wife?"

Again, the man shrugged. "Supposed suicides," Emil said skeptically.

"But you don't seem to think so."

"No."

"Why?"

"You don't take your own life after having survived the Holocaust."

A dozen heads nodded in agreement.

"Last known residence?"

"Peter, please," Barbara interrupted. "Give someone else a chance," she insisted.

"Last known address?" Harold picked up.

"Stockholm."

Angelica rounded the ball of her boot back and forth against the concrete floor.

"Where's that?" Jennifer whispered.

"Sweden," Karen whispered back.

"W-what h-happened to the ch-child?" Danny wanted to know.

"Anna. A beautiful little girl who grew up and had a family of her own," Emma said. "A handsome, rich husband with whom she had a gorgeous little boy."

Barbara's eyes were glued to Angelica.

"Wh-what hap-pened to the boy?"

"No one seems to know," Emma said.

"Is this boy who the government is looking for?" Billy asked.

Emil nodded. "All grown up now, I suppose."

"And the parents of this boy?" Pricilla queried. "Anna and her rich husband."

"Murdered," Emma stated.

"I still don't get it," Betty said, frustration furrowing her brow. "What was the connection to the work camp and those death camps?"

Barbara gestured for Emil to elaborate.

"The man's sister, Hannah Abramowicz, was gassed by the Nazis in Treblinka shortly after she gave birth to Anna," Emil explained. "The infant was smuggled out safely. Hannah's brother, however, was told that the child had died in its mother's womb. But Emma learned the truth through other survivors long after the war was over. Fearing for the safety of their own child, Anna and her husband raised the boy secretly, moving clandestinely across three continents over a period of several years."

"Why did Anna and her husband feel it was necessary to move around so secretly, especially after the war was over?" Betty pressed.

"Because of who fathered Hannah's child, Anna."

"Who?" Betty questioned.

"The Führer himself," Emma answered.

"Adolf Hitler?" Peter laughed hysterically.

Emma and Emil nodded solemnly.

"Then . . . this person who the government is looking for is the supposed grandson of Hitler, you're saying," Peter reasoned.

Again, Emma and Emil affirmed that it was so.

"What's this boy's name?"

"Angelo," Emma answered.

"I don't follow this," Karen said quietly.

"It's very complicated," Sharon agreed.

"It's really not that complicated once you see the big picture," Barbara Giordano said. "You see, I've been collecting bits and pieces of this remarkable family mystery for more than thirty years. But the trail continues with two people who apparently hold yet another piece of the puzzle. Emma and Emil. Few knew where these two were. Well, now they're here with us.

"It's not too hard to understand what happened if you knew how beautiful a woman Hannah was," Barbara continued. "So beautiful, in fact, that Hitler had to have her for himself. It was prophesied that for the next three generations a curse would befall the nations of the world, so long as any offspring from that original seed of evil remained alive. It was said that as malevolent as the German leader may have been, that was how benevolent a soul Hannah Abramowicz was to those whose lives she touched. Hence, the struggle of good and evil prevails. Believe it or not," Barbara added.

"Believe it," Emil Jewitt said emphatically. "Hitler possessed Hannah's body but never ever her soul."

"She must have been some looker," Harold said.

"From reports, she was said to have been the most beautiful woman on planet earth," Barbara maintained. "'A Jewish angel,' several Nazi leaders close to the chancellor had joked."

"As pure and as beautiful in here," Emma swore, tapping her breast firmly.

Barbara smiled satisfactorily, looking straight ahead at Angelica. "As beautiful as our very own angel."

"I'll s-second that," Danny said, getting to his feet.

Forty-eight soldiers rose and followed Danny's lead, smartly saluting their commander in chief.

Emil and Emma sat in stony silence.

Angelica's troops settled down.

"Very few people in the world today know that Hannah Abramowicz first bore the Führer three male children then conceived a late-in-life child before he sent her off to Treblinka," Barbara continued. "Unbeknownst to the chancellor, Hannah was already three months pregnant. Anna was the fourth child who miraculously survived the death camp as Emil has explained."

"And where are Anna and her rich husband today?" Gwendolyn asked. "Don't they know where their son Angelo is?"

"Anna and her husband divorced, and she married his younger brother. Her first husband was found murdered soon after, along with Anna," Barbara said. "Angelo was eleven."

"Did the stepdad take care of Angelo?" Priscilla persisted.

"He did indeed, before committing suicide, or so it was determined."

"What was the stepfather's name?" Betty asked.

"Anthony Reynolds." Barbara watched Angelica set her eyes on the ceiling. "After that, the trail turns cold, as does the whereabouts of Hannah's three male children," Barbara concluded.

Chapter 43

Barbara and Angelica sat together in the study—studying one another. It was six p.m., and the two had just finished discussing business. Barbara held a fine Austrian crystal stemmed snifter of brandy before her. Angelica sipped mineral water with a wedge of lemon suspended in an expensive water glass. The older woman shifted her eyes to the fireplace then spoke. "Quite an interesting afternoon, Angelica. Wouldn't you say?"

"Are you making any headway with the other witnesses?"

"Oh, they're watching the video of Joan and Carlos' candid performances earlier. I'm sure they'll be anxious to talk to us by tomorrow. I'm giving them the evening to sleep on it. But I'm very much interested in that couple. Emma and Emil. Aren't you?"

"You don't really believe that story, do you?"

"Every single word, my angel."

"You do?"

"Let me ask you something. How do you suppose those two survived the camps? I know for a fact that men like Emil, who worked in the quarry, didn't last two weeks. A month at most. How come he did?"

"Ingenuity. Good fortune, I guess. Emil did what he had to do to stay alive. They both did, I'm sure."

Barbara shook her head. "Instant obedience, that's how they lasted. They did what they were told to do and did so immediately, not having to wait to be told to do something. That's why they survived. I'm sure ingenuity and good fortune paid off in spades, too. But immediate obedience was the key to survival in those labor camps. This morning I witnessed such obedience—and truth—with respect to the interrogation of those two."

"You mean that far-fetched story? Four direct descendants of the Führer, for God's sake! You can't be serious."

"One of whom grew up, married, and gave birth to a beautiful boy. A boy that the most powerful government on the face of the globe can't find."

"That's because he doesn't exist."

"Oh, but he does."

"Then why can't they find him?"

"Because a certain faction of that government allows him to operate with impunity just as I operate the largest drug cartel in the country without fear of reprisal. Soon I will control the import and export of drugs across three continents. Perhaps, one day, across the board."

"And what is this faction that bestows such protection?" Angelica asked, setting down her glass.

"You know as well as I do."

"Presume that I do not."

"A ruling body headed by the direct descendants of the Nazi dictator himself."

"So you've actually bought into that demented couple's account."

"A true account, I told you. Each and every word."

Angelica leaned back in the leather chair and stared directly at the overhead oak beams. "And how do you know this?"

"Because the pieces of a fifty-year-old puzzle are beginning to form a picture. I know that one son had three of his brothers killed. Two of whom were priests."

"And what and who is this ruling body, Barbara?"

"The Triumvirate."

"The Triumvirate?"

"Yes. Karl Hitler, son of Adolf Hitler, a.k.a Karl Baceni, heads this Trinity."

"Karl and who else?"

"A mercenary who is known by few as Edward Baceni, and a monsignor at the Vatican who goes by the name of William or Bill Baceni; that is, when they're using surnames at all. Regarding this elaborate cover-up operation, Ed controls Tom Harden, who is the mayor of Macon, Georgia. Bill controls Sheriff Tom Hayes of Bibb County, Georgia. And Karl controls the governor of that state, Al Atkins, as well as the powers that be in forty-nine other states. A dynasty, my darling. The Triumvirate controls and therefore rules the world economy."

"The Triumvirate," Angelica said and smiled disingenuously, "who rules the world economy."

"Yes."

"Three men control the world in essence?"

Barbara nodded.

"And Karl Baceni is the son of Hitler, you say?"

"Along with Ed and Bill."

"A mercenary and the monsignor, you say."

"I say."

"How and when did they all come together?"

"They met many years after the liberation. Karl, the eldest, was groomed from a very early age to one day hold the seat of power."

"And where is this alleged seat?"

"Where it was and still is, Angelica. The Vatican."

Angelica stood and went over to the fireplace, gazing into the flames. "And why would you assume that I have knowledge of this body of three? This Triumvirate that you claim exists. You do assume that I know something, don't you?"

"Because your past parallels the mystery that I've been following for three decades. Because you operate with impunity as I do. Because you took your mother's given name and made it part of your own. Because you took and rearranged your given name and gave it feminine wings. Because your surname, sir, is actually Reynolds. Angelo A. Reynolds. Or as another document shows, Baceni, abridged from Bacenowitz, which was taken from your maternal grandmother's brother's wife's maiden name. Hannah Abramowicz was your mother's mother, second mistress, along with Eva Braun, to the Chancellor of Germany; Adolf Hitler. You are his grandson, and Karl is your uncle. Angelica Ann Manns is quite inventive, my dear. Really says it all. Doesn't it?"

Angelica stood in silence.

"Should I go on?" There was no response. "Your stepfather, Anthony Reynolds, had a first wife who bore him two sons. Carson and Butch-Lee. Your stepbrothers. Both of whom you killed, of course. For years I was busy searching for Anna's son. Only recently have I learned from a little bird that the son had an operation in Sweden.

Another of your well-kept secrets, dear. World governments were searching high and low for Hitler's grandson when it was his transsexual granddaughter that they should have been looking for since your return from Stockholm. Of course, it was Karl, your uncle, who protected you all along the line."

Angelica held her palms before the fire as if holding back a blaze.

"Of course, I didn't know for certain about Hannah's daughter, Anna," Barbara continued. "Emma's and Emil's testimony made it all clear. But you. You had everyone fooled, including me. That exhibition you put on in South America certainly erased any lingering doubt. But it was that trip many years ago to Stockholm with your parents that put things back in their proper perspective once I realized who your mother actually was. Oh, and that curious remark you made about never wanting a doctor or a dentist near you until the day you died. All perfectly clear now."

Angelica turned from the fire and stared directly into Barbara's eyes. "Angelo A. Reynolds is dead. The doctors in Stockholm killed him on the operating table. A little bit at a time. Operation after operation. Angelica Ann Manns emerged a woman. I am her."

"I fully understand," Barbara said softly and sincerely.

"Not in a million light-years."

"Have it your way."

"It is the way it is. The cover the operation affords me is unquestionably a benefit, but in no way was the reason for it. I knew that I was a freak of nature from a very early age. I knew that I was different. I knew nothing about my ancestry. Not until my stepfather's mother's friend visited. She was one of the survivors who knew the secret. She and Mother fought bitterly one evening. I overhead things. I was anything but a stupid child. By then I had had the operations and believed I could handle anything. Anything but Mother's lies. She was the daughter of Adolf Hitler. The fourth child. She lied about that and everything else. I found out about my uncles through a woman whose mother helped raise the brood until they were taken away from her and placed in some sort of state military institution for privileged children. Uncle Bill went off to a seminary. The only thing she knew beyond that was that the three boys would rise to a station in life beyond expectation and that they would want for nothing. I had asked her why everything was cloaked in such secrecy. She smiled and said that Hitler was Germany, but that Hannah, my maternal grandmother, was a Jew. She told me that my grandmother's beauty was known far and wide. All through Europe, in fact. She told me, too, that my beauty far exceeded all expectations.

"I murdered my mother that very evening. Made it look like an accident. It wasn't so much the omissions of truth as it was those outright lies when I confronted her. I also knew I had to eliminate anyone who knew the secret. I killed my father, too."

Barbara got up and stood before Angelica. "And now, *I* know," she said without expression.

"I know."

"I'm your confessor, too."

"I know."

"We have important work ahead of us, Angelica."

Angelica nodded.

"Will any of this get in the way?"

Angelica shook her head.

"You would rest easier, though, if Robert Redler and Liza Downs were dead. Yes?"

"Yes."

"I sanction it. Your people or mine?"

"Mine."

"Good night, Angelica."

Chapter 44

Four male soldiers bore Robert Redler's height, build, and coloring. Half a dozen females could have filled Liza Downs' shoes. Sharon practically demanded the part, but Angelica had said that she just wasn't right for it. Harold and Betty were chosen for the assignment. Sharon wanted to scream.

"You're too skinny," Harold said and laughed.

"It's winter. I can put on a heavier coat."

"Your hair is all wrong," Karen put forth bluntly, flipping Sharon's curls as she passed by the budding would-be actress.

"I could wear a wig."

"You'd have to learn to walk with stilts," Betty badgered.

"You?" Sharon snapped. "You'd probably forget your fucking lines."

"What lines?" Bobby wanted to know. "Just three words. How could anyone screw that up? 'You're dead, motherfuckers,'" he bantered pleasantly.

"Yeah, how could anybody blow that performance?" Priscilla giggled. "Tell me."

"'Yo-your de-dead, mo-motherfuckers,'" Danny said with a straight face. A good five seconds passed in dead silence before he cracked the faintest smile. The barracks suddenly exploded with hilarity that lasted several minutes. Harold's loud and infectious laughter kept the group going until everyone finally caught their breath.

When the troops finally calmed down, Harold spoke. "Well, you could always rush in with radio in one hand, handgun in the other, Danny boy," the Midwesterner said decidedly, grabbing his good friend around the neck and shoulders in a playful headlock and hug.

Warm smiles and light laughter continued as Danny's and Harold's wrestling antics played to conclusion. Even Sharon and Betty had quit their bickering and were caught up in the mirth.

"First, Redler and Downs have got to turn up," Guadalupe reminded everyone. "Otherwise, there's no show. They've been gone forever."

"Few weeks," Allan said. "They'll turn up soon enough."

Peter came in from the hallway and plopped himself down on a bed. "Well, you can raise the curtain, folks. They're heading back. Robert Redler and Liza Downs."

"Back from where?" Carol asked.

"Back from God knows where. All I know is that they'll be landing at Islip Airport sometime late tonight before heading home."

Harold and Betty looked at one another momentarily then went off together to prepare. Sharon shook her head and left, too. Most of the others headed off for lunch.

"What's the game plan?" Paul asked quietly.

"Where you been, fella?" Bobby questioned.

"Sick bay, dude. Caught Betty's cold."

"You been swappin' spit when no one's lookin', boy?"

"Like to swap more than just spit with that one."

"Yeah, you and half the other guys."

"What about the other half?" Paul kidded.

"They all wanna bang Ms. M," Bobby said most assuredly.

"Don't let anybody hear you talk like that, dude," Paul said anxiously.

"Why not?"

"I think Peter's lookin' to dip his stick there. That's why."

"Nah, Peter ain't got the balls. He's sure smart as hell, but he ain't no cocksman."

"Keep your voice down, dude." The two of them looked down the line of racks toward Peter.

"He's just kissin' her ass, figuratively speaking," Bobby whispered behind with a big grin.

"So, what's goin' on with Sharon? She on the rag or what?"

"Man, you don't know shit, do you?"

"I know she sure as shit was upset when I came in before. I guess she really wanted that assignment."

"What she really wanted was to be with Harold."

"Sharon and Harold an item, dude?"

"Man, open your fucking eyes."

"They're like brother and sister. No?"

"Well, he may see her as a sister, all right. But I'm tellin' you she sees him as her Prince Charming. Sharon's jealous as hell that Betty's on that assignment with him. Tell you something else. I think Peter's got the hots for Betty."

"He's a weird dude."

"But fucking smart like I said."

"Harold and Betty, too, for sure."

"Bunch of fucking intellectuals."

Paul laughed. "Yeah, who will probably help keep our dumb asses alive."

"Right on, fella," Bobby agreed, the pair smacking each other's palm loudly before grasping hands firmly in mutual accord.

Peter raised his head and looked their way before lying back down.

"So, how they gonna do it?" Paul pressed.

"Harold and Betty are simply going to walk in and wait for Redler and Downs to arrive. When they return . . . POW! A bullet apiece in their brains. It's what Redler had promised to do to Ms. M and Mrs. G in his second book."

"You shittin' me?"

"Man, you don't know shit. Don't you listen during lecture?"

"I listen, dude."

"I think you're payin' too much attention to Betty's boobs."

The two smacked palms again, laughing heartily.

"Come on. Let's go grab some chow," Bobby suggested.

"Right on, dude. But I'm buying," Paul kidded, beaming like a beacon, the two of them heading down the hall.

"What's that shit-eatin' grin?"

"Why, that's my million-dollar smile, my man. You forget?"

"Yeah, money you remember."

"Fuckin' A, dude."

"The A for Adolf, Paulie?"

Paul stopped dead in his tracks. "Bobby?"

Bobby came to a halt. "Yeah, man?"

"Listen. I, ah . . . you know all about that Hitler guy, right? I mean about the war and all."

"Sure, I guess."

"Well, I kinda made a fool of myself in front of Karen," Paul confided.

"How so?"

"Well, when she walked me down to sickbay, I opened up my big mouth about the Germans and World War I."

"Yeah, so?"

"Well, that's just it. I put the Germans in the First World War, and Karen said we fought them in the Second. I felt like such an ass an' all. She told me I oughta open up a history book before I open my mouth again."

"Karen said that?"

"Uh-huh."

"Well, I got a bulletin for Karen. We fought the Germans in both."

"Both what?"

"World Wars."

"You shittin' me or what?"

"Shit you not. We entered it late in the game. April of nineteen seventeen."

"Meaning the First World War?"

"Right. Kicked the shit out of them krauts. By November of nineteen eighteen, it was over."

"What about in the Second World War?"

"Well, where the First was mainly fought in Europe and the Middle East, the Second involved every occupied continent on the face of the globe."

"Wait a second. I'm getting a little mixed up. Was Hitler in World War One or Two?"

"Both, actually. He served in the First and was even decorated for bravery. During the Second, he was Germany's Nazi leader. Nineteen thirty-nine to forty-five."

"Bobby?"

"Yeah."

"I never graduated high school. I feel like such a dope next to you."

"I'll let you in on a little secret. Neither did Adolf Hitler."

"You shittin' me?"

"Shit you not, man."

"Bobby. Would you be my . . . you know. Like a teacher or somethin'?"

"Your tutor?"

"Yeah," Paul said excitedly.

"Be happy to."

"Cool, dude," Paul beamed. "Positively cool."

The young man was absolutely ecstatic. As a matter of fact, there was nothing cool, calm, or collected in Number Forty-seven's character to suggest any kind of composure save when the lad was sleeping. At all other times, Paul Dominguez was a high-strung individual who sought acceptance and definitely found it in Ms. M's body of believers.

Chapter 45

Betty and Harold got out of their wetsuits and fins and stepped into sets of thin but insulated garb. Each grabbed a waterproof bag of equipment and made their way in the dark along a hedgerow toward the back of the house. Three federal agents patrolled the rear of Robert's and Liza's home. Two feds surveilled the front property.

Betty came out of nowhere and put a black steel kempo karate blade to an agent's throat and drew a deep dark line. Harold felled another and crawled toward a third man who stood against a raised shed, hands buried deep inside his parka pockets. Number Twenty-two pulled him quietly from his perch and thrust a razor-sharp Raptor four inches into the base of the man's skull, twisting the handle sharply for good measure. The two assassins moved cautiously toward the front of the waterfront home.

An agent stood as still as a statue beside a juniper at the northwest corner off the road. Betty took him down in an instant and drove the kempo through his throat. A gurgling sound emanated from the body as she rolled him beneath the sprawling branches. Another agent appeared from the shrubbery adjacent to the stoop; two extended arms and hands sweeping the area in front of him, the front sight of his weapon settling on the back of Betty's head.

"That you?" the agent whispered.

"Shh," Betty urged, her back still toward the man, her hand raised for silence.

A vehicle was heading west along Riverside Drive. Coming toward them, high beams both lighting and pointing the way. As the automobile approached the sharp curve, the pair of headlights lit the scene, revealing the two figures standing on the lawn. Another figure lay flat on the ground beneath the coniferous shoulder-high branches. The agent's forefinger was about to terminate the life of Betty Jenkins, cult member Number Thirty-nine, when Harold sprang into action, sending his Raptor rapidly through the air but not in the nick of time. The agent's round caught Betty across the cheek as Harold's blade hung from the back of the man's jacket, just below the nape. The agent spun around and leveled his weapon at Harold. But Betty's kempo flew at the speed of light and, with the pinpoint accuracy of a laser, found its mark at the base of the man's skull. The agent fired a second round into the frozen ground before his body hit with a thud.

The car picked up speed and was gone in an instant as Harold and Betty proceeded with their mission, first moving the bodies beneath the juniper.

Within two minutes, the assassins were safely inside the dark house, waiting for Robert and Liza's return.

"They just took out five federal agents," a driver reported.

"Who took out?"

"Redler and Downs."

"I can't believe this shit. Are you sure it was Redler and Downs?"

"I saw them with my own eyes as I drove by. I could see and heard shots as I approached. When I came back around again, they were gone. They've got to be inside the house."

"Describe them," the merc ordered.

"Redler: Six foot. Dirty blond. Average build. Downs: Shoulder- length brown hair. Shapely. Five nine or ten. Both wearing one-piece suits."

"Jumpsuits?"

"I think."

"What about a vehicle?"

"Negative."

"Obviously came in from the back. Maybe by boat or on foot. All right. Listen up. I want you to be certain it's them in the house."

"Yes, sir."

"If they are, you know what to do."

"Yes, sir."

"If any of the neighbors saw, heard or reported anything and called the police, I want them to do a drive-by. That's all. A drive-by. Keep everyone away from the area. No one goes up to the house, including Police Chief Grear, state troopers, or anyone. Got it?"

"Yes, sir."

"I repeat, once you know for sure it's Redler and Downs in there, you've got a green light."

"Yes, sir."

Harold was tending to Betty's cheek wound by the night-light in the upstairs bathroom of the Redler home.

"What about that car?" Harold asked. "You think it was them?"

"I saw the driver. Male. Short. That's all. Probably just some guy coming home from partying."

"Let's hope."

"Probably doesn't know what the hell he saw or heard."

"What I'm concerned about is the house across the street. It was dark when we hit this place, but their upstairs is lit up like a Christmas tree."

"This is the holiday season," Betty said, leaning forward and giving Harold a kiss on the cheek as he applied pressure to hers. "Christmas is only four days away."

"Hurt?"

"Not a bit right now," she lied.

"Neighbors had to have called the police."

"Would have been here by now. This is not the city, you know."

"Guy in the car could call them when he gets home."

"Probably wants to go home and go to bed. People don't want to get involved anymore. He'll tell his wife or girlfriend all about it in the morning. And as for the neighbors across the street, I know how to put their minds at ease," she said, removing his hand from the bloody batch of gauze pads.

"What are you doing?"

"Watch."

Betty hit the light switch, then turned and opened the blinds. Next, she pulled Harold to her and kissed him fully on the lips, one hand at the back of his head, fingers spread, her other hand pressing the gauze pad back against her cheek. "Know what I want for Christmas?" she whispered.

The neighbors across the street believed they saw Liza and Robert embracing in the window. So did the driver of the car that had passed by moments before. The neighbor's husband had just switched

247

off the bedroom light as the passenger in the vehicle turned a remote-control Daihatsu key-entry device. Instantly, a magnificent brightness seemed to illuminate the entire neighborhood. The sound that immediately followed was a stupendous rush and roar of unimaginable power from which giant five-foot flames leapt simultaneously on all three levels of Robert and Liza's modest six room Cape. The basement as well as the first and second floors defined the shape of hell and heaven. Hues of yellow-orange to blood-red blues and purples beheld the conflagration as well as the acid test of Betty's burning desire for Harold. The two clung to one another in that final moment of cremation.

"They're barbecue," came the transmission from the vehicle in transit.
   "Clean?"
   "Like a put-away plate and just about as flat."
   "Secured it?"
   "Nobody's going in, nor certainly coming out. I can feel the heat from here, and I'm half a block away. It's an inferno. I hear the sirens in the distance."
   "Go on then. Get out of there," the voice said calmly. "We'll take over from here."
   "I'm en route."
   The merc got off the phone then stretched his arms and sighed satisfactorily.

Detective Sergeant John Kenny, commanding officer of the Arson/Bomb Squad, when asked for comments concerning the 3:15 a.m. blaze at the Riverside Drive home in Riverhead, emphatically called it, "Suspicious, suspicious, suspicious."
   It was 9:00 a.m. before fire officials along with plain-clothes officers from the bureau of special operations released any information to the press.

Liza and Robert sat in shock, watching and listening in disbelief to the coverage of the fire on the six o'clock news that evening. Details were sketchy. The report was live from the scene. Liza Downs and Robert Redler were reportedly very dead. The couple saw their neighbors who lived across the street. The wife was in tears, relating what she had heard during the early morning hours . . . something about what sounded like a gunshot shortly before the fire. The husband told how they had both witnessed a bright white light before the implosion.

"Both Liza and Rob were in what was the window up there," the husband explained, pointing to where the razed two-story structure had stood just fifteen hours earlier. "A light went on, and then a short time later, poof. Suddenly, they were gone. It was like spontaneous combustion. Then fire everywhere at once."

"Did you hear any explosion?" the female reporter asked the Cott family.

Both husband and wife shook their heads in unison.

"Like a big wind. Whoosh!" the wife replicated with a wave of an arm.

The husband nodded nervously. "Never saw anything like it in my life," he put forth. "The house just fell in on itself."

Instantly, the camera panned the charred remains of the former residence, zooming in on what had been a large barren red maple in the backyard that stood in line with a ramp and pier running out to a floating dock. Behind and off to the right of the property, stood a scorched shed.

Liza got up and turned off the set, then sat back down and wept.

"Well, at least the Cotts across the street have an unobstructed view of the water for the time being," Karl noted with relish, switching off the picture by remote.

The monsignor invoked a blessing and put his hands together in peaceful satisfaction.

The merc nodded approval, brushing away some crumbs off a soiled and tattered Hawaiian shirt.

Chapter 46

Sharon was stricken with grief, her emotions running between the poles of sadness and sorrow before being escalated beyond the bounds of anger to an incomprehensible rage. Her body trembled, and her voice thundered a single syllable. "WHY?" she shouted, shivering uncontrollably.

Angelica peered into the young woman's swollen fiery eyes.

Sharon shook her head violently from side to side. "Why?' she repeated in a whisper.

"I know how much you care and how much you must hurt," Angelica said compassionately.

Sharon nodded abruptly, burying her head in the crook of Angelica's arm, weeping bitterly as their commander stroked the soldier's shoulder and soothed her anguish with a series of shushes and sound assurances.

"We'll find those responsible, Sharon," Angelica promised. "We'll find Robert Redler and Liza Downs, too. Whoever is responsible for Betty and Harold's misfortune will pay dearly. We'll punish them unmercifully. We'll drive them to the depths of hell. I swear."

"It won't bring them back," Sharon managed.

"No, it won't," Angelica agreed. "But it will help ease the pain. You'll see."

"You should have sent me," Sharon said quietly.

Angelica shook her head above Sharon's. "No," the commander in chief said firmly. "Not for all the Nazi gold enshrined in the Riksbank," she put forth enigmatically.

Rumors ran rampant through the barracks as forty some odd soldiers voiced their opinions concerning the deaths of Harold and Betty. Sharon remained silent, sitting in front of Harold's footlocker, sifting through his personal effects.

"What do you think you're doing?" Charlotte asked, staring down from her bunk.

Sharon ignored her. From a wooden tray, she picked up a small silver cross attached to a filigree chain.

"Hey!" Charlotte snapped, watching Sharon pull the item down around her neck. "You have no business with that."

Sharon stood up, closed the lid of the locker, pushed it back under the rack with her foot then fixed her eyes on Charlotte, challengingly. "Say what?"

Charlotte shifted her eyes to a corner of the room where most of the troops were gathered. "Look," she said, setting them back on Sharon.

"I'm looking," Sharon replied acidly.

"You know we're not supposed to wear any rings or necklaces or jewelry of any sort," Charlotte whispered. "Besides, it's not yours."

"Nor yours, nor your business," Sharon stated, tucking the artifact beneath the collar of her cotton shirt before turning away.

"I'm supposed to report any violation of the rules, Sharon. You know that."

"You do what you have to do, Charlotte," Sharon said, heading out of the area.

"Shit," Charlotte said under her breath. She wanted to say much more. She wanted to remind Sharon of the fact that she had kept her mouth shut when Sharon and Harold had gone off together several weeks after arriving at Mrs. G's. A serious infraction of the rules.

A red linoleum line down the center of the barracks divided the squad bay. Males on one side. Females on the other. Separate lavatories were the only facilities that provided the sexes their privacy. Other than that, the young men and women lived together as a single unit. Although the troops shared the common area daily, no one was to cross the line once the lights went out for the evening. But Sharon and Harold had. Nothing of a sexual nature occurred. Sharon simply declared her feelings for the young man. Harold was amused at best. As time went by, Sharon believed that Harold was taking an interest in her.

She held fast to that belief as she did the cross at her throat, ascending a series of stairs that evening at the western wall leading to a tower. Danny saw her from the parapet and called out to her. He raised his people on the radio; he screamed for her to stop. A moment later, her body fell to and rolled along the pantile roof, hitting the frozen earth forty feet below the outside wall.

The following morning, Sharon was buried in the courtyard without a ceremony—without so much as a condolence spoken.

Priscilla protested. "It's wrong," the freckled pig-tailed girl of sixteen persisted. "She is being treated no differently than Philip was after Ms. M shot and had Danny bury him. Remember?" Priscilla insisted. "Sharon was one of us. Philip wasn't."

"Or wasn't given the chance," Bobby interjected.

"She's right," Karen said. "Sharon was given a million dollars one moment then treated like a pauper in the next. Even a pauper is entitled to a proper burial."

"Sharon was weak," Gerald said. "There is no room for weakness in our organization."

"And I suppose Harold and Betty were weak, too," Carol suggested angrily. "Is that why we didn't have any kind of service for them as well?"

"When you're dead, you're dead," Paul said. "What difference is it gonna make?"

"You're so stupid," Karen came back with pure repulsion.

"I'm stupid? You didn't even know that the Germans fought in both World Wars," he said and laughed with a degree of satisfaction written across his face. He glanced over at Bobby and winked.

"Oh, so now you're an expert on the wars, are you?' Karen retorted. "Only soldier I know who doesn't know his left foot from his right unless Bobby boy's around to help remind him which is which. Had him put a *rock* in his *right* hand as a *reminder.* Only problem being was that the rocks in his head couldn't get the message to his feet. Rrrright, Paul?" Karen giggled, parading erratically along the barracks before purposely bumping into a wall, several racks, and a fire extinguisher mounted near a doorway. "And the next time Peter calls out cadence for us, Paul, ask him if he can accommodate you with a *clippity-clop,* you horse's ass," she concluded with a prolonged and baleful snort.

Karen's clique was practically on the floor. Paul wanted to

somehow disappear under the very floorboards. Forever. He masked his mix of anger and embarrassment with a silly grin and looked across at Bobby who surrendered a shrug.

"I feel Sharon deserves a proper burial," Priscilla maintained.

"Absolutely," Karen agreed. "I'll go talk to Ms. M about it before we go to lunch. Let me see a show of support. Raise your hands if you agree." A good many hands went up. "Somebody confirm the count."

Peter was in conference with Angelica when Karen came to the door.

"It's open," Angelica answered to the knock.

Karen entered a small but neatly furnished room.

"Have a seat, Karen," Angelica said. "We're just finishing up. How about a glass of juice?"

Karen shook her head.

Peter smiled. "You look so serious. What's up?"

"I'll come right to the point. Thirty-three of us request that Sharon receive a proper burial. We voted a few minutes ago. Maybe we can have a small service. Say a few words for Betty and Harold, too. That's what's up, Peter," Karen said, looking at the two of them forthrightly.

Peter rose from his seat. "I don't know about that, Karen," he wavered.

"Well, I do," Karen remarked.

"That's not how we conduct—"

"It would be good for morale," Karen continued, setting her eyes on Angelica in earnest.

Angelica seemed surprised. "I didn't know we had a morale problem."

"Unless Karen's creating one for us," Peter said, narrowing his eyes.

"Who's us, Peter? You and Ms. M?"

"Now that's enough of that," Angelica ordered. "Sit back down, Peter. Karen, take a seat. Now, both of you listen to me."

When Peter and Karen were seated, Angelica began her sermon, settling back comfortably into a wing chair.

"I'm not talking to two children, here. I'm talking to two members of an elite assassination team. Soldiers. We have an important mission to accomplish, and our timetable has just been moved back by the deaths of Harold and Betty.

"Those two took out five federal agents who were assigned to protect Robert Redler and Liza Downs. But another faction, besides us, wants them dead. Betty and Harold had gained entrance to the house and were dead not long after one of them turned on a light switch in the upstairs bathroom. What were they thinking? They had no business turning on any lights. They were told to wait in darkness for Redler's and Downs' return. However, someone set a trap that was electrically and chemically engineered and meant to fry the writer and his housemate the moment they arrived home. You with me so far?"

Karen nodded.

"We had the assignment sanctioned by Mrs. G. But another group had the same idea. Apparently, they hold the same concerns that we do. They mistook Harold and Betty for Redler and Downs."

"Who the hell are these people, really?" Karen demanded.

Angelica smiled. "You're on a need-to-know basis, and right now, you don't need to know."

"Does Mrs. G know?" Karen pushed.

"Knows the people involved; professionals," Angelica answered honestly. "But of course Mrs. G didn't know that they were on a collision course with us."

"But if these people are supposed to be professionals, how could they make such a mistake?" The question was out, but of course Karen already knew the answer. From a distance, especially in the dark, Betty had been mistaken for Liza Downs, just as Harold had been taken for Robert Redler. Angelica had certainly made sure of that, for her team was comprised of professionals, too. Still, things did not sit right in Karen's unsettled mind. "Perhaps if Sharon had gone in, instead of Betty, maybe . . . ." Karen paused in mid-sentence.

"Meaning if Sharon didn't quite resemble Liza," Angelica elaborated for her, "perhaps the other faction might have aborted their mission. Is that what you're thinking?"

"Something like that."

Peter jumped in. "You don't send in an actress to do the job Betty was trained to do. That wasn't a stage out there. That was the real world, with seasoned professionals. Not a damn performance."

"So it doesn't mean a thing to you that Sharon and Betty and

Harold gave their last."

"Sharon had a crush on Harold," Angelica explained. "It would have gotten in the way as apparently it had with Betty. Again, Betty and Harold had no business turning on a light. Furthermore, if that faction had suddenly realized that Harold and Betty weren't their mark, do you believe they would have simply sent them packing?"

"I think she thinks that Sharon should have died in Harold's arms instead of Betty, Ms. M. I also think we've got an incorrigible romantic on our hands," Peter expounded.

"Go to hell!" Karen exploded.

"Can you two see that what's done is done and that we have to get on with our work? Not dwell on what might or should have been."

"I can. She obviously can't."

"Emotions, children. They cloud your thinking. Dead is dead. A proper burial or a service with a million words of sentiment behind it is not going to change what is. Betty and Harold disobeyed orders and, as a result, may have brought attention to ourselves. Sharon took her own life. What kind of an example would I be setting if I seemingly condoned such behavior by allowing a ceremony as thirty-three of you request? Hum?"

"We're not robots," Karen disputed.

"Not yet, Karen. But in time," Angelica chided behind an ice-cold smile.

"I don't believe this. I thought we were a team."

"Oh, but we are, dear. Each like a tooth on one gigantic gear. All working in unison."

"Three of the teeth are gone," Karen put forth melodramatically. "Four, if you add Philip Glover to the body count."

"But the machine still runs."

"Coldly. Calculatingly. Emotionlessly. Is that it?"

"As how it must."

"And you're the machinist."

"An accurate metaphor if you insist."

"To do your bidding? Blindly? Without question?"

"You're not stupid, Karen. You knew what was expected of you when you came under contract. You're one of the brighter ones. Betty was bright. One of the brightest among the females. But she let her emotions get in the way. Once again, and for a final time, they had no business turning on that light and displaying themselves like they had as their neighbors from across the street told reporters. Think about that. What if Redler and Downs had seen it? Get the picture? Even if the place wasn't booby-trapped, do you think they would have marched right in? You need time to reflect on that."

"Maybe they had a good reason."

"Not to follow orders?"

Karen felt exasperated. Drained of all emotion. Burned up. In a flash, her pent-up anger had dissipated to nothing more than annoyance. What kind of power did Angelica hold over her? An easy enough answer to such an elementary question. The power of life and death. Suddenly, she grew afraid but hid it. A trick of the trade that Sharon had taught her. Karen pretended that she was Joan of Arc. Fearless. Intrepid. Both b*efore* and *after* having been tied to the stake.

"You said something about our timetable being moved back," Karen managed.

Angelica nodded. "We had a date set in July to join forces with Mrs. G's people and initiate a first strike."

"Aimed at?" Karen asked apprehensively.

"Peter, tell her."

"Imperialism," Peter said firmly.

"Our government," Angelica clarified.

"Its overthrow," Karen acknowledged, an inner voice telling her that Joan of Arc's knees would never knock.

"It's practically toppling now." Angelica illustrated, bending her arm at the elbow out of the perpendicular. "Just needs a little nudge," she said firmly.

"And you feel we'll be ready to accomplish that?" Karen asked in astonishment.

"Not alone, but with over a million troops that I command in addition to another two million connected to Mrs. G. Those who collided with Betty and Harold the other night represent a faction of renegade loyalists in federal, state, and local governments who work under the auspices of a tribunal made up of three individuals who run the world like a fine Swiss timepiece. The world, Karen! Not just this nation. They hold high court as well as a grip around the globe. The single Church of all continents." Angelica took a sip of juice before continuing. "I've just given you what you need to know, Karen.

"But before we move in the direction I've outlined, we are going to put the control of Mrs. G under my command. Three million strong. With weaponry to immobilize any nation on the face of the earth who opposes us."

"Jesus Christ!"

"He, too, Karen, if need be. He, too."

"And this powerful faction that you speak of—"

"The Triumvirate."

"They're just going to let you walk away with the prize?"

"Their powers have been compromised by the likes of Redler and Downs and people like them. Individuals with a special gift. A gift to see beyond the senses and perhaps alter events. That's why we're going to find Redler and his kind and terminate this threat. I will soon be given license to do just that."

"By Mrs. G?"

"Gee, no, Karen." Angelica smiled coyly.

"Then who?"

Angelica looked at Peter. Peter shook his head.

"I think she needs to know, Peter. I'm going to give her Betty's spot. That is, if she wants it."

Peter looked down at the floor.

"I'll soon be sanctioned by The Triumvirate," Angelica said confidently.

"But Mrs. G doesn't know this." Karen knew. "Does she?"

"Correct."

"And you're not going to tell her."

"Mrs. G made the fatal mistake of going after Robert and Liza on her own, without consent from The Triumvirate. That might have been forgiven. Might have," Angelica emphasized. "What is not forgiven, however, is Mrs. G's prying into matters that did not concern her. Matters that could further compromise the power of The Triumvirate. A classic example of being too smart for one's own good, I'm afraid. And believe me. It's good to be afraid. Are you afraid at this moment, Karen? You seem so tense. Hum?"

"Yes."

"And why is that?"

"Because I have a feeling that you're going to ask me to do something. Something I may later regret."

"Oh, I am. And do you know what that is?"

"Kill Mrs. G."

Angelica shook her head slowly and deliberately. "No, Karen. Peter has already taken care of that. Would you like to have a proper burial for her, too? Perhaps a service?"

Karen shook her head.

"Good. Now, what I'm going to ask you to do is go back to the barracks and convince those thirty-three that there is no time for such humanity. That they have been paid handsomely to perform as a machine. A killing machine. You go tell thirty-three while I prepare to tell two million that I am their new benefactor and commander in chief, that Peter is my second, and that you, dear, are Peter's right hand. Think you can handle that?"

"Yes, Ms. M."

"I know you can. Peter, go back with her only to help set the stage. We're going to be heading out of here soon. I want them packed and ready to move at a moment's notice. Any questions?" Angelica took another sip. "Good. Cranberry. Cleans the kidneys," she said before smacking her lips.

Chapter 47

It was Christmas Eve day. Kathleen Grear, the Riverhead police chief's sister, emerged from her room in upstate New York's oldest psychiatric center. The woman looked ten years beyond her age. She reminded Robert of his matronly aunt. Dignified, yet unassuming in speech and manner. She wore an open full-length cotton housecoat over a pair of green pajamas with beige slippers that matched the outer garment. Her silvery-gray hair was pulled straight back in a long ponytail and held in place by a yellow band. She politely excused herself from a circle of friends who had gathered around her in the hallway, stroking her hair and robe. Kathleen reached out and took Liza's hand without breaking stride.

"Come," she insisted like an eccentric businesswoman on the go. Liza craned her neck toward Robert. "Oh, he can come along, too, if he behaves himself." Kathleen giggled. "Most men are really bad little boys that grow up in body only, and it's our lot in life to remand them when we must. Yes?"

"Absolutely," Liza agreed, laughing and loving the woman immediately.

Kathleen led the couple into a large sitting area, removed a key from her pocket, locked the door, then went over to the window and drew the drapes. "There," she said, seeming quite satisfied, taking Robert's hand before turning him around 360 degrees.

The couple stood in matching blue pajamas. Robert's were one size too big. Liza's fit perfectly.

"Sit," Kathleen said. "Sit and let us sort things out. Yes?"

"Yes," Liza agreed, taking a seat in the center of a well-worn sofa.

Robert sat to Liza's right. Kathleen agilely went to the floor in front of them.

"So," the woman said decidedly, leaning forward and putting the pajama bottoms into the tops of Robert's socks. "There now. Before you trip and kill yourselves. Let's see. I guess the first thing we have to do is establish mutual trust. All right?"

Liza smiled and nodded. Robert scratched an ankle.

"Stop that!" Kathleen insisted, smacking Robert's hand. "Let's begin now. Close your eyes, Rob."

"Yes, ma'am."

"Call me Kath. I don't like formality."

"Kath."

"I want you to concentrate on me. No! With your eyes closed. Doesn't listen well. Does he, Liza? That's better. Rob, are you thinking about me? Focus. Picture me at twenty. Sylph. I never had a man. Not in all my fifty-six years on this planet. Picture me. Think of the most outrageous thing you can. How did I get by, you're thinking? I'm not a nun, you know. I took no vow of chastity. Come on. An outrageous picture is forming in that brain of yours. Push the envelope. Let me see what I can see. I said outrageous, didn't I? Oh, you're so bad, Rob. Sick is what I should really say. The administration here would have you committed in a heartbeat. You see me fantasizing with fanaticism . . . hood ornaments of early model automobiles. Yes. A Packard in particular . . . inserting a cold, phallic metal projectile into my vagina. Yes?"

Robert opened his eyes in sheer embarrassment and amazement. "Color of that car," he challenged stupidly, not knowing what else to say.

"Candy apple red with specks of gold," Kathleen said without hesitation.

"Jesus."

"You are a sick bastard," Liza said and sneered, shaking her head in disgust.

"No, that's actually pretty good," the woman insisted and nodded. "Symbolically and all. Automobiles were, especially in those early years, considered to be motels on wheels. Interesting you should pick the Packard, though, Rob. Tells me lots about your whimsical side." Kathleen grinned from ear to ear.

"Am I competing with a Packard?" Liza asked of either, a feigned scowl engraved across her face.

"More along the lines of a fifties Oldsmobile, Liza," Kathleen teased.

"Pretty good lines on that one," Robert kidded.

"Oh, you're about to receive four flat tires, bozo," Liza remarked, all kidding put aside.

"No, he's all right from where I'm sitting," Kathleen conceded. "And believe me, I can size them up." She fixed her eyes on Robert for a good ten seconds before she spoke again. "And that's coming from a long-time misandrist; got over it not too long ago. The fact that the two of you aren't married yet says there's still some hope for you, Liza," she added for insult.

Robert still did not know whether or not to take the woman seriously. He couldn't ever remember feeling so vulnerable. Indeed, she was remarkable.

"The fact that you lost the gift tells me you're falling by the wayside, Rob. So Liza can either carry the ball from here on out, without your running interference, or you're both going to fall flat on your faces. Mark my words. Two Toyotas," she digressed. "Yes? A Camry and a pickup truck with a cap; four by four," Kathleen rambled. "Better think God and Country, Rob. The terrorists are circling the wagons as we speak. Middle East. Not the Germans or the Japanese. Although we had our hands full with that latter bunch, believe you me! We worked very hard to keep the Big Three afloat. GM, Ford, and Chrysler. But Toyota, Honda, and Nissan are still kicking butt, even with our import restrictions, duty, et cetera. No. It won't be the Occident this time around. Won't be a joke when you'll *have to* walk a mile for a Camel."

"I haven't lost the gift," Robert slid in argumentatively as Kathleen Grear took a breath.

"Yes, you have! When was the last time you had a reliable revelation? Something solid? Certainly not when I looked Liza's way. Or you would have known what Liza knows."

"And that is what?" Robert asked, looking skeptically between Kathleen and Liza.

"Say it, Liza," Kathleen coaxed.

"That Kathleen . . . ."

"Say it!" she demanded.

". . . has the hots for me."

"But knows . . . Go on. Tell him."

"That I don't have those kinds of feelings for her. So she poses no threat."

"All right, Rob?" Kathleen smiled satisfactorily.

"Oh, much better, thank you, Kath," Robert replied.

"Mutual trust we're building here, yes?"

Liza nodded nervously.

"Good. Very good. Now. Let's get down to it. Shall we?"

"Please," Robert said, sitting on the edge of his seat, his palms already clammy in spite of the sixty-degree temperature of the room.

"Liza knew to bring you to me, yes?"

"Yes," Robert conceded.

"The window which she sees through is not as narrow as yours. Want to know why?"

"Yes, Kath."

"You're agitated inside. All wound up. You're in the middle of this whirlwind and fighting it. Let it whirl around you. Hold still. When you were writing your second book you were sitting back, letting those perceptions come through you. Right?"

Robert nodded.

"Liza's more in *touch* right now. Her window is very clear. Give me your hand," she said, reaching up to Liza. Liza gave Kathleen her hand. "Now, see what I see. Tell him the painful news that you both need to know. Do it now."

Liza suddenly began to cry as if someone had turned on the proverbial tear duct faucet.

Kathleen Grear gripped Liza's hand tightly. "Tell him!"

"Joe is dead," Liza whined and wept.

"Who?"

"The postal worker," she blurted out angrily.

"And who else?" Kathleen insisted, squeezing Liza's hand until it hurt.

"Brid— Brid·get, Brid·get O'Reil·ly," she answered through a syllabic series of sobs. "She was, *was* my friend!" Liza let out in a measured stroke of fury that tolled like a bell.

Robert sat there stunned.

Kathleen released Liza's hand. "And now you are on your own. Don't look at me. Look out that window of yours and tell me whose death you also see."

"Barbara Giordano's," Liza immediately acknowledged, staring at a wall.

"Who killed her, Liza?"

"Number Eleven."

"What?" Robert said perplexedly.

"Peter: Number Eleven. They all have numbers."

"What are you talking about? What numbers?"

"She'll explain it to you later, Rob. Don't stand in her way. She has a wide enough window now. Let her *see*. All right?"

"All right," Robert agreed.

"Damn well better. Do you believe in the forces of good and evil, Rob?"

"Yes, Kath. I do."

"Of course you do. You illustrate those powers beautifully on paper as a writer. But do you *believe* in those powers as a man?"

"I do."

"And do you also believe as a man, Rob, that good shall triumph over all evil?"

"I truly believe that, Kath."

"And will you put your faith and trust in my instructions? A candy apple Packard with specks of gold, Rob," she reminded him. "You're not going to get a clearer picture than that," Kathleen Grear affirmed and grinned.

"I will."

"Then you must simply let Liza run this show. That's it. If you do that, the two of you will prevail. Falter in that regard and you'll stumble along the path."

"Why didn't you come to us?" Robert asked. "I mean call upon us sooner."

"You would not have come just then. I'm just a crazy old lady who's been locked away in here as long as I care to remember," Kathleen said sadly. "Liza had to see the light. Liza had to look long and hard through that window."

"How did you come to wind up in here?" Robert couldn't help but ask.

"I was wondering when you were going to get around to asking me that. You see, I worked for the Department of Defense, military operations, and freelanced for the feds. FBI's Behavioral Science Unit. I compiled profiles of certain criminals: war criminals as well as serial killers. One afternoon, I stumbled across an old document. A very top secret report sent to the Office of Strategic Service in 1946, detailing large numbers of shipments of gold trucked across Europe for the Nazis, which eventually found their way to Swiss and Swedish banks. My investigations led to other documents involving forced auctions of properties in Berlin between 1930 and 1940. In '46, the Swiss agreed to pay the Allies sixty million in compensation for the looted gold. What my investigation showed, unequivocally, was that the Swiss government colluded with the Nazis in siphoning off Jewish assets as well as the laundering of gold. And here's the kicker. Not to the tune of sixty million, but to the arrangement of six hundred million in 1940s U.S. dollars. Know what that's worth today? Fortune being built on top of fraudulent fortune.

"Now you know where the money came from to put The Triumvirate in an unprecedented position of power. Those of us with the gift of what is mistakenly referred to as clairvoyance were their major threat. Along came hundreds like yourselves. Richard Geist's cult and Barbara Giordano's cartel were expendable operations used to test your strengths and weaknesses. Right now, Angelica Manns is in the catbird seat. Soon we're going to show them all how powerful the three of *us* can be, working together toward a single goal. The pièce de résistance. *Our* final solution."

"What happened between Barbara Giordano and Angelica Manns?" Liza asked quietly, wiping her eyes on a sleeve of her pajama top.

"Mrs. Giordano went too far, confronting Angelica with things that did not concern her, Angelica felt. And that was that. You see, what you do not know is who Angelica Ann Manns really is; that, and how she is indirectly connected to the head of The Triumvirate, let alone who that man truly is. You need an awfully big window for that one, Liza my dear."

"A window that even Joe couldn't see through," Liza said.

"Oh, I think Joe saw, all right. Only he couldn't handle what he knew," Kathleen clarified, getting off the floor and sitting next to Liza on the couch.

Liza began nodding knowingly. "Yes, I know that he was

holding back something horrible when I asked him about the Baceni brothers."

Kathleen smiled.

"What really happened, Kath?"

"Well, it's really very simple. First off, Baceni is an abridged, borrowed name assigned to three boys who had their real surname changed at birth."

"But why?"

"Because of who they are."

"Don't do this to us, Kathleen. Please."

"Better hold on to your seat then. There won't be any turning back. You'll carry this burden to your grave, which might come early once you know; that is, if you two are not careful."

"We're already marked for death," Liza said bravely. "Who are they?"

"The sons of Adolf Hitler as well as uncles to a nephew who you already know, who is now their niece and not a very nice one," Kathleen unloaded.

Robert and Liza were staring at Kathleen blankly.

"That's insane," Robert Redler finally said.

"Why? Because the history books tell us that the Führer had no offspring? The history books tell us that Lee Harvey Oswald assassinated President John Fitzgerald Kennedy, period. And I know for a fact that you don't for a minute buy into that one, Robby boy."

"You're saying that Karl and his two brothers are the sons of Adolf Hitler, and that they have a nephew . . . ?" Liza paused, taking a position on the floor where Kathleen had sat a moment ago, looking deeply up and into the woman's eyes.

Kathleen nodded. "Angelo Reynolds."

"Who is now his niece?"

"Angelica Ann Manns."

"Who underwent—"

"Yes, a sex change operation," Kathleen continued. "Which is what threw most everyone off the trail."

"Karl and his two brothers are uncles to Angelica Manns," Robert worked over in his mind.

"Men are so thick," Kathleen said with amusement. "Explain it to him, Liza."

"Karl Hitler is uncle to Angelo Reynolds who had a sex change operation and—"

"I know. I know. I know what you're saying. But it sounds so, so crazy."

"Coming from a certified paranoid schizophrenic, I take that as a personal affront," Kathleen teased.

Liza laughed loudly. For the first time things were beginning to make perfect sense. "Do you know the monsignor's and the mercenary's given names?"

"Liza. I know virtually everything. The monsignor is William. The merc, as he's referred to by intimates—of which there are few—is Edward. And, of course, you both met Karl, spelled with a K. Robert, in fact, has met all three in a meeting at Riverhead P. D. with my brother, the chief of police."

"Do these three Hitler brothers have middle names?" Liza asked, wanting to know everything she possibly could about the trio.

"No, they do not. Then again, neither did their father, who was baptized a Catholic: Adolfus Hitler. You might find it interesting to learn that he had a second mistress, Hannah Abramowicz, who was Angelica's grandmother. More about that later."

"You learned all these things by way of your extraordinary gift, Kathleen?" Liza asked in awe.

"Nah, mostly through OSS, CID, and CIA documentation, along with classified reports."

"You must have been one helluva good agent, Kathleen Grear," Liza commented.

Kathleen giggled. "Agent? I was a snoopy, snotty little bitch."

Liza was laughing in her sleeve. "Excuse me for being blunt. But I have a rather sensitive question to ask."

"Be blunt."

"Why didn't they just bump you off, as they say?"

"They say liquidate," Kathleen corrected. "They like that one a lot. Well, they would have. You see, I shared what I had with one of my supervisors. He thought he had gold, and actually he did. Only he got greedy and wanted all the glory for himself. Told me I never saw this or that and passed my work on to his supervisors. Never mentioned me in his report. Guess what?"

"They liquidated him," Liza said coldly.

"Nope. Terminated him," she teased. "They used those two terms interchangeably for a while. Can get pretty confusing. Gave the guy two week's severance pay then liquidated him one week later for his trouble. I saw what was going on all around me. Key players from around the globe disappearing off the face of it. I had a nervous breakdown. I was examined and interviewed by doctors who weren't doctors, and by psychiatrists who were plainly nuts. One day, I was examined by a man in a white coat who was Karl. My gift kept me alive. I fooled them all. I stayed put. If any of them believed for a moment that I was sane and had any knowledge of this matter, or even shown the slightest sign of marked improvement, I'd have been dead before the day was done."

"What about your brother?" Robert asked. "Chief Grear."

"I don't trust him. You shouldn't, either. It's not that he's not a good man. God knows that he is. But he's easily taken in. He's in league with the devil and doesn't know it."

"You can't spend the rest of your life here," Liza said.

"I don't intend to. That's why you're here. It hasn't been so bad, though. The director is very good to me."

"She knows?" Robert asked.

"Everything but that I love her. *That* she would never understand. You see, I've become very adept at hiding my feelings and emotions, keeping things locked away inside."

Liza reached up and took Kathleen's hand.

"Watch it, Liza. I could become easily attached. I haven't had much contact with anyone except for a bunch of psychos who love to pull on my robe and hair. I haven't spoken a word to anyone about this but Dottie in over thirty years. You see, I've gotten worse instead of better." She smiled so sadly.

Liza's heart was breaking. "I was about to have a nervous breakdown, too," she said. "In fact, I think I had a mild one."

"Soon after little David died," she nodded knowingly.

"You know."

"I told you. I know most everything. And I know you're going to end this evil. You and Rob. That is, if he behaves himself and listens to you. Understand?"

Liza looked at Robert. "Rob?"

Robert bobbed his head. "What can I get you, Kathleen?"

"How about an old Packard brochure, buster," she bellowed and beamed.

Robert Redler rolled off the couch and down into Liza's arms. He was laughing up a storm. Kathleen smiled down at the two of them like they were her children. Children she never had nor ever wanted in the kind of world she knew.

"Now listen to me," Kathleen said very seriously. "We have a lot of work to do. I hope you like history because you're going to get an earful. Are you up to it?"

Liza and Robert nodded.

"I'm going to give you the ammunition you need to take Angelica's people down. All of them. One by one. Barbara Giordano is out of the picture. That will make it somewhat easier. But it's not going to be a walk in the park." She paused and smiled. "Dot loves that expression. And so do I. You're safe here tonight. But don't even think for a moment that they won't come. Because they will. No stone unturned. They thought you might have sought sanctuary on the East End of Long Island. The monsignor is pulling his hair out looking for you high and low. The merc's people have their eyes and ears open, waiting for you to show. They had a false alarm at Saint Isidore's in Riverhead. The priest and pastor almost came to blows." She giggled with sheer delight then winked. "Dot set that one up nicely. Oh, and by the way, Rob." Kathleen leered.

"Yes?"

"You look very stupid in those pajamas."

Liza laughed.

Robert said nothing, trying to hide his annoyance.

"Get used to it, buster. Most men are stupid. You just look the part right now."

"I like her more and more," Liza stated with a satisfactory nod. "How do *I* look, dear?" she asked, addressing Kathleen while getting up.

"Adorable, Liza. Just adorable."

"This is going to be a long night I can see," Robert mumbled to himself.

"Let's meet here in an hour. Meanwhile, I'll rustle us up something to eat. Then we'll talk some more. I want to know what you two think about Madonna. Do you like her, Liza?"

******

Liza locked the door to their room with a key suspended from a long chain. She turned to Robert in disgust. "How could you be so crass and think about hood ornaments and vaginas, Rob? How could you degrade women like that?"

"We have people out there trying to kill us, and you're worried about degradation. I'm worried about whether or not we can trust her. I'm worried about whether or not she has all her marbles. I'm worried about whether or not the authorities erroneously labeled her certifiable like she says. Well, she wanted me to conjure up something outrageous. So I gave her something to clean her clock and maybe at the same time cure those lesbian fantasies."

"No, I think she cleaned *your* clock, buster," Liza set forth rather coolly. "You're not satisfied that she's legit after what you just listened to and learned about your Three Musketeers? Well, I am. You better wake the hell up, fella."

Robert gradually gestured surrender with a peevish pout. "I guess she's legitimate," he finally conceded. But in truth, he really and truly wasn't sure about anything anymore.

Chapter 48

Karl slowly raked both hands through a thinning gray scalp—long, bony fingers beginning at the tip of his forehead and continuing back to the top of the nape—down along the neckline—palms tracing the contour of a prominent jaw, pausing abruptly at the chin—drawing old but taut skin together as though he were fondling a goatee. "Where?" he pondered aloud. "Where could they possibly be?"

"Anywhere but on the streets," said the merc.

"Nor seeking asylum in any house of worship within a thousand miles of here," the monsignor swore.

"I really thought that we had them boxed in at Saint Isidore's," the merc frowned.

"Me, too," the monsignor swore and sadly shook his head. "Father O'Hanley said that a woman called it in. Reliable. Said she was positive it was them."

"They're playing with us, Bill," the merc scowled, sipping a white zinfandel before picking up a piece of Brie.

Karl glared. "They're too scared to play, gentlemen. They're running for their lives would be my guess."

"Yeah. Pausing just long enough along the way to have an elderly couple, two teenagers, and a pair of actors make damn fools of us," the merc reminded them.

"That was before we attempted to roast them," Karl snapped, breaking a pencil between a thumb and forefinger.

"All we did was drive them deeper underground," the monsignor declared matter-of-factly.

"So how much of a threat can they really be?"

"They know too damn much already, gentlemen. Too damn much."

"We'll find them," the merc promised most assuredly. "Right now, we've got other matters to attend to. We have to decide what we're going to do about this Manns business."

Karl agreed. "I think *he's* gotten too big for *her* britches."

The merc chuckled. "Don't you mean his-and-hers pantaloons?"

"She's not to be underestimated." Karl went over to a window and looked down at the boulevard. It was Christmas morning. The area below was deserted. "If we don't support her coup d'état, now, we lose face."

"Since when do we care about saving face?"

"Since we raised the Iron Curtain, Ed. Since we lowered the boom concerning the Canal. Since we put the Swiss on call. China on hold. We're the force, but we have to face reality. Our father's grip on power lasted twelve years when he believed it would last a thousand. Our reign, however, has continued for almost fifty years and will last indefinitely, my two dear brothers. Why? Because we always told our generals which way the wind would blow. Because we don't bask in the limelight or even take an occasional bow."

"Karl, we're talking about a cult and a drug cartel, here. Not a major line of defense. We could simply pull the plug on both of them."

"And who steps in to fill their heels?" he snapped. "Not at all prudent, gentlemen."

"Keep in mind that if they had gone through proper channels, we wouldn't be having either of these problems," the prelate prattled.

"Maybe yes, and maybe no. I don't want either of you to lose sight of the fact that there are a few groups out there taking a closer look around these days. Giordano learned Manns' true identity. Angelica knew the position it would put her in, so our niece wisely had her benefactor silenced. She seized the perfect opportunity to put herself on top. She also knows that the only way we'd ever support her outright, if we choose to, is to denounce Giordano's action as irresponsible and foolhardy. Corrupt and therefore criminal."

"Come on, Karl. An unsanctioned assassination—failed or not —is not an end-all."

"No. But violating a direct order after being told to stand down on the Redler/Downs hit *is*," the weasel-faced dictator stated steadfastly. "Then all that need be done is to justify Angelica's subsequent action."

"How?" the monsignor asked.

"Under what pretext?" the merc zeroed in.

"By simply saying that *we* gave the order."

"You'd want that to be our official position?"

"I don't see another workable solution, Bill."

"Why support Angelica at all."

"Because she's the prefect candidate to fill the vacancy."

"Not because she's our niece?" the merc tabled then smirked.

"Not only did she protect her own butt, gentlemen. She safeguarded ours as well. The moment Ms. Manns became vulnerable, we three became vulnerable."

Ed and Bill looked at one another cautiously.

"Why would anyone believe that Barbara Giordano had gone against our will?" the merc put forth, setting down his glass.

"Doesn't matter. We simply say she did. We ordered her execution and the installment of Angelica Manns."

The merc carefully weighed the alternatives, holding his vote in abeyance for the moment, batting the matter back and forth across his brain like a Ping-Pong ball. A good minute passed before he hunched his shoulders. "Okay, I guess."

"Bill?"

Bill took in a deep breath. "All right," he finally said. "I'll be at the Vatican on Sunday. How do you want me to put it?"

"Simply. You tell them that certain confidences were on the brink of compromise. Period. They'll understand. I'll speak with Barbara Giordano's generals."

Chapter 49

Robert and Liza listened as Kathleen Grear finalized the plan.

"So we all know pretty much what we have to do. Correct?"

Robert and Liza nodded in unison.

"Don't look so sullen. It's just Angelica's army of forty-six against the two of you," she presented good-humoredly.

"Isn't there anyone in authority we can talk to?" Liza questioned apprehensively.

"As naïve at times as she is pretty," Kathleen answered with a weary sigh. "Sure. There are lots of people in authority to talk to, Liza. Positively no one in power who would help out on your behalf. They'd sell the two of you down the river or have you anchored at the bottom of some bay before sunset."

Liza nodded.

"Let me tell you a simple fact about our victory in both World Wars. Know why we won? Bottom line? We as a nation were inspired. Our faith in the notion that good shall triumph over evil, regardless of the odds, was unshakable. And believe you me, there were times that the odds weren't so favorable. You are about to declare war on an evil empire. You and Rob for openers. Right up there on the front lines. You are the good guys and have the gift, Liza. The gift from God. That gift will become more and more powerful as it did with Rob when he fought against Richard Geist and his followers. But Rob slowly turned away from his belief and sought some sort of intellectual explanation on a seductive secular plane."

"I'm an agnostic, Kathleen," Robert said defensively. "If that's what you're getting at. I simply don't know about these things. All right?"

"You were given more signs than Burma Shave has billboards.

Yet you see no higher than that man-made advertisement." She turned to face Liza and once again berated the writer as though he weren't standing there. "Men can be so thick, dear. Maybe he'll catch on along the second go-around."

Robert Redler grew annoyed. "All right, Miss Smarty-Pants. Explain this to me. How could I have been hearing the Word of God if God told me to crush Richard Geist and Michael? Which I did. In cold-blood," he added, playing devil's advocate.

"Was it *really* cold-blooded murder, Robby? Or was it self-defense? Would you have gotten off that island alive had you done otherwise? Ask yourself."

"I pursued them with malice aforethought."

"Says you or the prosecutors? You were God's messenger, Rob. He delivered you. Don't make anything more out of it than that."

"It was The Triumvirate and their people who got me off the hook."

"Oh, I see. Not a jury of your peers coupled with God's intervention."

"The prosecution didn't push the envelope."

"The prosecution would have lost that case had they had O.J.'s entire dream team in its corner passing out free advice like pabulum."

"Why all of God's games then, Kathleen, if things are predetermined?"

"They're not. God's still screwing around with you, isn't He? You have the freedom to choose whatever game you wish to play and by whatever rules you so desire."

"I go around in circles with this," Robert admitted.

"Well, if there's any comfort in these words, Rob, I believe Liza is going to guide you off that perpetual merry-go-round, plant your feet solidly back on the ground, then help you regain your equilibrium."

"That would be nice," Robert said politely.

Kathleen shook her head. "That would be bliss," she extolled. "So, are you ready to go hunting, Rob? Liza is, I know. Are you ready to take out forty-six of Angelica A. Manns' A Team with a bow and a box of arrows for openers? David stood up to Goliath with just a slingshot and a stone," she reminded him.

"Yes, but that was one-on-one," Robert argued futilely. *And it was only a story*, the writer wanted to dispute.

"I know the odds don't seem very favorable, Rob," Kathleen admitted. "But you will have the element of surprise working in your favor. You will have the power of goodness on your side. You have other distinct advantages, too. You know the area well. And you're deadly with a bow, I'm told."

"At putting down deer. Not human beings."

"Evil human beings, Rob."

"Misguided adolescents."

"So were most of Hitler's soldiers."

"Not the same thing."

"How is it any different? Right from wrong, Rob. Even four-year-old children sense the difference. Young adults certainly know."

"Where are they training?" Liza questioned. "You said you'd tell us when you knew."

Kathleen nodded. "I had to be absolutely certain. It's a camp," Kathleen said directly to Robert. "In Riverhead. Angelica's troops arrived there yesterday. All forty-seven including the commander herself. Three, as I told you, are already dead."

"What camp? Where?"

"The 4-H Camp property."

"Off Sound Avenue?" Robert asked in disbelief.

Kathleen nodded. "Toward the north. I told you, you know the area well. True?"

Robert nodded his head up and down mechanically.

"We're not forgetting what they did to little David," Liza stated quietly. "To our home and property. Everything we own. All up in smoke. And now they're training several miles away from the smoldering ruins."

"Time to put an end to this evil," Kathleen set forth frankly. "This is not going to be Armageddon or anything like it. Just a minor skirmish. But a first and decisive strike. It will send a clear message to those in power. Now that's a battle that will not be easily won. But it certainly won't be yours alone. It is the tradition and intention of The Triumvirate to soon hand the torch over to the incoming trio who have been groomed from birth and waiting in the wings. Preparations for that day are being discussed as we speak. Perhaps the people in this great land will open their eyes before it's too late. See the evil for what it is. Then act. Alas, I shall not be around to bear witness to that hour." Kathleen turned away from the two. She stared out a corner window and folded her arms across her chest. "Dottie will be coming for you in just a little while to see you out of here safely. She'll provide you with everything you need. Where you're going will have a kerosene heater and running water. Your accommodations will be rustic and sparse: a barn and a stable on the property where Angelica's troops will not dare tread. Too close to the road. All right?"

"All right," Liza answered immediately.

"That's fine," Robert said, squeezing Liza's hand firmly.

"Good." Kathleen nodded satisfactorily, turning back toward them. "Good for you," she added happily. "We're going to say our good-byes here and now."

Aboard the yellow mini-van, Liza and Robert climbed. The two went down the aisle to the middle then ducked in to take a seat. Liza put her face inches from the window and waved good-bye to Dottie. Robert was at Liza's shoulder, pressing a palm against the cold, damp glass. Dottie stood rigid, the raised collar of her coat held together at her throat, a stoic stare fixed firmly across a dark countenance. She raised a hand almost timidly and formed a cup, the tips of her fingers barely touching one another. Liza nodded bravely that everything was going to be all right. Dottie gave up a little smile and sank her hands deep into the pockets of her coat, never taking her eyes off the two of them until the van disappeared into the night.

"You know what I never learned from her?" Liza contemplated.

"Who?"

"Kathleen."

"What's that?"

"Well, we know that Angelica knows that The Triumvirate is the embodiment of the Third Reich. Right?"

"Right."

"But we don't really know for sure if Angelica knows that Karl, William, and Edward are her uncles who are the sons of Adolf Hitler. I mean, they could be the sons of the pope, for all she knows. No?"

Robert was shaking his head. "No, believe me. She knows

exactly who they are."

"But how do you know that?"

"You heard what Kathleen said, same as I. Barbara Giordano somehow learned the truth about Angelica Manns and probably confronted her. A secret that had to be kept at all cost: the fact that Angelo was the grandson, now the granddaughter of Adolf Hitler, and that her three uncles are, in fact, The Triumvirate. That's why Angelica had to kill her. Then there's that not-so-subtle message Angelica conveyed regarding the execution of Barbara Giordano."

"I'm listening."

"It was the method employed that tells me with certainty that she knows," he assured her.

"Angelica had one of her soldiers hang her. So?"

"But it's what she had the soldier use to hang her."

Liza waited patiently, knowing that Robert was taking delight in a piece of the puzzle she failed see. Finally, she kicked him in the ankle beneath the seat.

"Hey!"

"Kathleen said Angelica had the soldier use wire. So what?"

"Not just any wire."

"Well then what?" she asked, exasperated.

"Piano wire," he expanded.

"And what's so significant about piano wire?"

"It's what Hitler ordered used on those who conspired against him after their botched assassination attempt. A rather excruciating death in that the very thin gauge wire slowly cuts into their throats and —"

"All right, I get the picture. Enough."

"My window might be narrow, Liza. But I can still add up two and two."

"That's wonderful, dear," she said, feeling somewhat ill.

"You know. I don't know if you have the stomach for what we're about to do out there."

"Listen carefully to me, Rob. I'm going to, without a sound, pick them off one by one for what they did to little David. Not put piano wire around their goddamn necks. We have no law to go to. We have to take matters into our own hands. Everything that Kathleen said is true."

"Do you have any idea how close you're going to have to get in order to make a clean kill, Liza?"

"I watched all of your hunting tapes with you. Recall? Shot with you in the backyard from different heights, angles, and distances. I'll manage."

"You were shooting paper, not penetrating human flesh."

"I'll find the mark, hit it, watch them die, then do a little dance around them like that woman Margaret does who promotes her and her husband's tree stands in those videos of yours."

The bvan was dark, so he couldn't peer into her eyes; however, he believed that they had grown quite mad. "You used to say that *she* was sick; Margaret." he reminded her. "And that dance, may I remind you, was over the carcass of a deer, not another human being."

"Let me tell you something, darling. The Nazis not only gathered up Jews, all ages, both sexes, and sent them off to their deaths. They gathered up their property. Their money. Even the gold fillings in their heads. The remnants of that regime want those of us with the gift exterminated, too. Zachariah Ballard and all the others who died before him. Those who followed, like Joe. Even poor Bridget O'Riley whose curse was in helping us. You and I present a threat to their mastery, Rob. Would *all* their generals allow The Triumvirate to wield such power if the truth be known? My feeling is that full disclosure would weaken the power that those three devils wield.

"As Kathleen said," Liza went on, "we are about to engage in a skirmish, not a major war. The two of us are going to show The Triumvirate that Angelica Manns can't even lead forty-six troops through a winter training session let alone a legion of millions that she so desires to command."

"And we're going to do all this with a couple of antiquated weapons?" Robert tested.

"With a couple of antiquated weapons and your knowledge of the 4-H Camp, your tracking ability, military genius and might. How am I doing?"

Robert laughed. "Have I been shouting out orders in my sleep again? Listen. Like I said. This is going to be a lot different than putting down deer, dear. You have absolutely no idea. These troops have been trained extensively: hand-to-hand combat, martial arts, small arms, archery, explosives, and the list goes on. Granted, you have the window, but I can't afford to put you in harm's way anymore."

"She's right. Kathleen is one hundred percent correct. Men are thick. We *are* in harm's way. Right now. Sitting on this bus. We could be blown to smithereens in the next instant if they knew that we were sitting here. The more time that passes, the more danger we're in. Get it? I'd rather fight them on our turf than theirs."

"We gotta be nuts. You know that."

"We have little choice. We have got to be brave and see this thing through."

Robert sat in silence, staring at the driver's back. His name was Patrick, and the two had been told by Kathleen that he could be trusted with their lives. Liza snuggled up against Robert's shoulder and mumbled a Merry Christmas before she dozed. It was nuts he told himself again. In two days, he and Liza would walk into the woods off Sound Avenue and try to stop forty-six soldiers and their commander in their tracks. Or more precisely, in their trees, he knew. For that was what Phase One of the troops' advanced training entailed, they had learned. Pure madness was in the making, he also knew.

A few minutes later, Robert dozed off, too.

Chapter 50

It was the dead of night. Cold and raining heavily. Within a rustic lodge overlooking Long Island Sound, Angelica sat in front of a large stone fireplace. A north wind ripped across the waters at forty knots and tore mercilessly at the bluffs. Two loose windows at the northwest corner of the building rattled menacingly. A sentry stood posted just inside each of the five doorways. Weapons ported smartly across the front of their bodies. Outside, several soldiers walked the perimeter in ponchos. Rifles slung over each shoulder. Muzzles pointed at the ground; protected from the steady downpour.

Angelica stared into the fire. She was more than happy. She was thrilled. She was truly commander in chief of both cult and cartel. Recruiter of young men and women into her church of aggression. Chancellor of drug trafficking through three continents. Of course, this was her probationary period. She had officially been given a pass and a promotion. She would be watched closely. Her performance would be evaluated periodically. Profits were the bottom line. Customer satisfaction hung just above it. Barbara Giordano had been too conservative in her thinking. Angelica's radical approach would have suppliers busy trying to keep up with product demand. Then, when the time was right, and the changing of the guard put in place, she would, before the turn of the century, in one fell swoop, become the empowered. It was beyond destiny; it was her rite of passage.

"All right, captain my captain. How do we proceed?" Liza asked, stepping out of the van off Sound Avenue and into the heavy rain. She held a black plastic bow case in one hand and a large canvas bag in the other. Robert carried the same, sending Patrick away with a simultaneous nod and a confident tight-lipped okay.

"Straight ahead," Robert answered, heading due north.

"I can't see a blessed thing," Liza complained.

"Lift your feet high. It's mostly brush."

Liza tripped and went down to her knees, dropping the case and the bag from each hand. "Shit."

"Stay down. We got a car coming."

Headlights loomed from just around the bend. A moment later, a vehicle blew by.

"Okay, let's move," Robert ordered.

Liza got to her feet with the case in hand. "Where's the bag?" she squealed.

"Keep your voice down, goddamnit."

"It's pitch black. I can't see," she whispered. "Here we go." Liza grabbed the bag.

"Stay directly behind me."

"Feet high," she recited.

Robert shook his head in both despair and disgust.

Ten minutes later, they arrived at a building. A spacious barn. The door was padlocked. Robert put down the bow case and bag then took out a key and opened the lock and latch. He pushed open the door and led Liza inside, holding her by the wrist, guiding her across the space.

"Put the stuff down. I want you up this ladder and into the loft. I'll hand you up one piece at a time. Just put them off to the side."

"Can't we turn on a light? I'll kill myself up there."

"Listen to me. We're on the edge of a two-hundred-acre parcel. They're probably spread out just north and west of us. That's not a very large playing field. And we're playing for keeps. No light. No noise. In a few hours, this place is going to light up with farm animals. Roosters and chickens. Geese and turkeys. Goats and pigs. Horses and even bulls. It's the perfect place for what we have to do. But right now, not a peep. We store our gear and get some sleep. Take off your rain gear."

"Yes, sir!" Liza said belligerently.

Neither of them slept well but rather slipped in and out of a palpable state of anxiety, a cold black blanket of uncertainty bearing down upon them, a cover that could not be brushed aside. A chill ran from the top of Liza's shoulders to the small of her back as she slipped into a state of semiconsciousness before suddenly calling out in her sleep.

"What?" Robert sat up alert.

"Scared."

"Cold?"

"No."

"Try and get some rest."

"Right." Liza willed a cloud of consternation away but not its cousin, fear. "Rob?"

"What?"

"When you shot Richard and Michael, what did you feel?"

"Numb, like now. Now go to sleep."

Liza inched her way across the hay and snuggled up against Robert's back. "One more question?"

"What?"

"Are you scared?"

"That I might hurl you out of this loft and have to do everything myself come morning. Now, shut up and go to sleep."

Suddenly a strange sound came from the pasture below.

"What was that?" Liza cringed.

"A horse snorting. You woke him up."

The next thing the couple heard was the early morning alarm of several roosters serenading their feathered lady friends throughout the land. A few minutes later, turkeys were gobbling. Chickens were cackling. Ducks and geese were parading back and forth in front of the red barn. Robert was at one of the windows with a pair of binoculars, scanning the dusky fields and wood lot for any sign of Angelica's soldiers.

Liza crawled over on her hands and knees beside him. "See anything?"

Robert lowered the glasses and shook his head, moving over to another window in the north wall.

"Well?" she asked.

"*Nada.*"

"Thank God. I'd hate to kill anybody first thing in the morning on an empty stomach."

"There's a granola bar in your pack somewhere."

"A granola bar? This is a farm, for Christ's sake. With chickens and eggs."

"Good. Grab yourself a leg and a wing on the way out."

"Funny. I'm on a funny farm with a comedian who doesn't want to feed me."

"You ready?"

Liza looked at him and began to cry. "I don't know whether I can do this. I thought I could, but I'm so scared."

"Me, too," he admitted, crawling over and collecting her into his arms, comforting her for a couple of minutes before another rooster crowed rather loudly. "Snooze alarm," he kidded.

Liza laughed somewhere into his jacket, her face lost in a fleecy fold.

"Come on over here. I want to show you something. Come on." Robert moved to a window, removing the field glasses from around his neck. "Take these. Look down there," he said.

Liza took the binoculars and looked in the direction he was pointing. "Where?"

"That single tree across the road."

"It's still so dark out. I don't see anything."

"Got that tree?"

"Yes."

"Now look in it. Concentrate. Adjust your focus."

Liza turned the focus knob. "Jesus. What is it?"

"Look all through that tree."

"There's more. What are they?"

"Turkeys."

"Turkeys?"

"Turkeys roosting. That's how and where they sleep. Like Angelica's soldiers out there. Only you'll find one of them to a tree. That's how Richard Geist's followers eluded the authorities for years. They literally lived in the woods. Chief Grear and Sergeant Phelps found their tree stands. Empty, of course. But not today nor tomorrow. Not until each and every one of her soldiers takes a deer. Because if you can consistently put down wary whitetail, you can put down common men with confidence. Learn to hunt the whitetail successfully, and you can wipe out your enemy at will."

Liza lowered the glasses and looked at Robert squarely, realizing the moment of truth waited just beyond the tree line.

"I don't know if I can kill anything," she whispered, trembling like a leaf.

"You don't have to. You be my window is all."

"Not in cold blood, I can't," she clarified plaintively through a whimper. "I just can't."

"It's all right."

"I'm sorry."

"Nothing to be sorry about. Come on."

Liza tried to compose herself. "At least it stopped raining," she said.

Robert was sorry it had. Sorry that the wind had died down, too. Sorry he had brought her, yet at the same time glad that she was there. The ambivalence unsettled him more than what he knew he *had* to do.

"It's going to be light in a few minutes, and we want to cross into the wood lot behind that tree, unseen."

She understood and stepped backward down the ladder to the ground. He handed her the gear they needed.

"Careful with that bow," he cautioned.

"Hand me mine," she ordered.

"I thought—"

"I'll back you up." *Somehow.* "Don't argue."

He unsnapped the second case then handed down her bow.

"You have my release?"

"Got it," he said, climbing carefully down the ladder.

Onto his bow, he snapped the quiver that held six razor-sharp broadheads fixed to aluminum shafts. Liza did likewise. The two slipped on a pair of gloves along with a wrist-strap release, securing the wide band in place with Velcro.

"You do not take that release off for any reason or you might give away your position. Velcro is noisy. You can still nock an arrow on your string, but you'll have to do it carefully. You don't want to hit aluminum against the metal release trigger," he cautioned and demonstrated, touching the shaft against the trigger housing of the mechanical release. "Silence is golden. Got it?"

"Got it. Why don't we nock an arrow now?"

"Not in the dark. You'll wind up snagging or bending an arrow," he explained patiently. "When it turns light and we can see what we're aiming at, we'll do exactly that. Kind of trail your bow slightly in back of you as we head through brush and branches.

Remember how we protected our fishing rods working our way to secluded ponds?"

It came to her before he even said it. "Yes."

"And when you do nock your arrow, be sure to keep the broadhead away from the string. You could fray it and be in a world of shit. These are not like the target arrows you're used to."

"Yes, sir," she said respectfully.

"Let's do this." Robert went over and opened the barn door, scanning every inch of terrain with binoculars.

A minute later, the two were in the wood lot, heading north.

As daylight broke through slats of gunmetal-gray covering, a guard outside the lodge signaled that two were coming. The sentry inside the front door announced the news. Angelica went immediately to a window facing west. Karen and Elizabeth were hauling in a deer. A good size doe, Angelica noted, smiling handsomely from ear to ear. She grabbed her coat and went out and around the corner of the building to greet them.

"Who got her?" Angelica asked.

"I did, Ms. M," Elizabeth answered up excitedly. The two were elated but exhausted. "We had to drag 'er up half the bluff."

"I'm dead," Karen said, dropping the haul line, her hands moving to both knees. "She's got to weigh a ton," she added, puffs of white breath passing from her mouth and rushing south.

"One eighty on the hoof, I'd guess," Angelica declared, walking over to the animal and examining the entrance and exit wounds. "Less twenty after you field-dress her."

"One ton," Karen argued amicably.

"This was a beautiful shot, Elizabeth," Angelica congratulated the young woman sincerely.

"I took out a lung."

"You had no trouble tracking her." It wasn't a question.

Elizabeth beamed. "No trouble at all. She bled like bloody Friday."

Angelica laughed. "Where did you come up with that?"

"Bloody Friday? My father always used to say that."

"Go inside and warm up," the commander in chief invited.

"You want me to pull the tree stand first?" Elizabeth said

eagerly.

"I want you to go inside and wait for me. Then I want you to tell me all about your kill." Angelica turned to Karen. "Go back out there and bring me back a deer."

Karen started to say something but thought better of it. She turned and headed off in the direction from which she had come.

"Thank you for helping me," Elizabeth called out.

Karen put her hand in the air in acknowledgment.

"Inside," Angelica said again.

"Yes, Ms. M."

"Bobby. Paul."

The two young men came trotting over to Angelica. "Yes, ma'am," Bobby said.

"Think the two of you can get this deer hoisted on that meat pole—cleaned and skinned?" She gestured toward the rear of the lodge. "Without butchering it too badly, I mean?" she teased.

The two looked at one another. "Does a bear shit in the woods, dude?" Paul asked of Bobby.

"Does a ferret fart in a furrow?" Bobby threw back to Paul. Both soldiers nodded in agreement. "We can do that, Ms. M," the two comedians said decidedly, bobbing their heads in unison like the Bobbsey twins.

"That's very amusing, gentlemen," Angelica simpered. "Your good humor should easily carry you through a second watch after you've finished hanging Bambi." She turned abruptly and headed back inside,

When Angelica disappeared around the corner of the building, Paul turned to Bobby in confusion. "She wants us to pull another four hours after fuckin' with Bambi, dude?" he flared.

Bobby looked dumbfoundedly at his friend. "Hey, does a hickory horse have a wooden dick, *Dummkopf?*" he said in answer.

Robert and Liza were two hundred yards or so into the woods when he thought he caught a movement. His right hand shot back, fingers extended downward like the fletchings suspended from the quiver on the bow that he held firmly in his grip. Liza stopped dead in her tracks. Neither of them moved a muscle for the next five minutes. He studied the rising sun filtering between patches of thick cloud covering, the diffused light eerily breaking across the treetops, casting long tentacles of shadow before suddenly being swallowed up whole.

Several more minutes had passed before the sun shone through the clouds again, daybreak saturating the landscape. But a single shadow did not conform to the patch of camo cloth hunkered between the boughs of the forty-foot black oak set forty yards north-northwest of them. The pair dared not move. Liza's leg muscles ached from the crouched position she held. Robert so wanted to raise his field glasses but would not risk it.

Finally, the pattern moved a fraction to the left, and Robert knew he was looking at the back of a parka hood. Instantly, he raised the glasses and confirmed his sighting. Without taking his eyes off the figure, he lifted the strap from around his neck and put the binoculars away. Without a word, he communicated to Liza to stay put, remain quiet, and that everything was going to be all right. A forefinger and a thumbs-up sign did all his talking for him. Liza frowned but understood.

Robert circled to his right, taking cautious steps forward on the ball of each foot, setting a heel down carefully before moving ahead, alternately shifting his eyes from the ground to the tree in which his quarry sat. Robert took in the trees around him, too. It was twenty-two degrees Fahrenheit, and he was sweating as though he had run the quarter mile.

Liza lost sight of him. Twenty minutes later she began to panic. Her heart raced, and her breathing became erratic. She turned nauseous and wanted to lie down on the ground and die right there. And then she saw little David. Only it wasn't little David, she knew. It was a tree stump. But the outline of her nephew's face was in it, she swore. "Why are you doing this?" she whispered, knowing he was dead. And then the face was gone. Liza laughed nervously yet quietly. "Shh," she told herself. "Get a grip, girl."

A moment later, there came a crash that shook the forest floor. Liza froze. She could hear movement in the distance. Then silence. Liza was biting down on her glove. Someone was coming. She was sure that it was Robert, yet she would be ready just in case it wasn't. But Robert did not have a hood attached to his jacket, and Robert would never ever raise his bow and prepare to pull an arrow back, pointed directly at her chest. Before the figure ever came to full draw,

Robert had released an arrow from his 70-pound pull bow, the 90-grain scalpel-sharp broadhead cutting a path clean through the woman's ribcage and out the other side.

Number Thirty-three just stood there for several seconds as if an arrogant wind had failed to put her down, dropping her weapon painlessly before giving up her life. She toppled and Liza jumped a mile.

"Oh, my God!" Liza sounded, tearing insanely at a glove with her teeth before offering up an explanation. "I thought that was you." Liza shivered. "But you would never ever hurt me." She sobbed. "Never, ever," she continued, raising her pitch while waving the bow and arrow like a wild magician with a wand. The arrow had slid off the overdraw and was hanging precariously from her bowstring.

Robert grabbed the weapon from her, unnocking the arrow. Liza threw a fit. He put both weapons on the ground behind him. Before she could utter a single word, he slapped her with an open hand. Hard. She fell beside the body, immediately scrambling out of its way, clutching her mouth with both hands. He grabbed her by the back of the neck and pushed her face inches from the frozen face of death.

"That could have been you," he whispered. "Understand?"

She nodded violently.

"There's forty-four more out there. Just like this one."

"Why, why did you let her come so cl-close to me?" she stammered.

"What are you talking about?"

"She was over there." Liza pointed in the direction from where Robert had come. "She was in that tree. You let her get down and come after me." She wept, covering her mouth with her hand.

"This is another one. The other is lying at the base of that tree. This one heard you."

Liza shook her head.

"I heard you. You gave yourself away."

"I thought I saw little David over there." She trembled, turning in all directions until she saw the trunk.

Robert knelt down next to her. "Listen to me. I'm going to take you back now."

Liza shook her head. "No."

"You're a danger to yourself. And you're a danger to me."

"No, you need my window. I'll be good. You'll see."

Robert shook his head, lifting her chin to face him. "Look at me. You're not feeling well. I was wrong to put you in this situation. It's a stupid thing I did. You can't see through that window when you're all wound up like this."

"Yes, I can. Even better. You'll see. Trust me."

"Let's go."

"Where are we going?"

"Back to the barn."

"I want another chance. I'm calm now."

"No, you're not. I'm not. So how can you be?"

Liza stood her ground.

"Want me to carry you out of here?"

"Shh."

"What now?"

"Two more are coming. Walking toward us." Liza pointed due west. "Several steps and then they stop."

Robert took out his binoculars.

"You won't see them yet. Minutes away. Just behind the pineland. Coming through a field."

Robert couldn't even see the pineland through the lot, let alone the field. But he knew those two tracts of land were out there. She had never been up that way. He looked at her oddly. "You sure?"

"Pick up your bow," she said quietly.

"Listen to me."

"No, you listen to *me*. Kathleen told you that I'm running this show. I say we're a team. Pull her body out of the way, behind that knoll. And give me back my bow and arrow." Liza readjusted the strap on her release. "I said give it to me." She took back her bow then reset the arrow above the nock point, attaching the release to the string, drawing back fluidly, taking aim, concentrating on her breathing, her stance. "They'll be coming through that little clearing over there." She motioned, letting off on the string carefully. "I'll be behind this tree," she said, stepping toward it. "You take that one over there. When they reach that stump, we come to full draw, step out together, and release."

"You're sure?"

"I'll take the one on the left; you take the one on the right. Center of the chest. No prisoners."

Robert was studying her carefully. "You gonna be all right with this?"

"Right as rain." As if on cue, it began to drizzle. Liza smiled.

"I'm sorry I hit you," he said quietly.

"Shut up."

Robert pulled the woman's bloody body behind the knoll.

Fifteen minutes later, two giants came into view, better than seventy yards away. Robert realized that the pair was probably stalking deer, taking a dozen or so steps at a time in the hopes of catching Bambi in his bed. What unnerved him even more than the size of the two men was their sheer audacity. Snap-shooting deer on the move took inordinate skill with a bow and was usually reserved for very windy days so as to muffle the stalker's movements. Suddenly, a score of thoughts hit Robert all at once. Were they carrying bows or . . . guns? Something was strange with the configuration. He strained to see clearly but couldn't. A single shot fired from a gun could end all their lives in a matter of minutes. Were they poachers hunting out of season with guns? He tried to alert Liza. He could see that her eyes were glued to the two. She was totally focused.

At fifty yards away, the giants came into the narrow clearing, walking side by side. Robert could plainly see that the two men were carrying camo-finished crossbows fixed with quivers as well as telescopic sights. Surprising the pair as planned could trigger a deadly response. The pair was loaded for bear and looked as though they might fire in excitement in lieu of lining up a shot. Or might he and Liza become their intentional targets? Poachers were unpredictable. But were they piranha of another sort? Angelica Manns' people? Patrolling, perhaps, the periphery of the camp for any sign of trouble?

The two men now stood twenty yards away. Robert could sense that Liza was putting the same data through her brain. She did not look over toward him, though. Her stance told him that she was going ahead as planned. Her feet were firmly planted. Resolve was clearly written across her face. In seconds, the men would reach the stump. Robert put down his bow and arrow and pulled a pistol from his belt.

"Freeze, fools," Robert snapped, stepping forward of the tree, the handgun leveled at one of their faces.

One man's crossbow swung upward, aimed on Robert's chest.

"Freeze, my ass, motherfucker," the second thundered, pointing his weapon at Robert's head.

"Drop those toys or daylight will fill the void between your ears," Robert promised.

"Who the fuck are you, asshole?"

"Conservation Officer Carbone," Robert answered, holding a steady bead on the more menacing of the two.

"That a fact?"

"Fact, fool."

"You ain't no fucking conservation officer. And that ain't no standard uniform. Ain't no nine-millimeter issue, either."

"I wear and carry what I want. And right now I want you two to drop those weapons."

The redneck laughed. "A second ago they were toys."

"Let me tell you what I think," the other said. "I think you're a poacher just like us. I think you want this fuckin' place all to yourself. I think Jeff can put an arrow through you before you could bat an eye."

Jeff laughed. "Yeah, I think you're fucked."

"Now, let me tell you what I *know*," Robert retorted. "I know that I'm taking you out first, like I did the other two before you came. Look at the blood to your right."

"Your other right, stupid," Liza said, stepping out from behind her tree at full draw, a broadhead pointed at the shorter giant's center.

"Well, well, well. Will you lookie here, Sammy. I'd say we got us one of them Mexican stand-offs," the taller of the two trespassers declared with a grin. "How long can missy hold back that bow, boy, before her arm falls off?"

"All fucking day long, asshole," Liza responded. "Fifty-pound pull. Eighty percent let-off. It's like I'm holding ten. Understand? Now, like Officer Carbone said. Drop them."

"There's an awful lot of blood there, Jeff," Sam stated. "Leadin' back to that mound behind 'em."

"Why do you have a bow, lady, if he's a conservation officer?" Jeff demanded.

"Your arms getting tired, boys?" Robert interrupted, noting their shift in weight. "I'd bet good money those babies you're holding are every bit of ten pounds, too."

"Shut up," Jeff snapped.

"I know that name, Jeff," Sam piped up. "I think he's who he says he is."

"Shut up. I asked you a question, missy."

"We're dressed and carrying like this because we're on special assignment," Liza explained. "This is not a call-in complaint from some cranky farmer. We have two bodies back there. Two of several killers who are hiding out in these woods. We want to blend in, not stand out. All right?"

"We're not interested in pieces of shit like you," Robert rejoined. "You're just a lot of unnecessary paperwork to us. If we didn't have our hands full with this business," he said, gesturing back to the blood, "I'd run your sorry asses in this minute. Now drop those weapons and take a hike, and I'll just chalk this up to bad timing."

"I don't want no trouble with the law," Sam whined.

"Why would the cops send in two conservation officers, Carbone?" Jeff asked with a smirk.

"Because this officer knows these woods and gets the job done," Liza snapped.

"Yeah, well, I wanna see a body back there like you claim. If you've shot a deer, like I think you have, we're taking it. Maybe you too, missy. 'Cause I don't believe a fucking word you said."

"Then I'm telling you how we're going to do this," Robert ordered.

"You ain't telling me shit," Jeff countered.

"Then be prepared to die," Robert put forth plainly.

"Listen to him," Sam puled. "Please."

"On the count of three, we all lower our weapons. One of you can take a walk behind us and see for yourself. The other body is forty yards northwest of us." He could see the two were tiring, knowing that Liza had to be tired, too.

"Do what he says," Sam pleaded.

Jeff curled a lip. "On the count of three," he conceded. "No crap."

"No crap," Robert said evenly. "One . . . . Two . . . . Three."

Both parties lowered their weapons simultaneously.

"You go," Jeff ordered.

Sam followed the blood trail a short distance, stopping at the foot of the knoll. He tiptoed around it carefully then suddenly brought a hand up to his mouth. Liza's eyes were on the cowardly figure, dry heaving at the foot of the mound. Jeff's eyes never left Robert's.

"We won't bother with you," Robert swore. "We just want you the hell out of here. Today you're lucky on two accounts. Lucky that the others didn't kill you. Lucky we made you for what you are; otherwise, we would have cleaned your clock."

Sam came back all shaky, holding a bloody arrow in the air between a thumb and forefinger. "Clean through," he said, pointing to each side of his torso.

"Why didn't you just shoot the poor soul with that?" Jeff said, pointing to the pistol lying on the ground.

"You're not listening to me. There are others out there waiting."

"You're for real?"

"For real."

Sam started to pick up his crossbow. "Come on. They're going to let us walk."

"Those bows stay right there, fellas," Robert snapped.

Jeff scowled, holding fast to his weapon. "Six-hundred-dollar package. I don't think so, chump."

"How much is your life worth, Jeff?"

"Do we get them back?"

"They're illegal. You're illegal. You're trespassing on private property. Gonna cost you more than a grand in fines and jail time if you persist. So give it up and get the fuck out of here," Robert concluded, losing patience fast.

"That way," Liza pointed in the direction they themselves had come. "For safety's sake," she added.

Jeff stepped back. "I'll remember the two of you," he said threateningly.

"I would hope that you would," Robert agreed.

The two giants walked off in the direction Liza had sent them, never looking back. Robert picked up his pistol and bow and arrow.

"You were fantastic," he said, returning to Liza's side.

Liza forced a smile. "I just hope we did the right thing by letting them go."

"I wouldn't worry about those two creeps. They won't be back, and they'll keep their mouths shut. They'd be too embarrassed to tell anyone the truth about what happened here. They'll just make up some cock-and-bull story about how they lost their weapons."

"I hope you're right."

"Let's get those crossbows out of sight."

"Think we can use them?"

Robert shook his head. "Too cumbersome for what we have to do. Besides, they're low-end junk. Six-hundred-dollar package, my ass."

"If you say so."

Chapter 51

Governor Alexander Atkins paced his office, brooding over rumors of indictments about to be handed down within the next few weeks. The buzzards were circling the Capitol, he certainly realized. Atlanta was all abuzz. Mayor Harden and Sheriff Hayes sat waiting impatiently in the governor's outer office.

The governor pressed the intercom. "Sally, darlin', send them in," he muttered gruffly, champing on an extinguished cigar.

The two Toms were at the threshold. Immediately, the sheriff opened the door for the mayor, and both men quickly found a seat.

"Governor," the sheriff greeted.

"Al," the mayor managed.

"Gentlemen. Gentlemen. Auspicious times are ahead, I'm sure. I just don't know how far down the fucking road they lay. Do you?" he asked with considerable agitation.

"That's why we're here," the mayor assured him.

The mayor's smile appeared as an angel of mercy, the sheriff's repetitive nod as nothing more than a woodpecker picking away dispassionately at the governor's flimsy silver lining.

"What's the rub?" Al demanded.

"O'Sullivan gets the hauling contract."

"That fucking Irishman? Monte won't stand still for it; not for a second."

"Monte's out."

"What?"

"He takes the fall for bid rigging."

"How long?"

"Two to six years."

"He's seventy-four years old, Tom. He's my friend."

"We're your friends, Al," the mayor reminded him.

"Plus five-point five million in fines," Sheriff Hayes put in.

"Fuck the money. The money's nothing. Monte won't last a year."

"We'll work on that afterward."

"What about his son and daughter?"

"Probation. They're out, too. The family's out, Al. Lifetime ban from the carting industry."

"A fucking waste, Tom."

"Waste is what the district attorney's office is arguing. Waste and Mob influence."

"Fuck the district attorney. I'm the governor of this state."

"You won't be, Al. Not if those indictments are handed down. We said we'd fix it. Right? It's fixed."

"Is it ever," the sheriff added and chuckled quietly.

"I want that son of a bitch out of office, Tom, Tom. You guys fix that, you hear?"

"First things first, Al. You let this thing quiet down some."

"Monte's like family to me, boys."

"Monte feels the same way about you. That's why he took the deal. There's no other way. It's very fashionable these days for a young D.A. to go after the Mob, especially if he knows that he can make it stick. He'll take the biggest slice of bread, now, or simply have you for toast tomorrow. It's just that simple, Al."

"Everything's off my back?"

"Every last crumb. Business as usual. Auspicious times are here again, Al," the mayor swore. "Oh, and Al."

The governor looked at Tom Harden guardedly.

"You'll be in your office this afternoon till what time?"

"Till around four. Why?"

"Karl would appreciate it if you'd make yourself available for a chat sometime after two."

"Would that be a chitchat, Tom?"

Together, Tom-Tom rose to their feet.

"You really should thank him, Al. Profusely," the mayor underscored. "He went all out for you. One hundred and one percent of his support. He'd like to know that you're appreciative is all. He'll phone you."

"Sure thing," the governor promised, gnashing the cigar between his teeth. "What are old friends for?"

"Governor."

"Sheriff."

"You can rest easy now, Al," Hayes said comfortingly.

"Thank you, gentlemen," the governor mumbled, pushing himself back from his desk. "Let me see you old warriors to the elevator."

"Not necessary, Al. Sit."

"No, I insist. I sit around all day and worry. I want to get up and stretch these old legs. Get out and breathe a bit. Maybe even jog around the building. Backwards. Ever hear of Backwards Day? My grandson had on everything backwards this morning. Told me he'll be doing everything backwards in school today. I told him if it's anything like going downhill, I've been doing it for months. Told me I talk silly. Imagine? The governor of the great state of Georgia, silly. I told him he had some set for seven. Wants to be a talent scout. Where do these kids today get these ideas?" The governor opened the door for the two men.

"Thanks, Gov."

"Sally, darlin'. I'm going to see these men downstairs. Maybe take a little walk."

"Yes, sir."

"Did you ever see anyone so pretty, boys?"

The secretary blushed.

"Twenty-one," he told them.

"I am *not*," she scolded sophomorically. "I'm forty-four."

"Forty-four, and she still can't bring herself to tell a little white lie."

"Forty-four! That's ancient, Al. I don't know why you keep her around, Gov.," the sheriff teased.

"Because she still puts out, but not for me anymore," he bantered playfully. "Well, maybe twice a year; around my birthday and Christmas. Ride, Sally, Ride!" he sang out rowdily, bumping and grinding both his buttocks and groin to the lyrics.

The middle-aged woman put her blonde head down, smoothing the front of her skirt with both palms before turning away in humiliation.

At 2:15 p.m. the phone rang in the governor's office. The switchboard put it through on Sally's private line. Sally screened it and buzzed the governor.

"Yes, darlin'."

"It's him."

"All right. Put him through."

There was a long beep followed by a coded series of scrambled signals.

"Karl?"

"Hello, Al."

"Good to hear your voice, old friend. Hope you and your family had a fine Christmas, sir. To what do I owe this special honor?"

"Time to collect on an old debt, old friend."

"I see. Well, Karl. Lay it out for me, pal. But before you do, let me express my sincere thanks for all your support of late. I am indebted. I think you know that," the governor's voice trailed.

"It's about Millie, Al."

"Millie? Tom's wife?"

"Yes."

"Well, how can I be of service, sir?" the governor said, beginning to relax.

"Seems she's communicating with a certain party about matters of a very delicate nature. I want you to take care of that for us, Al."

"Take care of it?"

"Yes, Al."

"But you have people for that, Karl. I—"

"We want *you* to take care of it."

"Me?"

"Yes."

"May I ask why, Karl? I mean, it seems to me the mayor could take care of his own affairs, no?" he hedged and laughed uncomfortably.

"We brought that to his attention once already, Al."

"I see. Maybe I could speak to Sheriff Hayes about the matter. As you know—"

"We're lending our full support to Tom Hayes concerning the Ballard business. We feel he has enough on his plate right now. Don't you?"

"Right, right. Of course. It's just that the Montes have their hands full, too. And I was—"

"We're not asking for the Monte family's involvement, Al. We're asking for you to handle this matter personally. We don't want it to go outside the circle."

After a moment's hesitation, Al caved. There was little choice. "I understand."

"That's fine, Al. You have forty-eight hours. Take care."

There was silence followed by a long beep on the line. Governor Atkins put the phone down on its cradle then lay back in his large black leather reclining chair. Thinking . . . thinking about the truly high cost of good fortune.

Chapter 52

Seven deer hung on a meat pole in back of the lodge overlooking the bluff. But only one was a buck; a four pointer. Elizabeth's deer was still the largest, however. Yet, Danny's was considered the prize. The young man sat by the fireplace. He sipped hot chocolate, absorbed in a tattered copy of *The Wizard of Oz*. He was king of the hill thus far. But it was still early; 2:30 p.m. A good three hours remained in which someone else could tip the scale of domination. Too, there was always tomorrow and the next day.

Robert and Liza's immediate concern was the method in which Angelica deployed as well as monitored her troops. He focused his binoculars on the Cliff House, as the lodge was called. Several soldiers were milling around inside the main room. Through the south window, Robert could see a young woman holding a glass to her lips. Sipping. A man of about the same age was talking into a hand-held VHF radio, pacing the floor near the far wall. Suddenly, the front door opened and another young man stepped out. He looked no more than eighteen. A woman with a pistol on her hip stood just inside the doorway.

Robert and Liza made their way around the wooded area to the west side of the building.

"Stay low, and stay directly behind me," he whispered.

"How many?"

Robert showed four fingers then put one of them to his lips. Liza followed him quietly, planting her feet precisely wherever Robert stepped. Fifteen minutes later, they were seventy yards off the east side of the lodge. He raised his binoculars and focused through another window, down a long corridor.

"Anything?" Liza asked.

Robert stared at the empty space for a full minute before lowering his glasses.

"Well?" she asked.

Robert shook his head. "Come on."

The wind picked up and chilled them to the bone. He turned and zipped Liza's jacket to the top.

"We're going to take it very slow and work our way around to the rear."

"How?" she asked, seeing that there was no available cover.

"Along the cliffs. Just beneath the bluff."

"You're crazy. You're crazy, and it's getting cold."

"Let's go."

The two of them did a balancing act just beneath the bluff. Slowly, tediously, they made their way along the steep incline, digging into the sandy embankment with the sole edge of their boots. An endless wind whipped across the Sound and created whitecaps on the water far below. For a solid ten minutes the wind refused to die. Finally, it settled down.

"You stay here," he said.

"Where're you going?" Liza demanded.

"To have a look." Robert climbed to the rim of the northern precipice, figuring he was aligned dead center with the back of the building when something grabbed his leg.

"Jesus Christ," he cringed, losing his footing and slipping a half a yard. "Don't scare me like that," he bristled.

"You're not leaving me back here," she said defiantly.

Robert ordered her to stay put, inching his way to the top. As he reached its peak, he peered carefully along the ridge, using his binoculars only after determining that the area was secure. He didn't need the glasses to see the seven deer hanging from a long pole suspended between two trees. But he scoped the carcasses just the same.

"Gross," Liza whispered, her eyes an inch above the crest.

"Twice, I told you to stay put. What are you doing, dammit?"

"Taking in the sights," she said.

"The view is that way," he directed, pointing across the body of water to Connecticut. "Now get back down."

Liza stewed. "Think we'll ever make it back there this summer, alive?"

"Move!"

Liza moved back down a foot.

Robert shot a finger to his lips then pointed. A figure was coming around the west corner of the building, running straight toward them, a rifle at the ready. Robert pulled his pistol and held it inches from the peak. One report from either weapon and he knew that they'd be history. Angelica's troops would swoop down on them like white on rice. Had someone spotted them from inside? He could hear the footsteps fast approaching. Suddenly, the muffled movement stopped, no less than ten feet away Robert approximated. He heard the familiar sound of a magazine ejecting from its receiver, followed by a single cartridge hitting the ground. *What the hell was going on*? he wondered. The sudden rush of the weapon being reloaded should have revealed the relevance. But it had not. Only when Robert heard the cry for acknowledgment did he realize the significance of the drill.

"How'd I do?"

"Fifty-one seconds," a male voice called out from a distance. "Let's run through that once again," the fellow ordered.

"Yes, sir," the female soldier replied.

"Not bad, though. I'd like to get you down to forty-five."

"I lost time coming around the building."

"Why is that?"

"Thought I saw something move back there in that corner, Peter."

"Pick up that round, and let's go have a look."

Robert waited until the footsteps faded before he signaled to Liza to make their move. And move they did. Crouching low. Quickly heading west.

Four soldiers patrolled the northwest corner, so Robert and Liza had no choice but to head back down the bluff before swinging around in a westerly direction around the enemy, then south-southeast, back up the cliff and into the woods. The only problem with the approach was that it would put them in a section where Robert believed Angelica's troops were heavily concentrated. But they could not chance going back the way they came.

If Peter had been a bounty hunter, they might be in deep doo-doo, Robert considered. He prayed that the instructor was making his bones as a woodsman himself and that Liza and he could stay a step ahead. What concerned him equally, was the hour. Robert and Liza could easily make it back to the barn before dark if they were simply on a carefree walk, but stealth would be the name of the game, and he would have to scan every single tree before either of them ventured a step. That would take them well into the night. But that could also be their edge, Robert knew, for he had come prepared.

When the two were halfway down the bluff, Robert stopped and spoke up first. "If you sense something urgent," he paused to take a breath, "you tell me. Like with those poachers this morning. Otherwise, I call the shots."

"All right," she agreed breathlessly.

"Can't have two chiefs."

"All right, I said."

"We still gotta go west," he pointed. "Maybe a hundred yards. Then we swing south. Then east. We've got to be careful on the northern route. That's where they're going to be." He gestured. "All through there."

"Why don't we go way west, past them, then head south?"

"Time. It's going to be dark in a few hours."

"What if they're still out there?"

"They will be. Remember the turkeys this morning? Roosting?"

Liza nodded.

"We're going to pick them off, one by one."

"With ten arrows?"

"With six more added every time we take a prize."

"I can't shoot their arrows on my bow."

"Then we'll use their bows and their arrows."

"I can't."

"Why not?"

"Different draw weights. Different draw lengths. You taught me that."

"I also taught you how to decrease the draw weight by ten pounds with the Allen wrench tool you carry. You'll just have to size up the situation very carefully." Robert started heading out.

"Wait," she whispered.

"What now?"

"Tell me what that was all about back there."

"Peter and his pupil."

303

"Doing what?"

"Practicing."

"Practicing what?"

"How fast she could move around the perimeter of the building, fire then reload."

"What if some of them have guns out there?"

"They don't."

"How do you know?"

"Gunning season is over. Gunfire would draw the heat. DEC Officer Carbone and his people would be down here in a flash. So would the police. Only if there's real trouble would Angelica's troops call attention to themselves by firing a gun. That's one of the reasons that they picked this place. They feel safe. No one belongs up here this time of year. Now let's move it."

Down was easy. Over wasn't so bad. Up was the killer that told Liza that she was definitely out of shape. When they reached the top of the cliff, it was four o'clock. Robert decided that they would stay fifty yards east off the north-south trail. Every fifty feet, Robert raised his glasses and ran the optics along and through the trees. They hadn't gone a hundred yards when he spotted a figure sixty yards out and thirty some feet high, sitting with its head down, the bow across the knees.

Robert signaled Liza then circled wide, for if that person ever lifted his or her head, the couple would be spotted in a heartbeat.

As Robert moved furtively, he failed to see a gray form rising slowly from its seat, high and off to the right. Robert was thirty yards from his target. The ghostly-gray form stood twenty yards away from his new quarry, the bow held squarely at arm's length, arrow nocked securely on the string, release in place.

Before Robert closed the gap, his target turned to life. It raised its head and smiled prettily, extending a pair of open arms as if offering a last embrace. Robert raised his bow and arrow as the gray form off to his right drew its.

The whiz from Liza's arrow put a sudden pang of fear upon the pretty girl's face as she saw her partner fold in two and leave the tree. The girl immediately raised her bow and nocked an arrow, but not in the nick of time. Robert put an arrow in her chest. The fall shook the forest floor.

Robert went over to Liza's victim and pulled the camo face mask from its head. Male. Maybe twenty-two years old. Robert went through all the pockets. Liza went over to the other body and did the same. Next, he quickly removed and compared arrows from the soldiers' quivers, closely matching what they would later need as replacements.

"This one will do nicely for me in a pinch. You take these two: Easton 2216s. A little bit heavier than what you're shooting. Same length, though. Take them. Just as a backup. Let's get out of here. Any ID on that one?"

Liza shook her head. "Oh, my God!"

"What?"

"That one's still moving."

"Let him be. Come on. I said, come on."

"I feel like I'm burning up. Sweating. I thought my heart was going to jump out of my chest. I had such a rush."

"The adrenaline. Now be quiet."

The pair made their way south, fifty or so yards at a clip. Soon they would lose the light. A million thoughts were racing through Robert's brain. Would Angelica leave her soldiers in their trees overnight? Unlikely. Would she collect them one by one at a designated time and place as Richard Geist had done in training sessions with his own soldiers years back? Or would the troops head back to the lodge on their own just before or after dark? Would there be a mass exodus within the hour? Would Angelica send out a search party for four of her missing soldiers or assume that they were out tracking a wounded animal through the night?

He now had answers to earlier questions, though. For most of the soldiers would be found along acreage he and Liza were presently covering. The group hunted in pairs, male and female it appeared; they wore the same clothing and basically had the same equipment.

Robert believed that no more than a dozen soldiers secured the lodge, leaving approximately thirty troops spread out west of them, along the north-south trail. In another hour, he'd have a clearer picture.

Liza was tapping him on the shoulder.

"What?" he whispered.

"I have to go to the bathroom."

"You hold it."

"I can't."

"Then I'm going to leave you here."

"Then leave."

"Number one or two?" he soured.

"That's personal."

"We're out here killing people, Liza. How less personal can it get?"

Liza said nothing.

"Do you need toilet paper?"

"No."

"Then go behind that tree, and don't make any noise."

"Piss on you."

"Behind that tree, I said."

He couldn't help but smile. He was scared to death but could somehow manage to grin and bear it. He pictured the smile on the pretty young woman that he had shot only moments ago. Maybe he'd just go mad and end it. Maybe he'd just shoot Liza in an act of mercy while she peed behind that tree. She just saved his life, and he hadn't even thanked her. Maybe he'd thank her just before he'd shoot her. Maybe he wouldn't even thank her at all. Ever! He waited.

"Okay," she said sullenly.

The two were on their way again.

A bevy of quail kicked up just ahead of them, and Liza thought she'd have a heart attack. "I'm cold," she swore, stepping carelessly and breaking a branch she should have seen.

"Why don't you just formally announce your goddamn presence?"

"I've been in these woods eleven fucking hours. And I'm cold."

"Of course you're cold, squatting behind a tree with your pants down. What do you expect?" The sun was now behind cloud cover, and he could see that she was starting to shiver. "Toes cold?"

She shook her head.

"Hands?"

She nodded.

Robert opened his fanny pack and pulled out two cellophane packages containing chemical hand warmers. Using his teeth, he carefully started a tear in a corner of one package, quietly peeling away a strip along its top. He removed the bag and shook it several times before handing it to her, then did the same with the other package. "These'll warm up nicely in a minute." Sliding a camo muff from back to front around her waist, he inserted one of the bags, the other inside her left mitten—flat against her palm. He pulled her right mitten off and stuck it in her coat pocket. "Stick this hand in your muff," he instructed. "Can't pull a bow back with freezing cold hands, now can you?"

Liza shook her head.

"Better?"

"Much."

"Good, now move your ass and stop complaining."

Twenty minutes later, the sun dropped behind the treetops. Soon it would be dark. The two made their way south without incident. Robert stopped and broke out his compass to confirm their direction. Liza moved up ahead and paused to take a breather. The warmth from the chemical bags felt good against her skin. She wondered how in God's name anyone could sit in a tree stand all day and into the evening, even with chemical hand warmers and toe warmers. For the moment, she felt safe and warm when suddenly a *whoosh* went by her right ear. Immediately, she hit the ground and rolled behind a tree, her bow and arrow held outward then upward and at the ready.

Robert saw Liza near the base of a tree and signaled her to stay. Sinking a hand silently into an inside coat pocket, he removed an expensive pair of Steiner night-vision binoculars, bringing them slowly to his face. He switched on the instrument and ran the optics once across the treetops; twice back and forth beneath the dark umbrellas; thrice along the ground. In the emerald-green light, Robert caught the image, pulling away his mask, having already descended his twenty-foot perch.

The man was making his way toward Liza, taking full advantage of all available cover. Picking up a stick, the soldier tossed it near her. Liza spooked and rolled another three feet. Instantly, the man loosed a broadhead that buried itself in a low limb an inch from Liza's arm. Immediately, she took cover behind another tree.

Robert had no shot unless the man stepped forward, five or six feet. Suddenly, he did. But Robert wasn't ready. He couldn't hold the binoculars in one hand and shoot a bow with the other. He could wait until the assassin shot off another arrow and then rush him before he had a chance to nock another, but the last shot had been frightfully close. Or he could simply shoot him with his pistol and wake the living dead.

Robert could barely see the outline of the trees or even Liza. All light was fading fast. For the moment, Liza had cover. Think, he told himself. For the love of God, think. Robert ran the glasses along a narrow trail, deciding which tree the man might run to. No obstruction between the tree the soldier hid behind and the one he would likely rush toward for the kill.

Robert put away the binoculars and immediately drew the bow, holding the twenty-yard pin on the point the man would hopefully cross. Suddenly, the soldier broke from cover, heading for the tree. Robert squeezed the trigger on the release, sending the arrow to its mark, dashing the man's brains while in furious flight. The body crashed heavily into the thicket and dropped. The world around them was dark and silent.

Robert pulled out the binoculars and found Liza in the sea-green emerald light. She was standing perfectly still, an arrow nocked and ready, the release locked securely beneath the nock, a knife blade fixed firmly between her teeth. How could he approach her in the darkness without getting arrowed or knifed himself, he wondered? He certainly couldn't or wouldn't dare call out to her. Not even in a whisper. Robert put away the glasses, turned his back, then smiled.

It wasn't a minute later before Liza came to him. "You never could piss quietly in the great outdoors," she whispered.

"Just sounds that way at night. Everything's magnified."

"Not everything," she swore.

"Complaints, complaints," he bantered, zipping up his fly.

"I'm not complaining about that bulls-eye, though. How in God's name could you see where you were aiming?"

"I really don't know, Liza. But I'll tell you one thing. I had an angel riding on that shot."

"I wonder if his partner's still— Lights!"

"What?"

"Look." Liza pointed.

"Get down."

Several points of light, like little stars, were moving toward them through the dark. Robert and Liza moved back some sixty yards. Two minutes later, a series of lights swept and danced and darted and flooded the pineland floor. Beams from flashlights, head-lamps, and lanterns brightened the night. Yet, not a single syllable was spoken by anyone.

The troops moved from south to north, heading toward the lodge. Robert counted thirty-one warm bodies, adding to that a body count of five that were strewn throughout the wooded area, getting cold. Liza was crouched behind Robert. The two of them watched until the lights became faint, finally disappearing in the distance.

"Tell you what's bothering me," Liza said.

"Our victim's partner," Robert guessed. "Probably female."

Liza nodded. "Think she's still out there?"

"What does your window tell you?"

"Window is dark, Rob."

"The guy could have been by his lonesome."

"An odd fellow, huh?"

"I don't know."

"I don't, either."

"What do you think?"

"I think she would have called out to one of the troops if she were still around here."

"Not if she was scared," Robert reasoned.

"Scared of what at that point?"

"Scared that I might shoot her."

"In the pitch dark?"

"It was pretty dark when I dropped that guy. I'm sure she would have heard that sound. Point is, if she is out there and gets back with the news, we're dead. There has got to be over forty of them all told. And they're good. But like Kathleen said, we have the element of surprise going for us. Let's pray the guy was off by himself."

"So what do we do? If you didn't see anyone else with those night glasses . . . which reminds me, why are you holding on to both pair?"

"Weight."

"Believe me. I can hold my own."

"Give me your light."

"Now he wants my light."

"Hand it over."

Liza handed him her mini flashlight. He reached inside his fanny pack and took out his own flashlight, along with a roll of tape. Finding a long sturdy stick, he secured her mini-light to one end, wrapping it with the tape.

"Take this and this," he said, handing her his flashlight and the stick with the mini-light attached.

"I don't get it," she said there in the dark.

"If anyone's still back there, we're going to flush 'em out."

"How?"

"You start heading back in that direction."

"Where?"

He turned her around. "There. Straight ahead. About seventy, eighty yards back to the trail."

"Got a tape measure?"

"Don't be cute."

"Not in this outfit, honey."

"Leave this on," he instructed, switching on the larger, longer light. "Now, when you hit that trail, right back there," he assured her, "you turn right, heading north."

"Right is north."

"Right."

"Got it."

"As soon as you hit the trail, switch on the mini-light on this stick. But I want you to hold it like this. Furthest from the side of your body. In your left hand. I want it to appear as though I'm walking beside you."

Liza looked at him in fascination. "What movie was that from?"

"The movie in my head."

"And where are you going to be?"

"Not too far behind till you reach the trail. I've got you covered. Ready?"

"Wait! How far should I go after I hit the trail? You didn't tell me that."

"Well, not up to the lodge, for crying out loud. Unless you think they're holding dinner for us."

"Be serious."

"About another seventy to eighty yards up the trail to where the terrain suddenly drops off big time. Switch off both lights when you reach the bottom. Wait for me there."

"How will I know it's you?"

Robert was fast becoming irritated. "I'll be the one with the white carnation between my teeth."

"No," she said angrily. "You'll be the one pissing in your pants."

"Probably. Now, get moving."

Chapter 53

The four- by four-foot fireplace was roaring and crackling away noisily. A large black wrought-iron ring stood off to one corner, filled with seasoned, split hardwood logs. A half-dozen of Angelica's soldiers huddled before the hearth, absorbing the powerful heat that gradually thawed their bodies. A dozen more crowded in close proximity. Wood snapped, and sparks shot in every direction while orange-red flames leapt upward, lapping the inner chimney wall.

"Didn't know that hell could be such heaven on a day like this," Rebecca said to Charlotte.

"This is nothing," Malcolm interrupted, his palms extended toward the fire about as near as he could bear. "Tomorrow the temperature is supposed to dip well into the teens."

"Shit, does she know that?" Charlotte complained with animated body language, her head and shoulder gesturing toward where their commander in chief reposed in a comfortable chair across the room.

"Think she'd even care?" Rebecca rejoined.

"You don't believe all that crapola about her and Geist's band of badasses spending practically the entire winter in the woods, do you?" Malcolm asked skeptically.

"Sure, if they were all out there humping one another for body heat, I suppose."

Malcolm and Rebecca giggled at Charlotte's remark.

"See any deer?" Doug asked, stepping between the two young women. His question was directed at Malcolm.

"Nah. Just a bunch of squirrels."

"I had one actually run right across my lap," Doug swore. "Chattered in the tree next to me for twenty minutes after that."

"That wasn't a squirrel, Dougie dear," Charlotte jeered. "Those were your nuts shivering in your britches every time you stood. Guy can't sit still for ten seconds. I can just imagine how he paid attention in school," she told the other two.

"Yeah, wanna know what my best two classes were?" Doug challenged.

"Duh, I dunno. Dougie. Were they gym and shop?" Charlotte mocked.

"Math and science. And let's see who gets a deer first, partner. All right?"

"Did you happen to note that there are nine nice deer hanging out back?" Rebecca smiled. "Seven of them taken by us girls."

Doug frowned. "You're kidding."

"Yeah, but Danny got himself a four-pointer," Malcolm boasted for the boys. "A buck scores more points."

"Way to go," Doug recouped.

"But Elizabeth's is still the biggest," Charlotte vaunted in defense, "even though it's a doe. A one hundred eighty-pound beauty," she added with satisfaction.

"Yeah, maybe with Karen sitting on its back," Doug heckled.

"Let's just wait and see what happens tomorrow. Us girls are gonna blow you guys away again. But first I'm going to ask Ms. M to have my seat changed," Charlotte threatened half-jokingly. "I'm telling you this guy scares all the deer away. He just can't sit still."

"All right, troops," Angelica announced, getting up from the recliner and walking toward the center of the room. "We have nine deadly archers present and accounted for, and from what I gather, six more out there probably tracking their trophies. I think that's extraordinary. It's like we've got other hunters out there driving deer for us. As a matter of fact, I was going to put on a little drive if you people didn't produce. But you've far exceeded my expectations." Angelica looked around the room in satisfaction. She stood very proud. "Yes, Elisa?"

"I understand that the women really outdid the men."

Several female heads bobbed in confirmation.

Angelica smiled. "Well, let's not get catty, girls. The tables can turn just like that," she responded, snapping her fingers loudly. "Besides, this is not a contest between men and women. How and to what degree you challenge yourself is what I'd like each of you to consider. The whitetail is a formidable creature in the sense that it will challenge most of you. When you become proficient in harvesting this animal, you will have developed a sixth sense, I can assure you.

313

"Now, before you take showers, eat, and get some rest, I want to reinforce a point that I've been making over and over again. A point that will lead to your success in taking white-tailed deer. And that is, once again, an awareness of the animal's keen sense of smell. Thousands of times greater than your own. So, I want to remind all of you to use your cover scent on your boots, tarsal gland scent around your kill area, and to shower tonight with unscented soap and shampoo that I've provided. You'll hang your outer clothing to air in the building next-door. Those of you who tracked, dragged, or handled deer today, in other words, sweated up a storm, everything gets washed and hung. You take another outfit. Everyone changes their undergarments daily, regardless of activity level. Got it?"

"Yes, Ms. M," the group answered.

"All right, there's plenty of hot cider for everyone to tide you over till dinner. I want to hear each and every war story," she encouraged with a prideful gleam in her eyes. "I want to hear how your hearts were pounding. Elizabeth, we'll start with you whenever you're ready, seeing as how you got the first and the largest deer."

Elizabeth was beaming.

"Yeah, girl. You did us proud," Charlotte called over, raising a fist high above her head.

Guadalupe seconded the motion, punching the air with spiraling fists of fury, spouting something in Spanish.

From her twenty-foot perch, Number Six carefully lowered the bow with her haul line before quietly climbing down the metal post. She shook like the single leaf that stubbornly clung to the majestic maple that had concealed her for the past twelve hours. Silently, she wiped away her tears, shivering violently as she looked around. Leaving her bow and haul line on the ground, she stepped back several steps and quickly unbuckled her belt, unbuttoned her pants, pushed the outfit and undergarment down, squatted—almost losing her balance—then finally urinated in pitch blackness before she thought her bladder would positively burst.

Still shivering, she fixed herself, checked her florescent compass, then headed west, out of the wood lot and toward the north-south trail, leaving her bow and arrows and haul line lying on the ground beside the prodigious maple. She had not forgotten them. She had purposely left the items behind.

Priscilla was deserting. Priscilla was walking away. She would have run to the main road if she could have seen her way, but she could barely see the ground. She dared not use her light for fear that the two killers would see it, although she believed the pair were far enough away to the north. *Who were they?* she wondered. They certainly weren't the police. The police would have called her partner down. The police would have given her partner fair warning. *Or would they?* she reconsidered. Maybe the police had been ordered to kill any of them on sight. But with a bow and arrow like hers? Priscilla couldn't stop crying, muffling the sounds of her sobbing somewhere within the sleeve of her waterproof, windproof, insulated garment. It was not so much the cold that Priscilla shivered from as it was the element of fear.

Robert heard someone or something approaching, coming to the edge of the trail. He drew his bow silently, setting the florescent sight pin upon nothingness. Nothing except the dark. Priscilla saw the yellow dot and froze.

"I'm unarmed," she said. "Please don't shoot me," the young girl added and trembled. "My hands are in the air. My bow is back there. I swear," she wailed.

Robert moved the pin a fraction, setting it just below the level of her voice.

"Down on the ground. Face down," he ordered. He had no vision to confirm the soldier's pledge. *No prisoners*, he had promised Liza and himself. How could they handle such responsibility? He prayed that it was just a trick so that he could kill her where she stood, but he couldn't even see that she was now lying on the ground.

"I'm sixteen years old," she cried aloud. "I never even had a date. I'm a runaway. Please, please, please don't kill me. I'm really not a bad person." She shivered and wept.

"Down."

"I'm down. I can't hurt you. Please don't—"

"Shut up. Spread your arms and legs out to the side. You have a flashlight?"

"Yes, sir."

"Put it on the ground level with your face. Turn it on. Do it."

Suddenly, he saw the light. He could clearly see her arm and

315

half her body. "Don't move."

"I won't. Please don't hurt me."

"Do you have any weapons?"

"A knife."

"Where?" He stepped closer.

"In my left pocket."

"Take it out."

She reached around and removed a penknife.

"Is that it?"

"Yes, sir."

"No more weapons?"

"No. I swear."

Maybe she was a weapon. Maybe she could take his head off his shoulders with a single roundhouse kick if she were standing upright.

"Where are your bow and arrows?"

"I told you. I left everything back there."

"Why?"

"Because I want to run far away from here. It's what I do best," she said as she continued, crying. "Run away from things. I'm so afraid."

Robert pitied her. She didn't look a day more than fifteen.

"Turn the light off. Put it back in your pocket."

"Yes, sir."

"Stay down. Don't you move an inch."

"Please, please don't do anything to me."

Robert reached back into his fanny pack for a line. "Put your hands behind your back and shut up."

Priscilla did as she was told, holding back her sobs. Robert tied her wrists together tightly, pulling her roughly to her feet.

"All right. Now, we're going to have a little talk, you and me."

The teenager trembled. "Please don't hurt me."

"If you say that one more time, I'm going to tie you to a tree and leave you here for the wolves." Priscilla stood absolutely still and quiet. "Understand?"

"Yes, sir."

"What's your name?"

"Lilly," she lied.

"Well, Lilly. I really think you want to live. Yes?"

Priscilla nodded. "Yes."

"So, I want you to answer all my questions truthfully. Some of the questions I already know the answers to. Some I do not. If I find that you're lying to me, I'm going to cut your throat." Robert pulled the knife from his sheath. Although it was dark, she could sense the nearness of the blade. "Do you understand me, Lilly?"

"Yes."

"That's good."

Priscilla started in with the crying again. Only this time she had trouble breathing.

"What's the matter, Lilly?"

She gasped. "My name's not Lilly. It's Priscilla, and I swear I won't lie again. You going to let me go?"

"One thing at a time, Priscilla. Let's see how well you do. How many are there of you?"

"Forty-five," she answered without hesitation. "Forty-six before two men killed my partner."

"What two men?"

"Two men that went that way," she said, gesturing north. "I saw one of them shoot him and heard the crash. Just a few minutes ago."

"So far so good, Priscilla. Where does that trail lead?"

"To a cabin."

"You mean a lodge, don't you, Priscilla?"

"Yes, I guess. Very big. I didn't mean a cabin."

"Just testing, Priscilla. Don't let me catch you in a lie."

Priscilla shook her head quickly. "I'll tell you anything."

"Who runs the show up there?'

"Ms. M. I don't know her name. None of us do."

"How many guard the lodge?"

"Nine or ten, I think."

"How are they posted?"

"One just inside each door; five in all. Four or five sentries patrolling the area outside."

"How often does the guard change?"

"Four hours if we're outside. Eight if we're in. We take turns and rotate. It's whatever she and Peter say."

"Who's Peter?"

"Her lieutenant. Her second in command. The two of them train us. Karen, another girl like us, sometimes gives us orders, too. She was just promoted."

"What kind of firepower do you have up there?"

"The guards carry rifles outside—.30-06s; .45-caliber handguns inside."

"How many rifles and handguns in all?"

"I think fifty rifles, with telescopic sights. I honestly don't know how many pistols."

"What about ammunition?"

"A lot of boxes. Hundreds, I guess. Peter keeps them in the back."

"What size boxes?"

Priscilla described the shape and size of the boxes with her arms. "Big cases."

"Where exactly?"

"First room on the right when you come in from the back. East side of the cabin. I mean the lodge."

"Any other weapons?"

"Half a dozen rocket launchers. Over fifty bows."

"Rocket launchers?"

"Yes, sir."

"For what?"

"Take down the aircraft, helicopters, tanks or trucks. Stuff like that."

"Rockets in the same room?"

"I think."

"You think?"

"I'm pretty sure."

"Any explosives?"

"I don't know, but if we do, Peter has to have them."

"Why Peter?"

"He's our bomb man."

"What kind of bombs?"

"All kinds. Plastics mostly."

"Any other specialty experts like Peter?"

"All of us, I guess."

"What's your specialty, Priscilla?"

"Languages."

"Languages?"

"Uh-huh."

"How many?"

"Nine."

"What other specialties are we looking at? Rattle off a list."

"Plastic explosives, small arms, kendo, judo, jujitsu, karate, communications, archery, knife and ax throwing, verbal terrorism by way of threat and intimidation, garroting and the application of piano wire for torture and electrocution, languages like I said, even acting and stunt performances, reconnaissance. You want me to go on?"

Robert stood in awe. "Enough for now. Now move." He moved her forward and along the trail.

"Where are we going?"

"Ballet instruction. I want to ask my partner how we're going to dance out of this."

"But you're heading north toward the lodge."

"Just move along and keep your mouth shut. But first, what's kendo?"

"A form of fencing using bamboo staves."

Robert smiled to himself. *Nine languages*, he thought. "And to think you could have qualified for placement in any decent college in the country."

"What?"

"Just keep walking." He asked her several more questions, learning that today's hunters would all report back at the lodge after darkness fell.

Robert and Priscilla hadn't gone more than twenty yards before he realized the two of them had veered off the main trail.

"I can't see where I'm going," Priscilla complained.

"I can't, either," Robert agreed, untying her hands in back then retying them in front of her, patting the pockets of her parka before removing and putting the small flashlight in Pricilla's hand, instructing the girl to keep the beam low and pointed at the ground. "Lead," he snapped, guiding the teenager back around the area, moving her ahead of him while holding on to her sleeve should she decide to run. "Move it."

The two of them were back on the main trail, heading north, the beam of light casting an eerie glow. An owl hooted ominously, and Robert thought about things that go bump in the night. He was worried about Liza, praying she wouldn't plant an arrow in his chest; hoping, too, that there were no stragglers on the path.

As they approached the descending slope, he wondered what Liza and he would do with Priscilla. What options did they really have? The possibilities unnerved him. Midpoint down the trail, Robert had Priscilla stop as he signaled three times with the flashlight, switching it on and off. He knew that no one from the lodge could see into the deep depression. He prayed that Liza would exercise extreme caution as captor and captive reached the valley floor.

Robert finally stopped. "Liza," he whispered. He heard nothing. "Liza," he called again a little louder. The wind seemed to answer up in Liza's stead. Priscilla was busy looking all around. "Liza," Robert snapped as the wind trailed off into the distance. "It's all right, Liza" he said, shining the light on Priscilla's wrists to show that his prisoner was restrained and that all was well for the moment. He put the light on himself for an instant before returning to the dark. No answer. "Shit."

"Too embarrassed to take a piss to sound your arrival in front of your newfound friend?" Liza asked while stepping onto the trail from out of God knows where.

Robert had practically jumped out of his skin. Priscilla was shaking in her boots.

"Jesus Christ. Why didn't you answer me instead of scaring the hell out of us like that?"

"Us? Couldn't kill her, huh?" Liza questioned with such hatred in her voice and eyes if Robert could have only seen them clearly.

"She was unarmed."

"So was little David."

"Liza, she's sixteen."

"My nephew was only five."

"You don't understand."

"I don't understand?" There was a sickening timbre to her tone. Priscilla started crying anew.

Liza went right up to her. "Which one of you put the snake in our mailbox?" she hissed in the girl's right ear. "Hum? Which one of you foul creatures is responsible for all our pain?" she demanded, stepping around the teenager and hissing in her other ear.

"Liza, don't."

"Don't what?"

Robert didn't answer.

"Tell me," Liza taunted the girl. "Tell me. Tell me. Tell me," she tarried with her tongue.

Priscilla recoiled.

Liza struck out, slashing the edge of the broadhead across the girl's parka hood, the arrow still nocked to the bowstring.

"Enough," Robert almost shouted.

Priscilla shrank from the pair, sinking to her knees.

"What's your name, bitch?" Liza lashed.

Priscilla winced. "Priscilla."

"The python squeezed the life out of him, Priscilla. Squeezed him until he was almost dead. He died before he ever reached the hospital. They wouldn't even let me ride with him." Liza's anger was mounting by the second. "Robert got to hold his little hand. Five years old, Priscilla."

Liza was about to strike again, but Robert held her wrist and took away the bow and arrow.

"I said, enough."

"Guadalupe," Priscilla said.

"What?" Liza snapped.

"Number Forty-eight. Guadalupe. She's the one who brought the serpent to your door."

"What does Guadalupe look like?" Liza demanded.

"Long black hair to the center of her back. Pretty. Scar across her left cheek. Spanish."

Liza looked directly at Robert, but Robert shook his head.

"All right. The three of us are turning around and heading south."

"You're not bringing her back with us," Liza declared.

"What do you propose we do with her?"

Liza gave a little laugh. "Why don't you read her her *rites*, like in *last*."

"Right now, we're all heading back to the barn. And then we'll decide what we're going to do."

Robert Banfelder

Liza took Robert aside. "You can't turn her over to anyone. You can't let her go. If you can't do what has to be done, Rob, I can."

"I got a lot of valuable information from her. She may be very useful."

"Oh, I see. Well, why don't you just swear her in and tell her she's on good behavior. If she continues to cooperate, maybe she'll make it till morning."

"You're not making any sense."

"No. You're the one who's not making any sense," she said in a low voice. "You're the one who's going to wind up getting us killed."

"We'll discuss this later. Right now, I'm hungry, tired, and cold. You're not?"

"Oh, Rob. I'm just getting warmed up."

"Well, now you're going to cool off, and that's it."

Liza was fuming, but she didn't say another word. She took her bow back and walked ahead in deadly silence.

"Let me go," Priscilla whimpered, "or she'll kill me. I know she will," she pleaded. "Please."

"You're all right for now," Robert told her. "Now, move ahead." Priscilla wanted to bolt, and Robert sensed it. "It will be all right if you behave and do as you are told."

Priscilla stood petrified. "Please untie me and let me go. I'll go so far away from here," she promised.

"I won't let her hurt you. I swear. But if you run, I'll let her take you down. I'll have to. Do you understand?"

Priscilla walked ahead in tears, believing firmly she was going to die by Liza's hand.

Chapter 54

Robert lit a kerosene heater as soon as the three of them entered the barn. A moment later, the noxious fumes dissipated from the area and the space began to warm. He retied Priscilla's wrists at her back and secured her to a wooden stanchion near the ladder leading to the loft.

"We have to talk," Liza said to Robert.

Robert turned on the water valve inside the building then filled a small pot, placing it on top of the heater. "So talk."

"We agreed we'd take no prisoners. Correct?"

"She's sixteen years old, Liza. She surrendered. She was unarmed."

"And if she had the chance back there, she would have killed you. But you killed her partner and she became afraid."

"That's right. So afraid that she was going to run away, not go back and warn the others."

"You don't know what was in her head."

"She could have warned the others on the path, but she didn't."

"Yeah, didn't want to die. She was one of the ones who took little Davey's life."

"One of fifty. You don't know her role."

"Her role is one of an assassin. A sick and demented mind."

"A mind manipulated by Angelica Manns," he said in a low voice. "A vulnerable child."

Liza shook her head. "You've had these kinds of kids when a few managed to reach college age. I've had them when their mothers wheeled them to school with their older brothers and sisters in baby carriages in Harlem. They're doomed from day one. They're street kids. They're on the road to perdition. They're on their way to a fiery hell but wish to first start trouble here."

"This kid speaks nine languages," he whispered.

"Oh, excuse me! I didn't know you were conducting interviewsfor such multilingual trash," she said, raising her voice. "Maybe she has nine lives, too, one of which I say we claim for openers."

"She got caught up in the wrong kind of crowd, Liza."

"That's right. The kind of crowd that goes around killing little kids."

"You know that that snake was meant for you or me. To scare us off. To make us stop. They weren't after David."

"Do you hear yourself? Does that make it any different? What are we going to do with her? Rehabilitate that piece of shit? Send her to finishing school? What? Tell me. You want to set up a POW camp here?"

"I want you to act rational."

"Rational. You released two Riverhead rednecks who may or may not return in a pickup truck filled with their fucking friends. Well, I went along with that against my better judgment if you want to know the truth. But if I were truly in charge of this chicken-shit outfit, like I'm supposed to be, I would have wasted those two on the spot."

"We're not murderers, Liza."

"That's exactly what we've become," she said, glaring over at the girl. "That's what they turned us into."

Priscilla cowered in the corner.

"Sixteen years old," Robert repeated.

"So was Amy Fisher. In what language do you need to hear that, Rob? Apparently, English isn't getting through."

For the next sixty seconds there was silence between them. Finally, Priscilla spoke.

"I'm not Amy Fisher," the girl said quietly.

Liza spun around insanely. "You shut your mouth, you hear?"

"I never hurt anyone. I wasn't at the Villa when they killed the nuns. I was waiting in the bus."

Robert looked at Priscilla with puzzlement. "What are you talking about? What nuns? What Villa?"

Priscilla proceeded to tell the story about the raid on the Villa and the killing of two nuns and two federal agents as it had been related to her when the others returned to the bus and fled. She continued with a firsthand account regarding the capture of those in the federal government's witness protection program: the torture of the woman who had initially refused to cooperate; the man who defied them; the two survivors of Nazi concentration camps, their stories of the war and elaboration concerning the direct descendants of Adolf Hitler; the government's endless search for the Führer's grandson; the recent assassination of their benefactor, Mrs. G, then finally, the installment of Ms. M as their new chancellor as well as commander in chief of both cult and cartel.

Robert listened in apparent fascination whereas Liza's concentration was clouded by anger concerning their moral dilemma. With every passing minute, it seemed more likely than not that Priscilla's status as prisoner was about to be elevated to that of Robert's protégé. At least in Liza's mind.

"Do you have any idea why your dear Ms. M, that's Angelica Manns, and the others are trying to kill us, Priscilla? Any idea at all?"

"No, sir."

"It's because we have a special gift which allows us to see great evil. Several hundred of us in this country had that gift, going all the way back to World War II. Many of these people have been killed off by a very powerful few. Ever hear of The Triumvirate, Priscilla?"

"No, sir."

"The Manhattan Project?"

"No, sir."

"How about the poisoning of our citizens with plutonium 239, some fifty years ago, along with other forms of radiation? Hum?"

"No, sir."

"What about Nazi gold?"

"No, sir."

"That's how their operations were initially financed. Blood money. That's how and when The Triumvirate was founded, formed and funded. Drug money supplemented the operations of the late Mrs. G's cartel and Ms. M's cult."

"That I know a little about."

"You do?"

"Yes, sir. We've all been paid a million dollars for our services. We know the money comes from drugs."

"A million dollars?"

Priscilla nodded, sending mucus back up her nostrils.

"Want to blow your nose?"

"Please."

Robert took a clean handkerchief out of his fanny pack and went up to her. "Blow."

Priscilla blew her nose noisily then started crying all over again.

"You going to wipe her ass, too, when she has to go?" Liza bleated.

"Shut your face," Robert shot back.

"Fuck you," Liza retorted.

Robert ignored her and began telling Priscilla a story. A story he and Liza had recently heard. A true story. A story with a moral to it.

"Sixty years ago, in 1935, a boy was born in West Germany. A boy who went by the name of Karl Baceni. But that wasn't his real name. His real name was Karl Hitler, the first of six sons born to Hannah Abramowicz, Adolf Hitler's imprisoned mistress, held in Munich against her will. A Jew. Hitler kept most of his personal life secret. You know who Adolf Hitler was, Priscilla? I mean apart from Emma and Emil Jewitt's recounting of their tale?"

"Yes, sir."

"Well, that's a start," he said and smiled, wiping away her tears on a clean corner of the handkerchief. "Anyhow, this boy, Karl, had been groomed from birth to one day hold power that no monarch, king, prime minister, or president in history has ever held. In 1975, at age forty, Karl assumed that power, handed down to him by the forefathers of Hitler's henchmen. You won't find any record of it in the history books, Priscilla. Two of Karl's younger brothers, sharing the same ideology, beholding to the beliefs of their father, Adolf Hitler, wield the instruments of power necessary to further the goal of world domination. These three men, collectively called The Triumvirate, virtually control the world's economy, govern politics here and abroad, and set both foreign and domestic policy. Consequently, every major market of importance around the globe is affected. In the year 2000, twenty-five years after faithfully serving and expanding their father's Reich, the trio shall fade into the sunset as their predecessors had, and three new monsters shall be handed the torch.

"Angelica Ann Manns, your beloved mistress of ambition and atrocity, was actually born Angelo A. Reynolds, son of Anthony and

Anna Reynolds. Anna, being secretly born in a Nazi concentration camp, was the daughter of Hannah Abramowicz. In other words—"

"Angelica is actually Angelo, the grandson of Adolf Hitler," Priscilla interrupted.

Robert smiled. "An A-plus for comprehension."

"Sex change operation," Priscilla put together on her own, "which is why Angelica had Peter kill Mrs. G. She knew!"

"Not many people do. Those who learn the truth wind up dead. Angelica wishes to usurp the power her uncles hold. She has a master plan. Always did."

"Who are the two other people?" Priscilla asked in fascination.

"Why are you telling her all this?" Liza hollered.

"Keep your voice down or I swear I'll tape it shut. Go make tea or something and stay out of this." He turned his attention back to Priscilla. "One is a most powerful monsignor who commands the pope like God commanded Moses."

"A monsignor?"

Robert nodded. "The other is a mercenary who commands generals like General George S. Patton commanded the armies in World War II. Ever hear of him?"

"The mercenary or General Patton?" Priscilla's eyes danced.

Robert looked at Priscilla for a full five seconds before he began to smile.

Priscilla cracked a smile, too.

"That's pretty good," he gave her.

"They're fucking buddies now," Liza said to the top of the rafters, throwing her camo face mask against the ladder leading to the loft.

"Liza lost her daughter to a cult," he continued in a low voice. "Splinter group of Richard Geist's Circle of Friends. Ever hear of them?"

Priscilla nodded nervously.

"Richard's people killed her."

Priscilla sniffled. "I'm so sorry."

"Liza's angry because I humanized you for her," he said softly. "She won't hurt you now."

"Let me go," she whispered. "I won't tell anyone, I swear."

"Can't," Robert said rather sadly.

"Yes, you can," she pleaded.

"You're going to help us."

"How?"

"I honestly don't know the answer to that, yet, Priscilla. But you are."

There in the low light cast by the kerosene heater, Liza glared at the teenager with a monumental hatred that belied any soothing words of comfort Robert offered concerning the personal safety of the girl.

"What languages do you speak?" Robert asked, making idle conversation for the moment.

"None right now," Priscilla said in a fearful tone, closing her eyes tightly while sinking down the post to the cold dirt floor of the one-hundred-year-old barn.

Chapter 55

When Karl was angry, he bore his father's eyes. The man was very angry at the moment. Cold steel-blue eyes surveyed the interior of the magnificent room. Eyes that pleaded, or so it seemed, to see well beyond the walls, the ceiling and the floor, as if searching beyond its barriers for pairs of eyes that might be peering back in: pairs of eyes belonging to the likes of Robert Redler, Liza Downs, and perhaps others. Karl's eyes came to settle on the two men seated before him.

"Our father, may he rest in peace, although I sense he is staring at us from beyond the grave at this very moment, never cared for Himmler. Never liked the man. Scoffed at his eccentric tenets: sorcery, homeopathy, glacial cosmogony, natural eugenics, clairvoyance." He let the last word settle in their minds like an annoying particle of dust drifting downward before coming to rest upon the polished surface of a highly-prized piece of furniture.

The merc stirred uncomfortably. The monsignor put aside his newspaper.

"Heinrich should have stuck with Lebenborn and his stud farms and completed the master race," the merc offered behind a grin. "Wouldn't have to be clairvoyant just imagining what went on behind barn doors. Masculine blue-eyed SS soldiers and suitable blonde-haired *Fräulein*. Too bad."

"Where could those two possibly be?" Karl pondered.

"They could be out of the country by now," the monsignor offered despondently.

"How? Where?" Karl exploded.

"Impossible," the merc stated emphatically. "They're right here. They have some help for sure. But we'll find them."

"Should have eliminated them the minute we knew," Karl railed. "Along with *all* the others, fifty years ago."

"We weren't in power fifty years ago. We were in lederhosen. Remember?" The merc smiled.

"You mean you were in lederhosen," the monsignor said dryly. "I was in knickers."

"I made suggestions and recommendations when I was in my twenties," Karl said, ignoring their banter. "Remember that?" he resounded angrily. "You two laughed. We should have warehoused them six feet under rather than in hospitals and asylums. We should have done it the day *we* came to power."

"Well, we still have three years to decide that issue, Karl," the monsignor said. "But there is little question in any of our minds concerning Redler and Downs. If Ed is confident that we're going to find them here, then we're going to find them here. My concern at the moment is Angelica. Is she fit to command? Is that awesome arsenal that she's in control of in good hands, or are we all sitting on a time bomb? You yourself admit that she has placed us in a compromising situation. Do we need to worry? Will she be satisfied with her command, or will she seek something further down the line?"

"Like what?"

"Like the seat you're sitting in, Karl, either before the year 2000, or when the power changes hands," the prelate put forth frankly. "It seems to me that a person with such ambition as Angelica would try and seize the opportunity sooner than later, gentlemen. Be interested to hear your thoughts."

"Why don't we wait and see how goes her probationary period and the training of her troops before we make any sort of judgment," the mercenary suggested. "Why don't we wait and hear what the cartel has to say about its new leader's performance in terms of dollar figures and customer satisfaction."

Karl was somewhat surprised by the merc's support in the matter, and nodded his appreciation. Usually, Edward was the more pessimistic, voicing skepticism and concerns beyond the scope of the monsignor's cause for aggregate worry. Perhaps the warrior was too concerned about Robert Redler and Liza Downs for the moment than to fault a situation that seemed to be going rather well, the leader thought.

In truth, Ed never liked Barbara Giordano's methods of operation. He thought her weak. A woman was not a plus in any business save prostitution, he believed. But a woman who was born a man intrigued him. Besides, it wasn't like his people weren't watching. They were virtually everywhere. Everywhere, that is, except on the heels of the writer and his domestic partner. Locating them was of paramount importance to the merc.

The monsignor reluctantly agreed with his youngest brother's assessment. "All right. Just remember that our father, gentlemen, would have positively frowned upon democratic rule," William said with half a smile.

"Ah, that was just a lot of propaganda, Bill," Edward teased.

Karl enjoyed the mercenary's joke alluding to Joseph Goebbels as 'der Führer's propagandist.' He sat back, relaxed, and even cracked a grin. "Three years, my friends. Three years and we will have done our duty."

"Meanwhile, I've got to do mine and be on an early flight to Israel," the monsignor yawned. "You guys think you can get along without me for a few days?"

"Just make sure Netanyahu's people forgive you for our transgressions, Bill," the merc kidded.

"They're not interested in forgiveness, Ed. Only our daily bread."

Karl closed his eyes. "If our father ever heard you two, and I'm not so sure he can't, he'd box your ears, you know."

"Our father would be very proud, Karl," the monsignor said most piously.

The merc laughed. "Not while we're sitting in the World Trade Center, he wouldn't."

Karl laughed, too. "Well, that won't be for a while yet, gentlemen."

The monsignor shrugged, getting up to leave. "It's late. Got to go."

"Oh, and don't concern yourself with Angelica's arsenal, Bill," the merc reminded himself. "It amounts to nothing more than crates of crude armaments is all."

"What about the hundred Scuds she has planted throughout the tristate area? What about the new plant just seventy miles from here?"

"Three-hundred-fifty-mile range, tops. And their guidance systems are from hunger. The worst she could do is take out the

Catskills. Put the borscht belt out of business for a month."

"I'm serious, Ed. What about the Soviets sending over parts via Iran, along with the technology that could effectively triple that capability?"

"So she winds up leveling the Adirondacks in addition, and maybe some of our northern Canadian cousins, too," he needled.

The monsignor was getting worked up. "I'm talking long-range, Ed. Twelve hundred miles plus. I'm talking nuclear warheads."

"You're talking the SS-4, Bill. But you're not talking sense. We'd never ever let that kind of capability fall into her hands. So, relax. Now, go to Israel. Kiss the Wailing Wall on your way to Tel Aviv."

"I'm so glad I inherited domestic trade," Karl trifled. "Foreign affairs are absolutely a bitch."

"And I'd change those pants before *you* go anywhere, Ed," the monsignor said to the mercenary before he took his leave. "I don't know how they ever let you into these buildings."

"Bless you, too, you hypocrite," the merc chided.

"The clergyman raised his middle finger as he reached the door.

The merc laughed, picking up and disappearing behind his brother's newspaper. "I wonder if he ever did that from the pulpit."

"Never ever when I attended services," Karl swore, stretched and listened to his bones creak as he stood.

Chapter 56

Priscilla had fallen asleep shortly after midnight. She laid there silently atop two bales of straw that Robert had placed next to one another for a makeshift bed. Her wrists were still secured behind her and to the stanchion but with a foot or more of rope added so that the girl could move to some degree. Additionally, both ankles were bound together tightly and tied vertically to the rope between her wrists. She wasn't going anywhere. Moreover, if Liza had her way, Priscilla's persistent, pesky little mouth would have been ducted taped, too.

"Again, I'm going to ask you what we're going to do with her," Liza droned, staring down from the loft at Sleeping Beauty.

"What time is it?" Robert moaned, stretching then turning onto his side to face the inquisition.

Liza pushed the INDIGLO button on her Timex. "Four."

"Feels like I slept an hour."

"I think the only one who got a decent night's sleep is your princess. Why don't you give her a wake-up kiss and tell her that her charming life is over."

"Kiss-off."

"You just going to leave her here?"

"Let me sleep on it."

"In case you've forgotten, we have forty plus people to kill today. I suggest you get into the swing of things."

"You make it sound like several grueling rounds of golf."

"Do you know what our chances of success are, Rob?" she asked hopelessly.

"Something like shooting par?"

"Slimmer."

"Look."

"I'm looking and listening."

"You want to kill them all because of what they did to David and us. I want to stop them because I want to put an end to Angelica's regime. If I could kill that he/she and save all the young men and women in the bargain, I would. But I know I can't. I also know that I just can't kill an unarmed teenager who wants to run away from this madness, no more than I could kill those two rednecks that were no part of this. *You* want revenge. Pure and simple. I want peace."

"Finished?"

"Finished."

"Good. We understand one another. Let's go do our job."

Liza got up, grabbed some gear then descended the ladder. Robert quickly followed.

From the center of the floor, the kerosene heater still threw out heat although the fuel gauge floated its little red marker near empty. Priscilla stirred then suddenly tried to sit up straight. She looked directly at Liza with frightened, bloodshot eyes. There were no tears this time but a cold expression of dread.

"I have to go to the bathroom," Priscilla said, turning her head toward Robert. "Please. I had to go last night, but I was afraid to wake you." Afraid was the key word. Afraid that it would be Liza who would lead her away then end her life.

"Do you speak German?" Robert asked Priscilla, picking up where their conversation had come to a close shortly before dinner; that is, if one could call a can of warm soup and two sandwiches, shared three ways, dinner.

"Yes, sir."

"How well?"

"Fluently. Why?"

"I'll ask the questions," Robert remarked.

"Speaking of questions," Liza snapped. "What time did Dottie say that the caretaker comes by to feed the animals?"

"Usually around eight in the morning then again at four p.m. The regular man is on vacation till after New Year's. The young fellow who comes around is usually in and out."

"So obviously she can't be here when he comes," Liza said, staring down coldly at the girl.

Robert nodded. "We'll have to take her with us."

"Jesus Christ. I knew you'd pull this shit. Shit!"

"Would you help us, Priscilla?" Robert asked.

"How?"

"Walk ahead of us. Locate your friends. Talk them down. Distract them."

"What then?" Priscilla asked, knowing the answer in advance.

Robert looked at Liza then back to the girl.

"I can't," Priscilla whined and whimpered. "Please. Just let me go. Please."

"You see?" Liza barked.

"If we were to let you go, Priscilla, how do we know that you won't contact them, or anyone? And what if you were caught? Angelica's people and the people who support her are everywhere. We'd be dead within an hour."

Priscilla was shaking her head in an exaggerated sweep. "I told you. I won't tell anyone. I swear. I want to be way away from here."

Liza threw up her hands in mock surrender. "I can't believe this shit."

"Well, why don't you place your hands on her like you do," Robert practically shouted. "Can't you tell if she's telling the truth or not? Where's that goddamn gift now?"

Liza went over to the bed of straw and started untying Priscilla's feet.

"What are you doing?" Robert barked.

"Taking her to the bathroom. Want to watch?"

"Watch you kill her?"

"What's the matter, Robert? You don't trust me?"

"No, I don't."

"But you'll trust her. Is that it?"

It was Robert now who threw up his hands.

Priscilla was crying bitterly as Liza pulled the girl to her feet. Liza led the teenager out the back of the barn and into an adjacent stable, directing her inside a stall and over to the latrine.

"I want you to stop your incessant whining," Liza ordered. "Do you understand?"

Priscilla's sobs subsided as Liza untied the prisoner's hands, stepped back outside the stall, closed the door and waited.

Moments later, the barnyard all about them suddenly turned alive. A rooster crowed in the distance and then another, nearby, did the same. A parade of chickens put up a squawk as a family of guinea fowl passed noisily by.

Robert thought he heard the sound of a truck coming around the back of the barn, but it was the sound of thunder rolling in from the south. A dog barked in the distance. A pall of black smoke rose from the kerosene heater, offending his nostrils as he went over and opened the little door to the unit, stooping and toying with a knob and lever, common sense telling him that the heater should not have been left to burn dry. He observed the burner's wick, its material turning to a white ash. Closing the unit's door, Robert made a mental note not to allow the kerosene heater to foolishly die out when suddenly a safety latch loudly snapped shut, turning off the unit. That noise, along with another round of thunder, totally unnerved him. *What's taking them so damn long?*

Finally, he left the barn and walked toward the stable. An unsettling feeling took hold of his mind and body as he entered. Heading toward the last stall on the right, Robert called out to them. "Everything all right in there?" Neither Liza nor Priscilla answered. He could hear whimpering and went over to the door. "I asked if everything is all right in there."

"Everything is fine." Liza sobbed. "Everything is just peachy-keen," she stated mournfully.

Robert tried to open the stall but couldn't. "Liza!" He stood back a foot before he kicked in the door. The rusty latch broke free and flew back against the wall. Priscilla sat positioned on the latrine, a shoulder against the partition, one boot off, her clothing fully intact, her face seemingly as white as the partial roll of toilet paper, the cut across her throat as red as roses. Liza, knife in hand, stood beside Priscilla, pulling the girl upright by the hair.

Robert looked at Liza as though she were stark raving mad.

"She had this hidden in her boot," Liza said, extending the bloody blade. "She pulled it when my back was turned." Liza let her go. The body slumped forward then fell to one side. "Why are you staring at me like that?"

"Why didn't you answer me? Why was this door locked?"

"It wasn't locked. It was latched. I heard someone coming. I didn't know if you were alone or with someone."

"I'm sorry," Robert said, dropping his eyes to the knife. It was a precision throwing knife. A balanced black blade of tempered steel.

"I thought . . . ."

"I see."

"I'm sorry," he repeated, staring down lugubriously at the girl.

"Sorry that you doubted me, or sorry that she won't be speaking fluid German anymore?"

"Maybe both."

"Well, don't feel too sorry for doubting me. I might have killed her anyway."

"Maybe she knew that. Maybe she saw no way out."

"You asked her if she would help us. She turned you down."

"She wasn't going back to them."

"Now, you can bank on it," she assured him.

Robert turned and walked away. "We've got to get this stall cleaned up fast," he ordered. "You look around for a hose, and I'll figure out a place to put her body."

"And then what?"

"And then we take out forty some soldiers, God willing."

"No more prisoners?"

"Not even if they wave white flags," he avowed. "Not even if they're twelve years old." *Not even if they're a hundred and twelve*, he said to himself with more than the hint of acrimony racing through his brain.

The bottom line was that he had put Liza in harm's way on more than one occasion. He was responsible for her, period, although it seemed of late that she had assumed the responsibility of protecting him. The fact of the matter was that they were responsible for each other. *That's what being a good soldier is all about*, he told himself. Liza had changed. She had the capability to shed her moral fabric and weigh the peril of a situation. She had the instincts to cut to the quick. To kill. Still, he had to intellectualize the moment as he was doing now. He would get them both killed if he wasn't careful, he knew.

War was more than hell. It was a *fait accompli*.

By late afternoon, twenty-three soldiers lay dead. A sum total of twenty-nine. Male and female. Ages sixteen to perhaps twenty-four. Both he and Liza knew there would be no easy pickings the following day. A search party would certainly be organized if it hadn't been already for the missing six from the day before. Robert and Liza were exhausted but somehow found the will to go on. Actually, the killings had been easy, for they had a good idea where along the line most of Angelica's soldiers had placed their stands. Dragging and hiding the bodies is what took its toll.

Robert knew that if Liza and he could raise the body count high into the thirties, they'd stand somewhat of a chance of killing off the rest, provided, of course, that they could lay their hands on one or two semiautomatic rifles before the penultimate hour. His pistol was no match against the sentries' deadly weapons set with telescopic sights.

Together, they had stealthily stalked the pineland on both sides of the trail. Thirty-one soldiers had been seen the night before. Robert reasoned that the others were probably set up deep in the wood lot to the west. He wondered if he and Liza would have time to bring down another one or two of Angelica's soldiers before dark. The late morning rain had quieted their approach throughout the day, having made it considerably easier for the pair to cover more ground in far less time. They'd chance it, he decided.

"Let's go that-a-way," Robert directed.

It seemed that Liza had read his mind or perhaps made up her own a second sooner, for she was already heading west.

Guadalupe was waiting in ambush for the couple as they left the pines.

The arrow smacked Robert solidly in the left arm, and he went down like timber. Liza loosed an arrow that grazed the girl's parka. Before Liza could nock another, Guadalupe leapt from the tree and caught a bough, breaking her fall before she hit the ground; instantly she went into a rollout, coming up short of Liza who floundered backward with her bow.

Liza withdrew a second arrow and swiftly nocked it but faltered, the arrow falling from its rest. Guadalupe drove a foot hard into Liza's stomach, doubling the woman over. The next kick landed against the side of Liza's head, sending her to the ground. But Liza was on her feet in a second, a second in which Guadalupe could have pulverized her, but the young woman chose to play.

Liza pulled Priscilla's knife. Guadalupe gave a little laugh. Liza crouched and tried to catch her breath. Guadalupe came in low with a foot sweep that made a mockery of the woman's stance. Liza was swept clean off her feet, again being dropped quickly to the ground. Guadalupe strutted in a semicircle around her, snapping up Liza's bow as the assassin's weapon had been left in the tree. The teenager removed a new arrow from Liza's quiver, nocked it upon the string precisely, giving Liza a rapacious, wolfish sneer. The girl looked over at Robert who lay semiconscious on his side.

"Tsk, tsk, tsk," Guadalupe teased, raising Liza's bow and grinning broadly, coming to full draw, the yellow sight pin aligned perfectly through the circular black peep, the broadhead aimed at hitting Robert's vitals.

Liza lashed forward, flashing the knife blade recklessly at the side of Guadalupe's face, but the young woman facilely pivoted clear. Liza lunged again, the tip of the blade sweeping the air glancing off the bow's limb. For Liza's trouble, she caught the heel of Guadalupe's left foot solidly across her face. Liza was stunned, crawling away on all fours in all directions like some sort of culled and half-crazed crab.

It was clear that Guadalupe was going to finish up with Robert before taking on the task of torturing Liza any further. It was apparent the girl was having fun. She couldn't help but to tease and torment.

"My name is Guadalupe, Liza. My number is Number Four. I sent you a special delivery. A very hungry snake," she said with a heavy Spanish accent. "You like?"

In one fluid motion, Guadalupe came to full draw, the lethal broadhead directed back on Robert's rib cage. She stood there easily holding Liza's bow—fifty-pound draw weight, eighty percent let-off—about to release the arrow when the bowstring suddenly snapped and the weapon's laminated limb shook eccentrically for a split second. Number Four stood numb as Liza rose and drove Priscilla's blade between the assassin's ribs.

"I think you're number's up, Lupe," Liza whispered short of breath, withdrawing the blade before thrusting it again—and again—and again—and for a final time before she slit Guadalupe's throat. "I think my little nephew Davey is looking down and smiling, Number Four. You like?"

Liza released her tenacious grip from the girl's parka before unsnapping its hood. "Little souvenir I'll need, seeing as how you're out of the loop," she said and sneered, immediately turning her attention to Robert.

The arrow had gone completely through his arm. He could

barely breathe, move, or talk. Liza opened Guadalupe's coat then fashioned a tourniquet by cutting and tearing strips of material from the teenager's turtleneck, tying the sections together. She pulled out the laces from Guadalupe's boots, removing them in addition to pulling off the extra pair of clean cotton socks from the dead girl's feet. Liza went to work on Robert, completely cutting off the bloody sleeve of all material right up to the shoulder, tying a tourniquet above the wound with the strips of cloth, using the socks and rawhide laces to form a pressing package covering both sides of the entry/exit wound. Next, she climbed Guadalupe's tree and retrieved the woman's bow and quiver, knowing full-well that Robert's bow was far too powerful to pull back and hold with any accuracy. She returned and removed the pistol and both pairs of binoculars from his pockets. Found the extra magazines. Took his wallet. Finally, she got him to his feet.

For the next forty-five minutes, she half-dragged him in the direction of the barn. He had lost a lot of blood before she could properly attend to the wound. Past the barn she pulled him. They were headed toward the road from where they had started out. She had to get him to a hospital. The application of a tourniquet always ran the risk of the loss of limb, she knew. It was over for Robert. But not for her, she swore. Not by a long shot. Both her gift and God were on her side, she firmly believed. She'd move mountains if she had to. But her legs were giving out. She had to stop and rest. Sixty seconds, she promised herself.

A car passed along Sound Avenue. Then another. Liza and Robert were a thousand yards from the road. Liza helped him back to his feet. "Try and help me, now," she insisted. "Try and walk. We haven't got far to go."

"Where?"

"To the road, then to a hospital."

"No." He shook his head and fell.

"Yes," she said. "If I have to drag you there myself. Let's go."

Robert began to walk.

"Listen to me very carefully. You have no wallet. No identification. You were robbed. Poachers. They shot you. You tell them your name is Richard Roberts. Easy name to remember. Say it."

"Richard Roberts."

"You make sure they take you to a local hospital. I'll come get you when I can."

"Police will want a report."

"You'll tell them you have amnesia. All you remember is your name. I think they'll leave you alone after that. At least long enough for me to come get you. All right?"

"What are you going to do?"

"The best I can."

Robert shook his head.

"You're in no condition to argue."

"You can't go back there alone." His words were strained as he wretched in pain.

"You have nothing to say about it."

"Say plenty," he swore. "You've got t-two choices."

"Correct. Either I put you at the edge of the road or in the center of it. Now, what's your name?"

"Richard Roberts."

"Friends call you Dick?" she said and smiled.

"Dickhead, after this."

"You'll be fine."

"I'm worried for you."

"Hey, I've got friends in high places," she reminded him through her tears, staring up at the sky.

"That's what I'm afraid of."

"What's that supposed to mean?"

"Don't want to, ahhh—" he cried out, stumbling in pain as Liza lost her footing.

"Sorry."

"Don't want to find you in heaven is what I mean."

"Better than finding me in hell, which is where I'm sending the rest of them."

"How did you get so tough?"

"Had a tough teacher. Now save your breath."

Liza and he finally made it to the road. A truck flew by then slowed down in the distance. A moment later it started backing up. Liza put the bow out of sight and waved excitedly. "I think this is where we say good-bye, Rob."

Robert saw the pickup and the single driver. "Just make sure you don't stick me in there if it's our buddy Sam or Jeff."

It was an old man with a look of consternation on his face. "What happened?" he shouted after reaching over and sending down the passenger window several inches.

"Poachers shot my husband with an arrow. Can you get him to a hospital here in Riverhead, fast?" she begged. "I have to stay and wait here for the police," she fibbed.

"Fast as this buggy'll go on four cylinders," he hollered. "Maybe firing on three. But I'll get 'im there. Don't you worry none. Can you help him in? Got a busted up back since the sixties. But I keep on truckin', too."

The old man opened the door, and Liza helped Robert up and into the well-worn seat. Robert was crying quietly, pretending his tears were solely from the pain.

She kissed him gently on the cheek, got down, closed the door then smiled up at him. "I'll be fine, Richard," she said, turning away before he could say a word. Immediately, the truck pulled away. Liza was crying, too, as she headed back north across the field. She couldn't remember ever feeling so alone in all her life.

"Poachers," the old man complained bitterly while making an illegal U-turn and heading east. "If I was twenty, I'd get me my ten gauge and have me a field day. Poaching is bad enough. Poaching out of season is blasphemous."

Robert watched Liza pass from sight.

Chapter 57

Liza had taken up the position along the north-south trail. Moving ever closer to the lodge. She was near collapse. The killing spree was over for the day. It was turning dark quickly. Liza was too tired to even kill the spider that crawled across her neck. She simply brushed it off with indifference. Her pants and jacket were probably loaded with deer ticks, but she couldn't afford the luxury of caring. If Angelica's soldiers hadn't killed her by now, contracting Lyme disease would certainly be the last of her concerns, she figured with a sardonic grin. She sat with night-vision binoculars, Guadalupe's bow, and an Allen wrench tool, having cranked the compound weapon down a good ten pounds. The day was turning dark.

A quarter of an hour later, Liza suddenly saw shafts of light flickering in the distance, approaching from a wood lot to the west. Six, seven, maybe eight beams were dancing in her direction, sweeping the area from left to right as if searching for something rather than simply finding their way. Liza moved backward into deeper cover. The troops suddenly veered from the trail, still heading in her direction. Suddenly, the group stopped no more than seventy yards away. A minute later, they proceeded ahead. At fifty yards, the group separated—four and another four abreast, fanning out before her. Forty yards and closing. A bright beam swept above her left shoulder, another slowly flooded the area a foot before her feet. A powerful shot of light from out of nowhere spotted a figure on the ground.

"Here she is," Karen called out excitedly. "Over here."

Seven others cast their light upon the subject then stood transfixed.

Liza's heart was pounding. It felt as though it was about to leave her chest.

"She's a beauty," Paul swore.

"Help me get her out of here," Doug said and grinned with

certain satisfaction, stepping forward with a hauling harness in hand.

"Make sure she's dead first," Allan said. "We wouldn't want to haul your ass out of here instead," he added, laughing like a hyena.

Doug approached carefully. He prodded the creature with his bow.

"Boo!" Paul exclaimed.

Doug jumped back a yard. "Fuckin' asshole," he snapped in anger.

Laughter and giggles went all the way around the ring of worshippers.

Doug stepped in and placed the harness over the head and around the upper body of the magnificent doe. "Puts Elizabeth's to shame, I'd say," Doug decided, very satisfied with himself.

"Fantastic deer, Dougie," Paul congratulated. "But tomorrow I'm getting me a ten-point buck."

Tomorrow, Liza thought to herself. *You'd never see tomorrow if I had you all alone*, she swore silently, crouched several yards away. *Never ever see the light of day.*

A quarter of an hour later, a concerned voice questioned several soldiers.

"Where the hell are the others?" Angelica demanded, sensing that something was terribly wrong.

The twelve of them looked at one another for answers. Six others walked the area just outside the lodge on guard-watch.

"May-maybe they w-went AWOL," Danny teased. "May-maybe they g-got lost," he said half-seriously.

"Maybe they're out tracking," Malcolm said on a more positive note.

"Thirty-eight of you?" Angelica questioned. "Thirty-eight of you suddenly all got goddamn deer?"

"Maybe a herd came through. Maybe a lot of us got lucky," Tanya said.

Angelica shook her head. "Nine deer yesterday. I thought to myself, couldn't be. Not without something or someone out there moving them about. Then six of us still out there last night. And now another twenty-four? What in God's name is going on?"

"I knew something was wrong when Priscilla didn't show last

night," Peter said. "I figured her for the first one back here."

"I'm taking two of us," Karen said. "We'll work the line back along the trail. See what we can come up with."

Half a dozen had their hands up as volunteers.

Angelica thought for a moment before she spoke. "All right. Take radios. I want the three of you in constant contact. You call in to Danny every ten minutes with the code. Peter, I want this area mined immediately. The entire perimeter. I want four pairs of eyes with night-vision glasses covering the cliffs. We double the guard. You and you on the roof, right now. You look for the invisible and listen through the cone of silence. That goes for all of you. We're on red alert. By morning, we ready ourselves for a full manhunt. We've got visitors."

"What about some sleep?" Paul whispered to Doug through a tunnel of murmuring.

"Most of you have been sitting on your asses all day," Angelica said as if reading Paul's lips or mind or both. "We'll rotate the watch, but don't count on more than a couple hours sleep at most. You'll soon learn what punishment the mind and body can endure when it has to. But you'll be fine. Karen, assign the watch to the rest of them till 5:00 a.m. Peter, come with me."

Liza had a revelation. It was a long shot. Literally. But she would need a rifle. Something powerful. Long range. She'd need luck, too. She'd need God's intervention for certain, she knew. Liza tried to fold then tuck away the cloak of fear into a cavernous corner of her brain, knowing too, that she couldn't quite bury fright forever. Desperately, she tried to summon forth a modicum of courage to help her up the mountain of uncertainty. Yet the clear voice of reason suddenly collided with a cloud of confusion, intuitively communicating that her mind and body were anything but on the mend. Liza momentarily marveled at all the men and women who had ever been in the heat of battle, wondering how on earth they ever clung to the flimsy cloth of sanity, how on God's green acre they ever found the strength, let alone the will, to go on in the face of all-out adversity. Liza wanted to surrender willingly to the dark demon of torpidity. Within minutes, she was sound asleep, shivering silently at the base of an uprooted tree.

Chapter 58

In her heyday, Millie Brown had been the prettiest girl in town. At fifty, she was remarkably attractive. She exercised at the gym daily, jogged four mornings a week, toiled in both her gardens and greenhouse on weekends, watched her waistline during every waking hour, perpetually counseled all her friends and family on nutrition while turning the rest of her attentions over to an all-consuming subject concerning the supernatural phenomena of parapsychology. Millie Brown-Harden, the mayor's wife, did not possess the gift or claimed to have any preternatural ability. What she did behold was a sound belief in its existence. What she excitedly talked about in private went beyond the realm of belief. For the past two days, Millie held irrefutable proof of its presence.

Mayor Harden was out of town, and the governor dropped by the manor for an unannounced visit. He drove his car to the back of the grand estate and parked.

"Come, come, come," the gracious woman insisted. "No bother. No trouble. A welcome surprise is all. Darlene! Put up tea and coffee after you see the governor to the study," she called out so sweetly. Millie pulled off a pair of gardening gloves and gave the man a big holiday hug and a belated Christmas kiss, less any needed excuse of mistletoe. "I've been in the greenhouse most of the afternoon. Exercising and planting. And now I'm going to plant my butt a spell. I welcome the break, Governor. You sit. I'm going up to shower and change. It's good to see you. I've got something I want to show you later," she said excitedly. "Came the day before yesterday."

Darlene came into the foyer quietly and took the governor's hat and coat. It did not take any powers except the power of observation to know that Darlene did not like the governor and that the governor felt the same way toward Millie's maid.

Thirty minutes later, Millie came downstairs in white jeans and a matching jersey. She carried a Manila envelope tucked under her arm. The governor was seated in the study, admiring the prodigious tree and all its magnificent decorations, not to be taken down in the Harden household until January 6th, the Day of Epiphany. He was enjoying a second cup of coffee when she entered the commodious room.

"So, Governor. No, please don't get up. Sit, sit, sit. You do not stand on ceremony around here. How was the holiday?"

"Oh, pretty quiet, I guess. God, but you're looking great, Millie," he said, sitting himself back down.

"Of course I look great. I work at it eighteen hours a day, seven days a week," she went on, putting herself into a comfortable chair across from her husband's old friend.

Darlene stepped into the room. "May I pour ya tea now, Mrs. Harden?" Darlene asked politely.

"You know I'm not a cripple, Darlene. Now, shoo. Go watch your soaps or just relax while the governor and I have ourselves a little chat. Later on, you can help me clean up. Now go," she insisted and smiled most pleasantly.

"Yes, ma'am," Darlene said then left the two of them alone.

"You spoil your help horribly, Millie," the governor declared. "Mine, I beat with a stick once in a while just to keep them in line."

Millie laughed. "Oh, you do not. Rumor is you simply shoot them if they overstep their bounds," she couldn't help but tease.

The governor looked surprised and tried to hide his uneasiness with a little laugh. "So much for rumors. So, what did you want to show me, Millie?" he asked with little interest, moving the conversation in another direction.

"This," she declared and beamed, holding up the envelope.

"What's that?'

"Proof."

"Proof of what?"

"You first."

"First, what?'

"Why you came to see me," she stated.

"Oh, I just knew that Tom's away and thought I'd come down and sneak a little kiss is all," he teased.

"Governor, if you came to flirt with me, I wish you would have called ahead."

"And?"

"And, I would have greeted you in my prom dress instead of gardening clothes."

Al Atkins laughed heartily, recalling the first and only time he had asked her for a date. "Could never get to first base with you, Millie Brown. Not with both Toms beating down your door," he added congenially.

"Well, I don't think you really gave it your all, Governor. I think you were too entranced."

"With whom?" the governor asked defensively.

"Not with whom, Governor."

"Then what?"

"With blind ambition."

The governor looked around the room uncomfortably. "You make that sound so base, Millie."

"Do I?"

"Anyhow, what's in the envelope?'

"First tell me why you're really here."

"Really. I just dropped by. A boyhood crush is all. I always liked you, Millie. You know that. I just thought we'd talk."

Millie smiled. "Well, I'm going to do most of the talking," she said, waving the envelope. "And you're going to do the listening. All right?"

"All right," he submitted, taking out a handkerchief and wiping his brow.

Millie opened the top of the envelope by bending up the two little metal tags. "I received this in the mail the other day." She took out a stack of papers, handing over a single photograph.

"What's this?' the governor asked, studying the picture.

"The wrecks of two wooden freighters sunk off the eastern coast of Long Island Sound in the late thirties. I believe they were towed there. That's Negro Head, renamed Friar's Head, probably because of pressure from the abolitionists prior to the Civil War. Those wrecks are still there, one hundred sixty-feet below the cliffs of the 4-H Camp in Riverhead, New York."

The governor's eyes rose from the picture. "Where?"

"Riverhead. On Long Island. You remember all that business

with Richard Geist and Angelica Manns. Two years back. That cult. Circle of Friends or something."

"Right, right, right," the governor nodded. "She hooked up with that Giordano gal. What about it?"

"Well, what you're holding there is the site of a little known battle figured into the War of 1812, when the British were blockading Long Island Sound."

He looked at her curiously. "And how does all this figure into —"

"The scheme of things? Well, let me tell you," she said excitedly, taking back the photo. "We're about to have another battle there. Only this one is going to be fought just a little to the left. This one is going to be fought *at* the 4-H Camp in Riverhead, Long Island, New York. May have even started."

"A battle between whom?"

"A battle between the forces of good and evil is all I really know."

"And how do you know this?"

Millie tapped the stack of papers.

"Well, what do you have there?"

"Letters from the Suffolk County Historical Society in Riverhead; the Department of Transportation, United States Coast Guard; text by an associate curator of the Division of Naval history at the Smithsonian Institution. Oh, and this here Xerox copy is a reproduction of a panel of the Coast Guard Academy Library's mural. All documenting that event."

"Well, I guess that supports the past battle there with the British. What about the present?" the governor asked pleasantly. "Above the cliffs, and all?"

"Don't know. But what I do know is penned in the cover letter. It's from a woman sitting in an institution in upstate New York."

"An institution?"

"Yes, like the kind Richard Geist and Angelica Manns exploited a few years back. A mental institution. The patient's name is Kathleen Grear."

The governor mopped his brow. "What did she tell you," he asked politely, "this Kathleen Grear?"

"She told me the reason why you're really here."

"Really?"

"Let me pour you another cup of coffee, Governor. I remember you could easily drink a pot all by yourself. Cigars and pipes and coffee. I kept telling you that one of them was going to kill you." Millie filled the governor's cup then poured herself some tea. "I guess it's going to be the coffee, Governor."

The governor looked pale.

Millie took a sip of tea. "Getting back to the battle, it seems that the Revenue Cutter Eagle wound up upon the eastern shore of Long Island Sound, just east of the Cliff House. That's the name of the lodge up there. See? Here's a picture. Anyhow, the ship's captain, Captain Frederick Lee, set out to rescue another vessel, the Suzan, which the British had captured. By all accounts, Lee's crew was outnumbered and outgunned. Rather than have his vessel fall into British hands like the other, Lee ran the Eagle ashore with the intent of having her stripped of guns, their carriages, powder, shot, sails and such so as to make her of little value to the enemy." Millie shuffled through the set of papers. "Here we go. Here's the remarkable part, Governor. Let me read to you from the pages of history." Millie picked up in the middle of the curator's document.

The governor's chin rested heavily on his chest as Millie read verbatim: "While exchanging fire with the brig, the barges and POMONE'S tender, which had reentered the scene, the Cutter's crew, her embarked volunteers, local fishermen and very likely folk come out from Wading River village, perhaps seventy-five people in all, proceeded at the same time to strip the EAGLE of guns, carriages, powder, shot, items of ships' equipment such as sails and cordage, to render her of small value to her captors. These considerable items were then manhandled up a 160-foot sand cliff and yet up another 80 feet to the summit of Negro Head. The pieces were emplaced, the national colors planted, and the British craft taken under fire."

Millie continued reading without looking up at the governor.

"If we are to accept the time interval noted by the DISPATCH log, this impressive feat was accomplished within no more than forty-five minutes! When one considers the time required merely to prepare the rigging to swing out the guns and their carriages into waiting boats, make the short passage to the beach, and get them from the boats to the beach, forty-five minutes would still represent a spectacular time just for that much of the operation.

"Two 4-pounders and their carriage represent an average weight of 900 to 1,000 pounds each, plus approximately 200 pounds more for each carriage. The 2-pounders weighed about 300 pounds each, including their carriages. Add to this the weight and bulk of the gun gear, ammunition and shot, plus sails and oddments of rigging, which still remained to be hauled up 200 feet of sand cliff under the fire of the enemy, and we are faced with no mean achievement, as any boatswain will testify!"

Millie put down the text. "Raw courage in the face of adversity, Governor. Talk to me."

Governor Al Atkins picked up his head. "Can't move, Millie," he mumbled.

"I know. It's paralyzing stuff. Tell me. How do you think Robert Redler and Liza Downs will fare?"

The governor shook his head with some effort.

"I guess it's anybody's guess. Darlene," Millie called.

Five seconds later, Darlene came into the room. "Yes, ma'am?"

"I think we're finishing up here," Millie said.

"Yes, ma'am," Darlene said, staring down at the governor.

"Did my husband call yet?"

"No, ma'am."

"You know what to tell him when he does."

Darlene nodded.

"I think we can clean up now, Darlene." Millie stood up and went over to the figure slumped in the chair. She opened the front of his jacket and saw the gun and shoulder holster tucked in the crook of his arm. A silencer was already screwed into place. "You help me carry him upstairs."

Darlene and Millie removed the governor from his seat.

Chapter 59

Liza Downs went up the cliffs at Friar's Head then traveled west toward the lodge. It was the direction that made the most sense; the approach that would put her at the east end of the building. Right up and out of the wood lot she would walk, God willing. From any other direction, the sentries would surely see her coming. There had to be close to twenty troops in and around the nest, she knew. The thought of having to overpower a guard, without being seen or heard by the others, terrified her. But she would have to manage somehow, for she had to secure a high-powered rifle.

Had to.

Cannonades of cauliflower-shaped clouds sporadically blocked the moon.

Thank God, Liza thought as she paused before making her way west along the pitch-black sandy cliffs. Thank God the troops didn't have noses like the white-tailed deer, or Angelica and her soldiers would certainly have smelled her coming from half a mile away.

Liza stopped and scanned the area with the pair of night-vision binoculars. She clearly saw two figures standing on the roof. She saw another sitting dormant atop a picnic table on a raised cinder block patio. She could not see the two soldiers patrolling the cliff just around the corner of the building. Liza put away the glasses and moved like a phantom through the night. A smelly phantom but a phantom nonetheless, she almost giggled although she fought to hold back a flood of tears. Would she ever see Rob again? she wondered. Would she ever see the light of day?

The toe of Liza's right boot squarely caught the corner of a crate that she almost tripped over if not for her moving dead ahead with extreme caution. The top of the shallow container lifted off easily, and what she found inside was truly godsent, for she had hoped to blow sky-high a pair of propane tanks situated near the front of the lodge with a blast from a high-powered rifle. But when Priscilla had told them of the troop's armaments, she had casually mentioned that C-4 does not explode when shot with gunfire as many folks believe, the young girl had elaborated; hence, the need for specialized incendiary blasting caps used in lieu of electronic-remote detonation. This eliminated the need for trigger mechanisms such as wire, remote radio, or cell phone operation.

Attached to the 2 x 1½ x 11-inch blocks of C-4 plastic explosive that Liza uncovered were loosely-taped packages of yellow incendiary-type blasting caps. A marksman could easily blow up targets from considerable distances. Earlier, Kathleen had mentioned the lodge's two propane tanks. Tanks for cooking the troop's meals, making hot water, and providing heat, supplemented by the occasional use of the cabin's fireplace.

Liza worked quickly and quietly, affixing a malleable, adhesive-backed block of C-4 plastic explosive directly between the two white cylinders standing next to one another along the lodge's front wall. Next, she inserted several of the blasting caps closely together within the center of the block so as to create a bigger bull's-eye.

Suddenly, a guard appeared well to her left. She raised Guadalupe's bow and set the pin on the sentry's back as the figure passed. Unless it was a clean kill, it would be *she* who would surely be dead, she knew. Too dark. Too far away to be certain she'd hit her mark. Liza reminded herself of one young boy she had shot earlier that afternoon who had squirmed and wiggled, moaning and groaning for a good two minutes before he finally succumbed.

As soon as the guard disappeared from sight, Liza moved stealthily ahead. She'd greet him or her on the next pass she promised herself, making her way toward a tree line, raising the night-vision optics to her eyes. The two figures on the roof were facing away from her. The sentry at the picnic table stood up and headed west.

Minutes later, two guards came within ten yards of Liza. They couldn't see her. The pair passed, talking quietly to one another. One of them turned around and started back. The other continued on ahead.

Armed with Priscilla's knife, Liza put down Guadalupe's bow and stepped out of nowhere, mumbling something in Spanish.

"Guadalupe?" Wanda questioned, somewhat unsure, snapping

her weapon to port arms.

"*Número Cuatro*," Liza answered.

"Christ, we thought—"

"Thought what?" Liza whispered, thrusting the blade straight into Wanda's windpipe, relieving the girl of her .30-06 Springfield, literally laying down her life. Liza found an extra magazine of ammunition in the soldier's pocket. She listened to the night wind pick up before dragging the body backward toward the trees, rolling it up against a log with her boot. Removing the girl's parka hood, Liza put it on, pulled and loosely tied the drawstring, then nonchalantly headed toward the road just to the right of the lodge, checking the weapon with a forefinger, making sure that the safety was off.

Liza felt great relief. She had a plan, and now she had the means with which to implement it. It was a simple plan. So simple that she wondered if it would really work. She would find out soon enough. Liza wished there was a way she could round up everyone directly outside the front door of the building. Immediately to the west would be nice. But she would have to do the best she could. Liza reached the beginning of the road when a voice called down to her.

"Hold it!"

Liza stopped dead in her tracks.

"Did you forget we mined across the road as well, stupid?" Doug warned.

Liza recognized the voice. She turned in the semidarkness as a cumulus cloud sluggishly gave way to light. "I guess my mind was on the biggest fucking deer," she answered in Guadalupe's accent, holding the rifle in one hand, tapping the top of Guadalupe's hood in a gesture of forgetfulness. "*Estupida*, for sure, Dougie."

"Hey," Doug called out to a small group gathered near the front of the lodge. "Lupe's back. She's finally back. Where the fuck are the others?" he piped down to Liza from the rooftop.

Liza shrugged, not daring to take another step.

"Where's Wanda?" one of the young men wanted to know.

"What is Guadalupe doing with a rifle?" another questioned.

"That isn't Guadalupe!" a female soldier shouted, her night-vision glasses fixed on Liza.

Liza snapped the rifle to her shoulder and blew Doug and another figure off the roof. Silhouetted against the sky, and with fine light-gathering telescopic optics, it proved a cinch. Her moving target wasn't anywhere near as easy, as Peter sent a round past the intruder's shoulder a fraction of a second before Liza flinched, fired and clearly missed.

The front door of the lodge flew open, and a woman inside opened fire. Short bursts blew by Liza's body before she found the protection of a fair-sized tree. Suddenly darkness began to fill the landscape. Two forms darted fifty yards to the left and right, trying to trap her in crossfire. Liza swept the rifle to the right and cut one of them down as easily as if she were buttering bread, two shots whipping through Bobby's torso before he hit the ground.

As Liza immediately crouched and darted from one tree to another, Peter opened with rapid fire at its base. A planted mine exploded, uprooting the last tree she had run from. And although she was already numb from fear, Liza felt the stinging pain in her right leg.

Inside the lodge, half a dozen soldiers held positions along the windows. Around the property, another six or seven soldiers circled. She cursed herself for not carrying out her plan sooner. But could she have? She only stood but fifty yards from the building at best. Not near the distance needed for what she had to do. Not without getting herself killed in the bargain. But time was running out, she knew full well. Where were the other soldiers who had fled before they tried to flank her, too? How many shots had she fired? How many cartridges did the magazine hold, including one round in the chamber? *Five!* she suddenly remembered, realizing she had shot her load. Had the enemy been counting? Why hadn't they rushed her? Would they attack the second they heard her exchanging magazines? Unless, of course, they believed the firepower came from the guns of two intruders instead of one bloody fool.

"Are you all right, Rob?" Liza shouted as a ruse. But, of course, no one answered back. "I said, are you all right, goddamnit? Answer me!" she screamed at the top of her lungs, cradling the weapon, and as she did so, released the empty magazine before slamming home another that housed the standard four. *Four not five*, she told herself, feeding a fifth round into the chamber.

From nowhere, Number Nine appeared with a rifle barrel pointed at the back of Liza's head, about to blow it off when a shot rang out and tore open the soldier's left temple. Karen dropped in a flash.

"No, she's not all right," a voice shouted. "Not by a *long shot*," Carlos punned and laughed, believing he had killed the enemy.

"Shut up," someone from inside the lodge snapped.

Liza went through the dead girl's pockets and came up with a hand-held in addition to another magazine. She turned on the radio and received a crash of static before she heard a male voice trying desperately to communicate with the dead.

"Nine. Nine. Come back. Come back," Danny called. "Come in Number Nine. Over."

Liza brought the unit to her lips and pressed the button for transmission. "Nine," she whispered.

"Code," Danny came back.

"There's a fucking army coming," Liza responded weakly. "Heading for the lodge."

"Code and position, damn you," Danny challenged.

"Hit bad," Liza babbled in half-truth, for her leg hurt severely.

"Number Nine is down!" Danny shouted. "No confirming code. No position. Is that a copy? Over."

"Copy loud and clear," a female voice came back. "I think I saw Nine take a hit."

Danny was off the radio then back on line thirty seconds later. "First squad; be ready to pull back," Danny ordered. "Copy, code and position."

There was no reply.

"Second assault team," Danny snapped. "Respond."

"Affirmative. White. King Rook Two."

"Copy that. Black. Queen Knight Four."

"That's a Roger, dodger. Code White. Queen Bishop Three."

"Affirmative. White. King Knight Two."

"Opponent's position? Team?" Danny asked of anyone out there.

"Black. Queen Five and holding," a male voice stated firmly.

"Confirmed," another figure concealed near the peak of the roof declared.

"Your codes and positions!" Danny demanded.

"White. Queen One."

"White. Queen Eight."

"Copy that," Danny transmitted from within the lodge, staring down at his chessboard-like sector chart rather satisfactorily. He nodded to Peter who was now back inside the building, and Peter sent four soldiers out the front door who took up positions on both sides in front of the building. A pair supported rocket launchers on their shoulders. Two others carried over a heavy wooden crate and placed it upon the ground between them.

Peter gestured from the front doorway, and two of the young men opened the crate, lifting out and feeding a projectile into the rear of each tubular weapon before stepping off to one side.

"Second assault team. Pull back now," Danny instructed.

Several minutes later, four warm bodies threaded their way back through the wood lots off each side of the road leading to and from the lodge. One by one, Liza picked them off, shattering four skulls to kingdom come.

". . . . *Thy will be done*," Liza said quietly, putting down the rifle and picking up Number Nine's. *Five and four more rounds in the extra magazine*, she told herself, her thoughts suddenly interrupted by another transmission.

"Listen up out there. You are outmanned and outgunned. We have firepower that can send you into next Wednesday," Angelica communicated. "I'm going to count to ten, and if I don't hear anything along the lines of an unconditional surrender, I'm going to lose my cool. Do you read me?"

Liza hit the button on the hand-held. "Loud and clear, *Angelo*," she answered.

There was a moment of silence. "Is that you, Liza dear?"

"Me and my angels, darling. We have this place surrounded. Coast Guard to the north. My people to your east and west, and I'm in your face with Robert and backup," she positively lied. "So give it up. There is no way out. I want all of you out and in front of the building. Got it?"

Angelica laughed. "Got it. Tell you what. Put one other person on the air. I mean besides Robert Redler—if he's even alive. Show me that you have a team out there. Or are you simply a team of one, tops?"

"With all the shooting, the local police will be here in minutes, too," Liza stalled. "And there are others out there listening in on us as well. It's just a matter of time, *Angelo*."

"Listen carefully to me, Liza. I'm counting. *One*. There are no Coast Guard cutters out there. We can see for miles. *Two*. No one is on that frequency. That's a very special radio you have on loan from Number Nine. *Three*. If you did have people out there, they would have said hello by now, dear. *Four*. Shots fired from up here are not at all uncommon as the local kids occasionally use the dunes as a firing range. And at all hours of night. Tracer ammunition as well. Also, poachers out there jack-lighting deer. A noisy nuisance at worst. *Five*. So when and if the police do come, sweetheart, know what they're going to learn? That we belong here. We've leased the property and lodge. I don't think they're going to listen to your tall tale. Especially when they understand that *you* do not belong up here, and that you and your domestic partner in crime went berserk and hurt some of my followers."

"We didn't hurt them, *Angelo*. We killed them."

"*Six*. An admission of guilt in front of many witnesses."

"And unless *you* give it up, we'll kill the rest of you. That's a promise, *Angelo*," Liza swore.

"*Seven*."

"How are you going to explain to the police all the weapons and explosives you've got?"

"My one phone call to Karl brushes everything else aside. *Eight*."

"You'll never get to place that call, *Angelo*. Not while I'm alive."

"*Nine*. This is your last chance to surrender . . . ."

Liza was in a prone position, the sling of the rifle wrapped securely about her arm and wrist. Her leg was bleeding badly. Sixty yards from the lodge was the point at which she was positioned. Her single black target lay set somewhere between two barely discernible propane tanks. There in the darkness, she could not discern her bull's-eye: the grouping of yellow blasting caps.

Considerably more destructive than any 20-pound liquid propane barbecue tank, the two 420s gradually came into view, each filled to near capacity with precious liquid propane gas.

Yes.

The two tall cylinders stood like sentries upon four-inch thick slabs of stone. A copper line led from one tank to the other, feeding through the wall of the building. Liza had slithered forward sinuously on belly and elbows to within forty yards of her objective.

She had stopped listening to Angelica's threats, as a series of clouds gave way to the magnificent moonlit night. Liza focused mightily on acquiring precise target acquisition. *White Queen to C-4— "Ten,"* Liza affirmed, squeezing the trigger and delivering one round into the bull's-eye that exploded both tanks in a ten-foot high, fiery, yellow-orange thunderous ball. The ground shook and nearly knocked her unconscious. The explosion had sent a *varoom* of fire that caught and instantly ignited the wooden walls of the lodge. And then came another explosion; a mine accidentally set off by a soldier on fire while running for his or her life.

In a daze, Liza dizzily witnessed the holocaust and listened to the sickening screams. "Checkmate, motherfuckers!" she declared in early victory. Exchanging magazines, she turned her back to the horror and made her way east, praying to God to lead her safely around the mines and whatever other madness Angelica's troops had prepared. She dragged her wounded leg behind her as if it were separate from her body. For a moment, she thought it was; thought that it, too, had caught fire.

How many of them had she and Robert killed in the past two days? she wondered. Was he safe? These were the thoughts that took her mind off worrying whether or not she would lose her leg. How many more soldiers were left? One thing she somehow *knew* for sure. So powerful was the vision embedded in her brain. Angelica Manns was still alive! Was that her gift from God for all her trouble? Was that what He wanted her to know? She hated God in that moment. She hated herself, too. Had she come this far to hate so solemnly? When, oh, when would she ever be delivered from evil? When would God just simply leave her alone? Why had He taken little Davey from her? Why was it still dark? Because God was back there with them standing in the light, she told herself. She was crying uncontrollably as she tried to run. Immediately, she fell.

Liza was panicking. She knew it but couldn't fight the dread. She also knew she was losing lots of blood. If only she could tie a tourniquet around her eyes and sleep. Forever. Yes! That could be God's gift to her. Eternal, blissful sleep. Then and only then would she make her peace with Him. Not a single solitary second before.

"I hate You," she mumbled, sitting down hard and opening her coat, somehow finding the strength to tear and rip strips of cotton from her turtleneck with her teeth, fashioning a tourniquet as she had done for Robert earlier. "Why couldn't God do for me in *my* hour of need?" she flared. *Because there is no God*, she told herself. No more than there ever was a Santa Claus.

Chapter 60

Mayor Tom Harden arrived home late. The housekeeper was standing at the end of the hallway as he passed through the foyer.

"Everything all right, Darlene?'

"Jus' fine, Mayor."

Tom Harden looked at Darlene curiously. "Nobody call or come by?"

"No, sa. Oh, jus' the paper boy. I lef' money in the envelope likes ya say."

"Where's Millie?'

"Upstairs in her room, I guess."

"You guess."

"Yes, sa. Mrs. Harden retired early. Says she wasn't feelin' real good."

"Governor call?" Tom Harden asked absently, shuffling impatiently through the mail on the marble tabletop beside the phone.

Darlene smiled. "No, sa. You asked me that earlier when ya called, and you asked me if anybody come or call when ya jus' come in. Someone as important as the governor, Darlene don't forget."

Mayor Harden put down the mail and smiled, too. "I'm sorry, Darlene. I've got a lot on my mind is all." He phoned the governor's home and spoke briefly with the answering service. Next, he called the governor's office. No answer. Finally, he punched in a coded number and let it ring forever before he hung up. "Darlene!" he shouted.

A moment later, Darlene appeared at the threshold and followed him into the dining area.

"Yes, sa?"

"Scotch and water. Rocks. Make it a double."

"Oooo-weee. We got us some worries and concerns, I can see."

"Never you mind."

"No, sa," Darlene said, shaking her head in earnest.

Tom Harden heard one of the doors open and close upstairs. He turned and looked around the corner toward the staircase. "Hi, sweetheart. Darlene tells me you're not feeling well. I was just on my way up."

"Don't trouble yourself, dear. I'm coming down." Down and around the wood and marble balustrade Millie came. Sixty steps along the staircase in all.

"It's pretty late. Why don't you go back and rest? I'll be right up. Darlene's making me a drink."

"Now that's what I need. A nice stiff drink."

"You?"

"Why not?"

"I think the last time you had a drink was when your father died."

"It's been that kind of a day, Tom. I feel like I lost someone who seemed like more of a father to me than a friend."

"Who's that?"

"We'll talk." Millie came up to her husband and pecked him on the cheek. "Come. Come. Come. Let's go into the study."

"What did you do today?" Tom asked.

"Oh, same-o, same-o. Exercised and read. Oh, and I started some seeds."

"It's January, sweetheart."

"Ah, but spring will be here before you know it."

Darlene came in with the mayor's drink. "Sa."

"Thanks, Darlene. Buy you a drink, Millie?" Tom kidded and smiled.

"Bourbon and coke, Darlene. No ice, please." Millie took a seat.

"Bourbon?" Tom declared. "Must have been some day."

"Come, sit."

Tom Harden took the same seat the governor had sat in earlier. He raised his glass and toasted his wife. "To the prettiest girl in Macon."

"Who's Baceni, Tom?"

The mayor put his drink down on the table across from her. "Come again?"

"Baceni," Millie repeated without expression.

Tom Harden shook his head, furrowed his brow, and searched the high ceiling with narrow eyes for the answer. "Doesn't ring a bell. Why?"

"Karl Baceni. Know him?"

Darlene came back into the room and handed Millie her drink, then left.

The mayor lowered his eyes and set them on his wife. "Can't say that I do."

"Can't? How come you can't?"

"Because I don't know anyone by that name. Should I?"

"How about the name Hitler, Tom? You know that name, don't you?"

Mayor Tom Harden's eyes turned as cold as January can get in Macon County. "Are you trying to tell me something?"

Millie smiled. "No, Tom. I'm trying to get *you* to tell me something."

"Like what?"

Millie took a deep breath. "Like who or what you really are."

"Me?" he questioned and laughed. "Who have you been talking to?" The mayor swilled his drink.

"Got a letter the other day from a woman in upstate New York. A women with a special gift."

Tom took another good gulp of his highball, set it down and tried to relax. He laughed. "That explains it, Millie. When are you going to stop with this business? Hum? No one has a handle on the future. Certainly not our stockbroker," he joked.

Millie smiled patiently. "I'm not talking about the future, Tom. Not anymore. I'm talking about the past. About the sheriff and the governor and what it is that you really do for them."

"What I do for the sheriff is to allow him to operate as he so chooses at the annual fair over in Bibb County, if that's what you're getting at. Little bit of gambling. Little bit of booze and a restricted area set aside for adult entertainment. Once a year. Nobody gets hurt."

"But somebody did get hurt in the parking area. As a matter of fact, a person was brutally murdered there, along with the man's dog."

"What is this all about, Millie?"

"It's about a person who calls herself Angelica Manns. It's

about a man and his two brothers whose last name was changed from Hitler to Baceni toward the end of the Second World War."

The mayor got up and walked about the room.

"Were you really just going to let the governor kill me and probably Darlene, too, then come home and go to bed?"

"What is this woman's name who you talked to? I demand to know."

"I didn't talk to her. She wrote me. Her name is Kathleen Grear. That ring a bell?" she mocked knowingly.

It was unclear whether the mayor was shaking his head in ignorance to the question or in sheer disgust. He did not answer.

"So. Where do you think we go from here?" Millie asked. "Hum? Stick me in some institution? I don't think you would have any trouble getting the three required signatures. Isn't that how many signatures they needed to put Kathleen and the others away? Or is that just up in New York, dear? What about Zachariah up in Milledgeville? How many names on the dotted line to hold him there for all those years? The signatures of three psychiatrists, or just yours, Tom's, and Al's?"

"Where is the governor, Millie?"

"Is that your first concern?"

"Where is he?"

"Upstairs."

"Upstairs where?"

"Upstairs in our bedroom, darling. Dead."

Tom's eyes ran up the spiral staircase. He headed back to the phone.

"What are you doing?"

"Calling Tom, Millie. You stay right there."

"You don't have to call the sheriff, dear. Tom's right here."

Sheriff Hayes came through the door and into the study. The sheriff held a gun.

"What the hell is going on here, Tom?" the mayor demanded.

"The governor came here to kill Millie tonight. She poisoned him instead."

The mayor looked over at his drink.

Millie giggled. "No, that's not what we have planned for you, Mr. Mayor. What we have planned for you goes back to the beginning, when the governor shot and killed his maid and butler. You remember that. You helped orchestrate that messy business along with the sheriff here."

"What do you think you're doing, Tom?" the mayor asked as calmly as he could. "Put that gun down. Darlene!" Tom Harden hollered.

"Darlene's gone for the evening, Mr. Mayor. So just cool your jets."

"Do you know what you're doing, Tom?"

"Yes, I do, Tom," the sheriff said.

"You two are crazy."

"Like my grandfather, Zachariah, Tom? It was like I put this gun to his head and pulled the trigger."

"He was nuts."

"No. He had the gift."

"What gift? He was nuts, I'm telling you."

"You're not telling me nothin' no more. You had the chance to tell me everything, Tom."

"Tell you what?" the mayor snapped with cold and angry blue-gray eyes.

"That Senator Atkins' butler was, in fact, my father, for openers."

"Jesus Christ, Tom. Who have you been listening to?"

"I'm just your lackey, Tom. I thought you were my friend."

"I am your friend. You are not my lackey. We made the senator into a governor. You and I. Together. We run this state. And when I step into real power, Tom, we'll run this country. We're talking just a few years. You're going to throw all that away?"

"What are you talking about? The governor is dead, for God's sake. If Millie didn't do it, the people would have done it through their vote come next election. It's over, Tom. We're dinosaurs."

The mayor laughed. "Do you know who I am?" he said pompously.

Sheriff Hayes shook his head. "I thought you were my friend," the man repeated.

"I told you, Tom. I am your friend. We go back to the days of the sandbox, for Christ's sake. Our families go back generations."

Sheriff Hayes was still shaking his head. "Friends don't keep secrets like that from one another."

"We share national secrets, Tom."

"Friends don't let other friends kill off members of their family. You knew the senator's butler was my father. Didn't you? You know why the governor was here today."

"Is that what this is all about, Tom?"

Again, the sheriff shook his head. "Not just any family, Tom. It's about *my* father and grandfather. About Millie and my mom."

"Your mother was a whore."

"And Millie?"

"They're all whores. She's whoring right now," he hollered, pointing an accusing finger at his wife.

"Just answer me one thing, Tom. Why? Why do you want her dead?"

"A national security risk. It has to be."

"She doesn't have the gift like my grandfather had, Tom. It doesn't explain things. Just, please, tell me why."

The mayor shifted his eyes between his wife and the sheriff.

"Well?"

"She makes a good case," was all that the mayor could manage.

"A case for parapsychology," Millie clarified.

"Put the gun down, Tom. You know you're not a killer."

"And do what? Give you the gun to kill Millie? Maybe me?"

"I wouldn't do that."

"But you would stand by and have someone else do it."

"Those were orders, Tom."

"From who?'

"From Karl to Al."

"Well, I'm in charge right now, and I'm giving the orders."

"And what are you ordering, Tom?" the mayor of the manor asked and smiled passively.

"Tell him, Millie."

"Well, first off, the sheriff here is going to shoot you dead, dear," Millie said placidly. "Then we're going to bring the governor back down here, put his gun, which is in the sheriff's hand, in Al's, and claim that he attempted to rape me at gunpoint. You came to my defense. The governor shot you, and the sheriff happened on the scene and shot the governor in self-defense. Is that about right, Tom?" Millie asked, checking with the sheriff.

"That's about it."

"And what do you propose to do then?"

"Well, Tom is going to help me take down and put away the Christmas decorations before we put out the tree; Three Kings' Day, yes?" Millie smiled. "You know that it's bad luck to do that before or after, don't you? That's what you yourself always said."

"And just how are you going to explain the poison in the governor's body? Tell me that. As executive head of state, the governor's body will be sent up to the medical examiner in Atlanta for a thorough, and I do mean a detailed, autopsy. Nothing but nothing will be overlooked. This is not going to be covered up by one of our cronies in the coroner's office, Tom."

"It's not going to be," the sheriff stated flatly.

"What do you mean?"

"It means that Karl has sanctioned me to kill you, and in so doing, has guaranteed no glitches in the investigation."

For the first time that evening, Mayor Tom Harden looked afraid. "That's not true!"

"Why not?" Millie said. "He's a murderer just like his father. He's had others killed. So why not you? He asked you to kill me. You told him you couldn't. He only asks once. Good for me. Very bad for you."

"Do you think for a second that he's going to let her live?" the mayor squawked before the sheriff. "He wants her dead. Why a sudden change of heart? And what about Kathleen Grear? You don't think she'll do something? Or Robert Redler? What about Liza Downs?"

"Kathleen Grear is dead. Robert Redler is lying in a hospital in Riverhead. And Liza Downs will probably turn up cold by morning. That's the latest, Tom," the sheriff elaborated.

"Who the hell do you think you are?" Tom shuddered, his eyes shifting from the sheriff to his wife.

"Why, I'm Mildred Brown-Harden. Your wife. Your widow in just about a minute. If you want to know the truth, and I certainly think that you're entitled to it, I've been asked to join the rank and file. You're out as next in line. Actually, you were never in the running, Tom. Oh, you might have been a contender once upon a time. But the

Triumvirate is more powerful than the Holy Trinity, dear. It's looking for a few good men. You're not one of them."

"Karl promised me!" the mayor screamed.

"Why? Because I just happen to be best friends with Karl's wife who believes very much along the lines that I do? You're behaving very silly. An expensive home and an important title do not make the man, Tom. It's his deeds. What have you done on your own? What street have you walked down that Karl hasn't paved for you in gold? Tell me."

"Who are you, Millie?"

"No longer the innocent schoolgirl whose books you and Tom, here, would carry home."

"WHO?"

"—who, through my research, for years unwittingly provided Karl's wife with lists of names, addresses, and telephone numbers of supposed kooks, cranks, and a few practitioners who actually possess the gift. People I corresponded with regularly. People like Kathleen Grear."

"And if that were truly so," Mayor Harden blared, "why would Kathleen Grear, whose window to the world was apparently as bright as Solomon's wisdom, write and reveal herself to you? Answer me that."

It was a question for which Millie Brown-Harden had no answer— the answer which nevertheless came to mind of the mayor of Macon with such clarity in the instant Millie gave the order.

"Kill him."

Sheriff Hayes shot the mayor three times in the chest.

Chapter 61

Liza had the sensation of floating, yet every so often she felt her body jar, followed by a pounding, as if being held at anchor in a thirty-knot current before suddenly breaking free in a following sea. She tried to open her eyes, but each time heavy lids closed them like a shutter covering a camera's lens, warning against even the gossamer condition of night. Where was she? On the sea of salvation . . . sailing heavenward? Liza gradually squinted to hold her eyes open for several seconds while they darted at the dark. Her leg throbbed against something which cradled her. She thought she could feel the beating of a heart behind her left shoulder that she swore was not her own, pounding away against a crashing surf she could clearly hear. She tried turning her body, but the hollow held her firmly in a protective embrace. It was as if the vessel were breathing and squeezing her for dear life.

Suddenly, the momentum stopped then abruptly changed direction. She could feel the sudden surge. Liza listened for the telltale slap of a sail or some sound of an engine but swore she could only hear and feel the beating of a breast, pounding away violently. Liza was swept forward again before she realized that the vessel that held her to its bosom was not one that transported people, but rather a body on the run, a body that was violently pumping blood through vessels of its own. Human vessels. Her own heart was quickening. Liza was being carried forward in someone's arms.

"Rob?" she cried.

"Shh," came the succinct reply.

Liza began to cry.

"Shh, y-you'll b-be s-safe soon."

The young man was practically out of breath she reasoned as she wept.

"N-no more s-soldiers," Danny promised. "I'm ta-taking you

far away fr-from here."

"I have to get to a hospital and find someone."

"F-first we h-have t-to get f-far away from here," he repeated. Danny began running with Liza held tightly in his arms.

Approximately five hundred yards further, Danny stopped to catch his breath again, setting Liza down as gently as he could.

"What's your name?" Liza whispered.

"Fr-friends b-back home call me D-Danny Boy."

"Where's home, Danny Boy?"

"K-Kansas."

It was still too dark for Danny to see Liza's painful smile. "Are you taking me back to Kansas with you, Danny?"

Danny chuckled quietly. "No. Not q-qu-quite that far."

"Why not?" she asked anxiously, resting her head involuntarily against his knee.

"Y-ya-you're not Dorothy, and I'm no wizard," Danny said and laughed in his sleeve.

"Danny?"

"Yes, ma'am?"

"If you were a wizard, would you be a good wizard or a bad wizard?"

Liza couldn't see Danny's tears as he wiped his eyes there in the dark. "If I w-was a wizard, ma'am, I'd b-be the v-very best wizard I could be."

"I really believe you would be, Danny. I really and truly do."

Danny reached down and lifted Liza into his arms again, then started running across an open field. The sky ahead of them showed the faintest hint of light.

Chapter 62

Robert awoke in a private hospital room. Two lengths of transparent tubing from inverted plastic bags fed his body. The room was dimly lit. In the corner of the ceiling on a metal shelf sat a television set. A commercial was running, but no sound. Robert had to crane his neck to note his early morning visitor.

"Where am I?" Robert asked.

"Not where you ought to be. That's for damn sure, Mr. Richard Roberts."

"How did you find me?"

"Well, I haven't got a crystal ball like you. But I had resident doctors, nurses, repairmen, and cleaning people on every floor from Greenport Hospital to Stony Brook University Medical Center looking for the likes of you and yours. Actually, I started looking in the morgues but figured we wouldn't be so lucky."

Robert noted that the door was closed, probably even locked.

"You're in Central Suffolk Hospital. We had you brought down from surgery a little while ago. Lost a lot of blood, but you'll be fine for now."

Robert said nothing.

Karl could plainly see the apprehension written across the writer's face but knew that Robert wouldn't ask.

"Liza's fine, too," he volunteered.

"I know. I got her the hell out of there. She's long gone," he lied. "You won't find her."

Karl smiled and shook his head. "No, we find anyone who needs finding. But in your case and Liza's, it took a little longer than expected. I will concede that. She's two floors below you."

He watched Robert's eyes gradually relinquish, not necessarily extinguishing their hatred.

Two solitary tears rolled down the writer's cheeks as he stared blankly at the TV. "Liar!"

Karl ignored the remark then continued. "You won't be pulling back a bow for quite some time, and she won't be running interference for you for at least for a month or maybe more. Nothing life threatening. Unless . . . ."

Robert shifted his eyes from the television set to the figure sitting beside him. "Let me make clear to you a single promise, Karl. Nothing that I can't keep. You fuck with me or mine once more, and I'll find you where you sleep. That includes the merc, the monsignor, Manns and company, Tom-Tom, and the governor of Georgia—and anyone else you work with, Karl. Promise."

The rhythm of the rhyme and its delivery momentarily startled Karl, but he recouped quickly, deciding not to inform his nemesis that he need not concern himself with at least two of the aforementioned. "Brave, I imagine. But rather stupid on the surface because—"

"Then look beneath the surface, Karl."

Karl sighed, lowered and shook his head sadly. "Look, Rob."

"It's there for *you* to see."

"Don't you know that I could have and still can have the two of you put out of your misery in a heartbeat," Karl stated calmly. "Do you doubt that for even a second?"

"And don't you realize that I have put the fear of God into you for your remaining days here on earth. Do you doubt that in the least?"

Karl stared at Robert for a good moment before he got up and headed for the door before facing about. "You'll find an envelope in the inside pocket of your coat when you're discharged. Something to help get you and Liza back on your feet. Take it to the bank where it was issued. Actually, any branch. You won't have a problem. Oh, and another thing. Next time, take out better insurance on your boat and home and cars," he added. "You never know." Karl unlocked the door and let it swing wide open as he left.

It was four in the afternoon when Liza found him. A tall black orderly wheeled her through the open door and right up to the side of Robert's bed.

"This gal of yours must have some real pull here, mister. Defied all the doctors' and nurses' orders and had the head of the hospital insist I bring her up. You guys got fifteen minutes, and then I put her back to bed. Or it's my butt." He smiled complacently and walked out.

"And where the hell have you been?" Robert griped.

"Sitting around here kicking ass," she explained, taking his taped and needled hand.

"What's that?" he asked, pointing to her own apparatus hanging from a pole above her chair.

"Just a scratch," she fibbed.

"How did you wind up here?"

Liza smiled warmly. "Clicked my heels together," she said, bringing the heel of one red slipper alongside the other.

"Did you have a visitor earlier?"

Liza nodded uncomfortably.

"What did he say?"

"Said he couldn't talk sense to you, so he'd try me."

"And?"

"And I listened to what he had to say."

"Which was?"

"That it's over. Said he's giving us a second chance."

"What did you say to him?"

"I told him we might see him at the Second Coming."

Robert squeezed her hand. "Good girl."

"We kicked their butts up there, Rob."

"I caught some if it on the news."

"You don't know the half of it."

"Going to keep me in suspense?"

"Angelica Manns is dead. Danny killed her."

"Who's Danny?"

"The one who brought me these red slippers."

"Oh, *that* Danny," he sighed, raising his other hand in a mock display of understanding.

"He's a stutterer."

"That's the one," he persisted.

"He was one of her soldiers, Rob." She put her head down then raised it back up, holding back her tears. "He practically carried me here." She squeezed his hand. "Twenty years old. He had to kill three of his own to get me out of there."

"Where is he now?"

"Someplace far, far away from here." Liza suddenly laughed.

"What's so funny?"

"He wants to be a radio announcer." She guffawed.

"I'm definitely missing something here. You said he stutters."

"Not when he's on the radio. Believe me, I know."

"And how's that?"

"He almost blew me to smithereens by calling out coordinates flawlessly. He had a grid of the 4-H camp set up like a chessboard." Liza was laughing hysterically.

"One minute he's trying to kill you. The next minute he's carrying you out of there. How come?"

"I think Danny finally figured out for himself that Angelica was once upon a time an Angelo; that is, after I raised the issue and got her attention on the VHF. Danny said she had the same look on her face as when Barbara Giordano was toying with her in front of the troops while they were interrogating Emma and Emil Jewitt. You recall Priscilla's account."

Robert nodded.

"Well, apparently Angelica and Danny had a thing going. She seduced him early on. Told him on more than one occasion that they were two of a kind in that they both had learned to overcome their handicaps. She was always evasive whenever Danny asked her what she meant. When I called Angelica, Angelo, and Danny saw her face, I think that's when he knew. He told me he loved her. Said he believed she felt the same. He also said she made him promise that neither of them would ever lie to the other. After the explosion, Danny asked her if what I said was true. She answered, yes. He shot her just before he ran out the back of the lodge."

Robert took her hand. "I saw the Cliff House on the news. How did you manage that?"

"You know those two tanks by the front door of the lodge Kathleen told us about?"

"The propane tanks."

Liza nodded. "I blew them."

"How?"

"Got ahold of some plastic explosive and a .30-06 and shot them."

"You kidding me, or what?"

"Kid you not."

"You know, I had my eye on those tanks, too," he swore.

"There he goes. Trying to steal my thunder."

"Not for a second, darling." He repositioned himself and winced.

Liza worked the wheels of her chair closer to the bed, laying her head upon the edge of his mattress, taking his hand and tucking it beneath her cheek.

"What else did Karl have to say?" Robert asked.

"'Forget about us and we'll forget about you.'"

"Anything else?"

"Told me to make sure that whatever you write and publish be presented as fiction."

"And you said?"

"I didn't say anything. I just shot my right arm out and saluted. When his back was turned, I gave him the finger."

This time it was Robert who laughed and laughed heartily as Liza sat there tittering. He laughed so hard that he cried because his arm hurt so badly. But he didn't care.

"You want to go to the press with this story?" Liza asked after they both settled down.

"We went to them before. Remember. Two years ago. Or did you forget?"

Liza shook her head.

"Do you remember how the press turned a blind eye, covered their ears, put a finger to their mouths and shushed me? Did you forget how the police railroaded me?"

"Do you want to go back to teaching?"

"Did you forget how the college turned their back on me? How even the chairperson of the English Department lied. 'No, we did not get rid of him because he refused to change a failing grade given to a student, reluctantly changing it to a passing D. No, we did not give him permission to use his novel in either manuscript or published form in the classroom for seven consecutive years. No, we did not get rid of him because there were criminal charges brought against him.' And then her one concession. 'Yes, he is a gifted teacher.' But I couldn't land a job after that. Did you forget those instances, Liza?"

"No."

"Did you forget who controls the police, the press, our institutions of higher learning, and our very government?"

"No, I haven't."

"Well?"

"Well, then what?"

"I'll continue writing. I'll tell the story in the only form it can be presented, Liza. Like virtually all fiction, embedded between its covers and its lines lies the truth. People see that. People are *not* stupid."

"The truth is that people like Karl are here to stay. The truth is that people like Barbara Giordano are the lesser of the evils. The truth is that people like Angelica come along maybe once in our lifetime. The truth is that we beat them. You and me, Rob."

"But we didn't beat The Triumvirate."

"No, not yet, we didn't. But it's not just up to us, Rob. You remember what Kathleen said? Not entirely our battle. We gave them a run for their money. We can't save the world."

"No. All we can do is make a dent in their armor. And if all good people make a dent collectively—"

"—then the world might be a safer place; you think?" Chief Grear interrupted, coming into the room with a tall vase filled with a dozen white roses in one hand, a tiny blue box in the other. "For you," he said, handing the vase to Liza. "And for you," he added, gently setting the small blue box upon Robert's chest.

"What's this?"

"Open it up," the police chief said with a stone face.

"Doesn't even ask how we're doing," Robert said glumly.

"Shut up and open it. I know exactly how you're doing. You'll just have to do things with your other arm for a while."

Robert lifted off the top of the box and found a golden key sandwiched between two pads of cotton. "What's this?"

"Key to your new boat. Well, almost new. Confiscated fifty-footer."

"A cop bribing a civilian?"

"It's tied up at your dock. You two will be living aboard it when you get out of here. You can supervise the building of your new home as soon as you approve the plans that I'll be sending over this afternoon. Keep you both out of trouble."

"And who's going to pay for all this?' Liza asked. "The taxpayers?"

"I understand there's a check waiting for you among your personal belongings," he said to Robert. "That should cover it. Listen, I've got to run. I'll check in on the two of you tomorrow. We'll talk."

"Where are you off to?"

"I'm in the middle of making arrangements, Rob. My sister Kathleen passed away last night."

Liza brought her hand to her mouth and, with the other, put aside the roses, taking the chief's hand. "Oh, I'm so sorry."

Chief Grear took his hand back gently and gave Liza a kiss on the cheek. "Gotta go," he said, forcing an awkward smile before exiting the room.

"I wonder if he knows," Liza spoke in a somber hushed timbre.

"I don't know what that man knows and doesn't, Liza. I swear to God I don't."

"What was that business about a check?"

"Apparently, Karl left us some money."

Liza shook her head in disbelief. "You're not taking it, are you?"

"I don't know."

"Think he and his people will really leave us alone?"

"I don't know that, either," Robert admitted, staring blankly at the door.

Chapter 63

The Three Musketeers sat across the table from three other men. A mid-January wind howled through a broken window at the far end of the tenement railroad flat. Karl tapped his pen impatiently on an 8½ x 14-inch legal pad. Ed sat behind his newspaper. With the edge of a hand, Bill swept a series of crumbs into the center of a napkin, bunched and stuffed it into a small empty Styrofoam cup, adding a tea bag then placing the plastic cover back on top.

"So," Karl began. "This meeting is informal in rather informal surroundings as I'm sure you've noted." He smiled warmly. "In less than three years, you will be handed awesome responsibilities for which you have been schooled," he addressed the trio. "Not in theory, but in its practical application. America has served as your proving ground. A microcosm in which you learned and grew painfully aware of the fact that the United States is in its infancy. A foolish nation, believing that it is the most powerful on the face of the planet; a people behaving much like an impetuous child from time to time. America is not your fatherland, my children, no more than Germany would be yours today; nor would any one country in the world, for that matter. Your home is global, gentlemen. Your house has seven rooms, inclusive of a cellar and an attic. Asia is your bedroom for the moment. I want you all to get lots of rest. You'll need it. Believe me. Europe is your dining room, right now. I want you to eat hearty, but not leave a mess. South America is your den of iniquity." He paused and grinned enigmatically. "Relax, but do not *be* lax. Bill and Ed will fill you in. North America? I'd like for you to renovate that room. Or maybe you'll find that you'll have to scrap it and start from scratch. You'll soon decide. On the other hand, Australia shall be your living room, my lads. There, you will live to see the wonders of a civil civilization, I trust. It's a room your work will keep you from, alas. Antarctica is like that extra room for storage, my students. You'll soon learn what secrets we have buried there. We haven't told you everything as yet. Africa? Your study. Not so dark as you may think. Why does the world still point an accusatory finger at my father and the German people? Ethnic cleansing is as old and as new a solution as any nation.

"Heaven and hell are your discriminatory boundaries, boys. Stay out of the cellar and the attic, but watch your flooring and your roof. You and you and you are the walls, gentlemen," Karl pointed a bony finger at each young man. "Your house has no doors through which others would otherwise pass in or out of. No windows for those with penetrating eyes to see within." Karl fixed his eyes firmly on the three before concluding.

"That about wraps it up, lads. I'm no speechmaker, so Bill and Ed will follow with an illuminating talk regarding the extremes of peace and war. I sit somewhere in the middle. That is the secret of our reign. Balance, my boys. Balance. A delicate balance will be the key to housekeeping in your new home. We'll take a moment before we hear from Bill."

Karl pushed back his chair, got up and went over to a dirty window, looking down into a deserted street. Bill and Ed remained seated. The three men sitting across from them stood and smiled warmly with one another, shaking hands and offering each other early congratulations. The senator's son from Virginia said something amusing to the steel magnate's boy from California. The third and oldest shared their laughter, yet remained aloof. They chatted quietly as old friends for several minutes then took their seats before Karl returned to the table.

The monsignor rose and smiled charitably at the three soon-to-be, incoming successors. "Peace!" he thundered. "Where in hell should I begin?"

Karl smiled and nodded over to Ed excitedly, who nodded back. Both of them believed William's speech on peace and harmony to be the prelate's most powerful sermon from the mount.

The three men in their mid to late forties sat enthralled throughout the clergyman's delivery. Karl and Ed enjoyed themselves thoroughly, studying the men's mood and manner. Wherever the senator's boy and the steel manufacturer's son found mutual humor and laughed aloud, the eldest would merely crack a smile. And at points along the line where the monsignor's lecture turned decisively moribund, the younger two went searching deep inside themselves, whereas the other man's eyes cast a light of understanding.

The cleric concluded his speech, and the mercenary was given the floor.

The merc's message was brief and to the point. War is hell, and in hell the devil is master. The man left no room for doubt. Cruel, barbarous, inhuman, and savage were but mere adjectives to describe varying degrees of necessary measures to be taken in order to seize and hold onto the seat of power. Diplomacy and negotiation, like treaties and other promises, were simply temporary cloaks to pacify the faint of heart. And when the man of war was finished, he handed each of the three younger men a carving knife, leading them to an open elevator door.

"Simply show us that no sense of meaningless morality will ever cloud your thinking," the merc said without expression as he stepped aside.

Suspended from the roof of the elevator car, three naked bodies hung off each wall like crucifixes. On the east panel hung a beautiful Russian girl in her early twenties. Slender arms secured high above her head. She stood on tiptoe. A thin but tenacious wire wrapped around her wrists, ready to cut to the bone. Translucent tape across her open oval mouth clearly explained her modified silence. Dark eyes monumentally expressing their terror.

A two-year-old male child on the back wall wailed a muffled lament, unlike his thirty-year-old mother to the left who was already strangling and bled profusely from her neck. Freshly painted in blood above the child was the Star of David.

The two younger men stepped into the car and quickly went to work on the Russian girl and baby boy. The third took his time and methodically mutilated the mother. The moans and muted screams that emanated from the solitary car were indeed much like the continuous wailing of the wind coming through the broken window at the far end of the apartment. In fact, from where The Three Musketeers stood and watched, the sounds at either end of the room were indistinguishable.

Taking up the entire top floor of the twenty-four story apartment complex, five hours and three thousand miles northwest of the carnage (via Cessna's Citation X) the six had left behind, the palatial penthouse far exceeded what would be described as grand. Utopian might be more on the mark. But attentions were not at that moment focused on decor or ambiance of any sort. Concentrations were given over to the phenomena of the preternatural; that is, the supernatural, parapsychology, clairvoyance and such. The problem was dilemmatic. The conversations were deadly serious. No one present had simply entertained the possibility that the events that so concerned and consumed them were simply a gift handed down from God. Of the six, not even the monsignor raised the possibility. Karl headed the discussion:

"When the three of us were once seated where the three of you now sit, soon to step into our shoes, we, on occasion, when asked, voiced our opinions as to what we thought about those who held the power to see beyond the six senses. Quite frankly, I feared them. So, I simply said that I wanted to see all of them dead, right then and there. But far wiser men sat where we are seated now." Karl smiled. "For several reasons, gentlemen, this final solution has not yet come to pass. As you know, most of the gifted were experimented on. Over the past twenty-two years, we three have vacillated between the poles. We've incarcerated some, institutionalized others, and even terminated a few from time to time. The results have always been the same. They have somehow gotten back to us, whether from a prison, a hospital room, or from the grave. Don't dare scoff!

"Anyhow, it took a good many years to bring Geist's cult and Giordano's cartel together, to mold their respective operations into a cohesive, precision piece of machinery. Robert Redler posed a threat. We tried to recruit him. We failed. Our people tried to find him and kill him, along with Liza Downs. He and she are still here. Well, I finally found them. I could have ended either of their lives in a heartbeat if I had half a mind to. But that's the point. The other half of my brain tells me that would be a terrible mistake." Karl deliberately shook his head. "Along the line enters his better half. Liza Downs. His gift wanes, and suddenly she comes into her own shortly after Angelica's people threaten her and unfortunately kill her five-year-old nephew, David. Together, that team of two—with a little help from Kathleen Grear," he added with a frown, "has been either directly or indirectly responsible for the deaths of practically fifty soldiers in training, not to mention two of its leaders: Barbara Giordano and Angelica Manns. The latter having killed the former. Two years ago, Redler took out Richard Geist and Michael. Those four individuals will be quite difficult to replace.

"Probably one of the most remarkable women with the gift to date was the police chief's sister, Kathleen Grear. She had all of us fooled. Her window was wider than anyone's I've ever seen. Her murder, by my orders, immediately resulted in Liza Downs' lethal blow, no pun intended, at the 4-H camp in Riverhead, New York. Of this I am convinced. We know precisely at what hour and minute Kathleen Grear's life was terminated. It is not coincidence that it coincided with the blast at the Cliff House where Ms. Manns had housed her troops for training. Hence, I remain prudent. Bill and Ed concur." Karl took a sip of water before continuing.

"At present, I believe Robert, Liza, and I have an understanding; that is, you don't come near us, and we won't come near you. I know. About as reassuring as an order of protection from a county court. But I think they'll keep their distance. Let Robert Redler vent through his fiction. If it goes beyond that, he and Liza will meet with a boating accident or such. We'll just have to monitor the situation very closely.

"Now, we've studied and tested Redler. We've given him sensitive information. He's good. But his window is limited as I've mentioned. Seems to be getting narrower. Downs' is indeed wider. Kathleen Grear's was extraordinary. Yet, it would seem she did not see her own death on the horizon when she confided in the mayor's wife, Millie Brown-Harden. Or did she? I think she did, and I'll tell you why. When our people performed an autopsy on Kathleen, guess what we found? Cancer. Inoperable. Six months she had at best. What did she have to lose? She set the ball in motion. Might have done it anyway. Who knows? Anyhow, she got Robert and Liza to go after Angelica and her troops. Got Millie to murder the governor and Sheriff Hayes to murder the mayor. If my information is correct, the sheriff is on borrowed time. Yes. Kathleen Grear exacted her pound of flesh all right. And so did that Ballard fellow in Milledgeville. Zachariah. It could all come crashing down on us if we're not careful. If Robert Redler and Liza Downs are still around when you three assume the watch, we want you to be careful, too. Damn careful.

"So. Enough said about that for now. Allow Bill and Ed and me to bring on the entertainment. A little R & R. We've all earned it.

We're dining inside with six of the loveliest young ladies you've ever laid . . . well, let's just leave it at that." Karl smiled broadly. "Imported," he told his three protégés. "The six women; not the wine." He giggled like a schoolboy.

Everyone got up and headed toward the dining room, which looked more like a ballroom, done up in floor-to-ceiling mirrors, crystal chandeliers, and sconces made of gold. Place settings for twelve were arranged at one end of the table that could easily seat sixty.

All six ladies were seated, their gloved hands poised on their laps beneath the single-length, hand-embroidered tablecloth on which you couldn't place a price.

As the men approached, they noted that three of the women were not particularly pretty. The other three were not at all what Karl had ordered. In fact, none of them were what one would call young.

"What the hell is this?" the merc questioned.

The monsignor frowned. "An obvious faux pas."

But Karl knew better. His instincts told him that something was terribly, terribly wrong. "I personally arranged this. This was not on the menu," he said quietly as if to himself.

The three subordinates stood leery. Transfixed.

A figure entered from the far end of the dining room where the six ladies were seated and took his place at the head of the table. Karl, the merc, the monsignor and their protégés glared, their eyes glued to the police chief.

"Good evening," Chief Grear said to the six who stood practically at the position of attention. The chief's eyes focused primarily on the oldest of The Triumvirate's charges. A cop. One of his own sergeants who had been transferred to the Riverhead P.D. shortly before Beau Hopkins had come aboard.

The sergeant made a move toward his shoulder holster, but the woman closest to him shot him in the upper chest. The cop fell over like a wall of lead, hitting the floor more noisily than the report from the assassin's gun.

"Permit me for a moment to introduce my ladies-in-waiting as yours are indisposed," the Riverhead police chief said evenly. "The one with the smoking gun is our switchboard operator, Doris. Doris, say good evening to the five fine gentlemen left standing."

Doris brought the muzzle of her Beretta smartly to the top of her bouffant in a short but snappy salute while remaining seated in her wheelchair.

Apparently, Karl was more concerned about how the seven had gotten through security than he was for the safety of his men or himself. "How did you get up here?" he demanded.

"By putting myself in charge of wardrobe and entertainment," was Grear's succinct reply.

"My men are all over this building," Karl blew.

"Your men are six floors below us with six lovely ladies. Partying. With your compliments, of course," Grear added politely.

"What do you think you're going to do?"

"Get on with the introductions," Grear answered with no change in expression. "Sergeants Hennesey, O'Shea and Deputy Chief Inspector Graves on your right from front to back. Gentlemen, stand up and be counted."

The three men rose from the table, two .380-caliber handguns and a .45 lifted from the lap of luxury and placed upon or near the fine linen napkins to their right.

"You will note that Angelica Manns was not the only one who knew how to put on makeup and sport an evening dress or gown," the police chief pointed out.

"Jesus Christ," the monsignor said and sweated.

"Relax," Karl said confidently. "They're not going to shoot us down in cold blood. The rest of us are unarmed," he made clear to Chief Grear.

"Unarmed?" the police chief questioned and laughed. "So were most of the six million European Jews who your father killed."

"My father acted on the will of the German people," Karl snapped. "My father only did what every good German wanted at that moment in history. To be led. To be told that it was all right to kill the avaricious, pernicious Jew! It wasn't only his soldiers, Chief Grear. It was the ordinary citizen on the cities' streets and country roads. It was the common man doing his duty by rounding up the vermin anywhere they crawled. From the grand estates to the most humble dwellings found throughout the hinterland. For every good German despised the Jew."

The woman seated closest to Doris stood, a revolver hanging loosely at her side, blocked from view. "My grandfather's name was Heller," she spoke. "He and my grandmamma hid a Jewish family from the Nazis for a good part of the war. I guess my grandparents were the bad Germans. Yes?" She smirked, stepping around the table and coming into full view.

"Disloyal. Stupid. What difference did it make? Had the war played out to its proper conclusion, my father and the German people would have killed six million more!" Karl said undauntedly.

Gretta Hoffmann extended the revolver out to arm's length and sped a bullet into Karl's right shoulder.

The monsignor grabbed his leader and led him to a seat against the wall. "Are you crazy?" the clergyman cried out.

"Are you prepared to administer extreme unction?" Gretta wanted to know, sending another bullet into Karl's other shoulder.

"For the love of God!" the monsignor screamed, reeling out of harm's way, his bloody hands and arms sheltering his head.

A light-skinned black woman seated beside Gretta rose. She was the tallest of the three. "How much could you love Him, Bill?"

"What?"

"I said how much could you love Him? God, I'm speaking of. The seven of us saw the aftermath of what you did to those three innocents back there. The mother and her son in the elevator. The Russian girl. What monsters you really are. Masqueraders. Sadistic torturers. Musketeers, my black ass." Clara Smith grimaced, leveling her Smith and Wesson in the monsignor's face. "Say good-by, Billy boy."

The cleric dropped to his knees, crawled then cowered in a corner. "Please," the clergyman pleaded, shedding anything but crocodile tears. "I'm so sorry."

"Yeah," Clara said. "Sorry we found your fucking nest." The policewoman turned merciful. She walked over and shot the cleric through the temple.

Karl was bleeding profusely, waiting for a miracle.

"So now you've met the girls, Karl: Doris, Gretta, and Clara," Grear said in a calm and even manner. "Seasoned policewomen, one and all."

Karl looked over and mumbled a profanity beneath a painful

breath.

From across the table, the deputy chief inspector stood and put a bullet in the leader's forehead.

"You don't mind if Doris remains seated," the police chief said to the remaining four. "You see, she has a disability."

Doris spun her wheelchair about, wheeling it around the table to face the remaining three.

The merc spoke up quickly; a pitch to save his life. "I have the power to make all of you rich beyond your wildest dreams. I'm talking millions of dollars. Each!"

Grear looked over at the inspector. "What do you think, sir?"

The mercenary and his three subordinates saw the sign of hope, looking pleadingly toward the man in charge.

But the rough-spoken inspector shook his head. "I'm afraid that I'm going to have to repeat myself." And with that declaration, he shot the merc smack between the eyes. Ed fell backward with a thump onto the plush carpeting.

The two souls still standing saw the handwriting on the wall and made their move. Sergeants Hennesey and O'Shea stood. A single round from a .380-caliber made a hole in the senator's son's throat. A .45-caliber exploded the top of the young industrialist's son's head.

The Triumvirate and its soon-to-be successors were positively dead.

Chief Grear went around both sides of the table and collected all six handguns from the cops, sandwiching the hardware into a shiny aluminum case between two sections of eggshell-shaped foam. Heading toward the changing room, the policemen and policewomen shed the borrowed dresses, peplums and ruffles, collecting their own weapons.

"You look positively divine," Hennesey said to O'Shea, helping the man unpin his wig.

"Yeah, like Andy Devine," Gretta teased.

"Nah, the two of you could positively pass for Poncho and Cisco, though," the inspector said of the pair.

"You? A dead ringer for Dale Evans," Clara decided of the inspector.

"Who me?" Hennesey threw back, taking umbrage.

"No, not you; the inspector," Gretta cried out in mild hysterics.

"All I want to know is how in hell the police chief got out of this?" the deputy chief demanded to know.

"That's easy," O'Shea offered. "Of the seven of us, who would *you* pick as a pimp?"

The five of them suddenly stopped their joking and jabbering as Grear entered the room. After an uncomfortable moment, the police chief turned to the deputy chief inspector. "John, what might one surmise from the sergeant's tone and comment concerning his commanding officer?"

"Chief, I'd have to say it sounds as though the man might be bordering on insubordination," the inspector answered without hesitation.

"Oh, really!" O'Shea retorted. "Then why don't the two of you so note it in today's report," he glared, tossing each of them an earring.

"I think he's got us there, Chief," the inspector decided.

"Maybe this time," Grear agreed and grinned. "Maybe this time," he repeated, handing O'Shea his garment bag.

O'Shea headed for one of the bathrooms.

"Good man," the police chief said to the inspector, nodding toward the sergeant's back.

"Salt of the earth," the inspector returned.

"Great buns," Gretta teased.

"And don't stay in there all afternoon primping," Clara called out after him. "We've got work to do."

Doris wheeled herself past the group, heading toward one of the other bathrooms in silence.

"What's the matter with her?" Hennesey questioned. "Hasn't said boo since the introductions."

"Hasn't gotten over Beau," Clara explained.

"None of us have," the inspector said.

"Got that right," Gretta confirmed.

"Amen to that," Clara concluded, her big brown eyes suddenly blinking away a tear or two.

Chapter 64

At police headquarters in Riverhead, Robert Redler sat before the chief. Grear looked absolutely drained but satisfied.

"How did you find them?" Robert questioned.

"I had a tail put on Patrol Officer Lakeland from the day Beau turned up dead. Took some time."

"How did you know it was Lakeland?"

Grear smiled sadly. "No one could best Beau. No one. Butch-Lee and Angelica had to be tipped off that Beau was coming. It had to be someone on the inside. One of us. Lakeland came to us so conveniently. When I had Hennesey and O'Shea pulled out of the 111th Precinct in Bayside, after the Queens D.A. cleaned house there two years ago, I wondered if I had made a mistake in judgment. But it was Lakeland who called in sick the day Beau went to Jersey. Not Hennesey. Not O'Shea. Lakeland was next in line; Karl's protégé. The officer was to become The Triumvirate's new leader in the new millennium.

Robert shook his head in disbelief. "A patrol officer. Who'd have thought?"

"Groomed from birth," Grear made perfectly clear.

"Listen, I realize it's the middle of January, and that it's as cold as a welldigger's ass, but Liza has some soup and sandwiches aboard. Nothing fancy. She insists that I bring you back with me if only for an hour or so. She wants you to see how she spruced up the interior. It's your gift to us, so you should really come and take a look at what she did."

The chief smiled. "Rob, I'm beat. Another time, like maybe in May," he half kidded.

Robert shook his head. "You're not five minutes away. Let's go."

"One hour, "Grear gave in. "I really need to get some rest."

Liza limped up from the galley with a hot seafood platter on a large tray holding plates, knives, forks, and napkins. "Champagne will be up in a second, gentlemen," she said, handing the tray to the chief, kneeling to adjust the height of the teak table, raising it a foot. "How's that?"

"Sandwiches, huh?" he said to Robert. The police chief set down the tray. "How about you sitting down here? I'll get the bubbly," he insisted, taking Liza by the hand, helping the first mate to her feet and onto the wraparound settee.

"I'm not an invalid," she protested mildly.

"No, you're on the mend. Robert's another story, however. You know, I was just thinking. He's going to need a co-captain *and* a mate when you head this hunk of plastic south."

"Got anyone in mind?" Robert asked in feigned ignorance, noting quite clearly where the conversation was headed.

"I could put in for an early vacation anytime," the police chief continued matter-of-factly.

"Could you, now?"

"Sure."

"And what would your wife say to that?" Liza asked.

"She said that we really wouldn't be much of a bother."

Liza smiled knowingly. "She hates boats. She said no such thing."

"No, she did. Really," Grear insisted, stepping down into the galley.

"How many times did we offer to take Blanch out for the day?" Liza challenged.

"Well, that's just the point. It was for the day. Not much room to speak of on that other boat of yours. But on this one, we really wouldn't get in your way."

"She'd really go?" Liza asked suspiciously, knowing Blanch feared anything over a one-foot chop, reminding herself of the time the woman sat beside her in the stern, heading out in Orient Point, white knuckled, afraid to cross the Sound, asking Captain Rob if he wouldn't mind remaining in constant sight of land, land she could barely see through the mist. "You're both certainly welcome to come."

"Well, actually Blanch wanted to know if she could meet us down there," Grear replied, carefully opening the other gift that he had given them in the hospital, the gift of expensive Champagne. Grear slid three stemmed acrylic glasses out from a narrow teak rack located just above and to the right of a double sink.

"Down where?" Robert inquired, smiling at Liza broadly.

"Port St. Lucie area."

Liza laughed. "Isn't that where your son-in-law has a small house near the water?"

"Coincidentally," Grear remarked, ascending the steps with the bottle and glasses, pouring the bubbly for the three of them. "What with that arm, Rob, and your leg on the mend, Liza, the two of you are definitely going to need another hand. True?"

Liza studied the overhead. "Let me see if I have this straight. Blanch is going to fly down there and meet us . . . and you want to do the Intracoastal with Rob and me. Then once down there, you'll leave Blanch behind, using our boat as your motel for overnighters with your daughter, your son-in-law and their dog. Is that correct, Chief Grear? Do I have it straight?" Liza put forth plainly. "A gift of a boat that you are sure to enjoy. Yes?"

Chief Grear smiled and raised his glass. "You know, Robert. She really is clairvoyant,"

Robert was truly amused. "Have you learned to plot a course yet, Chief?"

"Nope."

"Can you handle the lines on this lady?"

"Oh, you mean the boat. If you show me how, I can."

"When can you be ready to leave?"

"You just say the word."

Robert laughed happily and just could not stop.

Liza and the police chief joined Robert in his merriment, for the three were, indeed, happy and giddy for the moment. Happy to be alive.

"I guess I should know by now when I'm outnumbered," Liza conceded. "Happy belated New Year, gentlemen," she toasted warmly.

"Happy belated Christmas and New Year," the two rejoined, raising their glasses high.

"To our voyage," the captain of his new vessel toasted.

"To Beau," Grear said and saluted.

"To your sister, Kathleen, and Dottie," Liza said and sipped.

"To Bridget O'Reilly and all those who gave their lives to fight evil," Robert declared.

"To Danny," Liza toasted.

"Who's Danny?" the chief asked.

"Oh, that's another story, Chief," Liza remarked rather enigmatically.

"To six saviors," Grear pronounced, for he too had secrets that would remain as such.

"To the end of the Third Reich!" Robert sounded.

"Hear, hear," Liza and the chief seconded loudly.

And each finished their glass of Champagne and then another.

Police Chief Grear spent the remainder of the evening on the comfortable couch in the warmth of the spacious salon. Robert and Liza snuggled together in the commodious forward cabin. It was the first time in several months that the three slept peacefully.

BATTERED

THE STORY OF A WOMAN WHO MURDERED HER VICIOUSLY ABUSIVE HUSBAND

This work of fiction is an amalgamation of composite sketches concerning battered women whom I have interviewed at considerable length over the course of many years. Its fusion was additionally inspired by one battered woman's jury trial and her subsequent imprisonment for the shooting death of her husband. Therefore, this narrative is based both on fact and inspiration, a *roman à clef,* [translated, a novel with a key]; that is, a thinly-guised account of many actual events. The courtroom scenes are virtually verbatim. Back-and-forth bimonthly (in this case meaning twice a month) correspondence with one female inmate over the course of several years is closely transcribed as written; that is, the inmate's misspellings, poor grammar, et cetera, albeit instances of Caitlin Fitzgerald's (pseudonym) syntax have been altered for the sake of clarity. Too, all other names and locations were changed for obvious reasons. Again, this is a factual accounting framed as fiction. Be prepared to enter a dark world of spousal violence, murder, courtroom drama, a prisoner's *life* behind bars, and finally the woman's purported freedom, for cancer has reared its ugly head. This narrative is as real as it gets.

Photo by Barbaraellen Koch

Robert Banfelder is a mystery/thriller novelist whose Justin Barnes series won "Best Suspense Novels" from NewBookReviews.org.

Robert is also an avid outdoorsman, thereby penning approximately two hundred articles for such magazines as *Fur-Fish-Game, Deer & Deer Hunting, The Fisherman, On The Water, New York Game & Fish, Hana Hou! The Magazine for Hawaiian Airlines,* to name but a few. Robert's book on fishing titled *The Fishing Smart Anywhere Handbook for Salt Water & Fresh Water* has been endorsed by Lefty Kreh, internationally renowned angler and author. Robert maintains an online monthly report at *Nor'east Saltwater*; he is a member of the Long Island Outdoor Communicators Network and the New York State Outdoor Writer's Association. Robert weaves his knowledge of the great outdoors into the fabric of his fiction.

Along with Donna Derasmo, Robert co-hosts Cablevision TV's *Special Interests with Bob & Donna*, which broadcasts throughout the East End of Long Island, New York. Visit Robert at www.robertbanfelder.com, follow on Facebook, as well as Twitter @RBanfelder.

www.ingramcontent.com/pod-product-compliance
Lightning Source LLC
Chambersburg PA
CBHW071645260626
47170CB00001B/236